More Than Roommates:
Dani's Story

I0548076

ALSO BY BARBARA L. CLANTON

THE WHICKETT SERIES
Art for Art's Sake: Meredith's Story (Book One)
More Than Roommates: Dani's Story (Book Two)

THE CLARKSONVILLE SERIES
Out of Left Field: Marlee's Story (Book One)
Tools of Ignorance: Lisa's Story (Book Two)
Going, Going, Gone: Susie's Story (Book Three)
Stealing Second: Sam's Story (Book Four)
Out at Home (Book Five)
Tools of the Devil (Book Six)
Going Under (Book Seven)
Stealing Hope (Book Eight)

THE GRASSE RIVER SERIES
Quite an Undertaking: Devon's Story (Book One)
Rebecca's Story (Book Two) ... <Coming Soon>

THE GIRLS' SPORTS SERIES (Children's Books Ages 9-12)
Bases Loaded
Side Out
Live, Love, Lacrosse

MORE THAN ROOMMATES
Dani's Story

BOOK TWO IN THE WHICKETT SERIES

BARBARA L. CLANTON

Copyright © 2024 by Barbara L. Clanton

All rights reserved. No part of this publication may be reproduced, transmitted in any form or by any means, electronic or mechanical, including photocopy, recording, or any information storage and retrieval system, without permission in writing from the publisher, except in the cases of brief quotations embodied in critical articles or reviews. The characters, incidents, and dialogue herein are fictional, and any resemblance to actual events or persons, living or dead, is purely coincidental.

Paperback ISBN   978-1-953734-37-2

First Edition 2024
9 8 7 6 5 4 3 2 1

Cover design by Sarah (Forcoverservice)

Published by:
Bibi Books Publishing Company, LLC

Dedication

This work is dedicated to the people who befriended me in high school, college, and beyond. As a shy, introverted person, it is often difficult to reach out and make contact with other people. I'm grateful for those of you in the world who see the shy wallflowers and help them feel safe enough so they can experience the world.

Acknowledgments

Thanks go out to my friends and family, who helped me create this story. I need to thank my family for allowing me the space and the room to be creative. I also want to thank my awesome beta readers and editors. Jiske Bruijn has become a good friend and one of my dedicated beta readers, and I thank her for always answering my calls. I also have to thank Olivia, who sticks with me even though I'm still at the kindergarten comma level and seem to be remaining there. And then there's Audrey. Thank you for hearing the words and finding all the awkwardness within. Yikes. I am grateful for these three outstanding women.

Table of Contents

Dedication..v

Acknowledgments...vii

Chapter 1 1

Chapter 2 11

Chapter 3 20

Chapter 4 30

Chapter 5 43

Chapter 6 53

Chapter 7 60

Chapter 8 69

Chapter 9 81

Chapter 10 90

Chapter 11 98

Chapter 12 107

Chapter 13 118

Chapter 14 129

Chapter 15 137

Chapter 16 147

Chapter 17 155

Chapter 18 163

Chapter 19 171

Chapter 20 183

Chapter 21 193

Chapter 22 203

Chapter 23 215

Chapter 24 230

Chapter 25 242

Chapter 26 251

Newsletter Signup...262

Resources..263

About the Author...264

Books by Barbara L. Clanton 266

Chapter 1

The Strong One

Dani Lassiter closed the door behind her and then leaned back against it. She opened her arms for her tearful girlfriend to dive into.

"You okay, sweetie?" Dani pulled Meredith close.

Meredith's nod was at odds with her softly hitching breath against Dani's shoulder.

Dani kept one arm tightly around Meredith while the other stroked her back. Dani buried her face in Meredith's hair. Even though they had spent all day moving totes, boxes, and bags into their dormitory room, Meredith still smelled amazing. Dani let the love she felt for her girlfriend wash over her.

"You'll be okay, baby," Dani said to the young woman in her arms. "Did you know your dad told me to take care of you?"

Meredith sniffed back her tears. "He did?"

"Mm hmm." Dani kissed the crown of Meredith's head and then led her to Meredith's newly made, not yet slept-in bed. "Yep, just now, as they were leaving."

"I know they had to leave," Meredith said. "Mikey will be devastated when he realizes I'm not coming home for a long time."

Dani made soothing noises and then said, "Tell you what. Why don't we video chat with him once or twice a week?"

"Or maybe every day?" Meredith said with a hopeful lilt.

Dani chuckled. "Sure. Every day if that's what you want. He can mark it on a calendar or something."

"Mom would have to help with that."

"I teared up when my family left, too." Dani rubbed Meredith's back. "Leaving us was hard all around, I imagine."

"Yeah." Meredith wiped her eyes and brushed an escaped lock of long, wavy dark hair off her face. "I'll be okay." She managed a smile for Dani and added, "I just…" She sighed and said, "Today was a lot."

"And it's not even close to being over."

"I know," Meredith said with a groan. She took a deep breath, which Dani echoed.

Dani followed Meredith's gaze around their small dorm room. The newly painted white walls gave it an austere look, but the fresh paint smell gave it the mood of new beginnings.

"At least our families got us mostly moved in," Meredith continued. "Beds made. Clothes unpacked. Freshmen packets acquired from the Admin building." She gestured toward several folders lying in wait on her overflowing desk.

Dani didn't need to look at her own desk because it had the same pile overtaking it. Classes started in two days, so hopefully, they'd both have their acts together by then.

Dani brushed back Meredith's hair and then leaned down for a kiss. She meant it to be a soft, reassuring kiss, but things always heated up whenever their lips met. Meredith pulled back reluctantly.

"And how are *you* doing, baby?" Meredith asked. "You're always so strong and stoic. Nothing bothers you. And my dad was right. I'm going to be okay here because I have you."

Dani felt her cheeks get warm, and for the life of her, couldn't think of an appropriate response other than, "I'm okay." She checked her watch. "The dining hall opens for dinner in about forty-five minutes."

Meredith groaned. "I don't think I have the strength. And what if our dining cards don't work?"

"Shh, shh, shh," Dani said, stroking Meredith's cheek with the back of two fingers. "Let's lay down for a while."

"Okay," Meredith said and gave Dani a quick kiss. "But only if it's just a nap and nothing else, Danielle Anne Lassiter." She wagged a finger in Dani's direction.

Dani sniggered, sounding almost evil. "I'll be good. I promise."

They kicked off their sneakers, and Dani said, "I set an alarm. We're hitting the bookstore after dinner and video-chatting with our adopted grandmothers when we get back. Oh, then there's the RA meeting at ten o'clock for our floor."

Meredith groaned and pulled the hair band off her dark, flowing hair. She raked her fingers through and shook her head. It was one of the many endearing things Meredith did that made Dani want to pepper her girlfriend with kisses. But she held back. Sleep only. Darn.

They lay down, and Meredith wiggled back into Dani's embrace. In the three and a half months since they'd been together, they hadn't had many opportunities to be intimate. Living with their parents tended to thwart private moments. But now that they were away from home and roommates, they could finally explore each other. Spooning Meredith felt so natural that the contentment Dani felt almost overwhelmed her. She nuzzled against Meredith, placing a soft kiss on the back of Meredith's bare neck.

A hand reached around and smacked Dani on the hip. "Nap only."

Dani chuckled. "Yes, Ma'am." Dani thanked the Gods of dorm room assignments that they had scored a corner open-double room at the end of the hall with little traffic in front of their room. Dani chastely kissed Meredith's shoulder and allowed exhaustion to overtake her.

Dani's phone alarm woke them twenty minutes later. She sat up, yawned, and then laughed when Meredith did the same thing. Meredith brushed a lock of Dani's short blonde hair off her forehead.

"I remember when you did that to me outside Mrs. Levine's art room," Dani said. "I melted right there in front of you. Did you notice?"

"Yes," came the short answer.

"I already knew I was in love with you." Dani looked down. Why was she embarrassed to admit that?

"It took me a little longer," Meredith said, leaning in for a kiss and getting one. "But I finally came to my senses. Maybe if we're not too exhausted tonight, we can err…"

"You're so shy about sex," Dani whispered. "We have our own room. Real privacy. I only wish we had bigger beds."

"Mmm," Meredith said, still sounding sleepy.

Dani pulled Meredith into a quick hug, loving the calm, protective feeling she always got with Meredith in her arms. It was comforting. It was home.

"I'm hungry," Meredith said.

"Me, too."

Meredith looked down at her work clothes and made a face. "I need to change."

"You don't have to change for me," Dani quipped.

"Ha ha," Meredith said dryly and waved Dani away with a flick of her hand.

Dani was ready to go to the dining hall in no time. While Meredith fussed over what to wear to their dining hall debut, Dani took the time to send her parents a thank you text. Meredith had been emotional about leaving home for the first time, and Dani had been, too, but was doing her best to hold her emotions inside. She had to be the strong one, after all.

Meredith was finally ready to go and wore capri slacks with a loose, short-sleeved blouse. Dani felt underdressed in jeans and a Taylor Swift T-shirt. Oh, well. People were going to get her as she was.

It was weird taking the tunnel under their dorm to the dining hall, but it was kind of cool, too. Much needed in the winter, she supposed. Their dining cards worked on the first try, thank goodness, because they'd heard horror stories about malfunctioning cards. With that worry dispelled, they stuck together as they got in the crowded line for hot food and then another for the salad bar. Excited chatter filled the brightly lit dining hall, and Dani was intrigued by the wide variety of students there. There were so many different ethnicities and body shapes and sizes. They both skipped the dessert line and sat at the end of an uncrowded table near the beverage station.

"Beware the freshman fifteen," Meredith said, referring to the talk Meredith's mother had given them as they unpacked their new dorm. She held up a forkful of soggy green beans. "Yum."

4

Dani laughed and held up her own soggy beans. "We'll figure this out."

They sat alone, watching the other students mill about. Many already seemed to have an entire posse of friends. They must not be freshmen.

"I wish we could be out," Dani finally said, breaking the silence. "But we can't."

Meredith agreed. "Like you said. It's better to get the lay of the land before offending everyone's delicate sensibilities."

Dani laughed. Her smile faded when she noticed some guy a few tables over checking out Meredith. He had jet-black hair and a full beard and mustache. He looked older. Not a freshman like they were. She couldn't be sure he was ogling Meredith, but there was no way Dani was going to allow this. She started to stand up but caught herself in time. They weren't out. And he really wasn't doing anything.

"What's wrong?" Meredith asked. She looked around, trying to figure out what Dani had been seething about.

Dani sighed. "I'm just tired. And we need to hit up the bookstore."

Meredith nodded. "I hope we have time to squeeze in a Zoom call with Millie and Esther tonight before the resident advisor meeting."

Dani instantly relaxed at the mention of their adopted grandmothers' names. "They're excited for us."

"I can't believe the Randall-Bradley House for Women is opening in less than a month, and we won't be there."

"I know," Dani said. "They donated their house and put in so much hard work. I hope you and I are that strong when we're in our seventies."

"*You* will be," Meredith said. "You're the strong one in this relationship."

Dani chuckled. She often took the lead, and Meredith seemed to rely on her for decisions and to calm her down. "You're strong, too, my love." She whispered the last two words.

Talking about the older women they'd met while doing a research project together during their senior year of high school was a balm to Dani's soul. As they sat there eating in the noisy dining hall full of people they didn't know, Dani wondered what college would be like. Would Meredith get homesick? Would she find life as a Fine Arts major satisfying and not too difficult?

Would studying Political Science be all that Dani hoped it would be? And now that her lacrosse career was apparently over, she made a mental note to check out the fitness center and weight room. She had to find a way to get exercise and keep fit. Maybe she could work out tomorrow, but it might not be open on Sunday. Of course, she had to make time around the Poly Sci Orientation event. It was at the same time as Meredith's Fine Arts' event. So that was good.

"Hey," Meredith said. "You're a million miles away."

"Yeah," Dani flicked a lock of hair off her forehead with a shake of her head. "Just thinking about the million and one things we have to do before classes start on Monday."

Meredith groaned. "I hear that, sweetie." Meredith looked stricken. She whispered, "I can't call you that anymore, can I?"

Dani shook her head. "I have to watch myself, too. I hate this."

"Me, too." Meredith stood up. "C'mon, let's go bus these orange trays and find the bookstore."

Dani nodded and stood up. She looked over at the bearded guy, and sure enough, he looked away quickly. Damn it. He really had been checking out Meredith. That's not cool, dude. Not cool at all. She tried to give him a stern warning look, but he didn't look up again. The one thing she did notice, though, was that he was sitting alone. People were around him at his table, but it was clear they weren't his friends. And dressed in all black? What was that about?

"Are you coming?" Meredith said with a chuckle. "You're spacey this evening."

"I'm fine," Dani said without mirth. "Just fine." And if that bearded guy wanted to be fine, too, he'd better lay off looking at her girlfriend.

~~~

They made it back to their dorm room just in time to answer the video call from Millie and Esther back home in Whickett, a suburban town on the outskirts of Albany, New York, where Dani had grown up, and Meredith had spent her junior and senior years of high school.

"You answer it," Meredith said, gesturing to her bed. "I'll unpack the bookstore stuff and then join you."

Dani nodded and clicked the answer button on her tablet. "Hi, Millie," Dani said to the older woman who appeared on her screen. Millie's light silver hair was short and ruffled as usual, kind of like the woman herself. Dani hoped she would be as spry as Millie when she was that age. "We're all moved in."

"*Kind of* moved in," Meredith called from across the room where she was stacking Dani's books and supplies on her desk. Funny how Meredith had unpacked Dani's stuff before unpacking her own.

Esther appeared on the screen beside Millie. Esther's snow-white hair was wispy and not staying in the functional hair clasp she favored. Her eyes were bright, and it was obvious they were both excited to talk to their young friends. "Is that Meredith I hear?"

Dani nodded, smiled at the two older women, and then looked at Meredith. Yes, she had gotten lucky when she found out that Meredith returned her affections back in high school. Esther and Millie were the only ones who officially knew that Dani and Meredith were together and vice versa. It was fun having this secret between the two couples. "She's taking care of me."

"Aww," Millie teased. "Don't forget to come up for air now and then, you two. This new freedom might ruin you both."

"Millie!" Esther scolded. Dani laughed because scolding Millie was something Esther did often.

Millie smiled at her long-term companion. Although marriage was now possible for the two women since the laws had changed, both of them brushed off the topic whenever Dani or Meredith brought it up.

"It's young love, Esther," Millie protested and then fake swooned for Dani's benefit.

Meredith joined Dani on the bed and waved at the two women on the screen.

"There's our girl," Esther said. "You look nice with your hair pulled back like that. We can see your pretty face, dear."

"Told you," Dani said. It had taken quite some time for Dani to convince Meredith to stop hiding behind her hair fortress. Meredith's facial acne scars were the main source of her hesitation, but her shyness was another. Dani was still helping her come out of her shell.

"Hush, you," Meredith said to Dani, but her grin belied the fact that she liked the compliment. "Thank you, Esther."

"Millie," Esther said to her companion, "do you remember when we still had our original hair color?" She didn't let Millie answer, and Millie didn't seem to mind. "Mine wasn't as dark as yours, Meredith." She sighed and added, "Enjoy it while you can."

Dani laughed along with Meredith and then said, "So tell us about the Randall-Bradley House. How go the inspections?"

Millie took over. "We're juggling a million details, but we've got our checklist in our trusty old-school notebook right here." She picked up an old, tired-looking spiral. "Monday is the final inspection."

"No way!" Dani said at the same time Meredith said, "Good luck."

"And," Esther added, "we finally hired a live-in director. She accepted the position this morning. She's ready to move in once we get the final approval."

"That's fantastic," Meredith and Dani gushed simultaneously and then chuckled.

"I wish we were there for the official opening." Meredith sighed, and Dani understood the regret. They'd been there for a lot of the plan-making that summer.

"How's the security setup?" Dani asked. The four of them had had many conversations about workable security measures to keep the women and children seeking refuge from abusive partners safe and secure.

"Every window and door has an alarm," Esther said. "And we managed to get those magnetic locks installed." The magnetic locks were a source of pride for Esther. She was serious about keeping the residents safe.

Meredith leaned closer. "Someone inside the house has to hit a release button to unlock the door, right?"

"Exactly," Millie picked up the thread. "The security cameras have been installed, and the outside fences have been fortified and are now unclimbable."

"Fantastic," Dani said.

"Dani?" Esther said. "I have to ask this before I forget."

"Mmm?"

"You're majoring in Political Science, right?"

"Mm hmm."

"What does that mean? Why study political science? Not a criticism, dear. Not at all. I don't know anything about it."

"No worries," Dani said. "I'm going to study political ideologies in the United States and internationally."

"Ooh," Millie jumped in. "Maybe a semester abroad?"

"Maybe. I'm not sure what programs they have here." Dani shot Meredith a side glance to see what her reaction to this news was. They hadn't talked about the possibility of Dani taking a semester away. Meredith didn't seem phased by the news, so Dani continued. "I may want to go into politics or study law. But in the least, I want to understand our political institutions."

"You know she's always watching those streaming podcasts about politics," Meredith added, leaning closer to the screen.

"Boring, if you ask me," Millie said with a laugh. This, of course, earned her another scolding from Esther, but Millie just chuckled again. "But you do you. You have to follow your heart and figure out what you want. Now is the time to explore all those new ideas."

"So philosophical, dearest," Esther said to Millie. Her smile spoke volumes about the love and affection she felt for her longtime companion.

"Aww," Meredith said. "You two are wonderful role models for us."

"And you two keep us young," Millie said. "I don't know if we would have had the energy to make this project come to fruition without you two."

"Glad we could help," Dani said and pulled Meredith into a side hug.

They chatted for a few more minutes about the house and Meredith's plans to major in Fine Arts. Millie demanded regular updates from both of them, which they enthusiastically agreed to provide.

After a while, they had to wind down the call because Dani and Meredith had to get ready for their first-ever floor meeting in the Resident Advisor's

9

room. Meredith excused herself to go freshen up. Esther also excused herself due to a call of nature, as she put it, leaving Dani to close up with Millie.

"Dani," Millie said, her tone serious. "Take care of that girl of yours. She's not outgoing like you and I are. When I met my Esther, she was such a shy, introverted woman. I had to help her find her wings."

"I'll take care of her," Dani said. "There's no question about that."

"You're going to be busy with so many things. Going to school, starting your career in politics, taking care of Meredith."

"We'll be okay, Millie," Dani said, sensing that Millie was nervous for them. "I'll text you later in the week to set up another video call. How does that sound?"

"Good."

"And you, please take care of Miss Esther, and don't forget to take care of yourself."

Millie simply nodded. It looked to Dani as if she was tearing up. Was there something wrong? She wanted to ask, but Millie said a quick goodbye and ended the call.

Chapter 2

Just Roommates

It was late Sunday morning, and what a morning it had been. Dani took a deep breath to shake off her tension as she entered the covered walkway. The walkway was the most direct path from her dorm to the main campus and fitness center. Her goal that morning was a much needed cardio workout to clear her head and body. Next time, she was going to bring her workout gear with her so she wouldn't have to hike back up to the dorm, change, and then hike back down to the main campus like she had just done. That had been poor planning on her part. And to top it all off, her dorm was situated on a hill they called the Mount. It was one of two dorms connected by a shared dining hall. It was a cool design, but her dorm was far enough away that better strategizing would be in order.

That morning's welcoming meeting for Political Science majors at Eggers Hall had been…interesting. Five not-so-warm-and-fuzzy Poly Sci seniors ran the orientation and waxed on about how tough the major was. Apparently, their goal was to strike fear into the souls of incoming freshmen. *Strike all you want*, Dani thought as the seniors quoted statistics about dropout rates for that field of study. Dani wasn't scared, though. She was at Syracuse to study Poly Sci. She'd been in student government all four years of high school, culminating as senior class president last year, so she knew she could handle anything thrown at her. So why was this knot in her stomach still there?

"I can handle it," Dani said out loud in the enclosed walkway. The side walls were made from wooden slats spaced a few inches apart. The warm August humidity hung trapped in the tunnel. Sections of the tunnel were dim since the walkway cut underneath a dark canopy of trees and was surrounded by overgrown bushes. She'd been forewarned about Syracuse winters. Apparently, she would experience lake-effect snow and accumulations so high it couldn't simply be plowed. They had to load the snow into trucks to haul off campus. So, yeah, this covered walkway and the tunnels around campus made complete sense.

The probably-sanctioned graffiti dotting the wooden planks attempted to enliven the enclosed space and give it some color. Various clubs, sororities, and fraternities had left their marks there. Oh, look, Syracuse had a women's rugby team. How cool.

She was grateful for the colorful distractions, but thoughts of that morning wouldn't stay buried. The seniors with their pressed suits, impeccable business attire, and ramrod straight postures were probably greeted coldly as freshmen and were simply passing on the legacy. As they'd toured the classrooms that morning, it felt like a hazing as the older students quizzed them about political ideologies. It was as if they wanted to show the new freshmen how much they didn't know. Dani had to admit, she hadn't known much. But wasn't that why she was there? To learn? *I can handle it,* she told herself again. One thing became crystal clear in her mind as the morning wore on. She was not going to turn into one of these arrogant assholes.

Dani walked down yet another set of steps leading toward Sims Drive. How long was this walkway, anyway? It hadn't seemed that long when she and Meredith walked to the bookstore after dinner the night before. Did she take a wrong turn or something? And there was no way she was going to get out the map stashed in her back pocket. She could and would find the fitness center on her own.

She checked her phone for the time. Dang, she might not have much time to work out before meeting Meredith back on the Mount for lunch. The tightness in Dani's shoulder's eased somewhat when she thought of her awesome girlfriend. They had, indeed, christened their dorm room the night before. It had been their first night alone together, and they were eager for each other. They ended up sleeping side-by-side all night in Meredith's twin-sized bed. Dani wished they could push their two beds together, but they'd agreed to keep their relationship under wraps until they decided whether they could come out safely or not. For now, they were just friends—friends who'd gone to the same high school back home.

Meredith's mid-morning text sounded upbeat, so maybe her Visual Arts orientation had gone better than Dani's Poly Sci. The thought of someone hurting Meredith or making her feel dumb made Dani furious. She exhaled firmly through her nose at the imagined slight. Meredith's text said they were being taken on a tour to check out some artwork on campus and would take pictures if allowed.

Breathe, Dani told herself. *I'll find my place.* Before leaving the day before, Dani's mother had told her much the same thing. It had only been yesterday, but it felt like a week since her parents and younger sister Laney had left. Dani's mother had said, "If ever there was a time to try new things, it's now, honey. You might make mistakes, but you'll learn from them. I know you will. I remember feeling so lost during my first few months at Albany State, but you'll find your place. So will Meredith." Dani hadn't known her mother was so wise. A slight pang of homesickness hit her chest.

"Stop," Dani muttered. She didn't have time for that nonsense. She had to take this college experience by storm. The first step, after making sure Meredith was happy, was to dive full force into academics. Her plan included reading the first two chapters of her American National Government textbook. One of the tour-guide seniors hinted that reading ahead was not only a good idea but was expected. Dani refused to simply "call it in," as one of the seniors had cautioned against.

And she was going to join that PSLA club or group or whatever they called it. The Political Science Leadership Association was the group to join if you wanted to become active in on-campus politics. The group basically groomed its participants for on-campus political positions. It focused on things like campaigning strategies, debates, and fundraising. "Since time began," one of the seniors stated that morning, "every single elected officer has come out of the PSLA. And we do not expect that to change any time soon."

It sounded like a challenge to Dani, but she was on board because she fully intended to join that group. She wanted the experience. She had campaigned and given speeches in high school, but that was it. She'd never debated other candidates. It just wasn't part of the process in her high school. And, if truth be known, elections in her school were kind of popularity contests, so she wasn't naïve enough to think that her prior experiences would be enough to get elected to student government.

After forever, Dani finally saw the sunny exit of the tunneled walkway. Once out, she turned left on Sims, and the Barnes Center was right there. Yay. See? She didn't even have to consult her map. At least something had gone right that day.

She used her plastic SU ID card to gain entrance and was instantly overwhelmed by the multitudes of treadmills, bikes, elliptical machines, and who knew what else on the main floor. The floor wasn't exactly packed with students, but a fair number was there. A handful were actually working out. The rest seemed to be simply hanging out and socializing. Socializing at the gym? Dani scoffed soundlessly. That was not the point of the gym. These people seemed to be showing off their designer workout gear sans the actual workout. She looked down at her basic black workout shorts and Team USA Women's lacrosse t-shirt. It was just a workout, not a fashion show. Right?

She tucked her ID snugly into her pocket and spotted an open area with orange and off-white mats. She needed to stretch, partly to warm up her muscles and partly to ground herself from that troubling orientation. She looked around as she stretched her arms overhead. Yeesh, Syracuse colors were everywhere. School pride was a good thing, she supposed, as she bent over to touch her toes for a much-needed hamstring stretch.

"New?" a voice said from behind her.

Dani flew into a standing position. Oh, great, Dani thought. Whoever it was had chosen to walk up behind her and gotten an eyeful of Dani butt in greeting. She turned to find a tallish woman wearing an official-looking orange polo shirt with the fitness center name emblazoned on the left side.

"New? Yeah," Dani said. "Just looking to get in some cardio."

"Ah, well, you've come to the right place," the woman said, brushing her too-black-to-be-natural short hair off her face. Dani's gaydar pinged ever so slightly. "I can give you a tour if you want. My name's Joiee." She pointed to her nametag, didn't wait for a response, and launched into a tour. "On this main floor, you have all the cardio machines. They overlook the rock climbing walls that start down in the basement." She pointed toward the interior windows looking onto the colorful climbing "rocks."

Dani had no choice but to follow the woman past the exercise bikes to the windows. "That's impressive. But I really don't have much time for—"

"There are basketball and volleyball courts upstairs," the woman named Joiee with two e's continued as if not hearing Dani's plea. "And then one more floor above that is the running track that wraps around all the courts."

"That sounds like an amazing use of space," Dani said, not wanting to be rude. She looked at her phone. "I need to—"

"The pool and S-shaped hot tub are in the basement," Joiee interrupted again as if Dani had not spoken. "The bi-level weight room is there also. We have dumbbells, sprinting machines, upper body machines, you name it."

"I'll get a tour next time," Dani broke in, "but I don't have much time right now. I'm meeting my roommate for lunch and only have a little while."

"Are you on the lacrosse team?"

Dani inhaled sharply. "No, I'm not." That was her private shame. "They kind of stopped recruiting me." Why she admitted that to this tall stranger was beyond her.

"I'm sorry," Joiee said. "That's rough."

"How'd you know I played lacrosse?"

"Your shirt." Joiee nodded toward the USA Lacrosse shirt with her chin.

"Oh." Dani looked down at her chest.

"It's okay, newbie," Joiee said. "Maybe you can get an invitation to try out next year. That will be difficult, but let me show you something that might help get you noticed." Joiee didn't wait for a response and walked away, clearly expecting Dani to follow.

Dani didn't know what to do, so she did the only thing she could. She followed the fast-paced, most-likely-a-lesbian tour guide back toward the front entrance. She didn't know how this woman had gotten so far into Dani's personal life so fast, but there it was—her biggest embarrassment in her life was now out in the open for all to snack on. She had been on the Syracuse coach's recruitment list at one point but got dropped before anything became official. Over the summer, Meredith tried to make Dani feel better about the rejection, but still…it stung.

Joiee stopped in front of a large bulletin board. She smacked a few of the flyers. "Announcements for club teams, personal trainers, and things like that go here. But this is the sign-up sheet you need to look at. It's for the fall intramural league for women's lacrosse. The number of teams varies each year." She flipped up the top sign-up sheet. "Whoa, we might even get four whole teams this year."

"Do you play?"

"Nah," Joiee said with a laugh. "My girlfriend Laura plays. She was a varsity hopeful back in the day but didn't make the cut. I know. That sounds mean, but she's finally accepted it. The varsity women's team has been doing so well in recent years that Syracuse is attracting a lot of players from all over. But as you know, there are only so many roster spots available. And I'm sorry you weren't recruited, but there's a lot of competition out there."

Dani's shame at not being good enough tightened her chest, and all she could do was nod.

"Look," Joiee continued. "This intramural league is school sanctioned and a lot of fun. And," she poked the air with a sharp finger, "one of the varsity assistant coaches usually scouts for talent there. So, see? There's a chance to get recruited for next season."

"A slim one, but I get it," Dani said, not committing one way or another. Her head was woozy. She couldn't decide if she should sign up right now. She needed to talk it over with Meredith. Yes, delaying felt like a good tactic, mainly because Joiee sounded like a used car salesman trying to sell her something she hadn't known she wanted or needed.

A hand patted her upper arm. "Hey, just think it over," Joiee said. Her expression softened from hard-sell used car salesman to over-friendly fitness center employee. "Go do your workout. And if you want a personal fitness trainer, call me." A business card thrust toward Dani accompanied the last sentence. It had Joiee's name and phone number on it. "That's my personal number, by the way."

"Thanks." Dani wasn't typically reduced to one-word responses, but this woman was overpowering her.

"Have fun," Joiee said, spun around dramatically, and walked back toward the entrance—toward her next victim, no doubt.

Dani tucked the business card in her pocket and turned toward the line of treadmills.

"Fresh meat?" a male voice said behind Dani. She knew enough not to turn around.

"Yeah," Joiee said to the voice. "Scared wide-eyed freshman."

"That was a record."

"What was?"

The male scoffed. "The time it took you to give her your phone number."

"Shut up, Derek," Joiee said. "I was just helping her."

"Whatever you have to tell yourself. Did you at least get her name?"

"Nah. Not yet. She'll be back."

Dani was the one who scoffed that time. She may have lived a somewhat sheltered life in the suburbs of Albany, but she knew enough to know that Joiee was, in the least, a flirt and, at most, a player. The woman even said she'd had a girlfriend named Laura, yet she was flirting. Dani shook her head. She would never do anything like that to Meredith. She hopped on the treadmill farthest from the main entrance and wished she'd had the foresight to bring air buds to listen to music. She needed to block out all the weird stuff coming at her that morning. And the day wasn't even half over. At least Meredith was next on her schedule, and hopefully, Dani would get to enfold her in her arms and get the reset she so badly needed. But for now, all she had was a treadmill.

Dani increased the speed as if that would make her forty-five-minute run go more quickly. She pushed the workout to distract herself from all the fast changes coming into her life. She knew she would eventually settle in, but it couldn't happen soon enough. And classes hadn't even started yet.

Like an idiot, she hadn't brought any water. No worries. She would be meeting Meredith for lunch and would get some there. She snuck out a side door, so Joiee wouldn't try to corner her again. Yikes. Talk about coming on strong. Dani took a breath in the stifling August air and reoriented herself.

17

Ahh, Sims, right. The covered walkway was just up the street there. She headed toward the entrance, pulled out her phone, and texted Meredith that she was returning to the Mount. She noticed the time. Oh, shit, it was already noon. She broke into a jog, hit the tunnel entrance, and took each uphill set of stairs two at a time. She did not want to keep Meredith waiting. She wanted to spend every moment she could with her girlfriend because, very soon, they would be busier than they'd ever been.

She finally reached the top of the hill, popped out of the tunnel, and stopped momentarily to catch her breath.

"Look at you," someone coming toward her teased. "Overachiever." It was one of the students from her dorm floor. Right, right. She was the bubbly one with the long blonde hair and impeccable makeup from the Resident Advisor's meeting last night. She was girl-next-door pretty with her hair stylishly pulled back behind her head and somehow the style made her look more relaxed than last night when her hair was loose. "You're Dani, right?"

"Yeah," Dani said and blew out a breath. "Kate?" She squinted one eye, afraid she had gotten the girl's name wrong.

"That's me," Kate said. "Kate Evans." She smiled and added, "Come with. A bunch of us from the dorm are meeting at Schine for lunch."

"That's the student center?" Dani asked with a laugh. She was still getting her bearings on campus.

"Yes, and I'm literally dying to see what they have down there."

"I hope you're not…" *literally dying*. Dani stopped her retort just in time. Kate might not think Dani's jab was funny, so she amended her sentence. "I hope you're not waiting on me. I'm meeting my roommate at the dining hall." She pointed toward the complex ahead of her.

"Meredith's your roommate, right?"

"Mm hmm," Dani said.

"She's so nice in a quiet artist kind of way. Pretty, too. She's meeting us at Schine."

"She is?" Dani was confused. She pulled out her phone. There was a text message from Meredith stating the change in lunch plans and asking Dani to join them if she could. She groaned. "Ahh, yes, she is. Okay. Back down the steps it is."

"Excellent," Kate said and linked her arm around Dani's. "We have to get a group chat going for our floor. I know the perfect app."

Dani almost froze. What was Kate doing? Linking arms? Trying to be besties?

"I have been dying to get to know you guys," Kate said. "So, you two knew each other before, right? Did you decide on Syracuse together?"

Dani muttered something about attending the same high school and meeting Meredith in a history class their senior year. "We worked on a project together," Dani mumbled as they headed back down the covered walkway she had just come up. "And, no, we had no idea we both wanted to go to Syracuse."

"I see," Kate said, totally leading the way in both the conversation and the walking. "And I have been literally bursting to ask this question of you guys. Are you more than roommates?"

Dani literally choked on the question and coughed for several more steps. She pulled her arm out from Kate's to stop and bend over. She had to cough out her astonishment at the audacity of Kate's intrusion. *Did she really just ask me that?*

"Oh, my God." Kate patted Dani's back. "Are you okay?"

"I'm okay." Dani took a breath without coughing or choking or telling Kate to mind her own business. Did Kate hear them last night? Making love? Holy crap. Say something. She had to say something. "We're...we're just roommates," she stammered, totally failing any and all lie-detector tests.

"Just roommates," Kate echoed. Dani couldn't read Kate's tone. Did she believe it or not? It didn't matter because, for all intents and purposes, Dani Lassiter and Meredith Bedford from Whickett, NY, were roommates and nothing more.

Apparently satisfied with Dani's answer, Kate linked arms again and pulled Dani back down the walkway.

Chapter 3

Safe and Secure

The café was busy at that time of day, and Meredith's relieved expression at seeing Dani helped her take her own tight nerves down a notch. Unfortunately, they didn't have much time to share their mornings with each other as they navigated the boisterous and noisy student union.

Eight young women from Dani and Meredith's dorm floor squeezed around a table made for six, but no one seemed to mind. Hanging out with familiar faces seemed to be more important than physical comfort. Once seated, Kate commandeered any and all conversations. She seemed to want to know everything about everyone. She sure was a curious cat. Or maybe she was trying to gauge whether she measured up. A mixture of both, Dani decided.

"And what about you, Dani?" Kate asked, putting a lingering hand on Dani's forearm. "What language are you taking?"

"ASL," Dani said.

"No way," Kate gushed and leaned her arm against Dani's. "Sign language? How awesome. What does a political science major need with sign language?"

"You ever see those politicians giving speeches, and they have those sign language interpreters on the side?"

"Yes," Kate said, echoed by several other women at the table.

"If I ever run for office, I can be my own interpreter. And I can make sure my constituents with hearing issues are *heard*." Dani made air quotes around the word 'heard.'

Dani's face got warm as she watched Kate's expression turn to one of pure adoration. Kate cleared her throat, flicked her loose blonde hair over her shoulder, and turned away from Dani. "Did you guys know Petra's taking Chinese?" Kate bragged about her shy roommate sitting on her other side. Petra Alvarez wore her long dark hair back with a pretty wooden clasp, which showed off her darker skin and deep brown eyes. Her skin tone was quite in contrast to that of her roommate Kate's white alabaster. Dani wasn't sure what Kate's or Petra's heritages were, but both young women were truly beautiful.

Petra nodded in acknowledgment of Kate's statement but blushed furiously at the attention.

"She speaks Spanish, too," Kate added. "Fluently."

"Wow," Dani said, echoing everyone else.

"And she's not even a language major," Kate said. "She's a Poly Sci major."

"That's cool," Dani said to Petra, looking around Kate. "Me, too."

"I thought I saw you at the orientation this morning," Petra said.

"Pretty intense, wasn't it?"

Petra nodded but didn't add anything else. Dani felt Meredith's gaze on her. She turned to find Meredith's brow furrowed.

"Did everything go okay this morning?" Meredith asked.

Dani hesitated, not quite knowing how to describe her morning in words. "The seniors were intense. It kind of felt like they were testing us or something."

"I'm sorry that happened," Meredith said quietly. "Tell me more later, okay?"

Dani nodded, grateful that the conversation and focus had moved away from her. She wished she and Meredith were alone, but making new friends was important, too. Accepting those facts, she dug into her turkey wrap heartily as she discovered how hungry she was. With all the tempting food choices, it was easy to see how a fifteen-pound weight gain could sneak up on you.

"What about you, Kate?" Meredith asked. "What language are you studying?"

"Since I'm majoring in Social Work," Kate said, "my counselor here thought it would be good to have a working knowledge of Spanish."

"That's cool," Meredith said. "Maybe we'll be in the same section." Although directed at Kate, Meredith's smile almost melted Dani right there in front of their new friends. Yes, Dani was in love with the woman sitting next to her. Her heart felt full yet heavy at the same time. The heaviness was there because no one at their table or anyone at their new school knew their affection for each other. Even their own parents didn't know.

"OMG," Kate continued with a laugh. "I got so lost after I met with my counselor. I somehow got turned around and walked out a different door."

It seemed as if everyone had gotten lost on campus at least once already. Even Dani admitted she had been disoriented leaving the fitness center earlier. It was funny how Kate made sure everyone got a chance to share. She acted like the unofficial dorm director or something. Of course, Kate's constant touches on Dani's forearm and that one time on her thigh were beginning to wear a little thin, but Dani didn't know how to get her new acquaintance to stop. Maybe Kate was just one of those touchy-feely people. That might also explain the linked arms earlier.

Sitting at that lunch table in the awkwardness of making new friends, Dani got an idea of what it must have been like for Meredith when she transferred to Whickett High School in her junior year. She hadn't known anyone. She'd been the new kid. She'd once told Dani that her shyness and insecurities held her back from making friends, but you couldn't tell that now as Meredith joined in the conversations heartily. Dani flashed Meredith a smile and got a questioning look in return. Dani shook her head slightly as if to say, "It's nothing. I'll tell you later." Meredith smiled, indicating that she understood, and then went back to the conversation about what classes everyone had on the first day.

This somehow morphed into a conversation about everyone's high school accolades.

"In her high school's senior superlatives," Kate said, "my fabulous roomie Petra was voted most likely to become president."

"Never going to happen," Petra said with a scoff.

Dani could tell that Petra was shy, but there was a definite depth to her.

Never count out the shy ones, she thought, stealing a glance at Meredith.

"And Kate here," Petra said, "was voted most likely to be the first one married."

"Pfft," Kate said. "Doubt that. I'm a lot." She said this with a chuckle, which garnered polite laughs from the table.

"Dani was voted most likely to succeed," Meredith bragged about her own roommate.

"And Meredith was voted best artist," Dani countered and watched as Meredith's cheeks pinked up.

The other young women at the table offered their senior superlatives, including one who was voted for the best sneeze in high school. Kate jokingly demanded that she sneeze on cue, but that just made the woman and everyone else laugh.

Then Kate changed the subject to the topic of her boyfriend Stevie back home in Scranton and wanted to know about everyone else's love lives. Dani and Meredith excused themselves. Two other dormmates tagged along, and they headed back up the hill as a group. She wanted to hold Meredith's hand in the worst way but knew she couldn't. Not yet. And, although the two people with them probably wouldn't have made a fuss, Dani wanted people to get to know them first. She wanted to be Dani from Albany before inevitably becoming the lesbian on the fourth floor. You never knew what prejudices and fears people had. Even Meredith had been shocked when Dani told her she was into girls. Thankfully, she finally came around, but it had taken a while.

Once back on their dorm floor, Meredith walked ahead and unlocked the door to their room. She stepped inside and held the door open for Dani to enter. Before Dani knew what was happening, she found herself pinned against the door, the two hanging robes cushioning her back.

Meredith removed the distance between them and wordlessly locked her gaze with Dani's. Dani's heart sped up. She knew enough not to speak in this moment. Meredith ran her fingers along the neck trim of Dani's lacrosse T-shirt. The fingers moved lower and splayed themselves over Dani's heart, that sensual area just below her throat. A soft moan escaped as a rush of desire hit her body. The hand moved with purpose now, sliding over the T-shirt covering the tight sports bra. Her obvious excitement showed underneath the fabric. The hand didn't linger, though. It moved over Dani's stomach toward her lower abdomen. Dani held her breath. Was Meredith going to—? No. Instead, she grasped the hem of Dani's shirt and pulled it up and over Dani's head.

"You're way overdressed for this dorm room," Meredith whispered, her words breathy and unsteady.

Once the T-shirt was removed, Meredith reached behind Dani and locked the door. Dani's sports bra came off next. She was overwhelmed with desire, her breathing heavy. Meredith's smirk revealed the fact that she knew the effect she was having on her. Two thumbs hooked themselves on either side of Dani's workout shorts and yanked them down.

Meredith's appreciative exhale made Dani whimper. She wasn't used to whimpering, but Meredith did things to her. Her girlfriend usually wasn't this aggressive, ever. She was supposedly the shy one. Meredith, still fully clothed, pinned Dani against the door again. Soft kisses began on Dani's neck, causing chills to run through her. Meredith chuckled evilly. Dani was putty, and whoever this new Meredith was, Dani was fine with it.

Kisses landed on an ear, and an earlobe got sucked hard.

"Mmm, Meredith." Dani wrapped her arms around the woman torturing her. "What brought this on?"

Fingers reached up and clamped Dani's lips closed as the kisses continued along Dani's jawline and down to Dani's sensitive spots, usually hidden beneath sports bras. Dani's head lolled back against the robes as she gave in. The lips exploring her body finally made their way to Dani's own. Dani kissed the woman in her arms with such fervor that she almost lost control. She didn't. She couldn't. She wasn't in charge at the moment and merely returned Meredith's kisses eagerly.

A hand pulled Dani toward her bed. Understanding the unspoken wish, Dani leaped on the bed and lay back. Meredith deftly crawled on top, and the renewed kisses were now accompanied by soft caresses and eager stroking.

Dani fell back, letting Meredith make love to her. The sensations were exquisite. Making love. Yes, she could live for this, live for Meredith's touch. Meredith's fingers were sure and commanding. Dani climaxed quickly, devouring Meredith's mouth in an orgasm-fueled kiss. Meredith fell to Dani's side and caressed her face as Dani came down from one of the best orgasms she had ever had, ever.

"What brought that on, baby?" Dani asked again. "Not that I'm complaining. Not in the least." She reached for one of Meredith's hands, kissed its palm, and then splayed the hand over her heart.

"I missed you this morning," Meredith said, finally speaking.

Dani chuckled. "I noticed." She exhaled with a satisfied moan. "Let me catch my breath, and then I'll take care of your needs, okay?"

"No."

"No?"

"I'm content," Meredith said. "I just wanted you to know that I love you."

"I know that." Dani kissed the hand she was still holding.

"And I also wanted you to know that I'm the only one who gets to touch you this way."

Dani's brow furrowed. "Of course."

"So, Miss handsy little Kate Evans from Scranton, Pennsylvania, had better back off, or she's gonna get a knuckle sandwich."

Dani was floored. "Wow." She wasn't sure what else to say. "I didn't like her touching me, either. You know that, right?"

"I do," Meredith said and nuzzled closer. "Jealousy is a new emotion for me."

Dani scoffed. "I kind of like it."

"Mmm," Meredith said. "And she claims to have a boyfriend named Steve, Stevie, or whatever at home. Mm hmm. Sure."

"She could be exploring," Dani offered.

"She can explore all she wants, but not with you." Meredith climbed back on top of Dani, sitting across her hips. "You. Are. Mine."

"And you, my love," Dani said, pulling Meredith on top of her, "are mine." Dani flipped her over and began a slow but steady extrication of the cute outfit her girlfriend had worn that morning. Since they'd gotten together,

Dani had been learning Meredith's spots, and it didn't take long before Meredith was calling out Dani's name muffled beneath a pillow. Now, there was no denying that Meredith was content. They wrapped up in each other's arms and dozed for a while.

About forty minutes later, they woke up from an extremely satisfying nap to find several texts from Handsy Kate.

"She's serious about going to this welcoming party tonight," Dani said, putting on her robe. A shower was definitely in order.

"She mentioned it to me this morning," Meredith said. "The fraternities and sororities are sponsoring it. Greek-apalooza or something."

"I guess they want the freshmen to start thinking about pledging sophomore year."

"I don't know anything about that stuff," Meredith said as she rearranged her full bathroom caddy.

"We'll figure it out," Dani said. "We have time."

"Yeah, I can't afford extra costs, though."

"Neither can I," Dani agreed. "Go ahead and shower first." The bathrooms in the Mount dorms were unique. They were called pods; each was a single-serving room with a sink, toilet, and shower. That made things nice and private, making one less thing to worry about. Of course, her devilish mind wished the two of them could shower together, but that was a future bucket list item. One day.

Meredith pulled Dani into a hug. "See? I'm keeping you. You're always so thoughtful."

"And I'm keeping you, too," Dani said. "I love you, Meredith Bedford. You are my one and only."

"Mm hmm." Meredith's loving smile almost melted Dani to the core. "I love you, too, sweetie. Thank you for being patient back in high school when I hit my own prejudices head on."

"It broke my heart when I thought our friendship was over," Dani said. She kissed Meredith's forehead.

"But I came to my senses," Meredith said. "Now look at us."

Dani squeezed her tight and then let go. Changing the subject, she said, "I need to do some reading for my American Government class."

"Overachiever," Meredith said with a smirk and moved out of Dani's arms. "You go shower first. I need to organize my crap." She gesticulated wildly at the disarray that was their room. "And later, if that bothers you while you're reading, I'll start some required sketches for my Studio One course."

"Overachiever," Dani quipped and opened the door to head for a shower. "I'll be quick."

~~~

Dani and Kate held up Kate's drunken roommate, Petra, as they helped her walk back to the dorm after the Greek-apalooza party. Meredith walked behind them just in case Petra fell backward. Dani was still amazed at how huge the gathering had been. There had been way too much alcohol and who knew what else. That stuff just wasn't her thing. Kate was a little tipsy, too, but not to the magnitude of Petra.

"She didn't eat dinner," Kate said as they approached the covered walkway to the Mount. "Too many shots of fireball."

"You should probably get some food in her stomach," Meredith said. "Like a piece of bread or something."

"And get a bucket," Dani quipped.

"Dani," Meredith scolded.

"What? It's probably going to happen," Dani said without looking back. Another set of stairs was coming up, and she had to watch what she was doing.

"Good call, actually," Kate said. "I thought the party would be different." She sounded disappointed.

Dani had no clue what to say, and neither did Meredith since she didn't respond either. Parties and drinking had never been Dani's cup of tea. Before she met Meredith, she'd been to a lot of parties with her friends but would nurse one beer the whole night. And she wouldn't even drink the whole thing anyway. She had no clue why beer was so popular. It tasted terrible.

She was still lost in her own thoughts when they finally reached Kate and

27

Petra's room. Without warning, though, Petra broke free and ran to one of the bathrooms at the end of the hall. Kate ran after her. Dani and Meredith followed but at a slower pace.

"This is *not* fun," Meredith said quietly with a sigh. "But they both kind of need our help."

"Yeah." Dani shrugged. "We're like the designated drivers, but without cars."

Meredith chuckled and then amended, "We're the designated walkers."

It was Dani's turn to laugh, but she'd heard the tiredness in Meredith's voice. It had been a really long day, and even though it was only ten o'clock, Dani wanted to be back in their room cuddling with Meredith.

Once Petra emptied the contents of her stomach and was able to keep down a couple of bites of a blueberry muffin, Dani and Meredith wished Kate and Petra well and then finally headed back to their own room.

"Not fun," Meredith muttered again as she opened the door to their room. Once Dani was also inside, she amended. "Well, that's not true. The party itself was kind of fun. Seeing all those people? I have a ton of sorority flyers in my pocket." She pulled them out and tossed them on her desk.

Dani drew Meredith into a hug and sighed as she let go of her tension. "And now we can forever say we went to the opening party."

"Yep."

"Tired?"

"Yep. Shower. Now." Meredith pulled out of Dani's arms and got ready for a shower.

"Me, too," Dani said and also got ready. "I think I'm wearing more beer than I ingested."

"We'll need to figure out how to do laundry," Meredith said, putting on her robe. At least she wasn't shy about changing in front of Dani. They were getting used to seeing each other's bodies.

"Quick cuddle before bed?"

"Counting on it," Meredith said. "I'm almost rethinking our sleep rule, though."

"The rule about sleeping in our own beds on school nights?"

"Yeah, that one."

"We both need our rest," Dani said, sounding like the grand sage that she totally wasn't. "But we'll reevaluate in a few days. Okay?"

"Mm hmm." Meredith headed out the door to the shower.

It wasn't long before they were both showered, had their clothes picked out for their first day of classes, and were lying on Meredith's bed facing each other. The kissing had tried to heat up to more, but they were both too tired to follow through.

"I don't want to leave you," Dani said, looking back at her own bed on the other side of the room.

"I don't want you to leave." Meredith snuggled closer.

"It's a stupid rule," Dani said softly.

"Don't leave me. Ever."

"I won't," Dani whispered. "We'll catch up on sleep on the weekends."

"Mm hmm," Meredith murmured as her eyes closed, and she fell asleep safe and secure in Dani's arms, just where Dani wanted her.

Chapter 4

Enough Fodder

Nerves about the first day of classes kept both Dani and Meredith from getting a good night's sleep, and both were clearly anxious Monday morning, but having breakfast with Kate and Petra and a few others calmed them somewhat. And now, they had backpacks on their respective backs and were headed to the main campus for Monday classes. Neither expected to return to their dorm room until almost four o'clock. Yes, Mondays were going to be long. Maybe naps before dinner?

"Wait," Meredith said and stopped walking. "I thought you were going to work out." She pointed toward the fitness center they had just passed.

Dani kept walking down the sidewalk toward the HB Crouse building where Meredith's eight o'clock Spanish class was. "C'mon," Dani said cryptically. "You don't want to be late for your first class, do you?"

Meredith caught up and hooked her arm in Dani's. "Why, Ms. Lassiter, are you walking me to class?"

"I am," Dani said and stood taller.

Meredith didn't say anything for a moment and then cleared her throat. "You are the sweetest thing."

"I'm a thing now?"

"Mm hmm." Meredith unlinked their arms when they heard a couple of students behind them. "And you're *my* thing." This she whispered. "Don't you forget it."

"Glad to be of service, ma'am." Dani tipped her imaginary hat.

Once at the flat-roofed brick building, Dani reminded Meredith that she was on her own for lunch since Dani had her sign language class then. She wished Meredith luck in her first class and then also wished her luck and good vibes for her first-ever studio art class right after that. Thank goodness the building that held art classes wasn't too far since Meredith would only have ten minutes to get there.

Dani headed back toward the fitness center. She was a little sad about leaving her girlfriend, but then remembered that every day, except Fridays, they had at least one class together. And today's shared *Introduction to Women's and Gender Studies* class was at two-fifteen, so she'd see Meredith then. The course would not only satisfy one of the Liberal Arts degree requirements but also sounded really interesting to both of them. Dani wanted to read ahead, but there was no assigned textbook. None that she could find anyway. Apparently, they would read articles and watch videos using the Blackboard online system. They both had good laptops—high school graduation presents—but should either of those devices fail, their dorm had a computer study room. Happily, though, she had somehow managed to read the entire first chapter in her American Politics book the day before. After working out, she planned to find a quiet place on campus to read the second before her ASL class at twelve forty-five.

Dani swiped her ID card at the fitness center entrance and headed right for the bulletin board. She took a pen from her pocket and wrote her name, phone number, and preferred position on the intramural league lacrosse sign-up sheet.

"First group session is Friday evening at the Ensley Athletic Center off Comstock," Dani read out loud from the top information sheet.

"That's when the student captains assess your skills," a voice behind her said.

Dani turned, knowing Joiee would be standing there. "Oh, hey."

Joiee nodded toward the sign-up. "Glad to see you came back." She flipped up the sign-up sheet. "Ah, first home position. Nice." She nodded her approval. "You'll get snapped up fast by one of the captains. That's for sure. You don't happen to know any goalies, do you? They're in high demand."

"No. I don't know anyone, actually."

"You know me."

"But you said you didn't play."

Joiee scoffed. "I don't, but I'm one of the student trainers assigned there. It's part of my job." Her hand circled around, indicating her job as a fitness center employee.

Dani nodded and was about to excuse herself when she decided to get bold. "I want to get a weights workout in. Do you have time for that tour now?"

Dani almost took a step back when Joiee's entire face lit up.

"Yeah, yeah," Joiee stammered. "Let me just tell Derek."

"Cool." Dani pointed to the warm-up mats. "I'll be stretching over there."

After an hour of lifting, Dani's muscles were aching, and she was physically weary. She'd be sore later, that was for sure. The workout itself had been good, even though she had to turn down Joiee's repeated offers for personalized training sessions. Joiee claimed to have a girlfriend, so it was confusing that she was coming on so strong. Dani simply pretended not to notice Joiee's advances. It wasn't that Dani didn't know how to flirt. She did. She'd landed Meredith, hadn't she? She just didn't *want* to flirt. She wasn't the least bit attracted to the tall, dark-haired woman, and, besides, it would be cheating. She would never betray Meredith that way. Ever.

After her invigorating yet tiring workout, Dani cleaned up as best she could and made a mental note to bring a change of clothes next time. The locker room had lockers and nice-looking showers. On Dani's way out, Joiee gave her a friendly goodbye and reminded her about Friday's lacrosse practice. She also clued her in on what to wear and what to bring. All in all, Joiee had been helpful that morning, but, nope, Dani was not attracted to her.

Since Dani's first-ever college class was American Sign Language back in the HB Crouse building, she decided to catch some rays in the quad and read her American Government textbook instead of going back up to the dorm. She found an isolated bench near the edge of the quad and read for a while. Highlighting the actual textbook felt weird because marking up a school-issued book at Whickett High School was sacrilegious. Dani couldn't help wondering how many other ways her supposedly good high school had not prepared her for college. She had an electronic version of the textbook online, but since Poly Sci was her major, she wanted tangible hard copies of all books. Call her old-fashioned…well, no one ever did, but whatever.

After a good hour of reading about the Constitution and its origins, Dani was definitely ready for something else. She checked the time and briefly thought about checking on Meredith, who would now be in her Studio-Art class. She rejected the idea immediately. She wanted to be a supportive girlfriend, but not a stalker-type. Dang, she should have brought her lacrosse stick with her. She could have practiced cradling and stick skills now that she was going to play in the intramural league. She didn't see any kind of wall for wallball drills or a net for shooting practice, so that wouldn't have worked anyway. Maybe Joiee knew a place where she could practice alone. Hopefully, she'd find somebody to work out with at the lacrosse practice on Friday. She desperately wanted to stay in shape, and that wasn't happening sitting on a bench doing nothing.

"Uh uh," Dani chided herself and closed her eyes. "No panicking. Everything is fine." She took a deep breath, held it, and let it out slowly.

It was then that Dani realized the reason she wanted to check in on Meredith. It wasn't for Meredith's sake at all. It was for her own. She was nervous and unsure. Everything was new and unknown, and Dani felt out of her element. On the phone the other night, Millie told her to be strong for Meredith. Well, duh, Dani obviously would do that, but she also had to figure out a way to be strong for herself.

Too antsy to sit any longer, Dani stuffed the textbook in her backpack and headed to the student union to get something to eat, and then she'd head to her ASL class. She'd be early for the class, but maybe she'd look for a beginner's sign language video on her laptop or something. At least that would distract her from freaking out about…everything.

~~~

"Show Kate and Petra," Meredith said to Dani at the dining hall table. "They haven't seen your new skills."

Dani scoffed but pushed her chair back from the table. She signed, "Hi, how are you? I am fine. My name is D a n i." She spelled her name slowly using the letters her ASL instructor had taught them that very afternoon.

"Ooh," Kate gushed as she clapped and bounced in her seat. "That was so good. You're so far along already." She looked at her roommate Petra and said, "Wasn't she good?"

Petra's smile conveyed so many things, including awe and amusement. "Yes, very impressive," she said genuinely, but it was clear that her roommate's overzealous enthusiasm also amused her. Petra turned to Dani and said, "You know she's going to make you teach her all that."

Dani laughed. "I know."

"Yes, yes," Kate said, moving her fingers. "Show me."

"Can I eat first?" Dani pointed to her beef tips and salad. No pasta or potatoes for her. Carbs were going to be limited from now on. She had to keep in shape.

"Oh, duh," Kate said and smoothed down her immaculate hair that didn't need smoothing. Dani recognized it for the calming gesture that it was. "Stevie says I rush into things without pausing to assess." She looked down as if embarrassed. "Sorry."

"You're fine," Dani said. Not sure how to ease the situation, she said, "So, how was everyone's first day of classes today? Meredith and I have some reading and a video to watch for our Women's and Gender Studies class."

"You'll have to let us know how that class is," Kate said, now fully recovered. "It's not an 'all men suck' course, is it?"

Dani almost choked on her food. She coughed behind her fist, swallowed, and said with a laugh. "No."

Meredith added, "We talked about gender today and how it's basically a social and cultural construct. It's how the society you live in dictates what it means to be a woman or a man. They even talked about people who don't feel comfortable claiming any gender."

"Non-binary?" Petra offered.

"Mm hmm," Meredith said. "There are cultures that are cool with those with mixed genders. I didn't know that. I think I've been living in a bubble."

"Me, too," Kate said.

Dani picked up the thread. "Problems come up when a culture expects every person to conform to the gender role assigned to the biological sex they were born in. They talked about terms like cisgender, genderqueer, gender fluidity, and transgender. Today was a lot."

"Cisgender is when a person's claimed gender matches the sex assigned when they were born, right?" Kate asked. After both Meredith and Dani nodded, she added, "So I identify as a cisgender woman." Without taking a breath, she blurted, "Hey, how did they define 'woman'?" Kate asked. "I mean, is there a difference between woman and female?"

"Great question," Meredith said with a laugh. "We've only been in the course for one hour and fifteen minutes, so…" she glanced over at Dani as if to ask for help with her explanation. "They explained that 'female' means the sexual genitalia seen at birth."

"AFAB," Dani added. "Assigned female at birth."

"Right," Meredith said. "But the definition of 'woman' is trickier. This is where people all over the planet are arguing."

"Go on," Kate said, taking a sip of milk.

"Well," Meredith said, "the professors said since we needed to establish working definitions for the class, they asserted that the terms 'woman' and 'man' are related to gender identification and *not* to assigned sex at birth. I mean, the terms aren't necessarily related to sexual organs."

Kate and Petra listened politely, as did Dani, who was ready to jump in if necessary.

Meredith continued. "People interchange terms so often that it gets confusing, so please bear with me while I try to make sense of it."

"All is well," Petra said.

"So, the way I understand it," Meredith said, "the term *woman* can either mean a biological female or a person who identifies as a woman but is male biologically. You know, has male…" Meredith gestured to her lap as her face turned the cutest shade of pink.

"We get it," Kate said, coming to the rescue. "You're talking about a transgender woman, right?"

"Yes," Meredith said with a nod.

"The professors said that was just one way to look at it," Dani added. "But seriously, the professors are fascinating. Not preachy or condescending at all. I think we're going to like this course."

Meredith nodded her agreement.

"I might take that next semester," Kate said.

"That's probably a good course for a social work major," Meredith offered.

"I have that one on my schedule for the spring," Petra said. "Take it with me, Kate."

"Okay," Kate said amenably. "Save your notes for us," she added quickly, touching Dani's forearm.

Instantly uncomfortable, Dani pulled her arm away and simply nodded. She wasn't sure where the ethical line was for sharing notes or assignments, but she'd talk it over with Meredith later. She glanced at her girlfriend, who had begun an animated discussion with Petra about her first art class. Hopefully, Meredith hadn't seen Kate's lingering touch. She smiled at Meredith's description of the plethora of art supplies available to students from some big art grant or something. Dani's heart swelled as she watched how happy Meredith seemed to be.

Dani looked up to find Petra looking at her. Petra smiled. It was another one of those knowing smiles. Dani wasn't sure what it was that Petra knew, but one thing was certain—Petra wasn't eating her food. She was kind of pushing it around and cutting it up so it looked smaller. Maybe she still wasn't feeling well from the shots of Fireball the night before. Must be. Dani wasn't about to point it out, though. As far as Dani was concerned, the incident was over.

~~~

It was finally Friday, and her third Government and Politics class was just finishing. The Poly Sci seniors had been absolutely right about reading ahead because the extremely no-nonsense professor expected them to know the material in the first two chapters inside and out. Luckily, Dani was able to give back a reasonably informed response when the professor asked her a direct question during the first class on Tuesday. Reading ahead was the name of the game, for sure.

Petra stood up from her seat next to Dani's. "Did you get the professor's hint about reading the UPenn Law Journal Article about Federalism?"

Dani nodded and adjusted her backpack. "Summer 2023. The first one that finds it shares with the other?"

"I was hoping you'd say that," Petra said. "Are you going to the Poly Sci Leadership meeting?"

"Yep." Dani knew her muted response didn't match her enthusiasm for joining the PSLA club. She was eager to get firsthand knowledge about politics and leadership. It was just that it had been a long week, and she still had her ASL class after lunch and then the first lacrosse practice after dinner. She'd have to get some homework done somewhere in there. Or maybe since Meredith had no classes on Friday, she'd be in the mood to snuggle and cuddle and …

"You okay?" Petra asked. She had a bemused expression on her face.

"Hmm?"

"You looked majorly distracted."

"Just tired."

"I know the feeling," Petra said and jostled around a slow-moving student in front of them.

It seemed like their entire Government and Politics class was headed for the big lecture hall, and once they got inside, it was obvious that the club was popular. "This is the PSLA freshmen meeting, right?" Dani asked Petra as they made their way toward the front of the hall.

Petra nodded and chose to sit in the first row. Great. No hiding. Dani had no choice but to follow.

"Sit, sit," one of the seniors said. The seniors who had led the orientation were there and again dressed to impress.

Dani suddenly felt way underdressed in her cargo shorts, sneakers, and button-down short-sleeved print shirt. Meredith had picked out the shirt that morning for her, saying it brought out the blue in her eyes. So, if Meredith liked how she dressed, that's all that mattered. Right?

"My name is Mae," the tall senior said. She was big-boned and of East Asian descent. And she exuded the confidence that Dani hoped to have one day. "Student Association members almost always come from this group. Look around. The people who will be representing you in student government are sitting in this room." She paused for a moment and said, "But we need to get the frosh in shape. Don't we?" Her question was directed to the three other seniors standing in the front of the room with her. They all nodded. None of them smiled, which made the hairs on the back of Dani's neck stand up. She exchanged a concerned glance with Petra.

"Freshmen, you need to hone your debating skills. Many of you were senior class presidents in high school, but realize this." She jerked her head to take in one side of the room and then jerked it toward the other. "That was a popularity contest." She tapped the table in front of her with such force that it made more than one person jump, Dani included. "This PSLA will *not* show you how to be popular. No. Here, you'll hone your skills. We'll show you how to get elected." She gestured to a pale, skinny white guy with scraggly sandy blond hair and said, "Wayne will lay down the specifics."

"If you want to run for office, you'll sign up on one of these five old-school clipboards after this meeting," Wayne said without preamble and held up one of the clipboards. "We'll randomly pair each of you up against another candidate for speeches. Write speeches you think will get you elected, even though these are only practice. But don't get us wrong. They will reveal your weaknesses." He paused for the slightest of moments and added, "Hopefully, they will reveal your strengths, too. This is the place where your classmates will get to know you. Do well, and they will get behind you and get you elected. Do poorly, and they won't remember your name." He gestured toward Mae and the other two seniors. "We will give advice and try to help you as much as we can, but ultimately, your classmates sitting here will be the ones to decide your fate.

"When you give your speech, tell us how you'll represent us. Tell us how you plan to be the voice of the people." He swept his arm around the large lecture hall. "Find out what the issues are. Freshmen, you've been on campus for three minutes." He waited for the chuckles to die down. "So, you have a lot of work to do to determine the issues. What needs to change here? What shouldn't? What can *you* bring to the Student Association that will elevate our collective experiences here at SU?" He smirked, then added, "Figure that out, and you're a shoo-in."

He nodded toward Mae, who said, "Debates start next Friday during this club time. Random pairings will be posted on the PSLA webpage on Sunday evenings by eight pm." Mae nodded toward the two remaining seniors and then moved to the side. Wayne walked over to stand beside her.

The young black woman brushed imaginary crumbs off her suit jacket and walked behind the podium on the left side of the lecture hall. A short guy with dark, clean-cut hair moved to the right podium.

The young woman spoke first. "We're going to model election speeches for you. Who goes first will be determined randomly. You'll each have three minutes to get your points across uninterrupted. After each candidate speaks, you will then have one minute to rebut. Again, this is uninterrupted."

Dani was impressed at the way the young woman captured everyone's attention. Dani felt like the woman was talking directly to her. That was talent.

"Some say there is an advantage to going second. I'm not sure about that. But one thing I do know is that first impressions are everything. So, make them good." She tapped the podium and then stood taller as she breathed. "Hey, everyone. My name is Shela Unigwe. I'm a senior here at Syracuse and in my three and change years here, I've noticed some things that need our attention. Let me outline those for you."

Dani settled into the colloquial and friendly cadence of Shela's speech and found herself wanting to help Shela fix all those things she outlined in her three-minute speech. The agricultural garden seemed like it needed volunteers. Maybe Dani and Meredith could... Dani chuckled to herself. Dang if Shela didn't have Dani under some kind of spell because Dani was ready to cast her vote immediately, even though Shela was already an elected member of the student government.

Dani turned toward Petra, raised her eyebrows, and nodded to indicate how impressed she was with Shela's speech. Petra returned the nod. Yes, everyone in that lecture hall was getting schooled on presence and speech-giving.

Shela ended her speech with these words. "Help me make this place better. For one reason or another, we were all attracted to this community and the traditions associated with Syracuse University. Your votes for Shela Unigwe will help make this the place you thought it would be." She pushed away from the podium but kept eye contact with the crowd as enthusiastic applause filled the space.

When the applause died down, the dark-haired guy moved closer to his podium. "My name is Enrique Acosta. I'm also a senior and have been here for three and change years, just like my opponent. But what my opponent fails to see is that many of the issues she brings up will only affect a handful of people on campus. Perhaps this arises from the fact that she is a first-generation American from Nigeria. As I understand it, her family were poor farmers before moving to America, and perhaps this is what influences her love for the agricultural garden. Sure, sure, it is a good project, but is that where all of the energy of an elected official should go? I say no. Has she given you concrete steps for funding those projects? Again, she has not." He looked over at his opponent, who looked back at him without emotion or any kind of reaction at all. Dani thought Shela's stoicism was incredible, but now doubts were creeping into Dani's mind. Shela hadn't really talked about how to pay for any of these things, had she?

"Here are my thoughts," Enrique continued. "Everyone knows Syracuse sports are a major source of interest and income for the university. But do we know where the money goes? That's what we need to find out. I mean, who's lining their pockets on the backs of our hard-working student athletes? Division one sports are grueling, but are the athletes themselves profiting from their hard work? Are any of us? That's one of the first things I would look into."

Dani sighed. He was making convincing arguments. Once Enrique wrapped up his speech, both speakers had one-minute rebuttals. Shela picked apart the fact that her opponent had not already researched where the sports

40

income went. She asked the group if they wanted to vote for someone who was all bluster and no substance.

Dani was quite confused when the meeting ended. She had no idea who she would have voted for.

After signing up for spots on one of the clipboards, Dani and Petra walked toward the student union, where they were going to meet Meredith, Kate, and a few other dormmates for lunch.

"That was intense," Petra said. "I mean, when Enrique started out negative, I almost dismissed him as a candidate because of that, but…"

"But he brought up good points," Dani finished.

"He did," Petra agreed. "So, I guess our next move is to find out what the issues are here on campus and how we might address them."

"Exactly," Dani said. As she veered toward the student union, Petra didn't. "You coming?"

"No," Petra said. "I forgot my notebook for my next class." She pointed toward the Mount. "I have to run back up."

"Cool," Dani said. "I'll check for the article after my ASL class unless you have time to find it first."

"You got it," Petra said as she turned toward the dorm. "Say hi to everyone for me."

"Yep," Dani said and turned away. She took a deep breath, held it, and let it out slowly. She had no worries about public speaking; she was okay with that. The part that was troubling her was the content of her speech. She needed three minutes full of words and sentences that would convince her classmates that she knew what the issues were and that she had solid ideas for addressing them. She also needed to show them that she was leadership worthy. But what exactly did that mean?

As soon as she walked into the student center, both Meredith's and Kate's expressions lit up. Dani relaxed then, knowing that no matter what, she'd be okay with Meredith by her side. She desperately wanted to pull Meredith into a full-body hug and kiss her silly but had to make do with her soft smile instead.

Dani plopped her backpack in the empty seat next to Meredith and hustled to get her lunch. When she sat back down, she took advantage of Petra's absence and wasted no time by asking her friends, "So what do you all think are the major issues here on campus? What do you think needs changing around here?"

No one had an immediate answer, so Dani had to find ways to get them to really think about their lives at Syracuse. Once it got going, though, many other freshmen and even some sophomores overheard the conversation and joined them at their table. After an hour, Dani's head was full of ideas and even fuller with the research she now had to do. No worries. She was intrigued and up for it.

As her classmates left for their afternoon classes, Dani sat back and smiled at Meredith. Yes, all would be okay because she had Meredith. And because she now had more than enough fodder for her first speech.

Chapter 5

Shushed

The Ensley Athletic Center loomed large Friday evening as Dani approached the front doors. Her lacrosse gear was strapped to her back, the stick jutting up on the left side. When she wasn't being recruited to play lacrosse for Syracuse anymore, Dani wasn't going to bring her gear with her. On a weird impulse the day before they drove up, she stashed her lax bag and stick in the pile by the front door. Weird how she needed that stuff in the first week of college.

As Dani was leaving her dorm room earlier, Meredith said it was funny that Dani had two backpacks—one for school and one for sports. Dani laughed and listed everything she needed, like her mouthguard, goggles, water bottle, and towel. She was about to go on, but Meredith shushed her with a kiss. Yeah, that was an excellent way to be shushed.

Meredith. Dani took a deep breath as she reached the big glass doors. In her first week of college, she discovered how much Meredith calmed her. They'd tried to nap together before dinner, but Dani's nerves about the practice, the PSLA debates, and just everything kept her brain moving and her nerves jangling. She tried hard to keep her worries from Meredith, and she'd been successful as far as she could tell. Dani even managed to eat a decent dinner at the dining hall.

As Dani entered the athletic center, she heard the din of voices and activity long before she reached the indoor field. Dozens of women her age buzzed around having a catch or stretching. Did she get the time wrong? No. She was triple-sure positive that the flyer had said seven o'clock. She willed her racing pulse to chill out, and it did somewhat when she saw a familiar face across the field. Joiee was taping up an athlete on the far sidelines, so Dani headed that way. As she walked past the women getting ready to play the game she loved, she realized that all this noise and excitement was just the usual chaos before practice. She'd participated in many similar scenes back in high school. She grinned at her silly nerves and wondered if anything at college would ever feel comfortable.

"Hey, Dani," Joiee called and waved her over. She looked so official at the trainer's table that Dani almost forgot Joiee was only a junior, two years older than herself.

"Hey," Dani said once she reached her acquaintance, who had just put the finishing touches on an athlete's ankle.

"Glad you could make it," Joiee said, laying the athletic tape on the table. Her easy grin put Dani somewhat at ease. "I want you to meet Laura."

She tapped the arm of the woman standing nearby. The woman turned, and Dani lost her breath at her striking looks. Dani was pulled into her eyes. They were crystal green, like the color of Alaskan glacier water. Laura's eyes seemed to have depths beyond anything Dani had ever experienced. Her dark, long blonde hair was tied loosely behind her back, making Dani almost wish she hadn't cut her own hair so short. She was vaguely aware of Laura's hand reaching toward her in handshake. Somehow, Dani recovered enough to shake the offered hand but almost forgot to let go. She swallowed hard and then said something to Joiee's girlfriend. What she said, she had no idea.

"Joiee tells me you have experience at first home," Laura said.

"Yes," Dani said succinctly, floating back down to earth.

"Excellent," Laura said. "Listen, I hear you're hoping to get the attention of the varsity coaches for next year."

Dani nodded. She was a little tongue-tied in front of the amazing creature in front of her. She had never seen such an attractive woman in all her life.

"Getting good enough to get an invite to try out for that team will be your new job," Laura counseled.

Dani tried to stay focused, but the words were coming out of Laura's full pink lips. Dani yanked her gaze from Laura's mouth to her eyes. Ack. Not better. The swirling vortex of glacier green was pulling her in.

"Academics?" Laura continued. "Back seat to your training. And if you make the team next year, you'll have to resign yourself to having a lot of make-up work to do. Some professors won't accommodate you, and that's their prerogative, but most will. I redshirted freshman year. It was rough. I practiced with the team and even suited up for games but never played. I put in the same hours and sweat equity as the real players but never got my chance. My grades were for shit, too." Laura looked at Joiee, "I never saw my girlfriend."

Joiee laughed. "Yeah, we were like two ships passing in the night."

Dani smiled and glanced at Joiee. Wow, they'd been a couple since their freshman year, so that made two years so far.

"And," Joiee added as she poked Laura on the shoulder, "you put in a lot more training and practice time than the others, in my opinion."

"Yeah," Laura agreed. "Anyway, Dani, I want you to try like hell to get noticed by the coaches, but be realistic. I busted my ass to be deemed worthy sophomore year, but I didn't make it. I'm not saying you won't, but don't set yourself up for a fall."

Dani frowned. She couldn't imagine what that would feel like. That, she decided, was not going to happen to her. She was determined to make the team next year and not as a redshirt, either. Maybe not a starter, but still.

"Don't look so stricken, Dani," Laura said with a chuckle. "I was relieved, actually. Playing Division 1 is a major commitment. It's a job. It will become your career for however long you play. Nothing else will matter. So, my advice? Major in something easy. Take online courses with online assignments. During my freshman year, I had tutors to help me make up all the work I missed. And, seriously, if you're not already in a relationship, forget about having one. If you are in one, just know that it'll suffer." Laura's serious expression softened. "Play in this intramural league. Put in the work. Varsity assistant coaches prowl around now and then, scouting informally."

Dani must have gotten a stricken expression because Laura laughed and said, "Relax. They won't be here tonight."

"Is everyone here trying to make the varsity team?" Dani asked, finally finding her voice.

"No," Laura said with a laugh. "The rest of us are here because we love lacrosse."

Dani joined Laura's laughter. "Me, too."

Laura glanced at her watch, "All right. I have to get the other captains organized so we can get this practice going. We're hoping to have four full teams this year."

Dani couldn't help watching Laura walk away. Her running shorts hugged her muscular body, and her confident walk was mesmerizing.

A soft clearing of a throat brought Dani back to reality. She felt her face flush since she'd so obviously been caught ogling Joiee's girlfriend.

"Listen, it's okay." Joiee leaned closer. "She has that effect on most people."

Dani pressed her lips together and nodded twice. Her face must be flaming red.

Joiee laughed again and pulled Dani by the arm. "C'mon, let me introduce you to a couple of players."

And with that, Dani was immersed in the sport she loved for two incredible hours. At first, she was part of the newbie group being assessed by the captains. Everyone, including the newbies, ran, did conditioning, and performed drills. Dani took every activity seriously as if she were being evaluated with every move of her muscles.

When it came time for four-on-three scrimmage-like drills, Dani was tentatively put on the Team Indigo squad. Joiee seemed impressed by this designation, and Dani learned later that Team Indigo was typically the second-best group. Laura was captain of the Team Cyan squad, which was the top group. Joiee told her that everyone vied to be in the elite Cyan group. Secretly, Dani made it her goal to move up to Team Cyan as fast as possible so those varsity coaches might see her and take her seriously. Funny, though, she had naively thought the captains would try to make the teams as equal as possible so one team didn't dominate. Not true, then.

Dani finally felt at home on the Syracuse campus. That was because she was playing the sport she loved. Whenever she was on a lacrosse field, be it indoors or out, she was in her element right where she belonged. By the end of that first practice, four full teams had been formed, with Dani remaining on Team Indigo. And that was okay for now. The captains said there would be movement from team to team every week, so moving up through the colors to Team Cyan was perfectly possible. That gave Dani hope because if she had any hope of making the varsity team, she had to be on the best team in the intramural league. The coaches would notice her for sure that way.

Dani headed to the sidelines with some players who'd also made Team Indigo. They bemoaned the twice-a-week practices, and one of her teammates, Amanda, wondered out loud how she would handle practices and games and keep up with classes. She groaned that she was "tired already."

Dani and some of the other players consoled Amanda, but Dani had been thinking the same thing. That evening's practice had been intense. She was glad she had done daily cardio that week because she'd had good stamina. Many of the others were clearly out of shape and sucking wind.

As they said their goodbyes to each other, Dani couldn't help wondering how hectic life would be if she actually made the varsity team next year. No, that was negative thinking, so she amended her thought. She couldn't help wondering how hectic life would be *when* she made the varsity team as a sophomore. There. That was more optimistic. She tucked that worry into the back of her mind and lifted her water bottle. Empty. Dang it.

"Hey, Dani," Joiee called to her, "I'll give you a ride back to your dorm after I clean up my stuff." She gestured to all the accouterment that went with being an athletic trainer. Rolls of athletic tape, pre-wrap, bandages, ice packs, and a host of other stuff lay scattered on the trainer's table.

Dani wasn't sure what to say. She'd planned to simply walk back and wasn't sure if she should get in a car with a woman she hardly knew. Fatigue washed over her, and she heard herself saying, "Cool. Thanks. I'm going to hit the bathroom, fill up my water, and meet you back here." She'd rinse off her mouthguard, too, actually. There was nothing more disgusting than forgetting to do that.

"You got it," Joiee called back.

As she headed for the locker room, Dani hoped that by accepting the ride, Joiee wouldn't take that as a green light to make a move. She pushed that worry aside as she entered the impressive locker room. After taking care of business and washing her hands, she splashed water on her face to help cool her down from the strenuous workout.

"You looked good out there."

Dani bolted upright, water streaming down her face. It was Laura. "You scared me."

"And you look good in here, too." Laura moved closer.

Dani's nerves jangled. Laura was flirting. That much Dani understood. She didn't respond. She couldn't. What was she supposed to say to that? To buy time, she turned away from Laura and reached for a paper towel to dry her face. When she turned back, she jumped again. Laura, with her soft hair, green eyes, and commanding posture, stood inches from Dani. Dani's heart pounded, and not from the workout. She took an involuntary step away and found her back against the concrete wall. Laura moved quickly. She put both hands on the wall on either side of Dani's head, effectively pinning her there.

"You're very attractive, Danielle," Laura said quietly, her voice husky.

Dani didn't want this, but she couldn't get any words out. Her mouth was so dry she could barely swallow. She prayed that someone would come in. Laura would back off then, right?

No one came.

Laura's lips parted slightly, but she moved no closer. She searched Dani's face, for permission probably, but Dani wasn't going to give it. Laura's green eyes seemed to be growing darker, if that was possible.

Dani needed to move, but she couldn't. Her brain was misfiring. Her muscles weren't working. She didn't know what to do. She'd been ambushed—frightened into inaction. Thoughts raced through her brain, but she couldn't voice a single one. One thought was stronger than the rest. Laura was integral to her doing well in the intramural league and ultimately making the varsity team.

Laura leaned in but then bolted back when several noisy players entered the locker room in the nick of time. Rescued! Dani breathed a relieved sigh. Maybe she'd been holding her breath. She couldn't remember. One of the players gave Dani a weird look just as Laura was saying, "To be continued."

She poked Dani in the shoulder and, without a backward glance, waltzed out of the locker room as if nothing had happened. Dani recognized one of the players from her Government and Politics class. Shit. She must be thinking the worst right now.

Dani couldn't worry about that, though. She had to gather her wits. She was shaking and a little light-headed but somehow found herself at the sink. Not knowing what else to do, she splashed water on her face again. In one small moment, her happy place had been trampled. Defiled. Negated.

She punched herself in the thigh and blew out an angry sigh. She'd always imagined that she could fight her way out of an attack. No rapist would ever have his way with her. She'd had self-defense classes in high school, and she was strong. But she froze. Why didn't she react? Why didn't she kick Laura in the shin or something?

Dani had no answers, but the one thing she did know was that she was not about to get in a car with Laura's girlfriend. Maybe it was a setup. Maybe the two of them prowled on unsuspecting newbies or something. Maybe they were into threesomes. Dani was not.

She snuck out a back exit and practically ran the entire way back to her dorm. Her one goal was to get back to Meredith.

Dani's adrenaline wore out just as she reached the road up to her dorm. She slowed to a walk to catch her breath. She had to look normal in front of Meredith because Meredith could not know what had just happened in the locker room. To tell Meredith would be to create doubts in Meredith's mind. She'd always wonder if Dani had initiated the incident, or if not, maybe she'd think Dani sent signals that Laura reacted to.

Dani sat at one of the outside picnic tables. It was already dark, but the table was well-lit by outside security lights. Meredith must never find out. She'd think Dani was unfaithful. She wasn't, but it wouldn't matter. If Meredith thought it, then it was true.

Dani wiped angry tears from her face. She'd have to stop at one of the restrooms to splash her face. Otherwise, Meredith would know she'd been crying. She stood up from her brief stop at the table and headed into the dorm. Just as she was going in one door, she saw the guy with the beard coming out the other. He was the guy that had been checking out Meredith. What if he did to Meredith what Laura had done to Dani? Or worse?

No way. That was never going to happen. Dani wanted to rush at him and tell him to leave Meredith alone or she would...okay, she didn't know what she would do, but something. Something violent, no doubt. By the time all those thoughts had run through her brain, the guy was already headed down the path toward campus.

That path is isolated, Dani thought as she headed into the dorm lobby. There was no way she would ever let Meredith go down to campus alone. No way. Dani thought maybe she should set up a self-defense class for her dorm. A plan was coming together in her mind as she stepped off the elevator on her floor. She headed to her room but remembered that she needed to wash her face.

Alone in the pod bathroom, Dani finally understood many things. One was that she might not be as safe as she'd assumed. And it wasn't the Syracuse campus or anything like that. It was just that people could be unpredictable. They might have ulterior motives like Laura. Another thing she realized was the incredible shame she was feeling. Although she herself had done nothing wrong, a part of her understood what it felt like to be a victim. *What would people think*? And then there was the shame of having to retell the events and relive them repeatedly. And now that she thought about it, maybe Laura wasn't done. She'd even said, "To be continued," or something like that. Shit. That was, like, a threat. Dread filled her chest. If Dani told anyone, Laura would attack her in a different way, possibly ruining Dani's reputation. Dani couldn't even imagine the shame associated with an actual physical assault. In comparison to rape, what Dani had experienced wasn't even a blip on the radar.

She stared at her reflection in the mirror, momentarily stunned at this revelation. She suddenly realized what atrocities women experienced at the hands of other people. How can this happen? Where was the humanity? She wiped away angry tears and closed her eyes. She willed her new understanding of reality into the background. She had to face her girlfriend in a moment, and everything had to be okay and fine. After all, Dani was the strong one, like

Millie said on the phone when she'd told Dani to take care of Meredith.

Dani vowed to make sure that Meredith and the rest of her friends understood the threats out there. Laura had cornered her in a public place. It was isolated at the time, but Dani had not given it a second thought. She would from now on.

Feeling like she could face Meredith, she headed into her dorm room. The smile that lit Meredith's face was a balm to Dani's soul. Meredith silently waved her over, so Dani dropped her bag and complied.

"Guess who's here?" Meredith said to her phone. Ahh, she was video chatting with someone.

"Who?" came the unmistakable voice of Meredith's younger brother Mikey.

"Boo," Dani said as she popped in behind Meredith so Mikey could see her.

"Dude!" Mikey yelled. "Mom, mom," he called, "Dani here."

"Hey, dude," Dani said, leaning a soft elbow on Meredith's shoulder. "How was school today?"

"Fun," Mikey said.

"Hey, Dani," Meredith's mother said, coming into view. "Good to see you. Meredith says you were at a lacrosse practice."

"Yes," Dani said and explained the indoor field and her scheme for making the varsity team.

"I'm so proud of you," Meredith's mom said. "I'm proud of both my girls."

Something in the tone of Mrs. Bedford's voice hit Dani like a missile as homesickness washed over her. Tears hit her eyes instantly, and she stood up out of view.

Meredith looked up concerned. Dani simply waved her off and turned away to wipe her eyes. She picked up her bag where she'd unceremoniously dropped it by the door and tucked it away after pulling out her empty water bottle. She'd clean that later. Her phone chimed an incoming text. She didn't recognize the number.

315-555-5643: It's Joiee. You okay? Where'd you go?

DANI: I'm fine. I decided to run home. Get an extra workout in. Sorry. Forgot you'd offered a ride.

315-555-5643: Okay. I was worried.

Dani didn't want the text exchange to go on any longer, so she just put a thumbs-up emoji over Joiee's last text. And she didn't even wonder where Joiee had gotten her number from. She'd clearly gotten it from the sign-up sheet. Crap. That meant Laura had her number, too. Dani swallowed hard. This nightmare wasn't over, was it?

She faced away from Meredith as she undressed and put on a robe. She needed to take a shower. Meredith's calm and joyful conversation with her mother and brother helped her relax. These were people that Dani loved and who loved her right back. These were safe people.

She turned and smiled as she heard Mikey talk about the new school year as a seventh grader. He seemed to be managing just fine without his big sister there to walk him to and from school. Apparently, Mrs. Bedford had hired a couple of high school girls from their neighborhood to walk him to school, drop him off with his resource teacher, and pick him up afterward. It had put Meredith's mind at ease. Dani's, too, she had to admit.

Dani chimed in and said her goodbyes along with Meredith. Once Meredith ended the call, she stood up quietly and pulled Dani into a soft hug. She didn't speak as she rubbed Dani's back and rocked her almost imperceptibly from side to side.

After a full minute, Meredith finally asked, "Are you okay?"

No one can know, Dani thought as she shushed her own self. "Yes," came the outward answer. *No*, came the inward one.

Chapter 6

Safety

Dani woke up Saturday morning with dread, confused about why…until she remembered. She bolted out of bed and got dressed to walk Meredith to the art building to work on a project, even though she would have preferred to stay in the dorm to nurse her aching muscles, sore from the long lacrosse practice the night before. She lied to Meredith as they walked toward campus, saying she was going to work out at the fitness center, but that wasn't the truth at all, now was it? Dani wasn't going to risk seeing Joiee or Laura. She didn't know if they had some kind of game going on, one where Dani was caught in the middle, but nope, she was not going to play. She could go for a run but couldn't bring herself to. Who knew what could happen if her running path brought her to an isolated area? Maybe she was just paranoid, but maybe not. Look what had happened the night before.

The rest of Saturday and all of Sunday passed by quietly. Almost too quietly. Dani cringed every time her phone dinged an incoming text, but thankfully, neither Joiee nor Laura texted or called. Maybe they'd both gotten the hint that Dani wasn't interested. But what was Laura's 'To be continued' comment all about? That's the thing that had Dani on edge and looking over her shoulder the entire weekend. Meredith even shot her a funny look in the dining hall Saturday evening when Dani changed their usual table to one near the wall. She didn't tell Meredith that she wanted to have her back to the wall so she could see anyone coming toward them. It had made for an awkward moment, but Meredith didn't press it, and Kate and Petra didn't blink an eye at the table change, so maybe it wasn't so weird after all.

Monday was Labor Day, so there were, blessedly, no classes. To keep herself from thinking too much, she invited Meredith to go on a long walking tour of the campus. Unbeknownst to Meredith, their ultimate destination was the rose garden at Thornden Park near the campus. Dani thought Meredith might balk at all the walking since they did so much walking going to classes during the week, but she didn't and seemed to welcome the break. Dani did, too. The grass amphitheater was cool, and Dani wished she'd brought a blanket and a picnic or something. That would have been romantic. But once they found the rose garden, Meredith was over the moon and took a million pictures, saying she had an idea for her next art project in watercolors using something called a wet-on-wet technique, which made Dani burst out laughing. Meredith smiled when she realized what she'd said, and the blush on her cheeks was so cute.

"Thank you for this," Meredith said.

Dani desperately wanted to put her arms around her girlfriend and pull her close but didn't dare with so many people around. The closest she got was putting her arm around Meredith's shoulders for the selfies they took in front of some deep red roses. "I scored some big points, didn't I?" Dani asked.

"Yes, you did," Meredith said, keeping eye contact. "Maybe we should go back? You know we could…" She leaned in closer and whispered something in Dani's ear that made Dani's whole body flush with heat. Meredith commented that she'd never seen Dani so flushed; even her ears were red. Yep, Dani had gotten lucky last May when Meredith finally looked her way.

Monday afternoon's hours-long exploration of each other's bodies kept Dani blissfully distracted that evening and during classes on Tuesday. She tried not to let Tuesday evening lacrosse practice ruin her vibe. But it did. Of course, it did. She purposefully went out of her way to avoid both Laura and Joiee and didn't even say hello or acknowledge either of them. Joiee gave her a confused expression from across the indoor field, but that was too bad because Dani wanted no part of Joiee or Laura. She made it through the practice unscathed, except for a tired body, and walked back to campus with Amanda and a few of their new Indigo teammates. They even set up a group workout date at the fitness center for Thursday evening. Hopefully, Joiee didn't work then. Hopefully, Joiee and Laura would leave her alone if she were with other people. Right?

Her wishes were granted, and she had an excellent team-building workout at the fitness center on Thursday with Joiee and Laura nowhere to be seen. Friday evening's lacrosse practice was a repeat of Tuesday's, but this time, Joiee didn't make any moves to be friendly or even say hello. She wasn't hostile toward Dani, just indifferent. Good, that's the way Dani wanted it.

Every practice had a group meeting at the beginning and the end. Dani was becoming a master of averting her eyes whenever Laura led these meetings, except that one time when the hair on the back of Dani's neck rose. She forgot herself and looked up to see Laura watching her. Dani looked down immediately. Dang, that was *not* good, but at least Laura hadn't tried to corner her again. Dani was getting smarter. She was never going to let herself be vulnerable that way ever again.

With the second week of college completed, Dani once again walked Meredith to the art building on Saturday morning. Meredith thought it was chivalrous that Dani walked her all the way, but Dani wondered if Meredith might feel smothered after a while. Didn't matter, as long as Meredith was safe. This time, Meredith gave her a short tour of the art room and her dedicated workspace. It was neat and tidy, just like her girlfriend. A few other students worked on projects in the large space, so at least Meredith wouldn't be alone. Good. Dani let herself relax. This was Meredith's happy place. Also good. At least one of them had that.

"Text me when you're ready to get lunch," Dani said as she got ready to leave. "If you can tear yourself away, that is." Her smile was genuine. Dani was surprised at how easily she had been hiding her anxiety from her girlfriend.

"I will," Meredith said. "I'm setting an alarm because I may start that watercolor project, and you know how I get lost in my work."

"Yes, I do," Dani said. She leaned in and whispered, "In all things you do."

"Oh, hush, you," Meredith smacked Dani lightly on the arm. "Maybe we can nap later." The waggling eyebrows made her meaning clear.

"Sure," Dani said with a grin. Meredith was cute when she was frisky. "We could do that, or we could start our monstrous statistics problem set. We didn't do so well on that first one."

"Ugh, don't remind me." A semi-awkward silence followed, and then Meredith whispered, "I want to kiss you goodbye. You know, like normal couples do."

"I know," Dani said. "Guess we're not normal." She said this with a laugh but didn't feel the mirth. What she really wanted to do was move behind Meredith, gather her long dark tresses together, and put them in the hairband Meredith kept around her wrist. Today's was red. But that was way too intimate a move for such a public place. "One day."

Meredith simply nodded and then said, "Have a good workout."

"Will do," Dani lied. To cover her deception, she waved the goofiest wave she'd ever waved, making them both laugh. Grinning, she turned and headed out of the art building, taking the steps two at a time.

She didn't head for the fitness center like Meredith thought she would, but instead, she hung out near the entryway to the covered walkway leading up to the dorms. She pretended to be texting on her phone as she was waiting for at least one other female to head up to the dorm so she wouldn't have to go up alone. It seemed kind of stalkerish, and maybe it was, but she had her reasons. Finally, after the longest ten-minute wait in history, two female students headed her way. They'd obviously just come from the fitness center based on their garb. Unbeknownst to them, Dani was their personal bodyguard, and they were hers.

"Power in numbers," Dani mumbled to herself.

Once back in the safety of her dorm room, she settled in at her desk to write her speech for her eventual PSLA debate. The pairings would come out on Sunday evening, giving her plenty of time to research her opponent. At the last PSLA meeting, Shela made a point about not only knowing your opponent's name but also knowing something about them. It felt kind of invasive, but if that's how the game was played, she would do it. Her eyes widened when she realized her opponent would also be researching her. A quick internet search on her own name didn't come up with much. Just some high school lacrosse accolades. Good. There was nothing there for her opponent to use.

Once she'd gotten down a good outline of the issues she wanted to bring up, she closed the file and checked her phone. Nothing from Meredith yet. And, thankfully, nothing from Joiee or Laura either. Good. They'd gotten the message that Dani wasn't interested in either of them in any way, but that didn't mean she would let her guard down for one instant. No way.

The rest of the weekend flew by, and before she knew it, Sunday evening was upon them.

"Ready?" Meredith said and pushed her black-rimmed glasses back up the bridge of her nose.

"Yep." Dani bounced onto Meredith's bed beside her.

"Initiating call," Meredith said, sounding like an AI robot.

"Sounds like we're part of some FBI secret operation."

Meredith grinned and said, "Response in five, four, three, two—"

"Do I press the button again?" Esther said, looking toward the side. It was odd that Esther was answering the video call because Millie was the more technically savvy of the two and typically handled the calls.

"No, no," came Millie's soft voice off-screen. "Turn it so I can see." This she obviously said to Esther.

Esther adjusted the tablet so both she and Millie were visible on screen.

Dani exchanged a glance with Meredith. Millie looked pale. Had she lost weight?

"Hi, hi," Meredith chirped, hiding her concern. "How are you guys?"

"Well, funny, you should ask that," Esther said. Her usually tidy, snowy white hair looked disheveled and unkempt.

"What's going on?" Dani leaned toward the screen.

"Millie's got some tummy issues."

"Pah," Millie said with a wave of her hand. "It's nothing."

"What's the issue?" Dani asked again. "You look a little pale, Millie."

"She's not eating," Esther answered for Millie. "Losing weight, as you can see."

"The doctor thinks it's diverticulitis," Millie said, clearly giving in. "Which is something that I can totally manage with my diet and a healthier lifestyle." This she said to Esther as if they'd had this same conversation a few dozen times already.

"A healthier lifestyle includes less stress in your life," Esther scolded. Esther looked into the screen at Dani and Meredith. "Getting the shelter up and running has taken a toll, I'm afraid."

"On both of us," Millie added.

"We'll be all right, girls," Esther said. "Millie's exploratory scope is Friday morning. We'll let you know how that goes, so please don't worry."

"But we will, anyway," Meredith said.

"Yes, we will," Dani added with a steady smile. She didn't want the two older women to worry about them being worried. "We'll send positive vibes your way to both of you, and we hope Millie's tummy issues are minor."

"Your words to God's ears," Millie said. "So, how's college life, you two?"

Meredith took the lead and told them about her classes, including the two she shared with Dani, and her art projects. Dani picked up the thread and gave a quick summary of her classes and the intramural lacrosse league. She added that they had made some new friends in the dorm.

They chatted for another twenty minutes or so, and after they hung up the call, Meredith and Dani sat quietly for a few moments, each gathering her own thoughts. Meredith broke the silence with a sigh and said, "I hope she's okay. Both of them."

"Me, too." Dani jumped off the bed. "We'll call them Friday after her procedure if they don't call us first."

"Millie's the one that usually takes care of Esther, but now..." Meredith trailed off.

"Esther's going to have to look after Millie, I guess," Dani mused out loud.

"If Millie will let her."

Dani sighed. "Yeah, there's that."

They sat quietly until Dani smacked her hands together, making Meredith jump. "It's time."

"Noooo," Meredith groaned in protest.

"Yep," Dani said. "Your desk or mine?"

"Yours. Mine's got piles." Meredith climbed off her bed. "Let me go to the bathroom first."

"Don't be too long. You're not getting out of this. Our statistics problem set calls."

"Don't answer."

Dani chuckled. "Since we blew it off yesterday for other more, err, interesting activities, we have to at least start it now." Ignoring the tongue Meredith stuck out at her, Dani said, "I'll get us set up."

After Meredith left, Dani mused about their older friends back home. Esther and Millie were old enough to be their grandmothers, but their bond across the years was undeniable. She wished she could help the older women somehow, but they were too far away, and Dani and Meredith had their hands full at college. Strong, stoic Millie had been hiding her stress for a long time, hadn't she?

Hiding stress. Yep, Dani definitely took after Millie in that regard. As the distance from Laura's harassment episode lengthened, Dani slowly concluded that she had overreacted. To be fair, Laura hadn't even touched her. Dani hadn't been physically assaulted. She was acting silly about it. No, actually, it was kind of dumb to have been so bothered by being cornered like that. Dani just hadn't expected it. That was all. Laura had simply surprised her. Nothing more. No biggie.

Still, the incident brought up a valid point about safety. What if Petra, in her drunken state, hadn't had friends around to help her that day? What if Meredith got lost in her artwork and found herself alone in the art building late at night? Dani vowed to be aware of her surroundings at all times and continue to make sure Meredith and her new friends were safe. But seriously, she needed to stop feeling victimized by something that was really nothing. If it happened again, which it wouldn't, she'd be aggressive right back and tell Laura to back off and leave her alone. That's what she should have done in the first place. No one would believe that Danielle Lassiter had frozen like that. No one. Dani didn't even believe it, so it was best to forget it ever happened.

She powered up her tablet and was stunned to see an email from Shela and the PSLA. She was scheduled to debate some kid named Darius on Friday.

"Who are you, Darius Washington?" She started to type his name in a new search tab but quickly closed it when Meredith returned to the room. Later. She'd research her opponent later. Now was Dani, Meredith, and linear regression time.

Chapter 7

Getting Favors

They successfully turned in their statistics problem sets during Tuesday's class. They felt good about themselves until the instructor told the class that they would now learn how to use an online statistics package for weekly projects in addition to their paper problem sets. Dani commented to Meredith after the Thursday class that whenever it felt like they were getting a handle on things, something else popped up to keep them from getting complacent.

"I'm glad I have you to lean on," Meredith had said. Dani reached for her hand to squeeze but pulled away just in time. She'd decided long ago, even before they'd started seeing each other, that she would be strong for both of them. She simply nodded her agreement but wished they were alone. Physical touch, no matter how small, was somehow more meaningful than a head nod. Maybe one day the world would accept them, and they could be out.

On Friday morning, Dani found herself at the PSLA meeting, sitting next to Petra as two freshmen guys debated each other. Dani was slotted to go right after this debate. When her nerves started to ramp up, she thought of Meredith. She was meeting Meredith for lunch at Schine directly after, and that would mean that her speech had been given and her debate over. For now, though, she had to remain focused, interested, and confident. Or at least seem that way.

In the current debate, the taller guy with dark hair handily outclassed his opponent, a dweeby-looking guy with strawberry blond hair. Maybe it was the taller guy's posture or something because the shorter guy actually did make excellent points about the role of student government on a college campus.

One of his points was that elected officers only served for at most four years, so it behooved each of them —yes, he used the word behooved—to act with clear and decisive action. He pointed out that his opponent was still auditing several classes, clearly indicating his inability to make "clear and decisive decisions." Dani thought his point was well played.

Her nerves were trying to get the better of her, but she reminded herself how clear and decisive her own actions had been at the lacrosse practices. No one bothered her there. No one tried to corner her. Yep. "Clear and decisive action" was now her middle name.

The debate in front of her ended, and when her name was called, she stood up decisively and confidently, hoping her jangling nerves didn't show.

"You've got this," Petra said and hit her on the thigh with the back of her hand.

Dani nodded and strode confidently toward the podium closest to her. She had her speech on paper but wouldn't need to look at it. She'd read it repeatedly during the week and even made Meredith listen a few times. Meredith had given her good feedback, too. Just one more thing to love about her girlfriend.

Her opponent, Darius Washington, strode toward the podium she'd clearly been heading toward. He got there first, so she simply grinned at him and headed to the far podium. It was a total power move if she'd ever seen one. Whatever. Cheap tricks would not intimidate her.

Dani was randomly selected to go first, so when Shela nodded for her to proceed, Dani said, "My name is Danielle Lassiter from Albany, New York. I am currently a freshman intending to major in Political Science."

Going off script slightly, Dani said, "A recent speaker said that the issues and their solutions must be clear and decisive. I agree wholeheartedly. But what are the issues? Most of us have only been on campus for a short time, so knowing what issues are prominent may not be obvious. I asked people what concerned them about life on campus academically, socially, or whatever they felt was important. My informal survey included freshmen, sophomores, juniors, seniors, grad students, and professors. And do you know what most of them said?" She looked up at the audience, trying to make it seem she was looking at each one individually. The expectant expression on Petra's face spurred her on.

"Most of them said, 'I have to think about it.'" She nodded a couple of times. "I took that to mean one of two things. They were either too busy to stop and talk to me or had no burning concerns. But once I prodded them without badgering them, I hope, they opened up. Others joined the conversations, and before long, I had a fairly lengthy list. The number one concern for first-year students, not just the women, seems to be campus safety, and I fully intend to work on getting isolated paths lighted and trimmed of overgrowth. One place that comes to mind immediately is the covered walkway from the Mount down to campus." A few claps followed her statement, which bolstered her confidence.

"Another concern is about communication. The first-year students I spoke with had no idea there would be elections or that a student council even existed. Non-freshmen said candidates were all over campus trying to get votes during election time but then nothing after that. They had no idea what the student council actually did."

Dani then outlined a few of her ideas for getting information out to students and creating simple ways to voice their concerns. She then spoke about a few other concerns her surveys had garnered, like exorbitant book prices and unequal housing opportunities for sophomores. She gave a few tentative ideas to address those but didn't go into much detail because she couldn't. She was honest and said she'd need to gather more information before suggesting viable solutions. That seemed to get a few head nods, so Dani was glad that she hadn't tried to bullshit her way through solutions.

She was about to bring up the costly burden on the student council for homecoming week when Shela called time. If she made it to the next round, she'd bring it up along with her fundraising ideas. Feeling confident, she nodded at Shela and turned toward her opponent.

"All good concerns," Darius Washington said with a nod. He stood taller, grabbed the lapels of his suit jacket, and rocked back on his heels. More power moves. Dani fought the urge to roll her eyes. "One point, however, is that it's called the Student *Association*, not the Student *Council*. So, perhaps looking for a more informed candidate might be prudent."

Dani stiffened when a few students scoffed in agreement. Of course, she knew it was called an association. She'd just used the familiar phrase from high school. She tried not to let her discomfort show. She had to seem confident, strong, and nonplussed.

"But that's a small issue," Darius said. "What's a bigger issue with this candidate to my right is her recent behavior, which certain sources have made known to me. It is alleged that this candidate cornered someone in a position of power to get favors. This happened two Fridays ago, right on this campus. She'd been here less than a week and already tipped her hand as to how far she's willing to go to get ahead."

Dani was stunned. He was referring to the incident in the locker room. But no one knew about that. Wait, one of those players who walked in was in her Government and Politics class. Dani's heart pounded as her gaze swept over the audience. Yes, there she was—that lacrosse player from the locker room that night. Her gaze was riveted on Darius. Mm hmm. They must be friends.

Dani took a covert breath, not wanting to seem affected by her opponent's accusation—a completely *false* one, by the way. Laura had cornered *her*, not the other way around. There was no way to defend herself without explaining the entire incident to this room full of strangers. They wouldn't believe her anyway.

Thank God Darius was finished blasting her and had moved on to lay out a few concerns of his own, which included more and better student seats at football games. She hadn't yet been to a football game; they were going to the team's first home game tomorrow, but she completely understood how huge Syracuse football was. There was no way she was going to go near that topic. And who knows? Maybe there was a need for more and better student seating. She would ask around at the game tomorrow. She and Meredith were going with Kate and Petra. Dani made it seem like a date when she asked Meredith to go to the game because Meredith loved that kind of stuff. Of course, she'd played the date angle cool when Kate and Petra were around. It was cute how Meredith and Kate were scheming about what to wear to show school spirit.

Apparently, Kate had lots of SU temporary tattoos that she planned to put on everyone's faces.

Soon enough, it was time for her rebuttal. It materialized in her brain before she'd given it much thought. "My opponent brought up issues that I hadn't considered. Some may think his concerns aren't justified. But I've learned that it's important to get all the facts before making assumptions. And this applies to making assumptions about someone else's actions or intentions." The last part was directed right at the lacrosse player who had clearly made assumptions about what she'd seen. "And this point leads to what I said earlier—Communication is key. Finding out what our constituents want is key to creating an effective Student *Association.*" She emphasized the word 'association' and grinned as she turned toward her opponent. The soft chuckle in the lecture hall punctuated her clear acknowledgment and acceptance of his correction. The fact that Darius looked stunned was priceless.

Dani wrapped up her rebuttal by stating her name again and saying she would work in the best interests of the students in her care. Darius seemed a bit off-balance when he countered for the last time and basically repeated his concern about student seats at home football games. Yeesh, maybe Darius really was super concerned about that. Dani almost wished she had one more rebuttal coming because she might just ask if he was as concerned about student seating at women's home volleyball games. She almost laughed out loud but held it in, knowing that her amusement could clearly be seen in her eyes.

When he finished his rebuttal, the students clapped, and Dani walked over and put out her hand. Darius, once again, looked startled by her show of good sportsmanship and shook her hand. Dani nodded to him and then returned to her seat next to Petra.

"Dang, woman," Petra said, "you were awesome. You were cool and calm when he threw that accusation at you."

Dani knew that Petra wanted her to explain what he'd meant by it, but she just couldn't tell her. It was over and done with. She had measures in place to protect herself and was trying hard to get herself elected so she could make the campus safer for everyone. In the meantime, she would make sure her friends were safe first.

One more debate followed hers, and Dani soaked in everything she could about debating styles and the issues the other students brought up. As she and Petra stood up to head out, Shela, the senior leader of the PSLA group, walked right into their personal space and clapped Dani on the back.

"You were good," Sheila said to Dani, who was trying not to be overwhelmed by Shela's height. "A little rough, but you handled his stunts without getting flummoxed."

Flummoxed? Dani tried not to chuckle. She'd never heard a real live person use that word before. "Thank you," was all she could think of saying to the imposing senior.

Petra walked farther ahead as Shela sidled up to Dani's side. "You need a bit more bite in your delivery, though. When you find out who your next opponent is, get something on them. Don't get me wrong, we can get people behind you, but we need to know that you can go on the offensive."

"Like he did?"

Shela scoffed. "Like he *attempted* to do. Of course, I'm dying to know what he was referring to, and if it's bad, you'll need to get ahead of it to control the inevitable gossip grapevine, but that's your call. I'm available if you want advice in that regard, by the way."

"Thank you," Dani said. "What did you mean when you said you can 'get people behind me'?"

"No candidate gets elected on their own, Danielle," Shela said quietly. "We—the seniors—we watch the newbs and find the talent. We nurture them. Get them elected."

"I see," Dani said, although she really didn't.

"Okay, listen," Shela said, patting Dani's arm, "I have to talk with the rest, but I know they'll agree that you're the front-runner from today."

"Wow, thanks."

Shela turned to go but looked back over her shoulder and said, "More bite."

"Yes, Ma'am," Dani said and saluted. *Oh, crap, did I just call her Ma'am?*

She's only three years older than me.

Shaking her head, Dani caught up to Petra, who was waiting in the entryway for her.

"What was that all about?" Petra asked, one eyebrow raised.

Dani linked arms with her dormmate and said, "I'm not really sure." As they headed out the door and made their way to Shine, Dani did her best to relay what Shela had told her. She couldn't quite believe it herself.

"I hope I can impress them as much as you did. You were so calm and stoic. And you handled yourself very maturely."

Dani burst out laughing. "Mature? Me? Be sure to tell Meredith that."

Petra laughed, and then the two new friends fell silent. Petra cleared her throat and said, "So, if it's private, I'll understand, but what was Darius talking about when he accused you of…whatever that was."

Dani saw an unoccupied bench and gestured for Petra to sit. She needed a minute to figure out what she was going to say. Maybe Shela was right. Getting out in front of the incident was probably best. It clearly wasn't going to go away on its own.

"I wasn't going to tell anyone what happened," Dani began and stopped. Words weren't coming.

"You don't have to—"

"No, I think I need to," Dani admitted and took a breath. "I haven't told anyone."

"Not even Meredith?"

"Especially not Meredith." Dani searched Petra's face and found concern mixed with compassion on her face. "I'm not sure I was assaulted because she didn't actually touch me, but I was cornered by one of the lacrosse captains at the first practice."

"What do you mean by 'cornered'?"

Dani explained what happened with Laura in the locker room. She even included her relief at the three players walking in, basically stopping any forward advancement. "And one of them is in the PSLA," she added. "She was in the audience today."

"No shit?" Petra scoffed. "So that's how Darius knew about it. Assholes.

What Laura did to you was clearly harassment, Dani," Petra said compassionately. "I'm sorry that happened to you. And now I understand why you've suddenly been so vocal about us never walking alone and always being aware of our surroundings." Petra pivoted on the bench to face Dani. "You must have been scared."

"I was." Dani took a breath and sighed. "And too embarrassed to tell anyone. You're the first."

"Wow." Petra flicked her head, effectively moving a lock of hair out of her eyes, and added, "Can I share something with you?"

"Of course."

"I..." She hesitated as if deciding how to say what was on her mind. Before Dani could prod her, she blurted, "I have an eating disorder. I'm set up with a therapist here on campus but haven't started yet. Stressful situations, like starting college, being far from home, the PSLA—all of it can set me off again. And I've been..."

"Struggling?" Dani offered.

"Yes," Petra said. "I mean, I finally got back to the healthy weight my doctor set for me. I was eating well and had sane exercise regimens, but all that was back home in a very structured environment. Mom cooked and helped me with my workouts, but now that I'm on my own, I need to find some structure."

"I'm not sure how I can help," Dani said, "but I will if I can. We can go to the fitness center together if you want."

"Thanks," Petra said. "I'd like that. My therapist back home says it's good for me to talk to close friends about it, so I figured since you were sharing, I would also."

"Thanks for trusting me," Dani said, truly moved. "Does Kate know?"

"Yes."

"Meredith?"

"Not yet," Petra said. "But I'll fill her in. I don't like having secrets from friends." Petra gestured beyond Dani. "Speaking of Meredith."

Meredith and some unknown guy were turning the corner toward them. Dani stood up, concerned. Who was he? Was Meredith safe?

"Hey," Meredith called over to Dani and Petra. "I'll be right there." She turned toward her walking companion and said something Dani couldn't hear. They both laughed, and she patted his arm as they parted ways. Hot green jealousy surged through Dani's veins. How dare that jerk laugh with Meredith.

"Breathe," Petra said quietly. "It's okay. She's okay."

Dani glanced at Petra, confused. What did Petra know? Dani clamped down her emotions and put on her best poker face.

"Hey, roomie," Meredith said when she got closer. "Hey, Petra." They turned toward Schine, and Meredith asked, "How did the speech go? I almost crashed so I could watch, but this one," she pointed toward Dani, "told me not to. She said she was nervous enough."

"She did fine," Petra said. "The best one out of today's group, for sure. But don't take my word for it. Shela said so, too."

"One of the large-and-in-charge seniors?" Meredith asked.

"Yes," Petra said.

"Dani, that's so good," Meredith gushed. "Wow."

Dani felt her cheeks flame hot but covered it by darting ahead to open the door for Meredith and Petra to walk through. Following behind her two friends, she took a deep, calming breath. Sometime before lacrosse practice that evening, she had to tell Meredith what had happened in the locker room. Maybe after her ASL class, but like Petra said, secrets among friends weren't cool. And Meredith was a lot more than a friend.

Chapter 8

Tell Her

Dani sprinted up the steps in the covered walkway toward her dorm. There were plenty of people meandering back up from classes, so she felt safe enough to chance the typically isolated walkway. The burn in her quads felt good from her afternoon run. She could have run on the track in the fitness center, but she wasn't going anywhere near that place, so she created her own route outside that wasn't too isolated but wasn't on the beaten path, either. And the weather was decent. True to everyone's predictions, it was turning colder, even though it was only the first week of September.

She slowed to a walk at the top of the steps to cool down on her way to the front door of her dorm. She was a little out of breath and at first thought it was due to conditioning or the lack thereof, but she'd been training hard, so it wasn't that. No, it was stress. Instead of talking to Meredith about the incident, she went on the run after her ASL class. She'd left Meredith in their room doing her Spanish homework. Petra was graciously going to stop and help Meredith with the subtleties of the Spanish language.

Dani skipped the elevator and took the four flights of stairs to her floor. She took one last calming breath. She was going to tell Meredith now. Right now. Dani put her key in the lock and let herself in quietly. Meredith turned, her face lighting up at Dani's arrival. An odd combination of joy and dread hit Dani's core. She couldn't tell Meredith now. Later. After her shower. Before dinner, for sure.

"I love it when you get all sweaty like this," Meredith cooed.

Dani scoffed. "Oh, sure. Until you get close and smell me."

Meredith's devilish smile relaxed into an easy one. "You never smell bad, Dani."

"Why, thank you, Ms. Bedford. But I think I'll hit the showers anyway."

"You're the only person I know who showers, like, three times a day."

Dani scrunched her face and counted. "Yeah, on practice days, I guess."

"Can I come to the practice tonight?"

"It'll be cold," Dani said as she stripped in front of Meredith and then put on a robe.

Meredith's appreciative gaze made Dani blush. "I don't care. It's on that field over by the rose garden, right?"

"Mm hmm," Dani said with a nod. "We either have to eat dinner now or afterward. You're call."

"Do you mind if I go?"

"Mind? Of course not. I just don't want you to be alone and bored in the stands. I never want you to be uncomfortable."

Meredith pulled out her phone. "I could invite Kate and Petra to come with us. They can keep me company."

"Perfect," Dani said. She closed her robe tight and leaned in for a kiss, not letting her sweaty body get anywhere near Meredith. "Let me go…"

"One more," Meredith said, leaning in for another kiss. If Dani weren't careful, the shower would be abandoned, and one of their beds would be occupied for the next hour.

"Only one more, you hussy," Dani teased.

One soulful kiss later, Dani was dizzy. "I love you, Meredith," she whispered.

"I love you, too, sweetie," Meredith whispered back. "Now go shower so I can hug you properly. Oh, and I haven't heard from Millie or Esther yet about the scope. We'll call after your practice."

"Sounds good." Dani grabbed her shower caddy, a gift from her sister Laney, and headed out the door. Petra was just coming out of her own room, a small envelope in her hand. She headed Dani's way.

"Hey, Petra," Dani said as she opened the door to the pod restroom but waited for Petra to reach her.

"Did you tell her yet?" Petra asked this in a low tone.

"No."

"You need to."

"I know."

Petra's silence was deafening. Her expression didn't betray whatever it was she was thinking, but Dani knew anyway.

"I will," Dani said again. "After practice."

Petra pulled out her phone and wiggled it back and forth. "Kate and I just got invited to watch you play."

"She's quick," Dani said. "Early dinner if you want to join before we head down there."

Petra looked down.

"Join us," Dani said. "I won't spill the beans, but it might be good for you to have some checks and balances, you know?"

"You'd do that?"

"Of course. Maybe I can help you with your eating plan or something."

"Keep me honest, eh?"

"Sure."

"Tell Meredith," Petra said, totally deflecting the thinly veiled conversation about her eating disorder.

"I will," Dani said. "Let me…"

"Go, go," Petra said. "I'm heading to your room anyway to help your roomie learn all about the preterit tense in Spanish."

Dani laughed. "Sorry I'm going to miss it."

Petra simply smiled, tapped Dani on her shoulder twice, and headed toward Dani and Meredith's dorm room.

Dani knew she was taking an overlong shower, but she was hoping to give Petra enough time to finish with Meredith and be out of the room before Dani got back. As soon as Dani walked in, her heart sank. Nope. They were knee-deep in Spanish verbs.

"We won't look," Meredith quipped without turning around.

Petra only laughed and remained focused on Meredith's notebook.

"Nothing much to see anyway," Dani said and then went about getting changed for the first outdoor practice. Laura told the group on Friday that tonight's practice would be the last official practice before the one-hour games started on Monday. Games would run on Mondays, Wednesdays, and Fridays for seven weeks, with a playoff schedule during the seventh week. Games were to begin at five o'clock sharp each week except the last playoff week, with games starting at four because the sun would set early in that last week.

Dani ignored the two women studying behind her and thought how far she'd come since the incident. Although she didn't look at Laura directly during the group meetings before and after the practices, she listened to the information.

"Danielle," came a loud voice.

"Hmm?" Dani whirled around to find Meredith and Petra smiling at her.

Meredith rolled her eyes, but her grin said she was more amused than upset. "You were a million miles away."

"Sorry," Dani said. "Did you say something?"

"Petra's going to get Kate, and we'll meet at the elevator to go to dinner."

"See you in three," Petra said and headed out the door.

Once Petra was gone and the door to their room closed tight, Dani said, "Sorry, I was giving you guys some privacy."

"Thank you," Meredith said as she wrapped herself around Dani's warm and now-clothed body. "Kiss?"

"Mm hmm," Dani murmured and let herself be kissed silly by her very attentive girlfriend.

The walk down to the outdoor practice field was filled with laughter and friendship. Dani was pleased that she and Meredith had made some good friends so quickly. The field finally came into view over the hill, and the sight took Dani's breath away. The green grass, the goals, the lined field. All of it made firm her resolve to continue to play this game she loved.

"Bleachers," Dani said, pointing out the ten-tier set of bleachers on the far side of the field. "I have to get ready to play, but please promise me that you'll all stay together."

"We will," Meredith said. She turned to Petra and Kate and said, "This is her new thing. She's afraid we'll be kidnapped or something."

Petra and Kate laughed, and Dani did, too, but it wasn't really kidnapping she was worried about. She caught Petra's questioning expression when Meredith's attention was diverted by something Kate said.

"I will," Dani mouthed to Petra. Out loud, she said, "Okay, I have to get to it."

"Good luck," Meredith said and hesitated. Meredith clearly wanted to say so much more, and Dani found herself wanting her to. Maybe one day that could happen.

Dani headed to a spot on the sidelines where her Indigo teammates had gathered. She plopped on the grass and put on her cleats before stretching. Her teammate Amanda asked if she wanted to have a catch. Amanda wore her highlighted blonde hair pulled back in a functional ponytail and even wore makeup, making it look like she was going out on a date and not about to sweat for an hour and a half. Dani never understood why players put on a ton of makeup before playing. They were just going out to get all sweaty. Were they trying to impress the other players? Dani had never worn makeup. Well, just that one time when Laney put mascara on her, and they both laughed their heads off. But that was it. Meredith wore makeup and had only once teasingly offered Dani her eyeliner. Was it like war paint? Dani squelched her giggle and tossed the ball back to Amanda. It felt so good to throw, to feel the weight of the small yellow ball landing in the pocket and then launching it back. She couldn't wait to run, though, to dodge defenders and flick the ball into the goal.

A whistle blew, and Laura called all the players together. Dani snuck a peek toward the bleachers. Kate was seated in the middle between Meredith and Petra and was talking animatedly with her hands. Okay, good. Meredith wouldn't get bored.

Dani looked down at her feet, not wanting to make eye contact with Laura, especially with Meredith there. Petra was probably up there trying to figure out which one of the people on the field was the one who had ambushed Dani in the locker room. It was probably best that no one knew.

Dani wasn't sure why keeping Laura's identity hidden was a good idea, but she decided that it was, and that was that.

Dani glanced up when Laura started speaking. Laura caught her eye and held it overlong. It took all of Dani's strength to look away.

"It's our first time outside," Laura said in her usual commanding tone. "Do not go crazy out here. We don't want anyone getting hurt. Joiee's busy enough over there."

Joiee nodded animatedly without looking up as she taped up one of the Team Magenta players. Maybe the player was on Team Teal. Dani couldn't remember. It had taken her a minute to realize that the teams were named alphabetically in terms of ability. Laura's Team Cyan was at the top of the food chain, and Dani's Team Indigo was right behind. Magenta and Teal followed in that order. Dani had high hopes of moving up to Team Cyan as quickly as possible. Roster changes would be announced after each week of play, so as early as Friday evening, she could be on Team Cyan.

"Hashtag goals," Dani muttered under her breath.

"How's that?" Amanda asked quietly.

Dani waved her off to say it was nothing and listened as Laura handed the information-giving to Stephanie Aldridge, the captain of Dani's Team Indigo. Stephanie was a senior and looked like she'd just walked out of a fashion model magazine. Her long dark hair was pulled back into the most stylish ponytail Dani had ever seen. Maybe Meredith could try pulling her hair low on her neck like that with a wide wooden barrette. Ooh, too bad Dani had a ton of reading to do after the practice because she suddenly wanted to play with Meredith's hair. Soon. This weekend, maybe. No, definitely.

Focus.

Stephanie spoke about the structure of the practice. They were going to stay in their own team units from now on and rotate stations every twenty minutes or so. Dani breathed a sigh of relief. Laura would be busy with her own team and nowhere near Dani.

When the meeting ended, Dani jogged with Amanda and the rest of their Indigo teammates toward the north end of the field. Stephanie said this station was designed for each team to learn its pregame warmup routine.

Their next station in the middle of the field would be for pure conditioning. Joy, Dani thought glumly. She just wanted to play.

Stephanie said, "I hear that at least one of you has hopes of making the varsity team next year. Good for you. The assistant coaches sometimes come by and scout for players. But please remember not to be a ball hog or try to impress them. They hate phonies and can spot a bad attitude a million miles away."

Stephanie was looking right at her. Dani swallowed hard. "WTF?" she mumbled under her breath. She wasn't a ball hog. She wasn't a phony. It had to have been Laura. How immature. Laura couldn't get what she wanted and was trying to sabotage Dani's dreams. Not cool. Even though it made Dani hopping mad, she took a deep breath and decided that she was going to do her best to play the game she loved without politics or mind games.

Stephanie ended her "pep talk" by saying, "Goggles up." It was almost comical how all the Indigo players obeyed instantly. Maybe they were afraid to be seen as phonies, too.

"Weaving drill," Stephanie called. "Goalie in the goal." She turned her back, assuming the Indigo players knew what she was talking about. Dani didn't.

When Dani didn't move, Amanda motioned for her to take the first home position. Silently, all the other players moved into various offense and defense positions. Stephanie tossed the ball to one of the attackers and then blew her whistle. Dani was completely lost. The other players moved down the short section of field toward the defenders like they knew what they were doing.

"Dani," Amanda called over, "weave behind Hayley."

Dani moved, and Hayley scooped the ball to her and then moved to the spot Dani had just vacated. Amanda headed toward Dani, who tossed the ball to Amanda. Okay, the weaving part was a drill for ball and player movement. Got it. She'd never done this drill in high school. Apparently, everyone else had.

"Defenders," Stephanie called. "Crash in. Get a stick on a stick. Good. Good. Offense, shoot when you've got a shot. Our goalie needs practice, too."

Amanda took Stephanie to heart and sent an airmail shot high over the goal.

Stephanie blew the whistle and pointed to one of the defenders whose name Dani didn't know yet. "Defender. That's a shooting space violation. You can't run into the path of a shooter. You approach the shooter, not the attacking lane. Subtle difference, I know, but it's for everyone's safety. Normally, we'd set up for an eight-meter shot, but we'll tackle that after the conditioning segment in our rotation. For now. Reset and weave again."

This time, Dani had an open shot, but just as she was ready to release the ball, a defender's stick hit hers and knocked the ball to the ground. Dang it. That was embarrassing. She hadn't even seen the defender behind her. They reset and worked the weave over and over again until Stephanie called time for a quick sip of water.

"Attackers, here," she called and pointed to a spot right in front of her. Her voice didn't sound very pleased. "Indigo is number two. That's not good enough. Do not be satisfied with that." She paused for a moment and said, "Attackers, you have to widen up and create space. Make that defense work. First home," she said, looking right at Dani, "come on. Have you never learned to change the level of your stick? You haven't scored once. The defense has your number already. Change the level. Use deception. Fake one way, go the other. You're using brute force and telegraphing every move. That's not going to work in this intramural league and definitely won't work on a varsity level." The fury in her eyes scared Dani. "Understand?"

"Yes," Dani said with a curt nod, even though she thought Stephanie was picking on her. Some of the other offense players hadn't scored either. Amanda had, so at least she was in the clear.

When Stephanie walked away, Dani turned toward Amanda with raised eyebrows as if to say, "What the heck was that?" Amanda simply shook her head as if to answer that she had no idea.

Dang. This wasn't fun. Was Stephanie really trying to help her, or was she mad at Dani because of the lies Laura told her? Or had the back-assward story of Dani being the aggressor gotten out from that PSLA meeting? Is that what everyone was thinking? She snuck another peek toward the bleachers.

Kate and Petra sat alone. Where was Meredith? Dani was on high alert and didn't even care that Stephanie had just blown her whistle. Dani frantically scanned the bleachers. Meredith wasn't there. She widened her search and felt instant relief when she saw her. She was behind the south goal, retrieving errant balls. It was just like her little brother Mikey used to do as the manager of Dani's high school lacrosse team. Dani's heart melted in love for her girlfriend all over again.

"Danielle," a sharp voice called. It was Stephanie's. "Care to join us?"

Dani didn't respond verbally. She simply turned and joined the team in another pregame drill.

The ultra-long hour-and-a-half practice finally ended, and Dani was exhausted. She wasn't sure if it was all from physical exhaustion, either. Stephanie seemed to get on her case for every little thing. Dani didn't know how to do half the things Stephanie told her she should know how to do as a college-aged lacrosse player. Dani wasn't sure how to 'change levels' or 'shoot across the body.' And she didn't have the nerve to ask Amanda or anyone else how to do these things. That would just show her ignorance. She had some serious research and practice to do. And that would be done on her own. No one was going to see that Dani Lassiter couldn't measure up. No way. She wanted this and wanted it bad, despite Stephanie's badgering and Laura and Joiee's games.

Dani tried to remain upbeat on the walk back to campus with her friends. Kate asked her who the person taping ankles was, and Dani's answer was short and maybe not so sweet. "Her name is Joiee. She's a student trainer who helps the intramural league. Maybe she gets paid. I don't know."

"Oh," was Kate's short response. After a few beats, she added, "That's cool."

Once back in the dorm, Dani and Meredith excused themselves to call home and then catch up on some reading. Petra was going to head to the study lounge on their floor and work on her PSLA speech, but Kate seemed a little lost.

"Guess I'll go to the dining hall and see who's hanging around," Kate said.

"Just be safe," Dani said like a big sister.

"You're so funny with that," Kate said.

When Dani looked at her like a school teacher, Kate put up both hands, "Okay, okay. I'll just go there and come right back if no one's around."

"Thank you," Dani said, knowing a look of relief crossed her face.

Kate's nod conveyed the truth to her intentions. "See you gals tomorrow. Noon. My room. We have to get ready early for the football game." And with that, she and Petra headed back to their room down the hall.

Once inside their dorm room, Meredith said, "You were so good out there. I was giving myself away, admiring the way you move. That's why I helped out on the far end of the field."

"Giving yourself away?" Dani pulled her mouthguard out of her bag and then leaned her gear against her closet door. She needed to shower before she called home and then called Millie and Esther.

"Yeah, me drooling over your lithe body was giving me away."

Dread spiked Dani's chest. "Did they notice?"

Meredith laughed. "No, but you need to shower. I am finding myself needing to run my hands over a selection of your muscles before we call our adopted grandmothers."

"Mmm," Dani said, her high-alert mode decreasing down to normal. "Which muscles?"

"You'll find out," Meredith said, her deep brown eyes full of mischief. She turned away, took the hair tie out of her hand, and shook her hair free.

"I want to play with your hair later," Dani said. She waggled her eyebrows and turned to get ready for her shower.

"Permission granted," Meredith said with a chuckle.

Dani loved the private banter between them. Meredith was becoming increasingly honest about her needs and desires. There were no games, no falsehoods, and no pretending, unlike a certain crystal green-eyed, dark blonde-haired lacrosse captain.

The calls home to their families caused a little bit of homesickness to well up in both Dani and Meredith, but they held each other for a few moments and felt better. The call to Millie and Esther turned out to be a non-video call to Esther. Millie's scope had been done late that morning, and Millie did indeed have diverticulosis, which meant that part of her digestive tract had become inflamed. An infection had also developed, Esther told them. Because Millie was in her mid-seventies, they wanted her to stay for a night or two at the convalescence wing at the Hudson Pines Senior Center. The Center was the place Dani and Meredith had first met Esther and Millie while researching a history project about the old Victorian house on Main Street they owned. Esther had been a patient at Hudson Pines with a fractured hip.

That night, though, Esther was clearly not up for a long chat, so Dani and Meredith said their goodbyes and ended the call after wishing both Millie and Esther good health and healing.

"I hate that we're not there to help," Dani said.

"I know," Meredith said and tucked her phone in her pocket. "I'm not sure there's anything we can do anyway."

"Yeah," Dani said as they sat in a momentary silence. Dani reached over for Meredith's hand and squeezed it. When she tried to move her hand, Meredith held on. And that was okay. Sometimes you needed a little more.

"I can ask my mom and dad to go over and check on them," Meredith offered.

"They would love that. Let's call them back tomorrow and suggest that. We can check on Millie's progress, too."

Meredith didn't answer verbally. She reached over and ran gentle fingers down Dani's cheek. Dani's eyes fluttered, not in arousal but in contentment. She sighed against the hand touching her and released the tension she hadn't realized she'd been holding.

"Cuddle?" Dani suggested.

"Mm hmm." Meredith maneuvered them so that Dani was the big spoon, as usual.

"Mmm," Dani murmured to the back of Meredith's head. "I love this."

"Me, too," Meredith said. "I love you, Dani."

"I love you, too, Merry."

Meredith chuckled and said, "Mikey calls me that. Now I miss my family again."

"We can call them again tomorrow if you want. Video chat."

"Yes, and your family. I need some screen time with your family."

"Mine?" Dani was surprised. Meredith had been kind of shy and reticent around Dani's family in the past.

"Yeah," Meredith said. "I mean, I think my parents know, so it's a good chance your parents might know, too."

"I guess. But I've never told them I'm into girls." Dani's arm pulled Meredith closer as she added, "Well, just this one in particular. She's an artist, and she is the most beautiful young woman I've ever seen."

"I'd like to meet her one day," Meredith said with an amused tone. "No, but seriously." She rolled over so she could look Dani in the eye. "I think I'm ready for your family to get to know me better. Not to come out to them or anything crazy like that, but so that they know who I am. Is that making sense?"

"It is." And right there was a perfect place to segue into telling Meredith about the incident with Laura in the locker room. The perfect place. Dani held her breath. The words wouldn't come.

Chapter 9

The Writing on the Wall

Meredith's smile was so big that it almost surpassed the one on Dani's face. The energy level in the JMA Wireless Dome was off the chain for the first home football game of the season. Their student seats in the endzone were amazing. Dani had no clue what her PSLA opponent Darius had been talking about when he said the seats were crappy. Kate, of course, was wildly energetic as she bopped and danced in place. And to top it off, quietly reserved, Petra was also smiling, clearly having fun.

Even though they had gone with a group of people from their dorm, Dani tried to make Meredith feel as if they were on a date. It was kind of hard, though. They couldn't hold hands or be demonstrative, and you could forget about a kiss for good luck. Meredith had never been one for crowds but seemed to be having fun so far. Good. Dani would make sure it stayed that way, too. If Meredith wanted something from the concession stand, Dani would run and get it. If she wanted to leave, no matter what, Dani would carve the way home.

"What?" Meredith said. "You're grinning like a cat."

Dani leaned in close and said low, "I just love you. That's all."

"Good." The blush that crept up Meredith's face was priceless. Her red cheeks clashed with the temporary Otto the Orange mascot tattoo that Kate insisted everyone wear on their cheeks. Even Dani had been powerless to Kate's insistence and sported one on each cheek. Dani craved a touch from Meredith at that moment. A quick squeeze of her hand or a light stroke on her cheek, but they couldn't. She knew that. Meredith's regretful smile conveyed that she wanted to do those things too but knew that they couldn't.

The pregame festivities in the quad had been empowering. Dani hadn't known that in addition to the marching band, there was a horn line, a drum line, and a color guard. There were even baton twirlers, and everywhere you looked, it was a sea of orange and blue. It was almost overwhelming. There also seemed to be a lot of alums milling about. Some were young-looking, and some not so. Dani wondered if she and Meredith would ever come back as alums to go to a home game. Would they meet up with Kate and Petra for a reunion, assuming they were still friends? Funny how an event like the football game made her feel part of something bigger than herself. Did she finally feel part of something at Syracuse? Did she finally feel like she belonged there?

"Here they come," Kate screeched, breaking Dani out of her thoughts. The banner bearers lifted their flags and ran toward midfield, accompanied by the cheerleaders. The team itself finally appeared from under the stadium as the players broke through the theatrical smoke, their orange home uniforms matching the sea of orange in the stands. Kate had her phone out, recording everything.

The fans were on their feet, Dani and her friends included, and erupted in a cacophony of noise matching the beat of the marching band's drums. Dani stomped her feet, clapped her hands, and yelled her excitement along with the thousands of other fans. They didn't call the Dome the 'Loud House' for nothing.

When the Western Michigan team ran out from their side of the field, the fans booed. Dani didn't. She didn't blame the crowd for booing since it was all part of the fun, but she always liked to show good sportsmanship whenever possible. The other team had trained hard, too. And as long as everyone played fair, let the game begin.

The game was a good one, full of twists and turns. Dani found herself explaining the rules to her friends when a whistle was blown, a penalty was called, or a touchdown was reversed.

Kate said, "You know a lot about football."

"I probably would have played if I'd had the chance," Dani said. "I mean, I guess I could have played in high school, but that would have been a lot of pressure, you know? To be the only girl playing?"

"You would have been good," Meredith said. "A running back or wide receiver, probably."

Dani was impressed. "I think someone here knows more about football than she's letting on."

Meredith smiled sheepishly. "I've logged a boatload of hours watching Syracuse sports with my dad and Mikey."

Dani pulled Meredith into a side hug and then realized her mistake immediately. She kept her cool, though, and simply winked at Meredith and let go. Wow, she'd gotten sloppy. She had to be more careful. For the last quarter of the game, Dani kept her distance and knew that Meredith felt it. She felt bad, but it couldn't be helped.

After the game, the excitement over the team's third win of the season followed them all the way back up to the Mount and into the dining hall. Meredith and Dani plopped their filled trays down at their now-usual table while Kate, Petra, and a few others were still getting food.

"It's okay," Meredith said. Her expression was one of compassion. "I understand."

It took Dani a milli-second to understand. "I'm sorry, baby. I don't think we're ready to be out yet."

"I know. I'm not sure I'm ready either. I mean, it's kind of like you deciding not to play football. Too much of the spotlight would have been on you. And you know how much I like the spotlight." Meredith framed her face with her hands.

"Not," Dani said with a slight scoff. "You're so cute." She leaned in but pulled away quickly. Petra was heading to the table. She had a small salad but had a selection of protein on top. Dani nodded her approval discreetly, and Petra nodded back. It was a silent communication, but hopefully, one that helped Petra, who had been doing so much better with food in recent days. She'd confided to Dani that she was starting therapy sessions on Monday. She wasn't crazy, she'd told Dani. She just needed healthy reminders, and she hoped her new therapist would be able to nudge her in the right direction. If not, then there were a billion other therapists in the world to choose from, right? Dani had laughed at that but absolutely agreed. Having friends to help keep her accountable was also important, Petra confided, but the ultimate decisions must come from her own brain.

Kate bounced over to the table. "I've been picturing you playing football, Dani. Just think about all those little kids who would have seen you play."

"We were just talking about that," Meredith said.

"Not only little girls but little boys, too," Kate continued as she sat across from Dani. "They would see a strong female playing a game she wanted to play despite the odds stacked against her."

"I do like to help people," Dani said. "That's why I want to go into politics, you know?" Petra and the rest of her friends nodded. "I mean, community leaders are supposed to help their constituents, help them lead better and more fulfilling lives."

"You like to see people living their best lives," Meredith said, leaning closer. She seemed to check herself and moved away. "Like Mikey. And me."

Dani smiled at her girlfriend. She absolutely did want Meredith and her brother to live their 'best lives.'

"You know what?" Dani said. "I do want that for people, but I don't think I could have handled being the subject of all that scrutiny." People might have concluded that because she was playing a typically boys' sport, she was a lesbian or a dyke or whatever mean, judgmental things they'd come up with. Sure, being out as LGBTQIA+ was supposedly okay now, but it still kind of wasn't. "All I want to do is live my life," Dani said, breaking the short silence at the table. "I don't think I could have handled that," she said again.

"We never know what we're capable of until challenged," Petra said wisely. "I'm sure you would have risen to the occasion, Dani."

Kate chuckled. "See why I love my roommate? She's so insightful."

Petra scoffed, and the conversation changed as a few of their dormmates joined the table. Everyone seemed excited about all the Syracuse traditions they'd witnessed firsthand that afternoon. The marching band's flute section hair flip in the pregame Quad show had been a surprising tradition that made everyone laugh, mainly because they weren't expecting the dozen or more flute players, including the one guy, to undo their hair ties and flip their hair back and forth like headbanging heavy metal fans. Seeing the marching band having so much fun almost made Dani regret never learning to play an instrument.

Dani felt at odds. She felt good in the company of her new friends but wasn't sure what to make of her own confession about not wanting the scrutiny of playing football. Not publicly acknowledging her relationship with Meredith fell under that same banner, didn't it? Meredith seemed okay with keeping their relationship hidden, didn't she? Did she want to be out? No, probably not. Because what if—

"You okay?" Meredith asked quietly.

Dani pushed her tray away. She'd lost her appetite. She looked over at Meredith, knowing they had to talk about their secrets. And that included the locker room incident. She'd had to tell Petra, "No," again as they walked back from the game when Petra asked if Dani had told Meredith yet.

"I'm okay," Dani finally said back. "Tired, I think."

"I'm done, anyway," Meredith said quietly. She stood up and said to the group, "Hey, we're going to head back up. I think I need a nap."

Easy chuckles accompanied the goodbyes, and just as they were almost out of earshot, Dani heard one of their dormmates say, "Where goes one, so goes the other." Polite laughter followed the statement, but it was confusing. What did that mean? Did they know? Or suspect?

Back in their room, Dani needed a few moments to get herself together. She excused herself to take a shower. Meredith seemed to know not to ask about her mood, which was good because even Dani didn't understand what was going on in her own head. Maybe she was just tired. Meredith was going to call her family while Dani was showering. Meredith said her father was dying to know what being at the game in person was like. Dani made a promise to herself to call her own family when she was out of the shower. They would probably want to know about the game, too. Maybe she was just a little homesick. Homesick for easier times, like when she was senior class president and a star lacrosse player? Things at college weren't as easy or simple. She hadn't expected to struggle at college. Well, she wasn't struggling academically; she had that. But other things weren't coming easy. Was it growing pains?

She growled as she shut the pod bathroom door behind her. "Chill out. Just…stop," she chided herself. She let the warming water wash over her head and body and breathed deeply. She was strong. Everyone said so, but somehow, she had to find the strength to tell Meredith about Laura's stupidity. She could overlook Stephanie's apparent dislike of her. And she could even figure out a way to bring more "bite" to the debates, but telling Meredith seemed to be the largest obstacle in her path.

But the debates were an issue, too, weren't they? Shela wanted her to go low and go on the attack. Dani wasn't sure how to do that and still stay "classy."

She scoffed when she tried to imagine showing good sportsmanship during a debate. Shela implied that if she didn't play the game their way, Dani would never get elected. And if Dani wanted to fulfill her dream of getting elected to the Student Association her first year, she had to play the game the way it was expected to be played. She'd find a way.

With firm resolve, she finished her shower and headed back to her room.

Her resolve faltered as she put her hand on the doorknob to her room. She had to tell Meredith. Tonight. Now. *No, after I call home.* She turned the knob and let herself back in.

"Feel better?" Meredith asked, making no move to come in for a hug the way she usually did.

"I do," Dani said and put on comfy clothes. "I'm going to call home."

"Oh, okay," Meredith said. "I'll go shower, I guess."

"You don't have to leave."

"It's okay. I'll let you have your privacy." Meredith gathered her shower caddy and robe and headed out the door.

Dani wasn't sure what had just happened. Was Meredith mad at her? She seemed upset. "Shit. I forgot to ask how her call with her family went. I'm an idiot."

Dani sighed as she hit her mother's cell number on her phone. She vowed to get out of her head and remember that Meredith might be going through some stuff, too.

87

"Hi, Mom," Dani said when her mother answered. Her throat tightened with instant homesickness. She did her best to keep her voice steady as she spoke with her family on speakerphone. Laney wanted to know everything about the football game. She asked if there were any cute guys in the dorm and a whirlwind of other questions. It was enough to knock Dani out of her sadness and into that familiar feeling of family. Dani felt the familiar sense of belonging as she talked with her parents, her sister, and even Brandy, the family golden retriever mix. She felt safe with them. They knew her. They knew her ups and downs, her moods, and what made her tick. Well, mostly. They didn't know who Meredith was to her, though. Dani's sadness hit her chest like a physical thing. They should know. Her family should know that she'd fallen in love that summer and had found her person. They should know that she now understood love songs and felt like she could write some of her own. But they didn't know. And that kind of sucked.

Meredith walked back in and gave Dani a smile that didn't quite reach her eyes. Dani put up one finger to indicate she was almost done with her call. It took more than a minute for Dani to wrap it up, and afterward, she took a moment to breathe in and let it out slowly.

"Everything okay?" Meredith asked. She was seated at her desk, brushing her hair.

Dani nodded. "Yeah. They're my goofy family. They're fine." She stood up and picked up her own desk chair. "May I?" Dani gestured to the hairbrush. Getting an affirmative nod, she set her chair down behind Meredith's. Meredith handed her the brush, and as Dani took slow strokes, she asked, "Your family okay?"

Meredith seemed to soften as she said, "Yes. They're going to take a family trip to visit Millie and Esther at Hudson Pines."

"That's awesome." Dani was relieved.

"And my Mom seems surprisingly relaxed."

"That's good."

"I think maybe I was part of her stress."

"You?"

"You know how I didn't fit in at good ole Whickett High."

"Mmm," Dani said. "But you did toward the end."

"Because of you."

Dani wanted to kiss Meredith's exposed neck but didn't dare. Things would escalate, and she'd never get her story out.

"You were ready to fit in all on your own," Dani said. "Remember the way you handled that bully in the hallway near our lockers?"

"The jerk who kept knocking into me?"

Dani chuckled at how incredibly awesome Meredith had been that day standing up for herself. "You told him you weren't going to put up with his shit anymore."

"I did, didn't I?" Meredith turned slightly to face Dani and waggled her eyebrows. "Having you as my protector helped, too."

"Nope. You did that one all on your own."

"Mmm," Meredith said and faced forward again. Good. Dani had to say it.

"I need to tell you something."

"Humph," Meredith said as if she'd been expecting bad news.

"Do you remember my first lacrosse practice? At the Ensley Center?"

"Yeah."

Dani looked down at the hairbrush in her hand. "Something happened that night."

Meredith didn't say a word or move an inch.

Dani hadn't expected Meredith to help her tell the tale, but the way she'd stiffened up meant Dani had to get it out fast. "It was after the practice. One of the captains—her name is Laura."

"Laura," Meredith muttered.

"Do you know her?"

"No, not personally," Meredith said as she stared out the window toward the Wireless Dome they could see from their room. "She was watching you on the field yesterday."

Dread shot through Dani's core. "You saw that?"

"Yes." There was an excruciatingly uncomfortable silence until Meredith added, "That was why I went down to that side of the field. I wanted to see who she was."

Dani knew she should move so they could look at each other face to face, but she was frozen. "I don't— She's not—"

"Something's different," Meredith interrupted. "*You're* different, Dani." She swirled around in her seat. "You don't want anyone to know about us. You've been cold to me lately when other people are around." She stood up. "You're giving off mixed signals." She tapped her foot as if weighing what to say next and then blurted, "She's very pretty, and I'm not stupid. I can see the writing on the wall."

"Wait, what?" Dani stood up, as confused as ever. What was happening? "Meredith, I love you. Laura cornered me. She—"

"See?" Meredith interrupted. "I knew something happened. I just didn't know what." Before Dani could respond, Meredith bolted out of their room, stifling a sob.

Chapter 10

No More Secrets

After an hour of frantically looking for Meredith in the dorm and dining hall, Dani finally headed back to their room to see if she'd returned there. The room was empty. Dani sat down hard on the floor, folded her legs, and rested her forehead on her knees. Meredith's phone lay on her desk, so calling was of no use. Dani's tour of every floor's study lounge, the basement computer room, the main floor lobby, and various student spots had all come empty. Maybe Meredith was in Petra and Kate's room. Dang it, she should have gone there first. But she didn't want to alert them that there was a problem.

Dani pulled out her phone and texted Petra.

DANI: Is Meredith in your room?

PETRA: Not anymore. She's on her way back.

Dani threw the phone down even as she saw another text coming in from Petra. She didn't care. Meredith was the only thing that mattered right now. She flung open the door only to find Meredith standing on the other side.

"I've been working up the courage to come back in," Meredith said.

Dani burst into tears of relief now that she knew Meredith was okay.

Meredith flew into the room and pulled Dani close. Dani hid her face in her hands as Meredith held her close.

"I'm sorry," Dani cried. "I should have told you right away. I was in shock and scared of what you'd think of me."

91

"Come," Meredith said, pulling Dani's head away from where it was burrowed against her chest. She kissed Dani's forehead and then led her to a desk chair. Meredith claimed the other. "Petra seems to know what happened but told me I needed to wait for you to tell me. Why Petra knew before I did is another question I have for you, but I'll reserve that for later."

Meredith's tone was a mixture of frosty compassion and something akin to 'this better be good.'

Dani spilled the whole saga, from the admitted initial attraction upon meeting Laura to the completely unexpected and terrifying scene in the empty locker room.

"I ran all the way home," Dani said, finally daring to look up. "I was jumping at shadows the whole way. I mean, I wasn't expecting to be harassed like that."

Meredith's expression had softened around her eyes somewhat, but her lips were still pressed together into a thin line, telling Dani that she wasn't ready to speak and that Dani should continue.

"I did nothing to spur her on or encourage her. Even Joiee said that Laura always gets what she wants. I didn't know what that meant. And I still don't, but I'm trying not to be alone with her or get cornered by her again."

Meredith's expression did not change.

"Meredith," Dani said in a whisper. "I don't want to be with her. I don't want to be with anyone but you. I should have told you right away. Honestly, I was embarrassed that something like that could happen to me. I was scared that you would think I encouraged it. Some players walked in on the scene, and then a rumor started. That jerk I debated yesterday used it against me, but they didn't know what they had seen. They twisted it to seem like I was the one who had cornered Laura. I didn't. I was rinsing out my mouth guard."

"Terrifying, isn't it?" Meredith said evenly. "Getting harassed? Not knowing if you're safe? Waiting for the next incident?" She blew out an angry sigh.

"Yes." Dani knew Meredith was referring to the regular harassment she'd had for the first year and a half in a new high school. A high school Dani had always thought was welcoming and nurturing of everyone. She was learning how wrong she was.

"And I do understand that embarrassment thing," Meredith said. "But I had no one to turn to for help. You did. Right here. It seems like you don't trust me—"

"I trust—"

"Or maybe you don't think I'm capable enough to help big, strong Dani. But I'm right here." Meredith stood up and paced the room as she continued. "I've been here since we arrived. I never knew you thought so little of me." Her back was to Dani as she picked at the edge of a poster on the far wall.

"I'm sorry," Dani said. "I was scared."

"Rightfully so," Meredith said as she turned around. "But you should have told me."

"I should have. I thought it would go away."

"It clearly hasn't," Meredith said. "Definitely not in her mind, anyway."

Dani grunted. She hadn't realized Laura might still try to do something. But Meredith saw it, and if Meredith saw it, how many other people did, too? Not that she cared what other people thought; it was just that... "I didn't know she was still, like, stalking me or whatever."

"And she has a girlfriend?" Meredith said, eyebrows raised to the ceiling.

"Joiee, the trainer."

"Hmm," Meredith said. "You should have..." She paused. "That you didn't confide in me hurts."

Tears sprang up from the depths of Dani's soul. "I never never never wanted to hurt you. That's why I didn't tell you."

Meredith groaned, hopped up on her bed, and patted the spot next to her.

"Really?" Dani said but didn't move.

Meredith nodded. "You're the little spoon."

"Okay." Dani climbed up to the platform bed and rolled away from Meredith.

Strong arms went around her as she scooched back to be the best little spoon ever.

"You're the little spoon because you have to learn that I can take care of you, too, Ms. Lassiter. I like it when you walk me to classes, but remember that I can walk *you* to classes, too."

"Okay."

"And…" Meredith grew quiet for a while, and Dani knew better than to interrupt the silence. "And maybe we both need to communicate better. I should have asked more questions when I saw you were hurting. I knew something had happened, Dani. I was just afraid to hear what it was. Those were my own insecurities, I think."

"I'm sorry."

"First thing. No more apologizing." Meredith said this with a chuckle and then kissed the back of Dani's head. "Mmm, your hair always smells so good."

Dani made a move to roll over so she could look Meredith in the eye, but Meredith said, "Uh uh," and held on.

"Second thing is this," Meredith continued. "I will be more brave and more assertive and put myself out there, and *you* will allow yourself to be a little more vulnerable by sharing your feelings and asking for help."

"Okay," Dani said and snuggled back into her big spoon. "Can I start sharing now?"

Meredith chuckled in surprise. She kissed the back of Dani's head again and said, "I'm all ears."

Dani slowly told her feelings about not telling her family that she'd fallen in love with Meredith. Meredith said much the same thing and also included the fact that their new friends on campus didn't know either.

"It's scary," Dani said. "It feels good to admit that."

"Vulnerability 101," Meredith said. "I think we need a few more weeks to acclimate, and then maybe we can start to tell people. Of course, as soon as we tell Kate, it will be all over campus."

"You don't know that."

Meredith burst out laughing. "I do know that. And so do you."

"Yeah, I guess you're right. So how about this? If we haven't come out before fall break, we'll tell Petra and Kate as soon as we get back."

"Okay, I think I can deal with that." Meredith sighed, breathing out against Dani's head. "It will be nice not to hide. It will be nice to be ourselves."

"Yeah, it will." Dani kissed the hand holding her close and then tried to roll over to face Meredith. She was once again thwarted by a tighter grip around her body. She'd never realized how much power the big spoon had. She laughed.

"What?"

"Nothing," Dani said, kissing one of Meredith's hands again. "This role reversal thing is weird."

"Yep, and something we both need now and then, right?"

"Yeah, you're right." Dani lay still for a moment and then said, "No nookie nookie?"

Meredith laughed. "I just want to hold you for a while, baby. Is that okay?"

"More than okay," Dani said, letting herself be held by the strong woman behind her.

They lay quietly and even dozed for about an hour when Dani stirred. Meredith was drawing swirls on Dani's back, probably trying to wake her up. Dani rolled over to see Meredith sitting up, a smile growing on her face. Meredith's fingers traced down Dani's nose and then over each of Dani's lips. She traced her eyebrows one after the other and then finally said, "Awake now?"

"Mm hmm." Dani basked in her girlfriend's touch.

"Did you see all those kids from the neighborhood hanging around at the practice yesterday?" Meredith asked.

"Yes," Dani said. "They were cute."

"Maybe we can enlist their help during games. Like ball retrievers or team managers?"

"Yes," Dani said and sat up. "Like my coach let Mikey do back at Whickett."

"Exactly," Meredith said. "You know, you, Petra, and Kate always think of ways to help people. Heck, Kate's even majoring in social work, and you and Petra are going into politics to help people. Am I selfish, wanting to do art?"

"What? Not at all. Art is your calling. And you're super talented." Dani wondered where all that was coming from. "I mean, look at how you helped Esther and Millie by doing their portraits for the Randall-Bradley House."

"I guess," Meredith said, not sounding convinced at all.

"Okay, okay," Dani said. "How about this? When you're this big famous artist, you can open your art studio up to needy people."

"People *need* art?"

Dani gasped in surprise. "You, of all people, should understand how good art is for the soul. Art makes people feel emotions, you know that. And doing art gives the artist a sense of accomplishment, right?"

"Mm hmm."

"Maybe you could volunteer at an after-school program for kids who need a boost in confidence or want more exposure to art—more than they get in school."

"I love that idea."

"And, and, and," Dani said, remembering something that might hit her point home. "Just look how Mikey thrives when we do arts and crafts at your kitchen table."

"He does. You're right about that," Meredith said with a nod. "Oh, hey, I didn't tell you. My mom told him that if he did well in school, he'd be allowed to be the team manager again this year. She already cleared it with your old coach."

"That is so cool," Dani said. Outwardly, she smiled, but inwardly, she wondered if she'd ever have a real lacrosse coach again. Would she make the team? She had so much to prove in the next six weeks of the season.

"Nope," Meredith said.

"Huh?"

"Tell me what you're thinking. You furrowed your brow like you were deep in thought."

"No more secrets, right?"

"Right." Meredith sat up and leaned back against the wall. She folded her legs and sat crisscross applesauce.

Dani maneuvered on the small bed and sat the same way. "I'm not sure

I'm going to be good enough to make an impression on the varsity coaches."

"Whoa, who put that BS in your head?"

"No, it's not that," Dani said and then told Meredith how she didn't know any of the drills and that the Team Indigo captain told her she should already know certain moves. "I feel a little lost out there. Amanda has been helping me."

"One of your teammates?"

"Yeah, she's cool."

Meredith grabbed both of Dani's hands in hers. "Look, maybe your high school career wasn't as all-encompassing as some of the other players. But I do know a few things about you."

"Like what?"

"You're smart."

Dani scoffed.

"Nuh-uh," Meredith said. "You don't get to berate my girlfriend. Understood?"

"Mm hmm," Dani said, a real grin creeping up her face.

"You're smart, and you work hard. Who cares if you didn't learn that stuff before now? You can learn it. Right? Ask Amanda to show you stuff."

"I could, I guess." Dani pulled her hands up, dragging Meredith's up with hers. She kissed the back of the hand on top. "I'd already kind of sort of been thinking along those lines."

"Other than encouragement, I don't know how else I can help you," Meredith said with a short sigh.

"I know how," Dani said and leaned back. Meredith yelped when Dani pulled her on top. It took a little maneuvering, but she finally got Meredith where she wanted her. "Kiss me, baby. Please?"

Meredith brushed a lock of hair off Dani's forehead and leaned down closer and closer. Their lips were milliseconds from touching when, bam, bam, bam, someone was pounding on their door.

"Hey, you guys," Kate called from just the other side. "Petra said Meredith wasn't feeling well."

Dani put a finger over her lips to keep them both silent.

"I just wanted to make sure you're both okay," Kate called through the door.

"We should..." Meredith said and pointed toward the door. "She sounds worried."

Dani groaned. "Okay, but you call out to her. Tell her you're okay. Maybe she'll go away."

Not only did Kate *not* go away after Meredith told her she was okay from inside the closed door, but soon enough, Kate, Petra, and four other dormmates joined them in their small room for a Saturday night hangout session.

At one point, Petra raised her eyebrows when Dani nodded that, yes, she had told Meredith, and things were now smoothed over. Petra threw a discrete thumbs up back.

"Truth or dare time," Kate announced.

A chorus of no's followed her announcement, much to Dani's relief. Instead, someone suggested they head to the study lounge to watch some Australian actor's new movie on one of the streaming services. It was kind of the last thing that Dani wanted to do, but Meredith seemed interested, so Dani went along with it. Everyone agreed to grab whatever snacks they had in their room and meet in the lounge in ten minutes.

Once everyone was out of their room, Dani finally pulled Meredith into a tight hug and whispered, "To be continued."

Meredith burst out laughing and pushed Dani away. "That's kind of funny, honey. Very funny."

Dani waggled her eyebrows and pulled out a big bag of popcorn she'd stashed for hard times. Meredith nodded approvingly. Just as Dani put her hand on the doorknob to open it, Meredith stopped her.

"Let's have fun, okay?"

"Okay." What was Meredith driving at?

"No thoughts of green-eyed lacrosse captains or even lacrosse. No thoughts of all the reading we have to do tomorrow or the project I have due Monday morning."

"You got it, baby." Dani opened the door and almost reached back for

Meredith's hand. She caught herself in time and hated herself for doing so.

Chapter 11

Lead With Your Heart

Dani was grateful to her friends for walking her to the first lacrosse game of the season. It was Monday late afternoon, and Team Indigo was slated to play against Laura's Team Cyan. Only Meredith and Petra knew about the trouble Dani had had with Laura that night in the locker room, and they both promised to keep their eyes open and watch for any weird behavior on Laura's part. They also promised *not* to tell Kate or anyone else about it. Flying rumors weren't going to help the situation in the slightest, so it was best to keep it under wraps.

At one point over the weekend, Meredith gently suggested that Dani confront Laura about the incident. *Hell to the no* was Dani's first reaction, but as they discussed it late into the night as they lay miles apart, each in her separate bed, Meredith chipped away at Dani's fear. Dani wasn't one hundred percent convinced it was a good idea but told Meredith she'd look for an opportunity. "No guarantees, though," Dani had said.

Dani's nerves ratcheted as they crested the hill and saw a million people in the stands and on the field. Holy crap. There were real referees, and the green grass field had been freshly lined. Dani had her usual pregame nerves, but these were compounded by her urgent need to play well. Her sights were set on moving up to Team Cyan. They were the best team and her best chance at being seen by one of the assistant varsity coaches. Syracuse varsity lacrosse was *the* best team and the one she ultimately had her sights set on. She just had to play well that evening.

Meredith stumbled into Dani, knocking her off balance. "You okay?" Dani asked as she offered Meredith a steadying hand.

"I'm fine." Meredith laughed at her own clumsiness. "First day on new feet, I guess."

Kate burst out laughing, and Petra chuckled in solidarity. When their two friends looked away, Meredith winked at Dani and then wagged her finger.

Dani rolled her eyes, sighed, and nodded, indicating that she understood. Meredith hadn't really stumbled. She had just been trying to get Dani off the negative thought train. The ruse had worked for now.

"So, as I was saying," Kate continued. "I love Dani's idea of personal defense classes for everyone in our dorm. We could start with our floor or something. Keep it small at first, and then branch out to other floors until the whole dorm is a bunch of crime-fighting Ninja warriors."

"That might be a stretch," Petra said.

"Gotta dream, right?" Kate said. "Hey, Dani, do you think your friend Joiee could teach us self-defense?"

"I honestly don't know Joiee that well, so I have no idea if she even knows self-defense."

"If she doesn't, then maybe she could find someone who does," Kate said.

Was it Dani's imagination, or was Kate's bopping becoming more animated?

"How about this?" Petra said to Kate. "Dani can introduce you to Joiee, and then you can ask her yourself."

"Nooooo," Kate said way too quickly. "No, no, no, no, no. I don't know her. I wouldn't know what to say." Kate looked down at her feet. Kate not know what to say? That thought was ludicrous. Something was amiss.

Dani exchanged a confused glance with Petra, who simply widened her eyes and shrugged. Clearly, Petra still hadn't figured out her roommate yet.

"Ooh," Meredith said, pointing to the sea of indigo-colored pinnies adorning her teammates' bodies. "I love that color. Of course, a cyan pinny would bring out your eyes more."

Petra burst out laughing, coughed, and then said, "You're on the purple team?"

"Indigo," Meredith corrected. One simply could not go around calling the color indigo purple in front of a Fine Arts major.

"Got it," Petra said, acquiescing.

Dani smirked at Petra, thanked her friends for coming, and headed toward the sea of indigo-colored pinnie-wearing lacrosse players on the sideline.

In no time, Team Indigo had warmed up and was heading onto the field for the first game of the season. Dani was amazed at how many people had shown up to watch. She recognized some of the players from the teams that weren't playing that evening, but there were a lot more people than that. And the young kids from the neighborhood were there, too. Some were in the stands, and some were wandering around the sidelines. Dani hoped they had parents or older siblings nearby that would keep them safe because one did not want to get hit by an errant lacrosse ball.

Dani headed out to her spot on the field and nodded to her mid-fielder, who was setting up at the center midfield line to take the game-opening face-off. Once all players from both sides were in position, the Team Indigo midfielder held her stick horizontally against her opponent's. The official put the ball in the nets between the two sticks held tightly against each other. She held the nets closed.

"No," the official said to the Team Cyan midfielder. "Keep it steady."

Another beat later, the Team Indigo midfielder yelled to her teammates, "I don't have it. She has it. She has it." She repeated the alert to her teammates that the ball was most likely going to pop out toward Team Cyan. Dani hoped her new teammates understood where to position themselves.

Sure enough, as soon as the whistle blew, the ball went exactly where the midfielder had predicted. A Team Cyan player picked it up, but a tenacious Indigo defender knocked it out immediately, and the race was on toward the Cyan goal.

"Create space, offense," Amanda called off to her right.

Dani widened her spacing between her teammates just as a long pass flew toward Dani from the defender, bringing the ball up field. Dani caught it, did a stutter step, and blew by the Cyan defender. Another Cyan defender was on her instantly. Dani stopped all forward motion, changed direction, and sent a flip-pass to Amanda. Amanda snatched it out of the air and, in one smooth motion, shot on goal. It was a hard shot, but the Cyan goalie stopped it easily.

It was a good opening run, Dani thought. Her blood was pumping as she ran back up the field. They had this. They just had to get to know each other as teammates.

"Way to work the dodge, Dani," Amanda called to her.

"Nice shot on goal," Dani called back as they moved back down the field.

Team Cyan was not fooling around and moved the ball quickly down the field. They moved it so quickly that Team Indigo's defense had to play catchup. A whistle blew for a foul.

"Eight-meter," the official called. The Cyan player lined up on the eight-meter center line to take the penalty shot. On the whistle, she sent a searing shot straight into the Indigo goal.

"Dammit," Dani muttered as the ball found the back of the net. Team Indigo was now losing by a score of 1-0.

As the first and second quarters wore on, Amanada managed to score twice, but Team Cyan answered each goal and then some. They scored five more times, making the score 6-2 in Team Cyan's favor at the halfway mark.

Dani sucked as much water from her water bottle as her body would allow. She toweled off the sweat from her face and arms and plopped down on the grass with the rest of her teammates.

Team Indigo's captain, Stephanie, paced in front of them, "Mathers is dialed in early for Cyan. Defense, get on her. Let's see if any of those other Cyan players can score." Stephanie waited for the defense to nod their agreement and then continued. "Mid-fielders, let's try to get something going in transition because we've got the speed and the moves to do it. Team Cyan might get complacent with their lead. They may decide to underestimate us, so let's surprise them by going right for the goal. But don't force it. If you don't have it, pull out. Set up. Offense, keep good spacing. Amanda, nice shooting. Danielle, your turnovers are killing us. Make sure your stick is free and clear when you attempt to pass. And don't hang on to it. Get the ball to Amanda. Understood?"

Dani nodded that she'd heard, but she was confused. Stephanie was basically accusing her of being a ball hog. She hadn't been. She knew when to pass the ball off. And she'd only had two turnovers, thank you very much. Two turnovers weren't 'killing' anything. Stephanie wasn't being fair, but there was no way Dani was going to let her captain ruin the game for her. No way.

Amanda clapped her on the back when they went back out on the field. "You got this, Dani."

Dani couldn't tell from Amanda's statement or her tone if she agreed with Stephanie's assessment of Dani's play. So, Dani simply nodded, did her best to shake off Stephanie's comments, and reformulated her game strategy. It was clear that Amanda was on today and was the go-to player, and since Dani was a team player, she would help feed Amanda the ball. But Team Cyan might realize that Amanda was a scoring threat and might double up on her. That would leave Dani open, so she had to be ready for some good looks on the goal. She'd only taken that one shot in the first half and missed. That wasn't going to impress anyone.

The third and fourth quarters progressed in much the same fashion as the first two, though. The Team Cyan players didn't let up, and they basically wove their way through the Team Indigo players and increased their score so much that all the bench warmers were now in the game for Team Cyan. Seeing that move, Stephanie put in Team Indigo's subs as well. Dani and Amanda hit the bench, breathing hard.

"Can't win them all," Amanda said and rolled her eyes.

"Nope, you can't," Dani said but hoped they'd be able to win next week's game against Team Magenta.

"Check it," Amanda said. She pointed to the field. Both Laura and Stephanie had put themselves in the game. They were both midfielders, the players that ran the most on each team. Dani had to admit that both Laura and Stephanie were good at what they did. Where Laura had leadership and team-motivating moves, Stephanie had finesse and cat-like moves.

Dani liked the vantage point from the bench at that moment. It gave her a chance to size up and kind of judge the two women who were in power to determine her fate in the league. The feeling was new to her. She wasn't used to the idea of someone so close in age having power over her like they did. It was kind of daunting, actually. So far in Dani's life, she'd only been responsible for her own actions. Okay, maybe she'd encouraged her teammates in high school, but she didn't determine their fate—not like Laura, Stephanie, and the other captains would. Even as senior class president, Dani hadn't wielded that kind of influence or power.

As Dani watched the game play out on the field, she wondered what a career in politics would be like. Every day would be filled with judgments affecting other people's lives. And she already knew that not everyone agreed on what was important or what was best. Just listening to the PSLA debates every Friday confirmed that. It was a lot of responsibility.

The final whistle blew, ending the game, and Dani leaped up to join the already-forming high-five line. She didn't look Laura in the eye when they slapped each other's hands. Instead, she kept her gaze unfocused, muttered the required "Good game," and moved on.

Dani was strolling back to the sidelines with Amanda when Dani heard her name called from behind her.

"Danielle," Laura said. "Can I talk to you?"

Everything in Dani's entire soul of existence screamed, "Nooooo!" But she was too polite for that and turned toward the voice.

"See you later," Amanda said, patting her arm.

"See ya." Dani looked toward Laura, who'd made no move to come closer. "What?" Okay, that wasn't polite, but it wasn't totally rude, either. Dani was walking a fine line.

Laura moved closer. Dani stood her ground.

"I just wanted to tell you that I liked what I saw out there."

I bet you did, you jerk. Dani scowled at the woman moving closer.

Laura didn't seem to notice. "You have good instincts, and you move well. It's Stephanie's decision, of course, but I'm going to recommend that she keep you on Team Indigo for at least one more week."

"Okay," Dani said. She understood. She hadn't had many opportunities to show that she was good enough for Team Cyan. Amanda had been the star of today's game, and Dani wasn't about to take that away from her. She wasn't a self-serving ball hog like Stephanie seemed to think.

"And just so you know, Stephanie is jonesing to move a certain player up from Team Magenta to play first home."

When Laura didn't continue, there was enough space between them for the words to sink in.

"Oh," Dani said as realization hit her solar plexus. "I have to go."

"I know," Laura said. "Keep practicing. You have a lot of potential."

Bile rose in Dani's throat, and she tried to swallow it down to no avail. She simply turned away from Laura and headed toward her bag on the sidelines. Her friends were waiting for her, but she needed a minute.

She took her time changing out of her cleats and back into her sneakers. She shoved her stuff into her bag but didn't bother sliding her stick into the holder on the side. She simply carried it like a weapon. She looked up and set her sights on the beacon of light in front of her. Meredith.

Although Dani hadn't yet seen Team Magenta play in a game yet, she knew beyond a doubt that she didn't belong there. Yes, she could admit that she should stay on Team Indigo and not move up to Cyan. But move down a level? No way. Uh uh. No way. She'd find out her fate on Friday evening.

"What happened?" Meredith asked, shooting a glance at Kate, who still knew nothing about the incident between Dani and Laura.

"Nothing much," Dani said as deadpan as she could. "Laura told me I'd probably stay on Team Indigo for next week."

"That's not a bad thing, is it?" Meredith said as they walked back up the hill toward the dorm. Dani wanted desperately to link arms with Meredith, to be comforted, but she couldn't. She had to be her usual strong self, but that was getting tiring as all heck.

"It's not a bad thing, no," Dani said after a moment. "But she also said I need to keep practicing."

"And I'll help you," Meredith said.

"You will?"

"I will."

"Aww," Kate said. "The artist and the athlete. Could be a kids' book." She stopped walking and said, "Uh, Dani, I think you have some fans."

Dani looked where Kate was pointing. A small group of elementary-school-aged kids were following them. "What's up, you guys?" Dani said to them.

One of the taller girls stepped forward and said, "Can you show us how to play sometime?" She was maybe in fifth grade, wearing an orange Tungsten Elementary School t-shirt and a pair of black sweats. Her dark hair was braided on her head in the most artful way.

"Absolutely," Dani said.

The sea of kids swarmed Dani and asked to see her stick.

Kate laughed. To Petra, she said, "Did you know we were hanging with a celebrity?"

"I did not," Petra said. "But I'm not surprised by this at all." Her hand swept to include the kids now surrounding Dani.

"Why do you guys wiggle your sticks when you run?" one of the younger boys asked.

"So, the ball won't fall out of the net."

A dozen or more questions were rapid-fired at her, and Dani answered each one until she finally had to say to the kids, "Hey, tell you what. There's a game here on Wednesday. Why don't I meet you here before, and I can show you some stuff." She briefly thought about the logistics of it but decided to worry about that later. "Make sure it's okay with your parents, though."

"We will," they chorused as they parted ways.

"Hey," Dani called back after them, "I'm Dani, by the way. What are your names?"

Dani and her friends just laughed as they shouted their names back to her in a cacophony of sound. The one name she did pick up, though, was Natalie, the first young girl to step up and speak for the group.

"See you all on Wednesday." Dani surprised herself by adding, "Bye, Natalie."

Natalie turned around with such a surprised expression that it almost made Dani laugh. "Bye, Dani."

Dani waved and smiled as the young girl waved back.

"That was so sweet," Meredith said as they headed back up to campus. "Have you ever thought about being a coach or a teacher?"

"Me?" Dani scoffed. "I don't think I have the patience for that."

"Of course you do," Petra said. "You handled that Darius guy so well. So calm. So cool."

"If you say so," Dani said. "Friday's your turn to be calm and cool."

Petra groaned. "Don't remind me."

"Don't let her fool you," Kate said. "She's been rehearsing her speech for a week now. And it's good."

"I'm sure it is," Meredith said. "This is my friend Petra we're talking about."

Petra's smile at Meredith was so endearing that Dani couldn't help but smile as well. Friends were a good thing to have.

"So," Meredith said, changing the subject, "we're going to have to figure out how to pull off teaching lacrosse to all those kids on Wednesday."

"Ugh." Dani groaned. "What did I do?"

"You led with your heart," Meredith said. "Like you always do.

Grateful tears stung Dani's eyes. One thing was becoming increasingly clear—she couldn't do this, any of this, without Meredith by her side.

Chapter 12
You've Got This

"You played so great, baby," Meredith said to Dani once they were back in their dorm room and alone.

"Thanks," Dani said deadpan. Even she heard the disbelief in her voice. "I didn't get a lot of looks on goal. Stephanie—"

"Team Indigo's student captain? The pretty one who wears way too much makeup and has a body I'd kill for? That one?"

Dani couldn't suppress a giggle. "Fair assessment, I guess. Yes, her."

"What about her?" Meredith asked as she took off her sweater and hung it up in the small closet.

"I mean, it was probably the right thing to do, but she wanted us to basically set things up for Amanda to score."

"And not you." It was a statement, not a question.

"Not me." Dani put her gear away after pulling her mouthguard out of her bag. "I mean, I had the green light if I had an open shot, but…"

"But you didn't feel confident."

Dani groaned. "Yeah, I guess not."

"Hey," Meredith said as she wrapped herself around Dani from behind. "Don't get discouraged. You know how to play this game, and you're good at it. Your chances will come, right?"

Dani pivoted so she could face Meredith. "You always know what to say." She leaned down and kissed Meredith's forehead.

"You missed."

Dani chuckled and lifted Meredith's chin with the side of her index finger so she could kiss her properly. On the lips. Where all adoring girlfriends should be kissed. Too soon, even for Dani, she stepped back, announcing the need for a shower and then some focused reading for their Women's Studies class due the following afternoon.

Meredith complained good-naturedly and teased about not letting Dani go but gave up the game soon enough.

In the shower, Dani let the hot water soak over her as she breathed deeply and let it out slowly. There were so many unexpected points of aggravation in college, none of which she had expected. She took another cleansing breath as the water cascaded over her head and down her body. She switched it up and mused on all the good things that she hadn't expected. Things like Kate and Petra becoming good friends. The surprising variety of food on campus. So far, she and Meredith hadn't gone hungry. Dani laughed out loud at that one. And the best thing of all was how close she and Meredith were becoming. Meredith was more than a friend in so many ways. As she toweled off, Dani felt deep in her heart that she could make a life with Meredith. That thought, however, she would keep to herself for a while. No sense scaring Meredith off, right?

When Dani got back in the room, Meredith whipped around in her chair and said, "Your phone has been blowing up."

"What's going on?"

Meredith rolled her eyes and pointed to Dani's phone on Dani's desk. "Kate and Petra texted me to see if you'd read their texts yet. I said you were in the shower and you'd check your messages when you got out. Go look for yourself. Oh, and that trainer named Joiee called you. I'm sorry I snooped, but I thought maybe your parents or Esther and Millie were calling, and it might have been an emergency."

"No, you were right to do that. And just so we're clear, you can look at my phone any time."

"Oh, good to know," Meredith said. "Some people are very private about their stuff."

At that moment, Dani had her back to Meredith as she put away her shower stuff but whipped around and said, "My stuff is your stuff, baby." She went over and picked up her phone. "We have no secrets between us, right?"

Meredith nodded. She waved her phone at Dani, "Same goes for you."

Dani smiled as she said, "Okay. Good." She took a deep breath, straightened her spine, and said, "Let's see what's going on here." Her text icon had a red number fifteen over it. "What the heck?" She clicked on Kate's text.

KATE: Petra and I made some calls. We have great news.

KATE: Can we come over? We have much to discuss.

KATE: Where are you?

Meredith rolled her eyes. "Impatient, that one. Isn't she?"

"I'd better get dressed before she bangs our door down with whatever it is." Dani tossed her phone onto Meredith's desk. "Can you read the rest and let me know what I need to know?"

"Mm hmm."

Dani had planned to get comfy and put on her pajamas, but it looked like their socializing might not be done for the evening, so she threw on a pair of jeans and a T-shirt.

"Well," Meredith said, "to summarize both Kate's and Petra's messages, it seems like they've convinced a few people to help out for your lacrosse clinic with the kids."

"What?" Dani was so confused. "It's just some kids, and it's not a clinic. Let me see." She read the texts from Kate and Petra. "Holy wow. Some of Kate's classmates in her social work class volunteered to help supervise the kids."

"That's incredible, Dani," Meredith said. "And Kate also knows a couple of physical education majors who said they could help."

Dani jumped when her phone dinged in her hand. They both laughed at the surprise of it. She showed Meredith her screen.

KATE: Are you clean yet?

111

DANI: Yes. We're coming over now.

"Oh, we're going to their room?" Meredith asked, getting up.

"Yep." Dani handed Meredith her sweater, ignoring Kate's answering text. "Millie told me once that it's easier to leave someone else's house than to ask them to leave yours."

"Wise woman she is," Meredith said.

"Yoda are you?" Dani asked with a chuckle as she held the door open for her girlfriend.

"Yoda I am not. Strange I am." Meredith broke out into a run down the hallway toward Kate and Petra's room. "Loser has to do the other's laundry," she called over her shoulder.

Dani jogged behind Meredith, letting her win. "I don't mind doing things for you."

The door in front of them burst open before Dani or Meredith could knock.

"About time," Kate said in a fake surly manner. "You take the longest showers."

Dani wasn't about to protest, knowing that she did not take long showers and was cognizant about wasting water. Instead, she cut right to the chase. "What's going on, you guys?"

Petra smiled big from where she sat at her desk. It was neat and tidy, just like she was. Dani recognized it as a way for Petra to have control over something. Hmm, Meredith got in those neat and tidy moods sometimes. Maybe that was a signal for Dani to be more attentive to Meredith's needs.

Kate gestured for Meredith to sit in her desk chair and then said. "We were talking and decided that there's no way you can teach all those kids lacrosse with your one stick, one ball, and the one *you*."

"So, we called around for help," Petra added.

"I went to high school with Marti, and she said they could bring lacrosse sticks, balls, and goggles from the PE storage lockers. She's a junior and a PE major." Kate barely took a breath and continued. "She has to get the okay tomorrow from her supervisor, but apparently, she and some classmates have this project—"

"A community outreach project," Petra interjected.

"Right," Kate said, pointing to her roommate. "It's for their class, and Marti said they hadn't figured out what they were going to do. It's a tailor-made perfect opportunity for them."

"Wow, okay," Dani said wide-eyed. "Is that Marty with a y or Marti with an i?"

"M-a-r-t-i," Kate spelled.

Dani wanted to ask why Kate and Petra told this Marti person about her promise to the kids, but she didn't know how to disrupt their obvious excitement. "I didn't expect all of this. We don't even know if the kids will like lacrosse."

"True, true," Kate said. "Marti said the same thing, didn't she, Petra?"

"Mm hmm," Petra said. "She and her group are going to bring some soccer balls, too. Just in case."

"That makes sense," Meredith added. "Maybe we can bring water or juice boxes for the kids."

Kate looked stunned. "Perfect idea. Maybe they have a big water jug in the PE storage locker. We'll need cups, though. Let me text Marti." Kate typed furiously on her phone. A text dinged back almost instantly. "Ha," Kate said, sounding victorious. "Marti's already got that covered."

"Wow," was all Dani could say. Kate had it all figured out. No. Both Kate *and* Petra. Just because Kate was the more vocal of the two and the one out in front didn't mean her quieter roommate hadn't contributed just as much, if not more. Petra was like Meredith, who often got quiet in groups of people.

Dani said, "Meredith suggested that once the game starts on Wednesday, we sit with the kids in the stands to explain the game to them."

Meredith beamed at Dani. Dani's core tightened. She'd just scored major girlfriend points. Hoorah.

"If they want to learn about the game, that is," Meredith added.

"Oh, shoot," Dani said and looked at Meredith. "You said I got a call from Joiee, didn't you?"

Meredith nodded. Kate made a funny noise, causing the other three to look at her.

"You okay there, Kate?" Dani asked and looked down to see if Joiee had left a voice message. She had.

"Mm hmm," Kate said, her voice high and tight. There was a slight flush on her face that Dani was fairly certain hadn't been there before. Did Kate have a crush on Joiee? Now was not the time to ask or tease her about it. And didn't Kate have a boyfriend back home? Someone named Stevie or something?

Dani took the focus back on herself. "Let me listen to her message." She put the phone to her ear, pressing it tight. She might not have secrets with Meredith, but Kate and Petra were a different story. She put a finger up and walked over to the window for a modicum of privacy.

"Hey, Dani, it's me, Joiee. I know you kind of don't want to be friends, but I have a thought about your lacrosse clinic on Wednesday before the intramural league game. My friend Marti told me what you were planning, and I think there could be a liability issue if any of the children get hurt. So, I want to help. How about I come down early and bring another trainer with me? Together, he and I can take care of any injuries to the kids or whatever. Just keep in mind that I'll have to get ready for the game at some point. I think I have three, maybe four people that need to be taped up."

There was a bit of silence in the recording, and Dani thought Joiee's message was finished, but then she spoke again.

"Listen, I think something might have happened between you and Laura. I haven't a clue what. But it seems that whenever I make a new friend, and they meet Laura, my new friend gives me the cold shoulder. So, I ... I don't know." There was a bit more silence. "Okay, let me know about the clinic thing. Thanks. Bye."

Dani turned to the group and said succinctly, "Joiee's going to come out early to be there for first aid and injury stuff."

"That's so cool," Meredith said. "Why are people doing all of this?"

Both Petra and Kate looked at Meredith in disbelief.

"What?" Meredith said with a laugh. "What am I missing?"

Petra spoke up first. She spoke directly to Meredith as she asked, "Who was the very first one to step up and volunteer to help Dani with the kids?"

"Meredith was," Dani answered for her girlfriend.

"Yeah, I was." Meredith was still clearly baffled.

"And just like you," Kate said softly, "we want to help."

"That's really nice," Meredith said.

"You guys are weird," Dani said, making everyone laugh. "Okay, so Kate. This Marti person seems to be heading up the PE group, yes?"

"Yes."

"Can you start us on a group chat? I want to give her a call to make sure we're all on the same page."

"Oh," Kate said, surprise in her tone. "That makes sense, I guess."

"I just don't want your friends to have the impression that hanging with the kids is bigger than it is."

"That's understandable," Petra chimed in.

"I mean, you guys are amazing for taking such a deep dive into this." Dani looked at Meredith for confirmation as she said, "You know?"

Meredith nodded her agreement.

"I just don't want to stir up trouble with…" Dani hesitated. She was about to say, "Laura," but decided not to dredge up that uncomfortable name and the stupidity associated with it. She looked over at Petra, who nodded, saying that she understood.

"I'm missing something," Kate said, her eyes narrowed.

"I'll explain it to you later," Petra said softly. She turned toward Dani and asked, "Is that okay?"

"Yeah," Dani said succinctly.

Kate looked from Dani to Petra and back again before nodding. "Okay, let me put us all in a group chat." Her fingers danced across her phone. "Petra? Meredith? Do you guys want to join this chat?"

"Nah," Petra said. "I get enough texts from my family as it is."

Everyone chuckled, and Meredith also declined the group chat invitation.

In an instant, Dani's phone dinged.

KATE: Marti – Dani wants to go over some details with you. She's on this chat, too.

MARTI: Oh, cool. Hi, Dani!

DANI: NTMU over text. Kate and Petra have been amazing getting the word out. Can I call you tonight?

MARTI: OFC. In 30 minutes?

DANI: Sounds good.

MARTI: We can group talk if Kate wants in.

KATE: She does.

Dani laughed at Kate's use of the third person. Kate waggled her eyebrows and smiled at her own silliness.

"What?" Meredith asked, probably regretting not being part of the chat. Meredith seemed to relax when Dani explained what they were laughing at, but Dani made a mental note to make sure Meredith was included in any and all plans for the kids' event. She didn't want Meredith to feel left out of anything.

MARTI: I'll initiate the call in 30. I'll bring Kate in first, then Dani.

DANI: Sounds good.

KATE: Yay.

MARTI: TTFN

"Thanks for this," Dani said to Kate and Petra as she waved her phone. "This is going to be cool. And not to be a doggy downer, but Meredith and I have a lot of reading to get to, and I'd like to get some in before Marti's call. We're going to head back."

Kate pushed off her desk. "Talk to you in twenty-nine minutes."

"Sounds good." Dani opened the door for Meredith to go through first. Once Meredith was in the hallway, Dani walked side by side with her girlfriend back to their room.

"When are you doing my laundry?" Meredith quipped.

"When they come up with more than twenty-four hours in a day," Dani said. Hopefully, Meredith wasn't serious about Dani doing all the laundry by herself because there wasn't much time in her days for things like that. And what the heck had she gotten into with this kids' event? She barely had time to keep all the balls juggled in the air without adding this one.

That Monday night and then throughout the day on Tuesday, Dani was on her phone taking care of the details for the Wednesday afternoon event, even though she really had no picture in her head of what it would look like. She'd have to wing it, as they say.

Late Tuesday evening, Dani mustered up the courage to text Joiee back. Meredith approved of the wording, and then Dani sent it.

DANI: Thanks for your offer to help. I appreciate it. I'm not sure how interested the kids will be in learning lacrosse, but there seemed to be a lot of them hanging around the other day. So, we'll see what happens.

A few moments later, Joiee's short reply came back in.

JOIEE: Glad to do it. I'll see you tomorrow.

Dani stood up from her desk, leaving the Women's Studies article about feminism half read, and walked over to show Meredith the reply.

"Short and sweet," Meredith said. She looked like she wanted to say something else, so Dani waited. "She seems like a good person, Dani."

"Mmm," was all Dani could muster.

"Give her a new chance, okay?" Meredith hugged Dani around her torso.

"Okay," Dani said. "But I'm not going to be alone with her, like, ever."

"Sounds like a plan," Meredith said.

"I'm nervous about hanging with the kids tomorrow. Everybody just jumped on board. They're making this into a whole...thing."

"Take control of it," Meredith said, looking up at Dani from where she sat at her desk. "You're good at that."

"I am?"

"Pfft," Meredith scoffed. "Uh, yeah, you are. Who else could have gotten a bunch of high school seniors with rampant senioritis to go to Hudson Pines and hang out with a bunch of senior citizens?"

"Anybody could have," Dani said.

"No. You're wrong about that." Meredith swiveled in her seat to face Dani. "You're charismatic. You draw people to you."

"Me?"

Meredith smiled knowingly. "Yes, you. You've got this, baby. And I'll be right by your side tomorrow for whatever it turns out to be. Two kids might show up."

"Or two hundred."

"Doubt that," Meredith said with a chuckle. "So, take a deep breath, okay?"

"Okay." Dani did as she was told.

"Now shut that phone down, and let's finish reading this article about feminism in the eighteenth and nineteenth centuries."

Dani didn't speak. Instead, she leaned down and kissed Meredith on the crown of her head and then walked back to her desk. She reopened the PDF on her laptop and said, "It's like history I never heard of."

"Brave women doing what they could with what they had for their own kind," Meredith said. "Despite the consequences."

"Mmm," Dani mused. "Well said, Ms. Bedford."

Meredith chuckled and then added, "Set a twenty-minute timer. I'll need replenishing at that point."

"Do my kisses really replenish your energy stores?" Dani threw an amused glance over her shoulder.

"Yep," Meredith said. "Set that timer if you know what's good for you."

Dani made an anxious noise and said, "Timer set. See you in twenty." She got back to reading after sending a brief but grateful thought to the universe for bringing Meredith into her life.

When the timer went off, Dani stood up and immediately wrapped her arms around her girlfriend. Meredith tried to turn around, but Dani had a theory brewing. If she moved this patch of hair off a certain roommate's neck, there might be plenty of skin to kiss. She tested the theory and was rewarded with a satisfied sigh from the recipient. Good theory, Dani mused as a dozen similar theories popped up in her head.

Soon enough, studying was no longer the priority.

Chapter 13

Take Control of That

Dani and Meredith bolted out of their Women's Studies class and hustled to the practice field. When they crested the hill, Dani breathed a sigh of relief. There were a few SU students there, but no kids yet. Her relief was short-lived.

"What if none of the kids come back?" Dani said to Meredith as they headed for the area where it looked like the physical education majors had set up a table.

"Hush," Meredith said and shook her head. "You've got this."

Dani nodded, not that she agreed with Meredith, but she had to get her nerves under control. A dozen or more fears rifled through her brain. I don't know these people. What if no kids show up? What if someone gets hurt? What if—

"Stop." Meredith bumped Dani with her hip again.

Dani groaned good-naturedly. "You always know."

"Mm hmm." Meredith increased her pace, making Dani hustle to catch up.

"I'm already doing your laundry this weekend," Dani said with a laugh.

Meredith laughed but didn't turn around. When she got to the table, she touched it and sing-songed, "I win. You lose. Now you have to buy me booze."

Dani reached the table and slapped it just as Meredith finished her taunting. "You don't drink."

"I know. I couldn't think of anything else that rhymed."

"And you two are underage, anyway," a young woman with an authoritative gait said as she walked up. "I can tell already that this venture, whatever it is, is going to be fun. I'm Marti."

"Dani," Dani said and stuck her hand out toward the short-haired brunette. They shook, and Dani introduced Meredith.

"Nice to meet you both," Marti said. "Now, listen, I think we should set up lacrosse here and soccer over there." She pointed to areas on and around the field. And then, if kids don't want to do those things, we can think of something else to do with the rest."

Dani was taken aback. She needed a moment to digest Marti's suggestions. "Great ideas, Marti, but before we get going on that, I'd like to meet with everyone first. The grownups, I mean."

"You're a grownup?" Kate said from behind Dani and then laughed so hard that everyone caught the fever.

"Shut up," Dani teased back. "I meant that I want the college students to meet. Not the kids. Does that make sense?"

"Perfectly," Meredith said and then greeted Petra, who was standing quietly behind Kate.

"Thanks for coming, you guys," Dani said.

"Wouldn't miss it," Kate said. Her long blonde hair was tied back into a tight ponytail. It looked like it hurt.

Dani looked at Marti and said, "Would you gather your people so we can meet and get on the same page?"

"Will do," Marti said and turned to call them over.

"Kate?" Dani said.

"Mm hmm?"

"I have a special assignment for you." Dani, not believing she was about to do what she was about to do, pointed.

"See the trainer over there setting up her table?"

"The dark-haired *grownup*?" Kate said with a chuckle.

"Yep. Can you go ask her to join our opening meeting?"

"Umm, okay," Kate said haltingly. All mirth was gone from her voice. Her feet didn't move, but she was looking in Joiee's direction.

"Ready, set, go," Dani said to Kate and pushed her gently toward Joiee.

"Come with me, Petra," Kate said and pulled Petra along with her.

Petra looked surprised but let herself be pulled toward the trainer.

When they were out of earshot, Meredith leaned in and said, "What are you doing?" She gestured with her chin toward Kate.

"Honestly? I'm not really sure, but sending Kate over there seemed like the right thing to do at the time."

Meredith narrowed her eyes. "Is this part of giving Joiee a second chance?"

"Maybe. I don't really know," Dani said. And she didn't know. "My instincts said to do that."

They couldn't continue the conversation because Marti came back with four people. Introductions were made, and two of the four were PE majors and part of Marti's outreach project group. The other two were Kate's social work classmates. The PE majors, including Marti, were all juniors, but like Dani, the social work majors were freshmen.

When Kate, Petra, and Joiee joined them, Dani said to the group, "This got started from an offhand comment I made to the kids on Monday. I said I'd show them some 'stuff' about lacrosse. That's all I said."

"And they got really excited," Meredith interjected.

"They did," Dani said. "So, I have no idea how many kids will show up, but if the number is manageable, I'd like to keep them all engaged in lacrosse at first. This way, we're not too spread out. I'd like to keep the soccer balls hidden for now."

"Oh, but I think we can handle the kids in different stations," Marti said. "One for soccer and one for lacrosse."

She was just about to say something else, but Dani spoke before she did. "No doubt about that. I want to set a cohesive tone with them first, though. We're not their parents, but we are kind of going to be responsible for them. Joiee came early to take care of any boo-boos."

Kate snorted, and the entire group chuckled.

"But," Dani continued, "I want to make sure they don't get those boo-boos in the first place. Once they get to know us and we get to know each other, we can branch out a bit. Does that sound okay?" Dani looked right at Marti when she asked the question. She didn't want Marti to think she and the rest of the volunteers were ganging up on her or rejecting her ideas.

"You know what," Marti said. "That makes sense. We can't get ahead of ourselves. You're right."

"Cool, cool." Dani was relieved she had been able to reign the enthusiasm into manageable levels.

Dani briefly went over some protocols with the group, such as never being alone with a child. Not making promises or giving them gifts. She reminded them to be professional in all things.

The head nods and murmurs of agreement made Dani relax a bit. Out of the corner of her eye, she saw a couple of the neighborhood kids squeezing through a hole in the fence and heading toward the field.

"Marti, since you're the expert on teaching, it just makes sense for you to lead the actual lacrosse teaching part, okay?"

"Will do, Dani."

"The kids have to wear goggles," Dani reminded the group. "And if you're playing, then you have to wear goggles, too."

"Okay if we finish setting up?" Marti asked.

"Yeah, yeah, yeah, in one second," Dani said, trying desperately not to lose control of the group. "Once again, I want to thank you all for coming today. Who knows what this will end up being, but let's remember to have fun, okay?" Dani reached her hand toward the center of the loose circle of people, and the rest followed suit. "We'll say, 'Have fun,' on three. Ready?" She didn't wait for them to respond and blurted, "One, two, three!"

"Have fun!" the group said and then laughed as they lifted their hands in the air.

"Whoa," Meredith said. "I've never done that before. That was cool."

"I guess that means you're on the team now," Dani quipped.

Meredith pressed her lips together and bugged out her eyes as if desperate to keep back a flood of emotions. Dani made a mental note to ask her about it later.

Dani called over to the retreating PE volunteers, "Hey, I'll be over in a minute to see what goodies you brought." Dani couldn't help the kid-in-a-candy-store tone to her voice. Meredith threw her a knowing smile when the

PE volunteers lit up at Dani's statement.

Dani asked Kate, Petra, and Kate's classmates to be general helpers and watch out for the kids' well-being. She asked them to go over and greet them and then usher them toward Marti's group. Dani also told them that they were more than welcome to pick up any spare lacrosse sticks and join in, but they were not to get hurt.

When Kate and her group left to corral the kids, numbering about ten at that point, Joiee turned to head back to her station.

"Hey, Joiee," Dani said, "can you hang for a second?"

"Sure." Joiee stopped in her tracks and turned around but made no motion to come closer.

Dani approached but kept a more than respectable distance between them. She hesitated for a split second because she hadn't planned on what to say. "I wanted to thank you personally for coming out today. You've been nothing but nice to me, and I haven't been very friendly. I'm sorry."

Joiee looked startled and didn't respond right away.

Meredith took that opportunity to say, "Whoa, look at all those kids coming through the fence. I'll go help Kate."

"Great," Dani said. "Thank you." And now Joiee and Dani were alone on the side of the lacrosse field.

Joiee took a step closer. "Listen, I got your message loud and clear that you weren't looking for a relationship. Okay? I just wanted to get that out of the way. I understand. I'm in a relationship anyway."

"Okay," Dani said, conveying with that one word that she understood and that she also knew Joiee had more to say.

"And I could also tell from the instant you met Laura you were attracted to her."

"She is striking," Dani admitted. "But I don't want a relationship with her either."

The surprised look on Joiee's face told Dani that she hadn't known that.

Dani continued, "And I'm not just saying that because you're her girlfriend."

Joiee looked down and grunted. "About that. Have you ever been attracted to something so beautiful it takes your breath away?" Joiee didn't wait for Dani to answer and said, "One summer, my parents took us on vacation to a beach in South Carolina. I don't remember which one, but I was, like, ten years old or something. I saw these amazing pink flowers and gathered a whole bunch of them for my mom. She put them in a vase in our vacation condo, but shortly after that, we both broke out in rashes on our hands and faces. Mine blistered." Joiee looked over at the crowd of kids and said, "I know you have to go, but let me just make this point." She swallowed a few times, clearly getting choked up.

Dani knew the most important thing for her to do at this moment was to hear the rest of Joiee's story. Marti, Kate, and the rest had things under control.

Joiee cleared her throat. "Mom was okay, but I had to go to the emergency room. The flowers I had picked, although stunningly beautiful, were pink oleander. The whole plant, including the flowers, is toxic. We didn't know."

"Hey, Dani," Kate called from the gathered crowd.

"You need to go," Joiee said and turned to walk away.

"No," Dani said and held up her index finger to Kate, indicating that she'd be there in a minute. "I need to be right here," she said to Joiee. "Go on."

Joiee continued despite her perplexed expression. "Laura is oleander, Dani. I didn't know that when I started dating her freshman year. I even moved in sophomore year when she asked me to. Is she still beautiful to look at? Shit, yeah, but—" Joiee hid her face behind her hands as tears flowed.

Dani didn't hesitate. She pulled Joiee into a hug and rubbed her back. "You're okay." After a moment, Dani pulled back and said, "Take a breath." Joiee did and seemed grateful that Dani was there.

"I need to get over there," Joiee said, pointing to her portable trainer's table.

"And I need to get over there," Dani pointed to the gathering crowd of kids. "But how about this? How about we meet for lunch tomorrow or whenever? But not as a date."

Joiee chuckled. "I know. I got that message very loud and very clear. But,

125

yes, it would be nice to talk to someone about this."

"Great," Dani patted Joiee on the arm. "Don't leave before we shore up details."

"Thanks," Joiee said. She turned and walked away without waiting for a response.

Dani felt weird about their unfinished conversation, hating to leave Joiee so emotional like that. But duty called, and she had to go.

Dani hustled over to the group and said to the tall girl she'd met on Monday, "Hey, Natalie," and put her fist out for a bump and got one.

Natalie beamed. She looked cute in her obvious PE t-shirt and shorts. "You remembered my name."

"Of course. And I see you brought a dozen friends with you."

Natalie looked around her. "These are the kids from my street. I told them you were going to show us some stuff about lacrosse, and they all wanted to come. I hope that was okay."

"Perfectly fine, kid," Marti answered for Dani. "What grade are you in?"

"Fifth grade. I'm ten."

"Perfect age to learn lacrosse," Marti said. "Right, Dani?"

Dani nodded over-enthusiastically, making Natalie laugh. She winked at Natalie and then introduced the SU student volunteers to the assembled group. "Miss Marti and her assistants will be the main ones teaching you about lacrosse, but the rest of us will be around to help."

"Will you help, too?" Natalie asked Dani in a shy voice.

"Of course. This was all my idea, wasn't it?"

"Mm hmm," Natalie said and then laughed.

"Safety is paramount, you guys," Dani said to the group. She then laid out the ground rules about always wearing goggles and always wearing the brand-new mouthguards Marti had brought over. She demonstrated with her own stick how not to place it near someone's head or any part of someone's body. "Miss Marti will go over everything again, I'm sure."

"Sure will."

Dani gestured for Marti to take over and was pleasantly surprised at how efficient and effective Marti and the other PE majors were with the children.

They were patient and kind, and the amount of laughter and goodwill flowing between and among the participants threatened to overtake Dani's emotions.

Marti showed them how to cradle an imaginary ball by moving the stick back and forth across their bodies. She exaggerated the movements, reminding them to have a tight grip on the top hand but a looser grip on the lower. The fun really began when the volunteers added balls into the mix. Balls went flying in every direction as the kids and college volunteers tried to keep the small yellow ball in the net. At one point, Marti widened the distance between the kids for safety reasons. That was a good call, Dani thought.

Meredith tried cradling a ball a couple of times and commented that it was way harder than it looked. Dani had learned how to cradle back when she was Natalie's age, so it came naturally, and she didn't even think about it anymore. Dani did her best to teach Meredith the finer art to cradling a lacrosse ball, but Meredith wasn't quite getting it. Dani was impressed that Meredith kept at it, though, and didn't give up at the first sign of failure. Good for her. She was a fantastic role model for the kids.

The next drill involved learning how to scoop up balls on the ground. Marti emphasized that their sticks had to be on the side of their bodies so they wouldn't impale themselves with the other end. Even Dani laughed along with the kids when Marti comically showed them how *not* to do it. Time was quickly running away from them, so Marti called the kids together and had two of her PE classmates demonstrate throwing and catching. The last five minutes were dedicated to letting the kids try. Dani enjoyed the mayhem way too much. Had she looked like that when she first started playing? Probably. Way too soon, though, Dani had to call an end to their session.

The kids groaned in disappointment, and Dani did, too. She felt like they had just gotten started. And she was pleased that not a single one of the kids opted out of the activities or left the group to do something else.

The intramural league players were arriving in droves, so they had to wrap up the clinic and get off the field. Yes, she called it a clinic. It seemed like the best word to describe what they were doing.

"Bring it in, everybody," Dani called. The kids and the college students gathered in a circle around Dani. "I hope you all had fun this afternoon. I did.

But yikes, the time went by so fast. Do you guys want to do this again sometime?"

A cacophony of responses filled the air. "Yes." "Tomorrow." "Do we have to stop?"

"Yes, unfortunately, we have to stop," Dani said with a laugh. "The college kids need the field for their game. Team Teal is taking on Team Magenta, as you can tell by their colored pinnies.

"That's pink," someone said.

Meredith jumped right in. "Technically, pink is more on the lighter spectrum of red, but I agree. Those pinnies do look pink."

Dani smiled at her and then said, "Hey, if anybody wants to hang in the bleachers and watch the game with us, we'll be in that middle section right there." She pointed to the bleachers at midfield.

"Can we still play with the sticks?" one older boy asked.

Dani looked over at Marti, who shook her head. Dani answered the boy by saying, "Not this time, Jayden. The PE folks have to put all this equipment away."

A chorus of disappointed whines followed her statement, but Dani only laughed. "You guys are hooked now, aren't you?"

"Yes," Jayden said. "You did this to us."

"We're willing to come back tomorrow," Marti said. "Right, you guys?" This she said to her PE classmates, who all nodded enthusiastically.

"Thursday it is," Dani said. She then told the kids that if they were able to bring their own lacrosse sticks and goggles, it would help. She also reminded them to wash the mouthguards thoroughly and to bring them the next day.

"Hands in," she boomed over the din of a billion conversations that had erupted.

Everyone put their hands in toward the center. Dani moved out of the center of the circle she'd found herself in and stood near Meredith. "We'll say, 'Lacrosse Rules' on three. Ready? One, two, three!"

"Lacrosse rules!" the group shouted and lifted their hands together. Dani laughed with the rest and smiled when she saw Joiee throw her a thumbs up from her training table, where she was taping up an intramural player's ankle.

128

"Help clean up, everyone," Dani said and picked up her own lacrosse stick where she'd dropped it earlier.

"That was so much fun," Kate said. "We're all coming back tomorrow, too."

Petra sidled up next to Dani and said quietly. "Except me. Thank you for this, though. I had a blast. I have a late afternoon class tomorrow, but if you do it again on another day, count me in."

"I will," Dani said. "We'll have to figure this out, won't we?"

"Yep," Kate said. "I feel a group chat with Marti coming on this evening."

"You're probably right," Dani said with a laugh. "You guys staying for the game?"

"No," Kate said. "We both have some reading to catch up on, and I'm literally starving, so we're going to head back up to the dorm and dining hall."

"Be safe," Dani said.

"I knew you were going to say that," Kate said.

"We'll stay together," Petra said, reassuring Dani. "No worries."

"Safety first," Meredith quipped. "Bye, you guys. See you later."

Dani felt Meredith's warmth and longed to put an arm around her. But she didn't dare.

"You were amazing, Dani," Meredith murmured now that they were alone. There was something akin to sparkles in her eyes.

"What do you mean? Amazing at what?"

"Handling this crowd of people." Meredith bent down to pick up a stray lacrosse ball. She tossed it over to one of the PE people. "I would never be able to handle this many people all at once. And the way you took the reins back from Marti right at the beginning? She's nice and all, but she was trying to take over a little bit."

"Yeah," Dani said, "but she meant well. I appreciate her help. We couldn't have done this without those guys or Kate and her classmates. Or you." The din of kids' voices faded a little as Dani took in Meredith's face. She groaned. "It's frustrating not being able to hold you right now. Or kiss you."

"I know the feeling."

Dani shook her head and wiggled her entire body to shake off her longing for physical contact.

"Miss Dani," Natalie called to her. "Can I sit with you and Miss Meredith?"

"Of course," Dani said and headed toward Natalie and Marti. To Marti, she said, "All cleaned up? I'm sorry. I didn't help."

"Next time," Marti said. "And besides. I had so many helpers, like this one here." She tousled Natalie's braids, making the ten-year-old smile.

"Group chat tonight?" Dani asked Marti.

"You read my mind," Marti said and slung the bag of lacrosse balls over her shoulder.

They set up a time for the chat and said their goodbyes.

Dani, Meredith, Natalie, and a trail of kids headed to the bleachers. Dani knew Laura was at the field but had managed to ignore her until now. Unfortunately, there was no smooth way to avoid her anymore.

"You look like a mother duck leading her little ducklings," Laura said as the group walked by.

Dani looked over her shoulder and grinned. The kids had formed a single line and were following her and Meredith to the bleacher seats. "Looks like it."

"Let's talk sometime," Laura said, her voice full of meaning. What that meaning was, Dani had no clue and no desire to find out.

"Enjoy the game," was the only thing Dani said back to her.

When they got to the top of the bleachers, Meredith leaned in close and whispered, "Way to take control of that."

Chapter 14

Why Shouldn't I?

Thursday afternoon's lacrosse session with the neighborhood kids should have lasted at least two hours, but they lost the use of the field at precisely five o'clock. Apparently, Laura had officially booked the field for a Team Cyan practice. Dani was frustrated because she felt they were just starting to get to know the kids and make some real progress. The fact that Laura was the one who put a stop to their fun made it worse.

The kids and the volunteers were disappointed, but at least they'd been having fun. The kids learned a lot in that one hour, including how to throw and catch more smoothly. Marti even had them try it on the run. That part wasn't as successful, but the kids were making great strides. Marti even asked Dani to demonstrate catching and throwing from both sides of the body. Dani tried not to puff up as she showed her skills, but it felt good to be recognized for doing something right. She realized after the demonstration that she hadn't been getting much praise or accolades or even atta-girls in the three weeks she'd been playing lacrosse in the intramural league. Not that she needed these affirmations, but it was always nice to hear.

To combat this disappointing realization, Dani made sure to praise each of the kids individually and tell them how impressed she was with them. She made sure to thank the volunteers, too. It was the least she could do for all the help they were unselfishly giving. If only more people had that giving attitude.

Back in high school, her guidance counselor once said to her, "Show me your friends, and I'll show you your future." This was right around the time Dani had met Meredith and they were becoming friends. It was also right around then that she'd become distant from her bestie, Ben. She had begun to realize something she'd kinda sorta already known. He wasn't very mature and had a bit of a mean streak, which he demonstrated when he made fun of Meredith on a couple of occasions. Although they had stayed in touch with each other since graduating, Dani knew she had outgrown him.

And if that guidance counselor wanted to see her friends now, well, here they all were volunteering. Meredith, Kate, and all of Kate's classmates had also returned to help. Petra would return when she could. Although none of them knew much about lacrosse, they were enthusiastic anyway. Even Meredith asked to learn how to throw, and Dani taught her personally. Meredith was still having trouble, and the funniest thing was when Natalie, an expert with one whole day of prior experience, corrected Meredith's techniques. Meredith was grateful for the help, and Dani was impressed with how quickly Natalie had been catching on. None of the kids showed up with their own lacrosse sticks, but Marti told her that most had remembered to bring back their mouthguards. Even though they didn't have sticks, the mouthguard thing told Dani that the kids were interested and eager to learn her favorite game. That was cool. Very cool.

After setting up the next session for the following Monday, the group said their goodbyes to each other and went their separate ways. Of course, Dani hoped to find out on Friday evening that she'd been moved up to Team Cyan and would be playing on Wednesday next week instead of with Team Indigo on Monday, but whatever. Marti and her crew could handle the neighborhood kids on their own if Dani had a game.

Dani, Meredith, and Kate walked back up to the dining hall, and Kate asked Dani why she wasn't furious with Laura for kicking them off the field. Kate even joked that she half expected to see steam coming out of Dani's ears. Dani explained that although she had been disappointed, Laura had every right to the field. She had reserved it officially. Laura explained to Dani how to officially schedule the field with the Department of Building and Property Use in the Admin Building. Laura said Dani would have to go down there in person the first time, though, to show her ID so she could get on the books officially.

Even after that perfectly reasonable explanation, Kate still maintained that Dani's ears should be steaming.

"You have to pick your battles," Dani said. Kate harrumphed good-naturedly, and the topic was dropped, much to Dani's relief.

"How was your lunch with Joiee?" Kate asked, changing the subject.

"Good," Dani said. "I told her what happened between Laura and me in the locker room, and she was hopping mad."

"As she should be," Meredith said. "As we all are."

"I know. I know," Dani said. "Joiee told me she broke up with Laura about a week ago."

Kate stopped walking. "What? Joiee and Laura were together? Hold crap. You'd never know they were a couple by looking at them. Oh, but I guess they're not now."

Dani pulled Kate by the sleeve to get moving. She was hungry and needed sustenance.

Dani was about to say more, but Kate said, "Do they live together? Why does Joiee still do the lacrosse stuff? I'd tell Laura to take a flying leap."

Dani chuckled. "I think she did tell Laura to do just that, but she told me this afternoon that she had already committed to the lacrosse intramural league and couldn't find anybody to take over."

"She's honoring her commitments," Meredith said. "That's noble."

"Very noble," Kate said as if to herself. "Noble, indeed."

Dani exchanged a confused glance with Meredith but just shrugged her shoulders. Kate was hard to figure out sometimes.

Dani tapped first Meredith and then Kate on the back and took off running toward the dining hall. "Last one there busses trays." She didn't look back, winning easily.

Friday morning, Dani showed up at the Department of Building and Property Use at eight o'clock sharp only to find that the office didn't open until nine. Disappointed, she shuffled over early to her eight-thirty Poly Sci discussion group in Eggars Hall.

She sat next to a very nervous Petra in the front row of the double-rowed circle. Petra was due to have her first debate in the PSLA meeting right after the class. Dani patted Petra on the shoulder twice, not hard, but forcefully enough to knock Petra out of her nerves, if only just a little. Petra glanced at Dani and nodded her understanding.

When the class was almost over, the teaching assistant leading the discussion group cleared her throat and said, "I think we've had a good discussion about Civics and the differences between that and what this Political Science and Government course is all about." She turned and looked toward Dani and Petra.

"Payton, would you please summarize our working definition of Civics?"

Dani stifled a laugh when the teacher's assistant student said the wrong name. There wasn't even a Payton in the class. Dani hid her grin behind her hand and didn't even jump when Petra smacked her thigh.

"Civics," Petra said, "comes from the Latin word *civicus,* which basically means anything that pertains to citizens in a society. Civics covers a lot of things, such as citizens' rights, but also expectations for citizen behavior and knowledge. One of those expectations is that citizens know and understand the government structure they're living in."

"Excellent," the TA said. She turned her head toward the opposite side of the circle and said, "Jason, can you please summarize 'Political Science.'" She used air quotes around the last two words.

Jaxon's eyes got big when he heard the TA botch his name. Dani sighed and got smacked in the thigh again by Petra. She glanced over at Petra and rolled her eyes. The TA was knowledgeable, that was for sure. Still, she was extremely disappointed that the TA wasn't making more of an effort to learn the names of her students properly, especially now that this was the fourth week of classes. That seemed disrespectful somehow. Dani made a mental note to get to know the names of all the neighborhood kids who came out to the lacrosse sessions.

Dani tuned back in as Jaxon was finishing up his summary. "So, Political Science is basically the study of observable and measurable political endeavors and behaviors."

"Excellent point," the TA said. "We can consider Poly Sci an actual 'science' because it's observable and measurable. Perfect." Air quotes had been used on the word science. This TA loved her air quotes. There was a guy who always sat in the back row who would state a number at the end of each class. Dani finally found out that he was announcing the number of times the TA had used air quotes in their hour-long class. It was funny, but still, it was kind of disrespectful, too. Hopefully, the TA wouldn't find out that some of her students were making fun of her.

The TA checked her watch and said, "Let me wrap up. In this course, we're not only understanding, but we're also analyzing the American political system and how it functions. We look at the political process everywhere, from public opinion to mass media to public policy. We study government leadership. Like the federal structure, New York State also has executive, legislative, and judicial branches. The Governor heads the executive branch. The state senate in the upper house and the state assembly in the lower house make up the legislative branch, and then there's the entire Judiciary branch, which interprets and applies New York State laws. A daunting task indeed."

The time was drawing near for the class to end, but the TA seemed to want to keep on speaking. The students around her were getting restless. Dani was, too, but she did a better job of hiding it.

"So," the TA continued, "even though we've been discussing Civics and discussing the political setup in the United States, we focus mainly on politics. Although we will cover the "nuts and bolts" of American government, our focus is on political science rather than civics, which means our task is to analyze and interpret political phenomena. What do our political leaders actually do? What observable things have we witnessed?" She pointed at Jaxon to acknowledge the point he'd made earlier. "And what influences those things they do?"

She paused for a moment and then looked down at her watch. "Oh, we're out of time. Don't forget that your written assignment on 'political influence' by the mass media is due at the start of Tuesday afternoon classes. Physical copy." She nodded once and said, "Have a good day."

The students stood up all at once as if choreographed.

"You ready?" Dani said to Petra.

"I guess," Petra said, resigned to her fate.

They headed out the classroom door and stifled a laugh when they heard their classmate yell "Twenty-three" from somewhere behind them.

"That is so rude," Petra said but laughed anyway. "Did you start your paper on the media?"

Petra was clearly trying to occupy her mind before getting to the PSLA meeting space.

"Not really," Dani said. "I've been busy with lacrosse clinics and just everything."

"I know what you mean," Petra said and held the lecture hall door open for Dani. "My high school was so regulated, so structured. I'm sure yours was, too."

Dani nodded in confirmation. "And college is so open-ended. I mean, you really have to know how to manage your time."

Petra nodded as they shuffled into their favorite row in the front. It wasn't long before Shela introduced Petra and her opponent, a freshman named Hailey, for their debate.

Petra had been randomly selected to go first, and she outlined many important issues she planned to help with, which included a more efficient way for students to feel seen and heard by the school's administration. She pointed out that several students had put in maintenance requests, but so far, nothing had been fixed, and no one had contacted them, either.

"So," Petra said, "I feel that communication is as important as the issues. And we need to—"

"Time," Shela called. "Thank you, Petra." She looked over at Hailey and said, "Your three minutes starts now."

"Thank you, Shela," Hailey said. "And thank you for your thoughts, Petra."

Oh, that was nice, Dani thought. She'd have to include that line for her next debate.

Hailey continued. "You're a Latina, Petra. Isn't that right? And I'm sure your way of thinking comes from that perspective. Let's be specific, though. You're a Puerto Rican, right?" Not waiting for an answer, Hailey said, "But here's the problem. You don't look Puerto Rican, so if people don't know your true background, then how will they ever know what your true motives are?"

Dani's eyebrows had almost reached the ceiling at this point. She scoffed in her seat. This Hailey was a jerk of the highest quality. Dani glanced at Petra, who was looking in Hailey's direction but not looking right at her. Petra seemed okay, but Dani would keep an eye out.

"My opponent's father is a New York State assemblyman somewhere down by New York City. Her street address is in a very expensive part of that area in New York City. She has a laser printer in her dorm room. A color laser printer. From what I hear, she prints photos for anyone who wants one. I can't afford a laser printer. I can't afford to give away expensive things like that. Maybe someone who feels they're privileged can. I don't know.

"Now, as an American born in upstate New York," Hailey said to the crowd, "I understand what kids our age want. Puerto Ricans probably want similar things, but from an outsider's perspective, I'm not sure my opponent can really know." She went on to discuss the lack of school dances, pointing out that her high school had one at least once a quarter, including the Sadie Hawkins dance, where girls were allowed to ask the boys to the dance.

Dani wondered just how sheltered Hailey had been growing up. One thing was for sure, though, Dani was not going to let Petra out of her sight at lunchtime. Petra needed her friends, even if she didn't know it.

Shela called time and said to Petra, "Rebut. One minute."

Petra didn't speak right away. Dani wasn't sure if it was her way of taking back control, but it was working. After several long seconds, Petra finally took a deep breath and sighed audibly.

"I was born in Queens. That's in New York state, which is in the United States, of course. My parents were also born in New York, and I'm proud of the Puerto Rican heritage I share with my parents and brother. And just to be clear, in case anyone has been living under a rock, people born on the island of Puerto Rico are United States citizens. Where I grew up in Queens, there are people from all walks of life and all cultures. All people, no matter who they are or where they were born, have the same basic need to feel safe, to make an honest life for themselves, and to be happy. The primary job of all government leaders is to make sure all of their citizens are taken care of and have their needs met. All citizens, regardless of origin or any other attribute that might separate them from the majority."

"Time," Shela called.

Take that, Hailey, Dani thought loudly in her head. Dani caught Petra's eye and nodded her approval. Petra's small smile was fleeting, but Dani saw it.

Hailey's rebuttal added nothing new, but at least she stayed away from heritage-bashing Petra again. Dani briefly wondered what Shela thought of Hailey's obvious ignorance. As a black woman, Shela was clearly not a white Caucasian of European descent.

Dani and Petra tortured themselves by watching the next several debates until it was finally time to head out for lunch.

"You're coming to lunch with us," Dani said. "I can't let you go off on your own after that."

"What was that all about anyway?" Petra asked the sidewalk.

"An ignorant, sheltered person," Dani said with a sigh. "But you did great defending against her stupidity. You pointed out indisputable facts. She was a living example of blatant ignorance."

"There are a lot of ignorant people out there, Dani," Petra said, finally looking up. "It's hard to ignore them sometimes."

"I know," Dani said way too quickly. That's exactly why she and Meredith hadn't come out to anyone.

They walked to the student union in silence for a while, both deep in thought. Dani's thoughts were disturbing. Hailey had gone low, very low, on her side of the debate, and a lot of people in the crowd seemed to like that. Dani had seen a lot of them lean forward in their seats when Hailey unleashed her negativity.

Shela wanted Dani to go low, too. She wanted Dani to find some dirt on her opponents and exploit those things. For what purpose? To show that the candidate was flawed somehow?

Dani sighed and said, "I just want to help people, you know?"

"I get that," Petra said, her pace slow.

"That's why I want to get elected." Dani didn't finish her next few thoughts out loud because she wouldn't know how to defend them. *If going low gets me elected, then that's what I'll have to do. They're all doing it. It's expected. So why shouldn't I?*

Chapter 15

I Know a Way

Sunday nights were study nights. Dani sat at the desk in her dorm room and snuck a peek over her shoulder at Meredith. Meredith had her hair up in a bun, with a few delicious tendrils falling down her neck. A surge of arousal swirling with something else, probably love, hit Dani, and she made a small noise, causing Meredith to look up.

The smile that grew on Meredith's face when she realized Dani had been looking at her made Dani tear up with emotion.

"Oh, honey," Meredith said and stood up. Her arms were soon wrapped around Dani from behind. "What's wrong, baby?" A kiss landed on the crown of Dani's head. "Are you upset because we have to do statistics next?"

Dani chuckled. "I'm okay. I just…You were—" She sighed.

"What is it?" Meredith moved to lean on the edge of Dani's desk so they could face each other.

"You were just looking so beautiful."

Now, it was Meredith's turn to make a small noise. "Back up."

Dani obliged and moved her chair back. She knew what was coming next, and true to her prediction, Meredith sat in her lap. "Tell Merry what's wrong." Her fingertips stroked Dani's cheeks, and then one index finger traced a path from Dani's forehead down her nose, over both lips, to beneath her chin. Meredith used that one finger to lift Dani's head. "You're not getting this kiss until you tell me."

"Dirty pool," Dani said but laughed anyway. She couldn't quite figure out what had gotten her so emotional, so she remained quiet. Meredith raised one eyebrow. Uh oh. She wasn't playing. Dani would never get that kiss unless she came clean. "Honestly, I was getting kind of bored reading this article for my freshmen English class essay and turned to look at you. The light was hitting you just right, and you always look so nice, regardless of how you do your hair. And," Dani shrugged, "I don't know. I guess I just realized how lucky I am that you want to be with me."

"That was the sweetest," Meredith said and then made good on the kiss. Okay, there were many kisses, but still, who was counting?

When they broke apart, Meredith stood up and said, "I need a study break. A short one because we do need to do the s-word."

"Statistics?" Dani asked with a laugh.

"Shhh," Meredith hissed. "Don't say it out loud. Ugh." She patted her bed and then climbed up. "Join me for a cuddle."

"I thought you'd never ask." Dani checked to make sure the blinds and curtains were securely closed and that their door was locked before joining Meredith on the bed. Meredith orchestrated their positions, and Dani found herself lying down with her head in Meredith's lap while Meredith's hand played with Dani's hair.

"You're not upset because you didn't get moved up to Team Cyan, are you?" Meredith asked quietly.

"No, not really. At least I got to stay on Indigo for another week." Dani sighed. "Stephanie didn't move anybody up from Team Magenta either like she said she was going to."

"See? You can breathe a sigh of relief then," Meredith said. "You know, I'm glad we got to talk to both Esther and Millie tonight. Millie looks so much better."

"She does," Dani agreed. "The mighty had fallen, but she got back up again, right?"

"Mm hmm," Meredith said with a chuckle. "Millie is a mighty force to be reckoned with. Esther said she was the worst patient."

"She's used to being the caregiver and the one calling the shots."

"Yep," Meredith said and then changed the subject. "You know, college is kind of different than I expected. Classes are so different than high school. They're impersonal. If you don't show up, no one notices."

"That's true, but you'd be shooting yourself in the foot."

"Mm hmm," Meredith said in agreement. "Some kids haven't figured that out yet, have they?"

"Nope," Dani said with a laugh. "And, seriously, it seems like every waking minute is taken up with something. Classes, homework, lacrosse, and then I go and invent lacrosse sessions with the kids because I apparently don't have enough to do."

"They love it, Dani," Meredith said, running her fingers through Dani's hair. Dani let her eyes close and would have purred if she knew how. "I do, too. It's a nice break from the lock-step routine we all seem to have here. It's almost like, hee hee hee, we're doing something the college won't grade us on or expect from us."

"So true. That Natalie is a cool kid, isn't she?"

"Kate said she's a latchkey kid. You know, like, she's home alone after school until her parents come home from work in the evening."

"I didn't realize that."

"Kate said she saw the key dangling around Natalie's neck. She thinks a lot of those kids are latchkey kids."

Dani sat up abruptly. "What's going to happen when winter comes? Like, we can't meet on the field. Can we reserve one of the gyms on campus or something? Teach them basketball or whatever?"

"Shh, shh, shh," Meredith said and forced Dani to lie down again. "We'll figure that out. Not tonight, but maybe this week, you can get on your hotline with Kate and Marti and try to figure something out."

"I can ask when I go to the Property Use office on Monday."

"There you go," Meredith said. "I knew you'd think of something."

Meredith then shared some of her own concerns about college, like the fast pace of all the classes and the art show during homecoming and Alumni weekend next weekend.

"I feel like we just got here," Meredith said, "and I'm already expected to show my work? I'm not ready."

"Let me help you."

"How?"

"No clue," Dani said with a laugh. "Carry your paintings? Help you set up? You'll tell me, okay?"

Dani got a kiss on the side of the head in response. But then Meredith added, "I'm going to have to spend more time in the Fine Arts building this week."

"Understood," Dani said. "Please don't feel obligated to come to my Wednesday game."

"And miss out seeing you run around and get all sweaty? Not on your life." Meredith stroked Dani's arm. "I'd pay good money to see that." This she said kind of seriously.

"You're too funny."

"I think I'm going to have to miss Monday's session with the kids, though," Meredith said. The disappointment was clear in her voice.

"I'll miss you. We'll all miss you, but you have important work to do." After a moment, Dani added, "I don't want to get involved, like at all, but Joiee is really hurting. According to her, Laura is a big player. Not a lacrosse player but a skirt-chasing *player*."

"Yeah, I got that," Meredith said with a chuckle.

"Joiee said she can't even count how many affairs Laura had in their supposedly monogamous year and a half relationship."

"That's really shitty."

"Right? Joiee said she was going to go to the housing office and see if she could get a dorm room in junior housing."

"That would probably be best," Meredith said. "She understands that you don't want anything more than friendship with her?"

"She does," Dani said. "And I guess we're becoming friends. I hadn't really thought about it that way."

"She seems like a good person," Meredith said. "If she knew about us, then maybe she'd know for sure that you were off the market."

Dani burst out laughing. "'Off the market,'" she repeated. "You're hilarious." After a beat, Dani asked, "Wait. Do you want me to tell her?"

"No. Not yet. We can make it two more weeks until fall break." Meredith sighed, so Dani waited. "I want to come out to my parents first," Meredith added quietly.

"Yeah, I think I want to come out to your parents, too." Dani laughed and got a smack on the hip for her actions. "Okay, okay, stop. I need to come out to my family, too."

"I hate to say it, but…" Meredith said.

"I know." Dani sat up. "We have to do our—"

"Don't say it!" Meredith jammed her hands over her ears. "La la la," she said, drowning out any of Dani's words.

Amused, Dani turned around and gave Meredith a kiss to remember. They locked gazes, and Dani whispered, "Can we? Maybe later?"

Meredith nodded as a sexy, devilish grin crept up her face. "But for now, we have to do our S-word problem set."

"Your desk or mine?"

"Mine," Meredith said. "Yours is too far away."

Dani burst out laughing and went all the way over to the far reaches of the tiny room to get her notebook. She pulled her chair over to Meredith's desk and plopped down into it. "That was so far. I need to rest," she said and faked being out of breath.

"Hush, you." Meredith opened her laptop and found that week's problem set. "It's amazing how much of this I actually understand now."

"See? Your college *edu-muh-cation* is working already."

Dani got a smack on the thigh for her attempted humor, and then they got to work in earnest. About a half hour and excellent progress later, someone pounded on their dorm room door.

Meredith put a hand to her chest. "What the hell?"

"Who is it?" Dani called out.

"It's Kate."

Dani leaped out of her chair and flung open the door. "What's wrong?" At first, she thought something might be wrong with Petra, but Petra was standing right next to Kate.

Kate walked in without invitation. Petra followed right behind. Petra turned and closed the door softly behind her.

"You haven't seen, have you?" Kate asked.

"What?" Dani exchanged a worried glance with Meredith. Had people found out about her and Meredith?

"Tell her," Kate said to Petra.

Petra sighed and said, "We're debating each other on Friday."

Dani's jaw dropped open. "What?"

"I know," Petra said. She shook her head and opened her mouth as if to say something but didn't know what.

"Shela," Dani said succinctly. "It has to be. She knows we're friends. It's the last day of debates. She put us up against each other, probably for her own amusement."

"Now that is just mean," Petra said. "The way they expect everyone to find fault with their opponent is so stupid. I hate this, Dani." Her lips were pressed together, and the scowl on her face spoke volumes.

"We just won't," Dani said. "I mean, c'mon."

Petra nodded and seemed to relax. "This part of the PSLA sucks."

"Yep. There's a lot about politics in general that sucks."

"You got that right," Kate broke in. "Right, Meredith?"

"Yeah, but she loves it," Meredith pointed to Dani with a head nod. "She listens to these boring podcasts about politics all the time."

"This one, too," Kate said, pointing to Petra.

"I use my air buds," Dani protested.

"Thank the living God." Meredith grinned at their friends.

Petra was the one to change the subject when she asked Meredith if she needed any help with her Spanish assignments.

"No," Meredith said and pointed to her desk. "We're just slogging through *that*."

"I love statistics," Kate said.

"Out," Meredith said with a laugh and pointed to the door.

"Fine, fine, but if you guys need help, I'm down the hall," Kate said. "C'mon, Petra." She grabbed her roommate by the arm and practically dragged her out of the room.

Before the door had closed completely, Dani heard Kate say to Petra, "See? I told you she'd be cool with it."

"I know."

The door closed, and Dani locked it.

"Oh, honey," Meredith said, pulling Dani into her arms. "I'm so sorry this is happening."

"You can't come."

"Excuse me?" Meredith looked aghast at Dani's statement.

"What?" Dani realized that Meredith had taken Dani's statement as some kind of out-of-the-blue sexual innuendo. "No, no. To the debate. I can't have you there. It will make me too nervous. I'll make sure Petra tells Kate not to go, too."

"You scared me, baby," Meredith said with a laugh. "Listen, that art show is Friday night, and I'm going to be way too busy to break away, anyway."

Dani nodded. That was probably for the better. She pointed to Meredith's desk. "S-word."

"Meanie."

They settled in, and before picking up where they'd left off, Meredith said, "I know you're nervous about Friday, but I know a way to relieve some, err, tension."

"You do?"

"Mm hmm," Meredith said. "And if we can get through this stupid problem set, I'll show you."

Dani's eyes grew wide, and she pointed excitedly toward the problem on the screen. It was probably the first and only time she'd been excited to do her s-word homework.

~~~

The very next Monday morning, Dani and Meredith were sitting in the dining hall eating breakfast with Kate and Petra when Meredith suggested that Dani stay in the dorm that morning to finish her Poly Sci paper instead of walking her to class. Dani was about to say that she didn't mind escorting Meredith, but then Meredith reassured her she would be safe walking to campus with Kate and Petra. When Dani protested, Kate shot Dani a confused look. Dani acquiesced instantly, knowing how controlling and possessive it made her seem.

"Okay, fine," Dani said. "Just be careful. Be aware of your surroundings at all times. All of you."

"Yes, *Mom*," Kate said while bugging out her eyes.

It felt weird saying goodbye to Meredith and just hanging around in their dorm room studying, but she settled into it. Kind of. It did feel almost like a rejection somehow, but maybe this was Meredith's way of giving Dani time to catch up on schoolwork. Dani had been complaining that there weren't enough hours in the day. Doing laundry on Saturday after the football game and festivities was, frankly, exhausting. Thank goodness Meredith had only been teasing about Dani doing her laundry, and they figured out the machines and the process together.

Monday evening was another session with the kids, but Dani had to leave them for her game against Team Teal. She was able to warm up with the kids for a little while but then had to get ready to play. It was so cute seeing all the kids flocking around Meredith, Kate, and Petra in the stands, cheering her on. She had her very own cheering squad. She waved big at her fans, who yelled encouragement back at her. She flashed them the *I love you* sign language sign, which they all returned. It made her heart swell.

She had to straighten up and focus, though. If she ever wanted to get noticed by the varsity coaches, she had to play well, score goals, and not make any mistakes. Meredith seemed quite amused when Dani did crunches or burpees in the limited space on their dorm room floor. She'd told Dani she was admiring the view, so on Sunday afternoon during a study break, she flung off her t-shirt and did her workout in just a sports bra and shorts. Meredith fanned herself comically, but the way Meredith kissed her afterward told Dani there had been some truth to the fanning. Nothing came of the kiss besides a reminder of their connection, and that was okay with Dani. She had no doubts that Meredith loved her. It was quite mutual.

Dani gave one last wave to her fans and caught Petra's eye. She nodded once, and Petra nodded back. Friday morning would bring the huge face-off debate at the PSLA meeting. Dani was not looking forward to that, but she was ready. Her speech had been reworked, and the only thing to do was to keep her nerves in check.

The game against Team Teal went well enough, but Dani thought she could have played better. At least she'd managed to score two goals to Amanda's three and only had two turnovers during the whole game. It was also nice to be friendly with Joiee and not have to avoid her. Maybe Meredith was right. Maybe Joiee could become a friend. Only time would tell, Dani supposed.

After saying goodbye to Natalie and the other kids who'd hung around to watch Dani's game that evening, Dani and her friends walked back up toward their dorm.

When they reached the driveway leading up to the dining hall, Kate burst out, "C'mon, you guys. I'm literally dying to know what dirt you've dug up on each other for that debate on Friday."

"Kate." It was one word, but it came from a very serious Petra.

"Fine," Kate said. "Don't tell me. I'll find out about it at lunch afterward anyway."

"And you are not to be at the debate," Petra said. "It will be stressful enough as it is."

"Fine," Kate said again. "I have a class at that time anyway. Whatevs." Kate's sing-songed reply let everyone know that she was cool with not being invited to the debate between her two friends. "Wait, you're not going, are you?" Kate asked Meredith.

"Nope. I've been uninvited, just like you. Humph." Meredith crossed her arms and looked away from Dani.

"Oh, it's getting thick out here," Dani said to Petra, who smiled. "But seriously, you guys understand, right? We're going to be nervous enough against each other up there without seeing you two cheering us on."

Meredith softened. "Dani, we understand. My art show is that night anyway, so I doubt I'll have any spare time. Let's see." She tapped a finger against her chin. "If I don't sleep for the next two nights, I might be able to get all my pieces done in time."

Dani wasn't about to lecture Meredith about the benefits of sleep, but she didn't. If anything, Meredith was the one who scolded Dani when she stayed up too late reading or working on assignments.

"Let us know how we can help you," Dani said to Meredith. Kate and Petra echoed that they would help, too.

"Hey, Kate?" Dani asked as she held the front door to the dining hall open for her friends.

"Yeah?"

"You're not *literally* dying, are you? Because I haven't brushed up on my CPR."

Kate burst out laughing and smacked Dani on the side of the arm, holding the door open. "You're a keeper, Dani," Kate said and headed inside.

"Yes, you are," Meredith whispered to Dani as she went by.

Chapter 16

Safe

For the fifth time in as many days, Meredith left for the main campus without Dani escorting her. She'd been spending a lot of time that week in the art studio. Although Meredith had come to Dani's game on Wednesday evening, she'd missed two sessions with the neighborhood kids that week. Even Natalie asked where Miss Meredith was, and then she seemed sad when Dani told her Meredith had a big project she was working on and couldn't make it.

And, truth be told, Dani was kind of lonely without her. And even today, Meredith said she was going to spend the entire day finishing up her projects for the art show, and she even brought clothes to change into for that evening's alumni event. Hopefully, she would be able to break away to meet the gang for lunch after the debate as planned.

Dani sat at her desk quietly, reading up on the assigned topic for her Poly Sci discussion group that morning. She *tried* reading, that is. It wasn't working. Her nerves were getting the better of her, and she was too antsy. The debate was later that morning, and Meredith's art show was that evening. But the most important thing was that, as far as Dani could tell, Meredith had forgotten that today was their anniversary. It had been four whole months since they'd gotten together. Meredith seemed to be singularly focused on the art show, so Dani gave her that out.

And, if she was being fair, Dani had been similarly absorbed with her own stuff. She hadn't done much to help Meredith get ready, not that Meredith had asked, but Dani decided to change that right now. She shoved her books and laptop in her backpack and headed to the Fine Arts Building.

She even broke her own rule and walked alone down the isolated walkway to the campus. Yeah, she really needed to get elected in order to somehow make this walkway safer.

She walked at a fast clip and made it to the Fine Arts building in record time. Shoot, she should have stopped somewhere to get Meredith flowers. No, no, a single rose. Yes, that would be the ticket. Oh, well. Later that evening, Dani would bring Meredith a dozen red roses. Dani reached the building and hoped she wouldn't be disturbing Meredith's concentration or something. She just wanted Meredith to know that she'd been thinking about her and find out how she could help. Sure, she could have texted, but she wanted to surprise her girlfriend. She'd been too caught up in her own stuff lately and wanted to make sure she paid proper attention to the love of her life.

Dani reached the undergrad workroom and was just about to yank the door open when she heard Meredith laugh. It was a great sound. It was one of the best sounds in the world. Hearing that laugh hopefully meant she wasn't tearing her hair out anxious about the show that evening. Dani didn't want to interrupt the laughter, so she spied through the narrow pane of glass.

Wait. What? Meredith was hugging someone. And that someone was a guy. Meredith pulled back from the hug with a big smile on her face. Dani's heart sank. That smile was meant for Dani only, not some random guy. White hot anger shot through her. No way. It was the bearded guy from the dining hall. She knew he was trouble. He'd been stalking Meredith. Dani pulled the door open a fraction, but her muscles failed after that. She couldn't open it any further.

"You're so funny, Edward," Meredith was saying as she rubbed the bearded guy's upper arm. That was such an intimate gesture, Dani thought. And just when it looked like Meredith was about to step back, she flew back into his arms.

A punch hit Dani's gut. Her relationship had been a lie. Everything she thought was true…wasn't.

She turned on the soles of her sneakers, ran down the hallway, and out the front door. Her backpack slammed into her back and kidneys as she ran. She could have tightened the straps but didn't have a spare brain cell to deal with it.

That jerk guy had been stalking Meredith, and she fell for it. Dani saw a bench and headed for it. She had to regroup. Funny how it was the same bench she'd sat on to read her Poly Sci textbook on the first day of classes. She crash-landed onto the bench, hoping to catch her breath, but the image of seeing them together wouldn't allow it. Meredith's grin, Meredith flying back into his arms, Meredith touching him—all of it played in a loop in her brain.

"'Stay in the dorm,'" Dani quoted Meredith out loud. "'I'll be fine on my own.'" Dani kicked the grass under her feet. "But you're not on your own, are you, Meredith?" How long had Meredith been seeing this guy? Had she kissed him?

"Oh, my God," Dani said to no one. "What if they've done more than kiss?" A slice of nausea hit her innards, and she let it. She deserved it for being so stupid, thinking someone as amazing as Meredith would ever be into girls for long. The world doesn't want it that way, so why would Meredith? It wasn't normal. It wasn't right. Meredith would do what was right.

Meredith had found a way out, hadn't she? Dani hadn't realized she'd had that fear until now. She found herself walking, even though she had no recollection of standing up. One concrete sidewalk led to another and then another.

Dani had served a temporary purpose in Meredith's life, hadn't she? She'd been there to help Meredith gain confidence and discover her worth. And she had found those things. She didn't need Dani anymore.

"Shit," Dani said out loud when she found herself in front of Eggers Hall. She looked at her watch. "Shit," she said again. "Late, of course. Make this shitty day even shittier." She slunk into the classroom of her Poly Sci Discussion group and found a spot in the back row of chairs next to the air-quote-counting guy. He nodded at her as if she were now a comrade in arms. Walking in late had apparently earned this guy's respect.

She didn't dare look directly at Petra because there was no way she could look at her friend without succumbing to her emotions. She had to go numb. She was already on her way, so tuning out the TA was easy.

She was going to have to move out of the dorm room she shared with

Meredith. There was no way she could spend another minute there.

Dani heard a soft clearing of a throat from the seat next to her. She looked at the guy, and he nodded his chin toward the TA.

"Sorry," Dani said to the TA. "I have a headache, and it's hard to concentrate." The headache part was true, she realized.

"Sorry to hear you're not feeling well," the TA said softly. "Should you be in class?"

"It's just a headache," Dani said. "I can answer. What was the question?"

The TA shot her a sympathetic look and then repeated her question.

"Ah," Dani said. She knew this. Dani took a deep breath as if gathering her thoughts, but in reality, she was stuffing down the images burning through her brain. "Lobby groups are special interest groups that try to influence policymakers. Their goal is to get politicians to support whatever they're pushing for. The National Rifle Association, for instance, spends millions in lobbying efforts. Blue Cross/Blue Shield hires lobbyists to represent their interests in an attempt to get laws passed in their favor." She stopped talking, hoping that was enough of an answer. It seemed to be.

"Excellent," the TA said with an approving grin and a slight head nod. Dani almost laughed out loud. She'd come in late, hadn't been listening, and still got approval from the teacher. Yes, this was an alternate reality, indeed.

When the TA's attention was diverted toward the other side of the large circle, the air-quotes guy flashed Dani a thumbs-up.

Dani threw him a return thumbs up and then scoffed. Yep, it was a weird day, for sure. It was like it wasn't even her own life but one of those many parallel paths your life could take. She didn't like this path. Not at all.

When the class was over, there would be no way to avoid Petra. She wasn't going to say anything about Meredith and the bearded guy, though. What would she say? And, besides, they had a debate to focus on, so that's what she would put her attention to.

"Oversleep?" Petra asked with a teasing laugh as they headed into the hallway.

"No, I just…" Dani hesitated. She wasn't sure what to say that wasn't an out-and-out lie. "I lost track of time." That part was true.

"We'll do okay, right?" Petra asked. The nerves about the upcoming debate were clear in her voice.

"Yeah, we got this," Dani said without looking at her friend.

As they walked the long hallway to the lecture hall, Dani was busy building walls to compartmentalize her life. Meredith's betrayal was going into one tightly sealed room, although Dani knew full well that nothing could keep it contained for long. The images were trying hard to paralyze her, but a small part of Dani's brain stepped up and somehow steered the ship in a different direction.

The two friends walked in silence, and once inside, Shela took Dani aside.

"Danielle," Shela said, "you're at the top of a very short list for backing from the existing Student Association members. You are well-spoken and cool under pressure. We just need to know that you can be tough when you need to be. The way to show that is to go on the offensive."

Something inside Dani woke up. A dozen interconnected thoughts raced through her brain—all with one common theme. Being the 'nice guy' wasn't working anymore. Had it ever? No, so screw that. Her gaze shifted back to Shela's.

"What's there to lose?" Dani said, standing taller. She'd probably be transferring back home to Albany State anyway.

"Yes, yes, yes," Shela said, obviously sensing the shift in Dani's demeanor. "You're up first. Go get 'em."

Dani nodded and found her seat next to Petra. She kept her head held high and didn't look at her opponent seated next to her.

Mae, the Student Association President, made a few announcements, including the election date in two weeks for first-year students, and then called Dani and Petra to the podiums to start the series of debates that morning.

A flip of a coin determined that Petra would go first. As expected, Petra delivered a smooth and thoughtful presentation. Throughout the speech, Dani disassociated. She sort of faced Petra's direction, but her gaze was unfocussed, and her mind was floating freely in the ether. She missed most of Petra's words.

"It's the Student Association's job," Petra said in closing, "to advocate for the needs of the student body in all areas of campus life, and this includes the need for accessible counseling services, as I outlined earlier. My opponent will advocate for safety on campus. And, actually, we should all advocate for that. The Student Association needs to ensure that all students have access to groups, clubs, and activities on campus as well as academic assistance and guidance where needed."

She paused for the briefest of moments, and Dani, sensing the shift, tuned back in fully. Petra continued, "To do all of these things, you need dedicated members of the Student Association. I am a responsible and dedicated person. My name is Petra Alvarez, and I'll be running for a position in the Student Association. Thank you."

Polite applause followed Petra's speech, and then Mae nodded for Dani to give hers.

Dani had a speech planned but decided to wing it. Yeah, she was in that kind of mood. She spoke about specific places on campus that needed to be fixed in order to make the campus feel safer. She spoke about methods for clear communication between the student body and the Student Association.

"The Student Association is duty-bound to look into matters brought to them," Dani said matter-of-factly, "but that's only if the students know how to find and interact with their elected representatives." She was about to go further along that vein but decided to show Shela and the others that she had the grit they were looking for. Her life had taken a turn that morning, and nothing really mattered anyway. Why should she be the nice guy? The old Dani was dead now.

Dani scoffed as she changed tactics. It came out louder than she'd expected. "It's interesting that many of you have come up here and talked about candidates' motivations for getting elected. 'Self-serving' was a phrase someone brought up. So, it's interesting that my opponent brings up counseling services today. She spent much of her allotted time on this topic." Dani wasn't sure if that was true, but she was winging it. "Counseling services," Dani repeated. "Why would a candidate be so gung-ho about this?"

Many of her classmates leaned forward as if waiting for Dani to go in for the kill, to spill the juicy gossip, to tear her opponent to shreds.

Dani's mouth went dry. She couldn't get any words out. She tried to swallow, but there was no moisture. Even her lips were cracked. Her headache pounded. She grabbed the edges of the podium as a wave of dizziness swept over her.

No. She couldn't do this. She looked toward Shela in the back row. Shela had a concerned look on her face yet egged her on silently as if saying, "Go for the kill. Do it."

Dani couldn't. Even in this alternate reality, she just wasn't that person. Petra was a friend. She couldn't out Petra's eating disorder. She couldn't out Petra's need for counseling. What kind of monster was Dani turning into?

"Time," Mae called, turned toward Petra, and said, "One-minute to rebut."

Dani looked toward Petra to apologize for what she had been about to do, but Petra was looking down at the podium.

Petra cleared her throat and said, "Safety can mean many things. Physical safety, as my opponent points out, is only one kind. Mental and emotional safety are also important, and they can be helped by counseling, as *I* pointed out. Case in point. I have two friends who are in a relationship. They're both women, but they haven't come out to anyone, not even their close friends. They're so cute together, always looking out for each other. They're affectionate in ways they don't realize they're broadcasting. But the fact that they don't feel safe coming out tells me we have a lot of work to do on this campus to make them feel safe." Petra exhaled audibly through her nose and added, "I want to make sure marginalized groups like the LGBTQIA plus communities are seen, heard, and acknowledged so they can feel safe here without having to demand—"

"Time," Mae called. She turned to Dani. "One minute."

Dani knew her face was beet red, but she didn't care. Quietly, she said, "This whole 'find your opponent's weakness' approach is counterproductive. To be blunt—it sucks." Shela wanted her to go on the offensive? Fine. She would. *Here it is, Shela.* "Why should we point out the weakness in others? Maybe these folks are going through something and are trying to heal. Holy crap, who are we to exploit that? That's what's making this country not-so-great these days. I mean, come on, everyone has…stuff. Instead, why don't we look for a candidate's strengths?"

Dani turned to face Petra. One hand gripped the podium, though, because she was a bit shaky. "This young woman right here, is amazing. In all the debates I've listened to, no one has brought up a specific group that needs help like she did today. She is really insightful. She didn't brag about herself, but despite her busy schedule, she's already volunteering to help out local kids in an after-school program. She used the word 'dedicated' before. She is. She tutors my roommate in Spanish on a regular basis, without pay and without expecting anything in return."

Dani took a deep breath and let it out slowly. "In my opinion, Petra Alvarez is one of the most thoughtful and dedicated candidates we have for a position in the Student Association. She'll have my vote."

Petra's grateful expression did Dani in. Emotion welled up, threatening to come out as a sob. Dani put a hand up as if to ward herself from her seated classmates and bolted from behind the podium. As she grabbed her backpack and jacket, she heard applause but couldn't register its meaning.

She didn't deserve Petra's friendship and decided that she wasn't going to spend any more time on the SU campus than she could reasonably manage. She had to pack and get the hell out of there. She'd figure out something to explain to her parents.

As she was jamming open the lecture hall door to leave, she caught the eye of her TA. The TA nodded and made a gesture that said she agreed with Dani and that it was about time it had been said.

Dani received the message but couldn't respond. She was already checking out. She'd never see that TA again anyway. Once outside in the late September air, she grunted long and loud to relieve her tension and then took two steps toward the walkway leading back to her dorm. She had a lot of packing to do.

She stopped after those two steps, letting her head throb. Something, she wasn't sure what, but something made her change paths. She set her sights on the Fitness Center. She had to talk to someone—someone who was safe, someone who might understand.

Chapter 17

What Do I Do?

"Where's Joiee?" Dani blurted to Joiee's coworker Derek at the fitness center.

"Hello to you, too," Derek said with a laugh.

"Sorry," Dani said less aggressively. "Is Joiee here?"

"No, no," he said. "She's moving into her new apartment today. That's why I took her shift."

"Where?"

"Well, uh," he hesitated. "Let me text her and see if it's okay to give out her address."

"Fine," Dani said. She yanked her phone out of her back pocket to text Joiee herself, something she should have done in the first place. She opened the chat window but hesitated. What was she going to say? Why was she running to Joiee anyway? She should be back up in the dorm packing while Meredith wasn't there. Or maybe she should just find the bus station and go home right now.

"She says it's okay, Dani."

"You know my name?"

"Yes," Derek said. "Joiee mentioned you two had lunch together, but 'not as a date.'" He laughed and then added, "Her apartment's about a half mile from here, maybe a ten to fifteen-minute walk. Here's the address."

Dani opened the maps app on her phone and set it to walking directions. "727 South Crouse Avenue Apartments," Dani read off his screen. "An apartment. Cool."

"Don't get too excited," Derek said with a laugh. "It's a studio. She's lucky they had something available right now. She really needed to get away from that cheating ex-girlfriend of hers."

"'Cheating ex-girlfriend,'" Dani repeated. She knew the feeling. "Thanks, Derek." She grunted, waved her phone, and bolted for the exit.

Once outside, Dani memorized the path laid out on her phone and took off on the run. She pulled the straps tighter on her jostling backpack and then broke out into a sprint. Making it to the address in under ten minutes, Dani looked around for Joiee in the parking lot. There was a car with boxes inside. That might be hers. She pulled out her phone and sent a text.

DANI: I'm in the parking lot. Where are you?

JOIEE: Whoa, that was fast. I'll be right down.

JOIEE: Can you help me move some stuff up?

DANI: Yes.

Dani knew she wasn't being very friendly or forthcoming, but she needed a minute to get her thoughts in order. She needed a safe place to do that in. Joiee had been the person that first came to mind, especially because she was also going through the whole cheating girlfriend thing.

Joiee appeared in less than two minutes.

"Hey, you okay?" Joiee asked as she patted Dani's upper arm.

"Yeah," Dani said and then thought better of her answer. "No." She didn't follow up and took a step toward what she hoped was Joiee's car.

"What's going on?" Joiee asked, heading toward the same car.

"I kind of need a minute," Dani said. "Let's get all your shit upstairs, and then maybe I can think."

"But you're physically okay?" Joiee asked.

Dani chuckled. She wasn't herself today. Not at all. "Yes, my pieces and parts are fine."

"Okay," Joiee said cautiously and led the rest of the way to her car. She hit the key fob to unlock the doors. "I'm glad the universe sent you to me right now. I need the help. Laura decided that since it was my decision to leave, I should pack up and move myself."

"She's a winner, that one," Dani said.

Joiee pointed to a box and said, "You." She pulled a different box out of the hatchback and said, "Me."

"Put that box on top of mine," Dani said.

"Really?" Joiee raised both eyebrows.

Dani nodded. "Yeah, the sooner we get this stuff in there, the sooner I can try to make sense of my life."

It took them a half hour to move the rest of Joiee's stuff to the top floor of the newly renovated apartment building. Dani welcomed the physical work. It took her mind off...things.

"This view is awesome," Dani said as she set the last few bags on the floor near the window. "What a cool kitchen area." She pointed to each thing in turn. "A bed, a couch, a private bathroom. How'd you score an eighth-floor apartment?"

"I have no idea," Joiee said, handing Dani a bottle of water. "The woman that lived here quit school or something. She moved out yesterday, I think."

"Right place, right time," Dani said. She moved a box off the couch and sat down. She took a long pull from the water bottle and then another.

Joiee moved a bag off the desk chair and sat down facing Dani. "What's going on?"

Dani sighed and looked down at her feet. She twisted the bottle cap off and on several times. She looked up at Joiee and sighed.

"I just now experienced the whole cheating girlfriend thing."

"Oh, shit," Joiee said and leaned forward. "Are you okay?"

Dani shook her head.

"Who?" Joiee asked softly.

"Some guy with a beard."

"Oh, shit." Joiee cringed. "What I meant was, who is your girlfriend?"

"Oh," Dani said and rolled her eyes. "Meredith. My roommate."

Joiee's mouth dropped open. "No shit? How long?"

"We got together on Memorial Day weekend back home, so, uh…" Dani tried to choke down a sob, but the sob had other ideas and spilled out of her soul.

"Oh, shit." Joiee bolted from her chair, yanked a box off the couch, and sat next to Dani. "C'mere." She pulled Dani into a hug and rubbed her back. "Tell me."

"Today is our four-month anniversary."

"Fuck," was Joiee's one-word response. She held Dani until Dani pulled back. "Okay," Joiee said with a serious tone. "Please rest assured that whatever you tell me stays with me, okay? Friends, real friends, that is, keep confidences." She searched Dani's face until Dani nodded. "Good." She let her hands drop and moved a respectable distance away on the couch.

Dani swiped the tears from her eyes and said, "I went to surprise her this morning at the Fine Arts building. There's this student art show tonight for the alumni event. Before I got in the room, I heard her laugh, so before opening the door, I looked through the window." Dani felt the numbness returning at the buried memory. "She called him Edward." Dani described seeing Meredith hug him and then smile. "It was so obvious that they were familiar with each other. Joiee, that smile had always been meant for me. Just me."

"I know what you mean," Joiee said softly. "And I completely get it. You think you know someone, and then they aren't who you thought they were."

They sat in silence for a moment, and then Dani explained how Meredith didn't want Dani to walk her to class that week. As if realizing it for the first time, she said that Meredith had definitely seemed preoccupied all week long. "She had been pulling away."

"Well, there is the art show tonight," Joiee offered.

"Yeah, but maybe there was more to it." Dani looked down at her sneakers. "I can't stay in that room with her now. Not for another second." She looked up. "I have to transfer. I can't stay at this school with her here. Albany State accepted me. It's probably too late to start there this semester, but I can start in January or something."

"Stop," Joiee said succinctly.

Dani looked up.

"You're in flight mode," Joiee said. "You've heard of fight-or-flight mode?"

Dani nodded.

Joiee took a breath, let it out, and said, "You can't leave Syracuse because of something like this. It's a big setback, I know. You've dreamed of going to this school, haven't you?"

Dani nodded.

"Since you were a kid, right?"

Dani nodded again.

"So, you're not going to run off half-cocked at the first sign of adversity. What Meredith did sucks. It positively sucks. But it's her loss, right?"

Dani nodded, not sure that was the truth. Dani wasn't that great of a person. Look what she'd done to Petra that morning during the debate. Petra was her friend. Probably not anymore, though.

"I think before you pack a single thing, you need to confront her." Joiee waited for a response but didn't get one. "You said she didn't see you, right? She doesn't know that you know?"

"Right."

"Use that to your advantage," Joiee said. "I've had practice with this, unfortunately."

"I know. I'm sorry about your situation," Dani said. "I'm not a very good friend right now. I haven't even asked how you were doing."

"You're okay," Joiee said. She sighed and said, "I am doing surprisingly okay. Derek's ready to kill Laura or at least seriously maim her, but I talked him off that ledge. Honestly, getting this apartment so quickly has helped ease some of my anxiety. The other stuff? Well, that's going to take a bit more time. I think I'm going to be single for a while."

"Sounds like a good strategy. And, listen, you can talk to me any time you need to," Dani said and meant it. "Seems like you could use a friend who understands."

"Thanks. I think Laura has already spread lies about why I moved out.

She's so manipulative. Not always, but if it lets her save face, then there you go."

Dani nodded her commiseration. "What do I do, Joiee?" Dani hid her face in her hands as the tears started flowing again. She felt Joiee get up from the couch, rustle around in a bag, and come back with a box of tissues. "Thanks." Dani wiped her eyes. She turned away and blew her nose. She grabbed a fresh tissue and wiped her eyes again. "This really hurts. I really love her."

"I can tell." Joiee's smile was compassionate. "I think you have to confront her and find out what's going on. because if you don't, you'll always wonder when she started seeing him, how they met, and all of that. If you don't find out, it will fester. I know personally how that feels."

Dani shot Joiee a sympathetic, closed-lipped smile.

"Okay," Joiee continued, "how about this? Act like you know nothing and get studded out for this art show thing. Bring your girl flowers. No, that might be too over the top. Anyway, this dude is bound to be hovering around, so you bump into him. Maybe not literally, but somehow, strike up a conversation with him. Find out who he is."

"I don't know," Dani said hesitantly.

Joiee laughed. "Wait. How about this? You introduce him to Meredith. Watch her reaction."

"Oh, that is so passive-aggressive," Dani said with a laugh. And, honestly, she really didn't want to hurt Meredith that way. She still loved her.

"Yeah, that's probably too much," Joiee said. "But I suddenly have no plans tonight so I can go to the art show. I can be your wing-woman supporting you in whatever way you want."

"You'd do that?"

"Of course," Joiee said. "You can use me to make her jealous if you want to."

"No, stop," Dani said. "I don't want to play games like that. She's a nice person."

"Who cheats on you."

Dani almost choked on the words and said, "Yeah, there's that, but she was the one who told me to give *you* another chance. She said that you might make a good friend."

"She said that?" Joiee seemed stunned. "I have to admit she seemed really nice when I met her at the lacrosse field. I thought there might be something between you two because you guys seemed to have some kind of cool chemistry."

A fresh batch of tears started, and Dani let herself be consoled, and that turned into another hour and a half of comforting each other. Joiee even relayed a message to Dani from Laura. It was an internet link to a series of lacrosse drills on YouTube. When Dani questioned Laura's motives, Joiee said that Laura did have a good heart, even if she was lousy at relationships.

They had a good laugh about that, and then Dani asked Joiee if she knew anyone who could teach self-defense. She said that she wanted the women in her dorm to learn some skills and strategies for personal safety.

"My friend Mo is certified to teach self-defense," Joiee said. "I'll talk to her about it. Can I give her your number?"

"Yeah, that would be great. Thank you."

"She's a hooker."

Dani's eyes grew wide, and Joiee started laughing. "She plays on the Rugby team here. That's the name of her position—hooker."

Dani slumped over in relief. "Wow. I mean, I'm open-minded, but that was out of left field."

"She's going to try to recruit you and all of your dormies to play on the team. It's a club team, completely student-run."

"Club team?"

Joiee nodded. "They have tryouts, practice a lot, and play other colleges."

"But they're not a varsity team?"

"Nope, but they get to travel and play competitively. So, I tell you all of this because she can be very convincing, and if you are determined to keep playing lacrosse, I'd try not to play rugby, too."

"Good thinking," Dani said with a laugh. Yes, it felt good to laugh, even if it was only temporary.

After a while, Dani felt grounded enough to head back to the dorm for a shower and maybe a nap. Or should she go for a run? Yes, a run and then a shower. And then a nap. She didn't want to skip her ASL class that afternoon, but she had to. Her mental health needed attention.

She doubted Meredith would be in the room for a variety of reasons. Art show. Bearded guy. Take your pick. And Dani hoped she wouldn't run into Petra or Kate, either. She wasn't sure she could deal with losing her girlfriend and two good friends on the same day, even though that had probably happened. Yeah, Albany State was looking better and better right now.

Dani made plans to meet Joiee at the art show later, suggesting they *not* show up together since that would look weird. When she got back to her blessedly empty dorm room, her inner reptilian brain wanted her to torch it, but she fought hard to stay in her logical-thinking brain and function like a sane human being. That stupid third part of the brain? The one that handled emotions? Yeah, that one was put on hold for a while, maybe permanently.

Chapter 18

Thumbs Down

After a short but intense run to the Ensley Athletic Center and back, Dani took a long, hot, water-wasting shower. She knew it was a small act of rebellion, but she didn't care. She'd be leaving soon anyway.

She tossed on shorts and a t-shirt and then crawled into her bed facing the wall. If Meredith did actually come back to the room, Dani would pretend to be asleep. Maybe Meredith would leave a note and go away.

When Dani woke, her stomach was growling. She rolled over, half afraid to see Meredith at her desk. She wasn't. There was no note either. Good, she hadn't come back to the room. Despite what Joiee said about not packing yet, Dani methodically moved all of her things that had gotten scattered around the room back into their proper places. It would make it so much easier to pack up later.

She purposely ignored her phone as she had been doing all afternoon. There might be texts from Meredith. There might even be texts from Petra or Kate. Best to be oblivious to all of that. Wait, Meredith wouldn't break up with her in a text, would she? Dani woke up her phone, thought better of it, and powered it completely off.

Instead, her logical thinking brain convinced her to focus on getting dressed. She pulled out the outfit she had originally planned to wear to the art show and methodically, almost mechanically, put on each piece of clothing. Whether her crisp button-down shirt, untucked, of course, and her slim black jeans with a matching blazer made her look 'studded out,' she had no idea.

Wait, the hair. A little gel and Meredith's hair dryer, and there was a cool slicked-back vibe going on there. Yeah. It was coming together. Dani grabbed the watch her sister had given her as a going-to-college present and slapped it on. It was a black stainless steel oversized man's watch and fit perfectly with the rest of the black outfit.

Dani took one last look in the mirror and scoffed. She was wearing all black, except for the white shirt. It almost looked like she was in mourning. She kind of was, wasn't she? Her gaze wandered to the background in the mirror. She saw Meredith's desk behind her. A cup of colored pencils sat ready for one of Meredith's spontaneous drawings. Her Spanish notebook was still opened to a recent assignment, waiting for Meredith's return. Meredith's desk looked lived in. Dani's now looked abandoned.

That emotional part of her brain broke free from its flimsy cage. Silent tears came unbidden. She allowed it for the briefest of moments but then grabbed a tissue, steeled herself, and headed out the door.

Her stomach rumbled again. She could stop at the dining hall, but the mere thought of food made her nauseas. She'd grab something later. And without much of a plan, Dani headed to the Fine Arts Building. She was already late for the art show, but that was just fine. She wasn't going to stay long anyway. She'd briefly thought about not going at all, but Joiee was going out of her way to be there, so she needed to honor that commitment, at least. And, besides, a perverse side of her wanted to meet this bearded guy in person. She wanted to size up her competition. Besides the obvious difference in genitalia, what did he have that drew Meredith to him? What was so great about this guy that Meredith would cheat on her?

"She told me she loved me," Dani mumbled to herself as she walked the campus alone, breaking all of her own safety rules. "She told me I was a good catch." If Dani was such a good catch, then why was she getting thrown back?

She had no real recollection of walking the paths to the Fine Arts Center, but the fun party atmosphere leading into the lobby woke her up. She'd forgotten it was an alumni event.

There was a big fancy schmancy reception going on in the lobby. Alums of all ages were dressed up, many holding drinks in their hands. There was a spread of food, too. Dani's stomach rumbled. A waiter came by with a tray of hors d'oeuvres. She probably shouldn't, but she needed some food so she wouldn't pass out. When he paused in front of her, she took that as a sign and grabbed three bacon-wrapped somethings. She thanked him, took a napkin, and snarfed down the first one in basically one bite. Oh, it was cream cheese wrapped in bacon. Nice. The next two went down just as quickly, and she was amazed that her stomach didn't protest and send the food back up.

Dani jumped when a middle-aged woman abruptly appeared at her side. "Are you a student here?" She took a sip of wine from the glass she was holding.

"Uh, yes." Dani swallowed the last bits of her snack. She wiped her mouth and fingers with the napkin and then tucked it in the pocket of her pants.

The woman wore a very striking and rich-looking suit. Her long honey-blonde hair was pulled behind her head. Like a lot of the alums at the reception, she looked elegant. "Are you showing at the art show? Are you an art student?"

Dani chuckled. "No, I plan to major in Political Science."

"Blah," she said good-naturedly. "You and my husband have a lot in common. Come, let me introduce you."

"Okay," Dani said, not knowing what she was saying okay to. It took everything in her soul not to blow past this woman, find the art show, and do whatever it was she was going to do when she finally confronted Meredith. But she didn't. Dani wasn't rude like that. She wasn't that person in the debate that morning who tried to ruin another person's life. And not just any person—a friend who probably wasn't anymore. And then again, neither was Meredith. Why had she come here?

"Roger, I found you a prospect," the woman said, approaching a distinguished-looking man dressed impeccably in an obviously tailored suit. The woman turned to Dani and said, "Oh, my goodness, I haven't even introduced myself." She stuck out her slim, pale hand and said, "I'm Witney Winthrop, and this is my husband, Senator Roger Winthrop."

"H-hi," Dani stammered. A senator? Holy shit. "Nice to meet you. I'm Danielle Lassiter. Everyone calls me Dani." Why she added that last part, she'd never know. She shook hands with the woman and then her husband as he launched into a dozen questions about her career goals and intentions. She did her best to answer them honestly. Paramount in her answers was that she wanted to help people live their best lives. He seemed to like that answer and went on to ask her about the courses she was currently taking and the ones she intended to take later. He gave her some advice about courses he had taken when at Syracuse that had helped him immensely in his own career.

"Oh, Roger," Witney said, "stop badgering the poor thing and tell her what you need."

"Right, right," he said and grinned. "I need a first-year intern. Obviously, you're in school, but we can work around your schedule. Weekends, school breaks, summer."

Dani was confused. What was he implying?

Dani was about to ask, but Whitney interrupted and said, "Did you know that Roger and I met here at Syracuse? Twenty years ago?"

"Um, no," Dani said. How could she have known that?

"Yep," Witney said with a knowing head nod. "He was Poly Sci, like you, and I was flitting about trying to find a major. I quickly found out that Psychology wasn't for me, but then he nudged me toward photography, and it was then I knew I'd found the two loves of my life."

"You did?" Dani asked, allowing herself to be amused by the couple. The way Roger beamed at the tale almost made Dani laugh out loud. These two were funny and cute.

"Mm hmm," Witney said and took a sip of wine. "I found my life's calling in visual art, and I also found him. Didn't I, Pookie?"

Dani's eyes grew wide. No, she would not laugh. And somehow, she managed to keep it together. How amazing it was to see two people who'd fallen in love in college who were still together and happy. Her elation at the cute couple deflated as she realized she wasn't destined to have that. She felt her face flush at the thought. Ugh. She had to find a way to excuse herself. She had to get publicly humiliated by Meredith and her new boytoy.

Roger was holding out a business card and a pen. "Write your name and phone number down, and I'll have Bennie call you on Monday about the details of the internship and where to submit an application."

"It's a paid internship, Dani," Witney said with a devilish grin. "Pretty good, right?"

"Uh, yes," Dani said as she carefully wrote down her name and number. "Thank you."

She handed the card and pen back to Roger, who tucked them into the inside pocket of his suit jacket. He then handed her a fresh business card. "Oh, how do you feel about interning in Albany?"

"That's where I'm from, actually."

"Even better," he said.

"Uh, thank you for the opportunity, Sir." Dani wasn't sure what the heck had just happened in this alternate life of hers, but if this were real, she'd take it. An internship with a state senator? Holy what-the-hell? Although it might mean sharing the SU campus with Meredith for a while longer.

"Hey, Dani," someone called from down the hall.

Dani looked up. It was Joiee.

"Oh, you have to go, dear," Witney said and patted Dani's arm. "Ooh, strong. Athlete?"

"Lacrosse," Dani said.

"It's nice to see young people engaged in activities," Witney said. "Isn't it Roger?"

"Absolutely," he said. "Oh, there's Marjorie Barnard. We must go say hello." He turned back to Dani. "It was nice meeting you, young lady."

"Likewise," Dani said. *Likewise?* Did she just say that to them? Who the heck was she turning into? It was an alternate reality day, for sure.

"Bye, Dani," Witney said as her husband dragged her away toward a group of wineglass-toting alums on the far side of the lobby.

Dani headed toward Joiee, who was politely waiting in the hallway leading toward the exhibit hall. Joiee waited for a couple of well-dressed alums to go by before blurting, "Holy shit, Dani, you know Senator Winthrop?"

"Nope," Dani said and kept walking. "I mean, maybe I do now." She gave Joiee the briefest of explanations about what happened and then blurted, "Is she here?"

"Yes," Joiee said succinctly.

"Did she see you?"

"No, I don't think so. I didn't get close to her section," Joiee said. "You look fantastic, by the way."

"Thanks." Dani took a few more steps, trying to harden her nerves, and then said, "It's what all the cool kids wear to get dumped by their girlfriends these days."

Joiee said nothing but patted Dani on the arm, probably in solidarity.

The hallway opened up into a spacious room with a ton of student art pieces on display. Alums, current students, professors, and who knew who else milled about talking, drinking, and checking out the art. Dani slowed her pace to a crawl. Joiee followed suit. There was too much to take in. There was pottery and paintings and all manner of art, including mixed media pieces that hung down from the ceiling. She'd need someone to explain it all to her. She used to have a person like that. Not anymore.

"Where is she?"

Joiee pointed to the far right side of the hall, and Dani lost her breath. Meredith was stunning in a red pantsuit with her hair pulled up high on her head in an elegant bun. Were those chopsticks coming out of the bun?

"She's beautiful," Dani murmured.

"She is," Joiee said softly.

"I can't," Dani said, wiping at her tears.

"I get it. But you've come this far." They moved off to the side and out of the way of the flowing human traffic. "Tell you what," Joiee said. "How about I go over and say hello? I want to check out her work, anyway. You can't see it from this angle. And then, when you feel brave, come over. I'll be right there if it turns sideways."

"Is that guy there?"

"I can't really see from here, but I'll give you a thumbs up if he's there. Okay?"

She really didn't want to meet the bearded guy. She really didn't want to see Meredith, either, who had probably gotten all dressed up like that for…him.

"Thumbs down might be a better signal," Dani said.

"I can't do that in front of Meredith's artwork."

Dani nodded. That made sense.

"I'll beckon you over when I feel it's safe for you, okay?" Joiee stood tall and confident. Dani wished she felt that way, too. Dani searched Joiee's face for a way out of this mess. "You'll be okay," Joiee said. "I'll be right there. I'll see you in a few minutes." She turned to head toward Meredith, but Dani stopped her.

"Wait. What if that guy is there, and she tells me she's been seeing him and she wants to break up with me? Then what?"

"Then you respect her wishes and remain calm, cool, and collected."

Dani's stomach lurched. Maybe those bacon-wrapped cream cheese things hadn't been a good idea. "I will. Of course. It'll suck, but I will. But I can't go back to the dorm room."

"No worries," Joiee said. "You can have the couch, and I'll take the bed. No funny stuff. I promise." She put her hand up as if giving an oath.

"Thank you. But what if she doesn't admit to being with him? I saw them. Caught them red-handed."

"That could happen." Joiee brushed a lock of her dark hair off her forehead. "Here and now is not the time to confront her, though. This is a reconnaissance mission. If she doesn't confess, then you'll confront her later in your dorm room. Or walking back to the dorm. Either way, you are welcome at my new digs."

"Joiee," Dani said and sighed. "You're a good friend. Thank you for this."

"I'm going over now." Joiee took one tentative step toward Meredith and waited.

"I'm okay," Dani said. "I'm going to stay here and wait for your signal." She exhaled, feeling her blood pulsing through her neck at high speed. Joiee walked away, and Dani took that time to breathe and slow her pounding heart.

She put her hands in her pants pockets, felt something weird, and pulled it out. It was the senator's business card. She took a moment to look at it. If she hadn't been in such a fog when she'd entered the art building, she would have realized that she had been talking to New York State Senator Winthrop from District 32 right outside of Albany. She didn't live in that district, but she was a political science nerd and knew who he was. His political views fit right in with hers.

"Alternate dimension, all right," she muttered and then looked up toward Joiee.

Joiee nodded at her and threw her a thumbs up. She had a smile on her face, but maybe it was a sympathetic grimace. Dani walked over as slowly as she could. Her heart increased its pounding and forced her to take a deep breath to slow it down. It didn't work.

Meredith was talking to some alums and had her back to Dani. Good. That gave Dani a bit of a reprieve. The proverbial shit would hit the fan any minute now.

Joiee beckoned her toward Meredith's displays. She mimicked breathing to try to get Dani to relax.

Dani took a breath, but she didn't plan to relax.

Chapter 19

Life Lessons

Dani had just about reached Meredith's display when a piercing voice sliced through her head. "Is this her?"

Dani stopped short. She had to. The bearded guy was blocking her path.

"OMG," he said, totally invading her personal space. Dani took several steps back. "Meredith simply cannot stop talking about you. Hun-ee," he said, dragging out the syllables, "you are more stunning in person. Let me look at you." He put his hand on his chin and then made a motion for her to twirl.

Oh, that was not happening. Not in this life. Not ever. Dani put a hand up to keep him away, literally and figuratively.

"Edward, stop badgering her," Meredith scolded from behind.

Dani was grateful for the disruption, but then she found herself looking straight into Meredith's baby-brown eyes, and all the worry she had packed into the last ten hours came rushing to the forefront. Meredith's face blurred.

"Dani!" Arms grabbed her. "Oh, my God!"

"Get a chair," someone yelled.

Dani felt herself guided to the floor. She thought she heard voices but was too tired to comprehend anything. She groaned in time to her throbbing head.

"You, pretty girl, get some water. Hurry." That was Joiee's voice. That much she knew.

Someone was stroking her forehead, almost petting her.

"You're okay, Dani," Joiee said softly. "I'm putting your feet up to help regulate your blood pressure. Dani felt Joiee's strong hands lift her feet and rest her calves on something hard. "Stress caused a sudden drop in blood pressure. You're okay," she repeated. "Keep breathing."

"Good idea," Dani joked. She heard a few relieved chuckles around her.

She opened her eyes and tried to sit up on her own but was a little weak.

"Joiee, should she be trying to sit up?" That was Meredith's voice. There was real concern there.

"Not yet," Joiee said. Joiee's voice sounded closer when she said, "Dani, I need you to stay where you are for a few more minutes. I need your body to readjust."

"K," was all she could manage. She kept her eyes closed and listened to the din around her. Opening her eyes would make Meredith and her betrayal real. Lying there on the floor was a brief reprieve from reality. She inhaled sharply when a cool cloth of some kind pressed against her forehead.

"You're okay, Dani." This was Meredith's voice. Meredith was wiping her face with something. Dani didn't want Meredith touching her and tried to sit up.

"Wait, wait," Meredith said, clear panic in her voice. "Joiee, she's trying to sit up."

"It's okay. I think she's recovered a bit," Joiee said. "And she's fairly lucid. We'll let her sit this way for a while, though. Until she regains her strength."

One of Meredith's arms went behind Dani's back, propping her up. At the touch, Dani's misery came rushing back. All of it. Meredith's betrayal, that bearded guy's very existence, Laura's aggression, Petra's humiliation.

Dani put two fingers to her throbbing temple and looked up at Meredith.

"Oh, honey," Meredith cried, tears in her eyes. "Are you okay? What happened?"

Dani couldn't form words yet. Her pounding head was taking up all of her energy.

"Oh, baby," Meredith gushed and kissed Dani's temple. Her kisses moved to Dani's forehead and then the cheek closest to her. "Tell me what happened."

"No," came the passive-aggressive answer.

"She didn't eat much today," Joiee said from her other side.

When Dani started to protest Joiee covering up the real issue, she was shushed from all sides. Outnumbered, she let herself be coddled. At Joiee's direction, she took a few calming breaths. A water bottle was thrust in her face. It was Kate. Dani smiled to herself. Kate must have been the 'pretty girl' Joiee commanded earlier.

"Thanks," was all the energy she had to say to Kate. "I'm okay," she said to Joiee, not daring to look at Meredith.

"She's okay, everybody," Joiee said as she stood up. "Let's all back up and give her some breathing room."

After a few minutes, Joiee and Meredith were able to get Dani seated in a chair off to the side of the room behind Meredith's artwork. Meredith was by her side.

"Baby," Meredith said quietly. She was squatting down close to Dani. "What happened? Are you okay?" She blew out an anxious sigh. "Did you forget to eat? Kate said you weren't at lunch."

"I wasn't." It was all she could muster up to say.

Meredith sighed. It was a nervous sigh. "I've been worried about you all day. You didn't return any of my texts. Kate said she saw you taking a run this afternoon, so I thought you were okay. But you're not okay, are you?"

"No." Dani took a swig of water, grateful that her stomach didn't churn at the intrusion. She looked up at Meredith. "Who's the bearded guy? Edward?" The name tasted bitter in her mouth.

"I wanted to introduce you to him tonight," Meredith said. "I didn't know..."

Dani simply grunted when Meredith didn't finish her sentence. *She knows that I know*, Dani thought.

There was another pause, and then Meredith said in a calm voice, "You look nice, Dani." She chuckled and added, "You clean up real nice."

Dani had heard enough. She let the now-empty water bottle drop from her hands and hit the carpet below. She turned her head slowly to glare at the now squatting Meredith. Blood pulsed through her head. Was Meredith really going to do this?

"Dani, you're scaring me. What's going on?"

"I asked you a question." It was abrupt and to the point. "Who is Edward?"

"That's what I wanted to tell you. He and I went to Greenspond High School together. He's a sophomore here, and he said he kept seeing me around campus but wasn't sure if it was me. He said I've changed a lot. He said I'm more confident and don't hide behind my hair anymore. He said he really likes this new me."

"I bet." Dani looked down. Hopefully, she could snag Joiee's moving boxes.

Joiee walked over unobtrusively with a matching chair for Meredith. Meredith thanked her and sat down to face Dani.

The confused look on Meredith's face changed as Meredith seemed to realize something. *Oh, yes, roomie, I know you're cheating on me,* Dani thought.

"Danielle Lassiter," Meredith scolded gently, a smile growing on her face. "I do believe that you're jealous."

"Humph," Dani scoffed.

"He's just a friend, Dani. You are so silly. And, besides, he plays on our team."

Her last few words were having a difficult time registering in Dani's brain. "What do you mean?"

"He's one hundred percent gay, my dear," Meredith said with a laugh. "The kids at Greenspond used to tease him mercilessly. They'd tease me, too, because I was shy and awkward, so that's how we ended up becoming friends."

Dani wasn't going to let it go. She was having a hard time accepting this explanation. She'd seen the hug and the smile. "Besties?"

"No, not at all, but we kind of looked out for each other in high school."

"And this morning's hug?"

"You saw that? Is that what started all this?"

"I came to see if you needed help," Dani said. It sounded weak even to her own ears.

"He surprised me in the art room. You must have witnessed the moment I hugged him when I realized who he was. You should have come in, baby. It would have spared you so much anxiety and non-eating." She tapped Dani on the knee in reprimand. "You've been brooding all day, haven't you?"

Dani felt her face flush with embarrassment. Even the tips of her ears felt hot. She nodded.

"Oh, baby," Meredith gushed. She reached over and pulled Dani in her arms. The hands rubbing Dani's back felt good. Dani hugged Meredith back. It was a perfect fit. She pulled Meredith closer and laid her head on Meredith's shoulder. The floodgates opened up. "I thought I'd lost you."

Meredith squeezed tighter. "Never."

Dani cried in Meredith's arms until she could breathe without crying. "I'm sorry." She pulled back so she could face her girlfriend. "I'm so sorry. I shouldn't have doubted you."

"No, you shouldn't have, but I get it." Meredith cradled Dani's face with both hands and then kissed her full on the lips. Dani returned the soul-affirming kiss, and it wasn't long before a clearing of the throat knocked them out of their reconciliation.

"Just roommates, huh?" Kate said, a grin on her face and a hand on her hip. Joiee and Edward were standing on either side.

Dani and Meredith touched their foreheads together momentarily, embarrassed at getting caught, and then sat upright.

"Guess it's time," Meredith murmured to Dani.

"A little ahead of schedule." Dani nodded. She reached for Meredith's hand, kissed the back of it, and held on. She looked up at Kate and said, "We're more than roommates, Kate. And it's about time everybody knows it." Fresh tears, happy tears this time, started, but Dani didn't care. "I love this woman with all my heart and soul, and I want everyone to know."

"Brava," Joiee said. "I'm proud of you both. Coming out is hard."

"Keeping my love for her under wraps was harder," Dani said.

"Aww," both Kate and Edward gushed at the same time and then laughed.

"They are adorable," Edward said.

"I know," Kate said. "I want that. What they have."

"We all do, hun-ee," Edward said. "We all do."

"C'mon," Joiee said to the other two, "let's give them their privacy." She ushered them away and declared, "After this, I think we can all believe in love again."

"You got that right," Edward whispered, almost to himself.

Dani and Meredith laughed at their friends' antics, and then Meredith's expression turned serious. "Dani, please understand that you're the only one for me. The only one of any gender or amazing hairstyle. How did you get your hair looking so fabulous?"

"I borrowed your hair dryer," Dani said with a laugh.

"Without permission," Meredith teased. "There may be spankings later."

"Whoa." Dani's face broke out into a slow grin. "This conversation took quite a turn." She took a breath, let it out as a sigh, and said, "I am a complete idiot. I hope you can forgive my presumption. But, baby, I was devastated."

"I would have been, too," Meredith said. "Remember when I assumed, you know, the whole thing about Laura?" Meredith patted Dani's thigh but didn't let her hand linger. "Our insecurities have been ringing out loud and clear, haven't they?"

"Yeah," Dani said. She stretched her neck from side to side, trying to relieve an entire day's worth of tension. It wasn't really helping.

"You have no reason not to trust me, Dani. I love you."

"Me, too," Dani said. "I don't ever want to be without you."

Meredith's smile melted Dani's heart. This was the smile meant only for her. The one she witnessed that morning was nothing like this one. Yes, she was an idiot.

"You haven't told me about this morning's debate," Meredith said, "but it's going to have to wait until after this."

"I know."

"We'll go get some food after, okay?"

"Yes, food would be good," Dani said and stood up with Meredith's help. She reassured Meredith that she felt okay. She felt steady.

"Are you ready to come out to this entire hall full of strangers?" Meredith asked.

"No time like the present."

They headed back to Meredith's displays hand in hand. Meredith immediately had to excuse herself to talk to some alums who were looking at her work. Dani walked over to Joiee, who stood by herself.

"All good?" Joiee asked.

"Yes, all good. Thanks for your help today. And on a day that was particularly shitty for you."

"I'm okay," Joiee said, sounding like she really meant it. "I think I needed the distraction. And, to be honest, my breakup was long, long overdue."

"You know what?" Dani asked and answered her own question. "I'm an idiot."

"I know," Joiee said matter-of-factly.

"Shut up," Dani said with a laugh. "You don't have to agree with me."

"You made an assumption. Something I've been guilty of, too. But heal from that. Talk things over with Meredith. Get to the place where you feel able to talk to one another about anything. No secrets. Let her see any and everything on your phone. No secret meetings with other women."

Dani narrowed her eyes and said, "Are we still talking about me here?"

"No," Joiee said, again matter-of-factly. "But Dani, just know that you're safe here. This campus is pretty accepting. I know it's hard to tell, but I speak from experience."

"Thanks," Dani said and then jumped when an arm went around her waist. "It's going to take a minute to get used to that," she said to Meredith, whose arm was pulling her close.

"Ready to officially meet Edward?" Meredith asked. "He's a lot."

"Okay, but I'm not going to twirl."

"What?" Meredith said, looking confused as heck. Dani just shrugged and let herself be guided toward Edward, who was chatting animatedly with Kate. To Edward, Meredith said, "Let's make this official. Edward, this is my girlfriend, Dani. Dani, this is my friend from high school, Edward."

"So nice to meet you, Dani," Edward said in a much calmer voice than before.

"Nice to meet you, too." The weird thing was she not only said it out loud but also signed it. She wasn't sure why she had done that. She hadn't been herself all day.

"Oh, you know sign language?" Edward asked.

"I'm taking a course now, so only a couple of weeks." This she didn't sign. She didn't have enough vocabulary yet to maintain a real conversation. "So, you knew Meredith from before, huh?"

"Oh, yes," he said, putting a hand to his chest. "She saved me from those idiots in high school. I knew I was gay since forever, but those jerks couldn't handle my fabulousness."

Dani chuckled at his over-the-top antics.

"My mother, I love her, but she wouldn't let me follow my boyfriend to Cortland. Whatevuh!" He flicked an imaginary lock of hair over his shoulder.

"She *made* you go to Syracuse?" Dani's grin was growing ever wider.

"You haven't met his mother," Meredith said. "She is quite the force of nature."

Dani chuckled for Edward's benefit but didn't know what else to say. She was still wound tight from her alternate reality day.

Edward leaned close to Meredith and whispered, "She's cuter in person."

Meredith pushed him away good-naturedly. Dani felt herself relaxing, not that the tension was completely dissipating because she'd spent all day wound up tight like a rubber band ball. That was going to take some time to undo. One thing was clear, though. Meredith and Edward were friends and quite obviously *only* friends.

"This has been a rough day for me," Dani blurted. She couldn't help it. She'd been up on a pretty high ledge.

"Oh, my God in heaven," Edward gushed, looking past Dani and Meredith. He hid his mouth behind the side of his hand and whispered, "Who is that gorgeous creature?"

Dani and Meredith turned to see who he was referring to. Meredith shrugged, but Dani burst out laughing. "That's Derek. He works with Joiee at the fitness center."

"Fit-ness," Edward repeated comically. "I'll say." He made no attempt to hide his head-to-toe perusal of Derek's bodybuilder physique.

Derek, who also cleaned up nice, wore a tight white T-shirt, totally showing off his pecs and biceps. Joiee must have invited him because he was heading right toward her. Wait, Joiee was still talking with Kate. Kate was twirling a lock of hair around one finger as she listened to whatever it was Joiee was saying. Well, that was interesting.

"Go introduce yourself to him," Dani said to Edward.

"I can't," Edward protested but then laughed. "Who am I kidding? Yes, I can." He took two steps, leaned back toward Meredith, and whispered, "Keep her."

"That's the plan," Meredith said and chuckled.

Dani was about to echo Meredith's statement, but one of the alums, a twenty-something guy with long hair, walked up to talk with Meredith.

"Excuse me," Dani said graciously and backed away. Meredith patted her on the arm. Dani took it for the hug that it was.

Dani's focus finally turned to Meredith's art pieces. In all the drama—caused by her, of course—she hadn't had a chance to look them over. Her jaw dropped open. Literally. If she'd had any doubts that Meredith loved her, they evaporated instantly.

"Meredith," Dani murmured under her breath. "What have you done?" Dani stood mere feet from six portraits of her own likeness in various mediums or points of view or whatever those art people called it.

She moved to the farthest painting on the left. It was a watercolor; that much she knew. Meredith had taken a lot of pictures that day at the rose garden, and the roses in the painting's background were an incredible frame for the subject in the foreground.

The subject in real life, standing in front of the artwork, shivered as something rushed through her. At first, she wasn't sure what it was and wondered if she needed to sit down again, but then an ethereal knowing replaced her confusion. Meredith was as much in love with Dani as Dani was in love with her.

Dani hadn't even looked at the rest of the art pieces and already knew that she and Meredith would be in each other's lives for the rest of their existence on Earth. It wasn't a wish or a conjecture; it was a hard knowing. She glanced over her shoulder at Meredith's easy-going stance and friendly demeanor as she talked with a circle of alums around her.

Meredith looked up as if sensing Dani's gaze and smiled. Dani's own smile grew bigger. Yep, she'd been an idiot to think Meredith had strayed. Meredith's attention was diverted back to her conversation, so Dani turned back to the artwork.

"How do you do all this?" Dani murmured to herself as she moved on to take in the charcoal sketch of her profile. She was at her desk, reading. When had Meredith done that? She was a sneaky girlfriend for sure, but sneaky in a good way. Ahh, Meredith's favorite medium was next. She loved oils. The small oil portrait of Dani smelling a rose with her eyes closed was incredible. It really captured the content feeling Dani had that day.

The next piece made Dani smile. She had no idea what this kind of art was called, but it was created from tiny bits of ripped colored paper in various sizes. They had been glued down to make a humorous portrait of Dani wearing lacrosse goggles and a mouthguard. It was too funny. And you could totally tell that it was Dani. The fifth portrait was in pastels and portrayed Dani laughing in the dining hall. Probably laughing at something Kate said, no doubt. The very last piece was a series of pencil sketches of Dani on one large paper canvas. Maybe Meredith had to show different sketching techniques to her instructor or something. She had complained one day that she was having trouble with her 'radial hatching technique,' whatever the heck that was. It just looked like a bunch of doodles to Dani at the time, but when a person like Meredith doodles, this is what you get.

"She is incredibly talented," Joiee said quietly as she moved to stand next to Dani.

"I knew she was, but this is just outstanding." Dani heard the awe in her own voice.

"As soon as I saw the portraits, I knew you two were going to be okay. That and sizing up Edward." Joiee laughed. "Flaming."

Dani laughed. "Yeah, he kind of is." Dani's smile waned as she gave Joiee a side-eye glance. "I was stupid. And impulsive. And just dumb."

"None of those things," Joiee said. "You felt threatened and reacted. Next time, get all the facts."

"Lesson hopefully learned." Dani glanced over at Meredith, who had an ever-growing circle of alums surrounding her. Yep, her girlfriend was popular, all right. And that was a good thing.

"Got a question for you," Joiee said. Her tone had turned serious.

"Shoot."

"Is Kate single?"

Dani burst out laughing. "So much for 'being single for a while.'"

"Shut up," Joiee said with a grin.

"You know," Dani said, "that's a tricky question. She claims to have a boyfriend back home or something, but she's been pretty flirty with me. So, I think you'll have to ask her yourself."

"I was afraid of that." Joiee groaned. "I'm not as in-your-face as Edward, though." She pointed over her shoulder. "Look."

Edward and Derek were standing very close together. It was too close for two people that had just met. "Is Derek—"

"Yes," Joiee interrupted. "And single. And looking."

"Wow," Dani said. "Today has been a weird day for everyone. Is Mercury in retrograde or something?"

"What does that even mean?"

"I have no idea," Dani said and burst out laughing. "I heard somebody say that this morning."

"Where were you at lunch?" Kate demanded, sidling up to them.

"I had a rough morning," Dani said, now serious.

"Petra skipped lunch, too," Kate said, clearly bummed out. "I had to eat with some other kids."

"Aww," Joiee said, "that must have been rough." There was a teasing lilt to her voice that Kate seemed to understand loud and clear.

"Oh, hush, you," Kate reprimanded. "They all abandoned me."

Before Joiee or Dani could say anything, Meredith came up behind them and said, "But we're all here now. Except for Petra, of course."

Dani turned to face her girlfriend and smiled. It was so freeing to think of Meredith as her girlfriend again. It was calming.

Dani turned to Kate and asked nervously, "Where is Petra, anyway?"

"She's doing a session," Kate said cryptically.

"Ahh," Dani said, knowing that Kate was covertly referring to a session with Petra's therapist. Dani hoped beyond hope that the debates that morning hadn't compromised Petra's mental health. Dani frowned. She shouldn't have run from the lecture hall. That whole flight-mode thing was totally counterproductive. Gah, she hated life lessons, and today's had been a big one, hadn't it?

Meredith nudged Dani with her hip. That was her signal to get out of her head and be present. Dani grinned back and felt her face flush. Yes, her girlfriend knew her well.

"In about fifteen more minutes, we can blow this joint," Meredith said. "Joiee, do you know a place we can get this one some food?" She put her arm around Dani's waist.

"I do," Joiee said, her eyes lighting up. "There's a 24/7 diner near my new apartment."

"Apartment?" Kate muttered as if to herself.

Joiee chuckled. "Okay if I invite the boys?" She lifted her head toward Edward and Derek, who were still standing too close.

"Of course," Meredith said. "Want to text Petra, Kate? See if she can join us?"

"I will," she said, glanced at Dani, and added, "but she won't."

Dani's heart sank. Yep, life lessons sucked, and apparently, she had a few more to learn. She was determined to make things right not only with Meredith but also with Petra.

Chapter 20

Push Play

Joiee waited in her car as Dani, Meredith, and Kate headed back into their dorm. Kate turned back and waved to Joiee, who smiled big, nodded once, and then drove away.

"What was that all about?" Dani asked Kate once they were inside the lobby, standing in front of the elevator.

"I don't know what you mean," Kate said innocently.

"She'll tell us when she's ready," Meredith said to Dani. "Just like we weren't ready."

"Oh, my God, you guys," Kate gushed as the elevator doors opened and she flung herself inside. "It took you two forever to come out. I knew you guys were a couple at the first RA meeting."

"You did?" Meredith looked stricken.

"Sixth sense," Kate said. "But then Dani denied it, and I thought maybe Dani had a crush on you, and that was as far as it would go." She shrugged, and then they all laughed when Dani comically pressed the button for their floor, a slight detail they had all overlooked after standing in the still elevator for over a full minute.

"I had a crush on her since the moment I saw the new girl in eleventh grade," Dani said, pulling a willing Meredith into her arms. "Still do."

"Took me a little longer," Meredith said and buried her face in Dani's shoulder. "A lot longer."

"Ooh, I want to hear the origin story," Kate gushed. "But I think I have to check on Petra."

They stepped out of the elevator, and Dani looked down the hall toward

187

Petra and Kate's room. She nodded, and then they said their goodnights and headed to their respective rooms.

Once inside their room, Meredith turned to Dani and said softly, "Something happened at the debate. That much is clear. Are you okay? Is Petra okay?"

Dani sighed. "It didn't go well. I'm an ass. I humiliated Petra. She won't ever forgive me, and I think I've lost a good friend.

"Oh, honey," Meredith pulled Dani into a hug. "All this in one day." She stroked the back of Dani's hair as if petting her and rocked her gently from side to side.

"At least I didn't lose you like I thought."

Meredith whimpered. "But you thought you did. And that made things so much worse for you, didn't it?"

Dani nodded. She took a big breath, sighed, and let herself melt into Meredith's healing warmth. After several long moments, Meredith whispered into Dani's ear, "I say we get into our pajamas and snuggle on my bed. I need you to rub my tummy."

"Too much diner food?"

Meredith groaned. "Why did I think I could eat that whole stack of onion rings?" She pulled back and groaned again.

"Because they looked amazing."

"They were so greasy," Meredith bemoaned. "I hope I don't break out."

"Tell you what," Dani said and gave Meredith a quick kiss on the lips. "Once we're snuggled, I'll tell you the tale of how big of an ass I was this morning. It's not one of my prouder moments, but I think I'm learning that I can't hold in this kind of stuff. Talking with you might help. Maybe you can help me figure out what to do."

"Vulnerability 101," Meredith said. "It's healthy. You want to wash up first?"

Dani waggled her eyebrows. "Let's go together."

Meredith looked stricken.

"Hey," Dani said with a laugh, "we're just brushing teeth and washing faces."

"But what will people think?"

"We'll let them think whatever they want," Dani said as if the mere thought didn't scare her to death. "We made a pact at that diner to be out and proud, to be ourselves."

"Like Joiee."

"Yeah, she survived being out here, so we can, too."

They each picked up their toiletry bags and headed to the Pod bathroom across the hall. Once inside, Meredith said, "I feel so bad about Joiee's breakup."

Dani had already started brushing her teeth but answered around her toothbrush anyway. "She knew it was time to eave Aura."

"Who's 'eave'?" Meredith said with a laugh as she secured her hair off her face with a wide hairband. "And who's 'Aura'?"

Dani laughed and then nudged Meredith away from the sink and spit out her toothpaste. She rinsed her mouth out and the sink before saying clearly and concisely, "Leave Laura."

"I know, silly."

Meredith smiled as she went about her face-cleansing ritual. She'd described the many-step process to Dani once, but this was the first time Dani witnessed it. Somehow, it was endearing. It was like something private and personal that Dani was finally allowed to see.

"What?" Meredith asked mid-scrub.

"You're beautiful."

Meredith scoffed and then rolled her eyes.

"It's true." Dani nudged Meredith out of the way again and washed her face quickly. She dried it on her hand towel and then realized she had a problem. "Uh, Meredith?"

"Mm hmm?"

"I have to pee."

"Go right ahead."

"Don't look."

Meredith burst out laughing. "Hadn't planned on it."

Dani felt kind of shy, and her bladder didn't cooperate for a moment, but then it finally did. Not once did she look toward Meredith, and when she was finished, she flushed and headed toward the sink with both hands held straight up like a surgeon going in for surgery.

Meredith bolted out of the contamination zone. Dani leaned over the sink but then turned her head to look behind her. Meredith was sporting the biggest grin. "You are so cute," Meredith said. "But I have to tell you. We're getting a double-sink vanity when the time comes."

"And what time would that be?"

"When we have a say in our living accommodations."

Dani felt her cheeks get warm. Meredith was thinking about their future together. Dani pursed her lips and waited. She didn't wait long as Meredith pursed her own and pecked Dani on the lips, leaving a touch of facial scrub on Dani's cheek. Meredith wiped it off with her finger and then with a washcloth. The intimacy of the move made Dani's core tremble.

"I love you, Meredith Bedford."

"And I love you, Danielle Lassiter." They pecked one more time, and then Meredith said, "I'm going to be a bit longer, so go on and get snuggly. Tomorrow's Saturday, so we can sleep in if we want to."

Dani knew exactly what Meredith meant by sleeping in. It meant they could stay up late. And staying up late meant they could be intimate. "Great idea, baby." She turned toward the bathroom door. "I'll see you in a little. Lock the door behind me."

Once Dani and Meredith were on Meredith's bed facing each other with the top sheet over them all snuggly and warm, Dani felt safe enough to relay the events of the morning—from the shock at seeing Meredith with the bearded guy to walking the campus in a daze, to showing up late to her Poly Sci class, and finally, the mood she was in heading into the debate.

"I was so afraid that you'd changed your mind about me, about us," Dani admitted. "I was afraid that you had a change of heart and wanted a husband and a house and kids and all that."

"Can you imagine Edward as my husband?"

Dani burst out laughing. "No. He's a good guy, but no."

They sat silently for a moment, and then Dani relayed the details of the debate. A heavy ache filled her.

"Petra didn't deserve that," Dani murmured.

"Two things," Meredith said. "No, three things. One, it sounds like that PSLA group has a mean mob mentality, you know, like those reality shows where they humiliate each other?"

Dani nodded.

"Two, it sounds to me like you never actually said anything about Petra. You never actually said a word about her eating disorder."

"But I started to. I mean, I didn't. You're right, but I implied…" Dani hesitated as shame took over. "I *implied* that she was going to therapy for something. People heard it."

It was Meredith's turn to nod. "Yeah, I have to give you that one. But I'm proud of you."

Dani scoffed. "Why?" It came out sharper than she'd intended.

"You thought your life had taken a rough downturn that morning, and even though you dabbled with your evil side, the good in you put a halt to it and pulled back."

"Not fast enough, baby," Dani whispered and snuggled closer, which encouraged Meredith to stroke her back.

They lay in silence for a while until Dani said, "What's three?"

Meredith took a breath and sighed it out through her nose. "You have to talk to Petra."

"I know. I have to apologize."

"You also have to tell her all these things you've told me."

"But that doesn't excuse what I did," Dani said.

"That's true. My mom says that to Mikey all the time. 'That *explains* your behavior, Mikey,'" Meredith imitated her mother, " 'but it doesn't *excuse* it.'"

"Your mother is wise," Dani said.

Meredith chuckled. "I'll tell her you said that."

"Please do. I need all the mother-in-law credits I can get."

Meredith laughed, but then Dani sighed and said, "I can't wait to go home. See everybody. See my room."

"Me, too," Meredith said. "Can we go home Friday after your ASL class? Or do you have a game?"

"Good question," Dani said. "Team Indigo plays on Monday."

"Against Laura's team, right?"

"Mm hmm," Dani said with a nod. "But, if they move me up to Team Cyan, then I play on both Monday and Friday, and we can't go home until Saturday morning."

"Have the new rosters been posted yet?"

"Oh, shoot," Dani said, bolting upright. "Let me check."

"Go on," Meredith nudged Dani toward the edge of the bed.

Dani knew her grin was kind of like a grimace as she slid off the bed in search of her phone. She stood next to the bed, tapping her foot impatiently as the lacrosse intramural website took its sweet time loading up.

"Week Three Rosters," she read off the screen and scanned the Team Cyan list. "Dang it," she said and grunted. "I didn't move up."

"Oh, honey," Meredith said. She was lying on her side now with her hand resting on her hip, elbow in the air. "But if we think positively, that means we can go home Friday afternoon."

Dani barely heard Meredith's words. If she thought this day couldn't get any worse, she was sadly mistaken.

Meredith sat up. "What's wrong?"

"I'm not on Team Indigo, either," Dani said as evenly as she could. "We have to go home on Saturday, after all. I'm on Team Magenta's roster."

"What?" Meredith leaped off the bed and peered over Dani's shoulder at the phone. "Laura demoted you? That lousy—"

"Stephanie makes that decision," Dani interrupted. Her blood pulsed in her head as her day-long headache threatened to return. She groaned.

"Baby, this really sucks. I don't know what to say."

"What is there to say?" Dani turned to face her girlfriend. "I mean, I have to take this demotion gracefully. Like I was going to do with you and Edward." She turned away from Meredith. "Like I'm going to have to do with the PSLA and with Petra."

A consoling arm went around her waist as a sympathetic head came to rest on her shoulder.

"Enough," Dani said, steeling herself. "I want to hear all about your day and the art exhibit and...all of it. Come on. Back up on the bed."

"So forceful," Meredith said but complied.

Once snuggle time was reinstated, Meredith's face lit up as she said, "One of the alums owns an art gallery, and he said my watercolor techniques were quite advanced for someone with my limited experience."

Dani smiled both inside and out as she listened to her girlfriend talk about the things she loved.

"I had so much trouble with the variegated transitions with the wet-on-wet technique."

Dani chuckled. "You know you're killing me with that."

Meredith smiled and bopped Dani on the nose. "My TA showed me a good technique for it, and I practiced and practiced until I got it. The alum even liked my mosaic paper piece. That is not my thing, though, that's for sure."

"But that's what your course is all about, right? Learning lots of different techniques and discovering ones you're good at?"

Meredith nodded. "You are so insightful. My favorite piece from the exhibit is the watercolor."

"Mine, too," Dani said. "Who am I kidding," she said with a laugh. "I loved them all. You're so good with oil paintings."

"The subject inspires me."

"I'm so..." Dani couldn't come up with the right word. "So loved."

"You are."

"So are you." That started a round of not-so-chaste kissing, which might have led to more, but Meredith broke away and said, "I forgot. I have something for you in my bag."

"Give it to me tomorrow." Dani tried to lean back in for more kisses, but Meredith pushed her away playfully. "No, I want to do it right now." Without waiting for a reply, she sat up, crawled over Dani, and made her way to her bag. She pulled out something and handed it to Dani. "I want you to have this."

"What is it?"

Meredith gestured for her to open the paper wrapping.

Dani pulled out something rectangular. She carefully undid the paper and was staring at the back of a picture frame.

"I will treasure it forever," she joked.

"Turn it over, silly," Meredith said.

Dani leaned in for another kiss, but her effort was thwarted again as Meredith stiff-armed her chest. "Aww, you're no fun."

"Turn it over."

Dani's heart melted when she saw the framed photograph. It was one of the selfies Dani had taken of the two of them at the rose garden that day. The beautiful red roses were the perfect backdrop for them, with their arms around each other's shoulders. She ran her fingers over their image. Tears filled her eyes as she looked up. "You're so thoughtful. You're so beautiful. Thank you for not wanting to be with that bearded guy."

Meredith smacked Dani on the shoulder playfully.

"And thanks for letting me be the epitome of Vulnerability 101 tonight," Dani continued. "I've always been the strong one in my friends' groups. The one who knows what to do and has it all together." She wiped her eyes because Meredith had become blurry. "But with you, I feel like I can…"

"Let your guard down a little?" Meredith suggested when Dani didn't finish her sentence.

"Yes. You understand me or seem to, anyway. I feel seen when I'm with you. And I'm beginning to slowly realize that I don't have to hold the world up for you. I mean, I'm still going to try, but you have to live your life, too."

"With you," Meredith added emphatically.

"Yes, I hope so," Dani said. She wiped at the last of her tears, hoping she had them under control. "Thank you for allowing me to not be perfect with you and to be…"

"Human," Meredith finished. "Come on. Snuggle time."

Once back in the bed, Meredith said, "Petra printed it for me on her fancy color laser printer. She wouldn't take any money."

"She's a good person. I have to make it right with her."

"Tomorrow," Meredith said. "Text her first thing, but let her set the time and place to meet. But she may not want to meet."

"I know," Dani said. "And then I'll spill my soul in a text."

"Yep," Meredith said. "And about Friday's game. You'll play for Team Magenta and keep your head held high as if this was a great thing. You'll meet new teammates, maybe learn new things." Meredith shrugged.

"Have you always been such an optimist?"

Meredith laughed. "Have you met me?" She laughed again. "Not at all, but I think it's the only thing you can do so Stephanie and Laura don't feel the satisfaction of trying to hurt you. Act like you don't care. Be that upbeat and cheery Dani I fell in love with."

Dani squirmed at Meredith's words. "I need to squeeze you right now."

"Oh?" Meredith said suggestively. "Need to boost your power center?"

"Mmm. Something like that."

Dani pulled her phone out of her pajama pants pocket and was just getting ready to power it down and toss it on her own bed when an incoming text dinged. She was about to ignore it, but she saw Petra's name.

"What is it?" Meredith asked.

"A text from Petra."

"Ooh, ooh, ooh," Meredith pushed Dani upright and then also sat up. "What did she say?"

"Let me read it." Before looking at the text message, Dani said, "I'm glad you're here with me for this."

Meredith rested her head on Dani's shoulder and rubbed Dani's arm with one hand.

"Okay," Dani said, ready to be blasted. "I bet she hates me."

"Just read it already."

Dani read the text out loud.

> PETRA: Kate told me I needed to send you this. She said you needed to see it.

"There's a link to a website," Dani said. "It's a video. She says she wants me to watch it, text her back *after* watching it, and we can set up a time before the homecoming game tomorrow. That's it. That's all she said."

"Click the link."

Dani's face flushed with fear. What was this? Petra's manifesto? Petra's public bashing of Dani?

"Click. The. Link," Meredith said again.

Dani clicked. It was a video of the PSLA meeting that morning. She watched herself on the tiny phone screen, bemoaning the caustic atmosphere created by the Student Association and then saying her words of praise for Petra. Whoever took the video stayed focused on Dani as she stormed out of the lecture hall, obviously fighting back tears. In the video, you could hear the door to the lecture hall close, and then the camera whipped around and zoomed in on Petra, who hadn't moved from her podium. She started to speak.

Dani couldn't mash the pause button fast enough. "I can't watch this.

Meredith squeezed Dani's arm in sympathy. Was there more of the video before this section Petra sent her? Was Petra saving the first part to shove down Dani's throat tomorrow? And what was Petra about to say in the video after Dani left?

"I can't," Dani repeated. "What if this is blowing up everyone's feed?"

"You can watch. And you will."

Dani looked Meredith in the eye and saw love and safety there. She took a deep breath but couldn't quite get it deep enough to calm her. Her heartbeat pulsed in her ears as tears fell down her cheeks.

"I hate this," Dani said.

"I've got you," Meredith said, pulling Dani close. "No matter what this is, I've got you."

Dani searched Meredith's eyes and again saw the security and reassurance she'd been seeking. She tried another deep breath and, this time, was able to calm herself enough to push play.

Chapter 21

Welcome to the Human Race

Dani held the door open so Petra could walk through it. It was Saturday morning, the day of the big homecoming football game, but that was the farthest thing from Dani's mind.

"Thanks for agreeing to go on a walk with me," Petra said. "My new therapist says it's a good idea for me to get exercise. Sane exercise. Not like I had been doing."

"I'm glad to help," Dani said. She didn't know what else to say. Seeing the video and texting Petra afterward to set up their meeting left her more confused than ever.

"Do you know a good route?"

"Oh, sure," Dani said. "I sometimes run down to Ensley and back, but that might be too far to walk."

"We'll play it by ear," Petra said and followed Dani's lead toward Mt. Olympus Drive, which would lead them past the Women's Building and onto Comstock Avenue.

They walked in silence for a while. Dani was absolutely going to let Petra lead this conversation.

"So, you watched that video?"

"Yes," Dani said succinctly.

"What did you think?"

"I'm not sure I deserved all those things you said."

"Hmm," Petra grunted and let it linger.

Dani couldn't read the tone, so didn't respond. Instead, she let Petra set the pace as they walked.

"Kate told me what you thought happened Friday morning between Meredith and her friend Edward," Petra finally continued. "I understand now why you were kind of cold in class and then weird at the debate. To be honest, I was surprised when you—" Petra stopped talking when a couple of students walked by, holding to-go coffees and chattering about the upcoming football game. "I was surprised, hurt, and frankly shocked when you were about to out me, when you were going to tell everyone something I had told you in confidence." Dani heard the anger and frustration in Petra's voice.

Remorse filled Dani's chest. "I know. I'm sorry. I am so sorry." She knew she needed to say more but couldn't find the words immediately. An uncomfortable silence grew until Dani broke it. "There are no excuses for what I did, Petra, and if you never want to talk to me again, I'll understand. But I'm grateful you're giving me a chance to explain some things. I thought my world had ended when I saw Meredith and Edward together. It was a reunion hug between two friends who'd found each other again, but I made immediate and erroneous assumptions. I misinterpreted what I saw."

"You know what they say when you assume," Petra said with a teasing lilt.

"Yeah, I know. And I did make an ass out of myself." Dani sighed and motioned for Petra to walk ahead of her on one section of narrow sidewalk. A tree's roots had decided to heave up the concrete on one side. "But that doesn't give me the right to ruin your life and betray your confidences. And just so you don't wonder about this for the rest of your life, I was never going to mention the eating disorder thing."

"Just the part about me seeing a therapist?"

"None of it was preplanned. I promise. I didn't go in thinking I was going to out you." Dani knew it sounded weak, but it was all she had at the moment. "You were talking about making counseling available to students, and I was fueled by Shela's insistence that I show some fierceness. But you know what? That pisses me off royally because I'm not the kind of person who is influenced by the crowd. I usually have my own thoughts. I was manipulated." Dani huffed. "But I can't blame them. I'm not blaming them. I'm just trying to figure out if I'm that kind of person. The kind of person who would attack a friend to move ahead, you know? Step on her back to get what I want."

"You're not."

"How can you be so sure?" Dani threw her hands out in front of her in obvious frustration. "I'm not even sure."

"I'm sure because I know you. And I also know I wasn't supposed to stay up there on the podium and take a third turn, but I could tell that you regretted your choice, and that's why you walked out. I needed the people in that lecture hall to know that."

"You told them I was a good person," Dani said quietly. "How could you defend me like that?"

"Because I knew something was off with you that morning. I didn't know what, and I wanted to make sure they didn't get the wrong impression of you." Petra cleared her throat and said, "Did you hear them clapping when you walked out?"

"Yeah."

"They were applauding because they were relieved that someone finally spoke up about the thing that was making everyone uncomfortable. No one liked attacking each other's weaknesses. Okay, that one guy, maybe."

Dani laughed because she knew exactly which guy Petra was referring to.

Petra continued, "I told them about your big heart. I told them how gracious you were telling them how I volunteered with the kids, but then I told them that it was you who had set up the whole outreach to the neighborhood kids in the first place. I told them how you make people feel seen and heard and that you listen, really listen. I told them how people gravitate to you because you're a natural-born leader, and you lead with grace. I've seen you, Dani. When Marti tried to take over the lacrosse clinic that first day, you handled it so well. I'm learning from you, and I told them that. And when I said that you will have my vote for one of the freshmen representative spots in the Student Association, I meant it."

Dani's chest tightened. Emotion bubbled up, and she had to stop walking as her tears began. "I don't deserve your kindness, Petra." She hid her eyes in one hand and tried to get her emotions in check. It wasn't happening.

Petra pulled her into a hug and murmured, "You're okay, Dani. I understand why you did what you did. I honestly do. I think we all learned something yesterday."

Dani shook her head and took a step back. "I keep reliving that moment, the moment I was about to go for your jugular. I was a crazed lunatic, Petra. What if that's the real me inside?"

"C'mon," Petra said, gesturing for them to start walking again. "I think we all have that fight instinct in us. That knock 'em down before they knock us down kind of mentality. It just makes us human, I guess. So, Dani, guess what?"

"What?" Dani wiped at her eyes again and breathed out a sigh.

"You just found out that you're human." Petra laughed and added, "Welcome to the human race, my friend."

Dani stopped walking abruptly. "Are we? Friends?"

"Of course," Petra said. "I'm proud to call you my friend.

"Same goes for me."

They started walking again, and Petra said, "Now, before you go and put me on some kind of pedestal, know that I'm human, too. That story I told about my two friends who were a couple but were afraid to come out?"

Realization dawned on Dani. "Oh, shit. You were talking about me and Meredith. I didn't even get that. Shit."

"Yep," Petra said. "I didn't exactly out you, but I put it right there for everyone to connect the dots. I'm not proud of that. And, so, I need to apologize to you, too."

"You absolutely do not need to apologize," Dani said and ignored Petra's insistence. "You know, the things you said about finding the people that don't feel safe was brilliant, and I'm still going to vote for you."

"You can't," Petra said. "I withdrew my name yesterday."

"No way," Dani said. "Because of me."

"No, not really," Petra said. "I realized that I'm not my dad, and I'm not really cut out to be a politician. Don't get me wrong. I love politics, and I'll find some other way to contribute. I have an idea if you're amenable."

"What's that?"

"I want to be your campaign manager."

Dani stopped all forward progress. "Wow, wow, wow. This is not how I pictured this talk going today."

"What do you say?"

"A million times, yes!" Dani hugged her friend and, when they started walking again, said, "You know, yesterday, when I thought I had lost both you and Meredith all in the same day, I was ready to pack up and leave. I was ready to transfer to Albany State."

"You were?"

"Yes. I couldn't bear to see your faces, knowing that Meredith never loved me and that I had betrayed a close friend. It was betrayal everywhere."

"Ah, but Meredith didn't betray you, and you didn't betray me." Petra stopped, turned, and said, "Let's head back. I suddenly have an appetite."

"I did kind of let the cat out of the bag about the therapy thing."

"But going to therapy shouldn't be a stigma," Petra said. "I mean, if more people understood that mental health is as important as physical health, then there wouldn't be so much shame around it."

"Ooh, ooh," Dani said, coming up with an idea. "You know the fitness center where Joiee works?"

"Mm hmm."

"That's a *physical* fitness center. What if there was, like, a *mental* fitness center you could go to? Just walk in and get a mental and emotional strength training session."

"Yes, yes," Petra said. "There could be little rooms where you get some counseling or simply have someone skilled and knowledgeable to talk to." She scoffed. "Wow, Dani, that is a great idea. I think you have something there."

"Maybe we could suggest that to the Student Association."

"And when you get elected, you can bring it up personally," Petra said seriously.

It was Dani's turn to scoff. "Doubt that."

"I don't know. A lot of people in the PSLA seem to like your style."

"Maybe not Shela and the seniors."

Petra laughed out loud. "It's time to change that culture."

"It is."

"How's lacrosse going, by the way?" Petra asked, changing the subject.

Dani's groan was so long that Petra finally asked, "What's going on?"

"I got put down to Team Magenta."

"That team you guys played last week? The pink team?"

"Yep."

"No way," Petra said. "You totally don't belong there. They weren't as skilled as you guys on Team Indigo. I was almost embarrassed for them, and now you're down there? No way. Something's going on."

Dani shrugged. "I think there's some kind of politics at work. Something to do with Laura."

"Are you serious?" Petra grunted. "Why do people think they can do shit like this? It's about power, you know. My dad says that all the time. 'Bunch of windbags,' he says when the assembly convenes. He says they just like to hear themselves talk and feel more important than they are."

"Could be something like that," Dani said. "Meredith thinks I need to talk to Laura, not only about this move to Team Magenta, but the whole incident that night at the first practice."

"You should. If nothing comes of it, then at least you'll have had your say, right?"

"Mm hmm," Dani said in a way that clearly conveyed how much she did *not* want to talk to Laura.

"So," Petra said in such a way that Dani knew that another subject change was imminent. "Kate told me all about you guys coming out at the art show. I'm so glad you finally did. She and I have known for a long time."

"You have?"

"Yeah. It's hard not to see two people who are so into each other."

"We were waiting to get a feel for things before coming out."

"Understandable," Petra said. "But I was one hundred percent sure that day when Meredith asked me to print the picture of you two in the rose garden. I thought to myself, 'Here are two people in love and not able to show it.' I felt so bad for you guys. You know? Afraid to come out and all. Kate and I were and still are rooting for you."

"Thanks," Dani said. "I'm not sure how our lives are going to change now that we're out, but knowing we have your support, and Kate's and Joiee's and Edward's and Derek's, we'll at least have a safety net."

"Who's Derek?"

Dani explained who Derek was and how Edward's eyes had almost fallen out of his face when he saw Derek at the art show. At Petra's urging, Dani told her a bit more about the evening at the art show.

"Oh, oh, oh," Dani said excitedly. "I forgot. I didn't even tell Meredith. I met Senator Winthrop last night."

"Holy shit, you did?"

"Yeah, he and his wife are SU alums. We talked politics and policy-making and all kinds of stuff. He gave me his business card." Dani paused for a moment and mused out loud, "Where did I put that thing? Blazer pocket, I think. Anyway, he wants me to call his assistant. I might intern for him this summer in Albany."

"Dani, see? Yesterday wasn't a complete wreck."

"Maybe you're right." They had reached the road leading back up to the dorms. "Hey, can I post to our group chat of four that you and I are okay?"

"Good idea," Petra said. "Kate is probably 'literally' dying to know what we're saying to each other right now."

Dani burst out laughing. "I bet she is. Meredith, too, but not the dying part." She pulled out her phone and tapped open the group chat app the four of them used.

DANI: All is well.

"Can't you just hear Kate and Meredith cheering in the dorm?" Petra asked with a laugh. "Let me add something to that."

PETRA: Meet us for breakfast in the dining hall.

PETRA: Three minutes.

"There," Petra said. "That ought to pique their curiosity."

Dani laughed, tapped Petra on the shoulder, and said, "Race you to the door. Last one there has to bus the trays."

Petra took up the challenge, and Dani wasn't sure how, but Petra beat her to the door. Oh, well. Bussing Petra's tray was the least she could do for her.

Over breakfast, Dani and Petra gave their roommates a summary of their talk, and Dani felt better about the events. She still thought of herself as a complete and utter jerk for doing what she'd done during the debate, but Petra had forgiven her. Kate had a million questions, of course, but Dani and Petra handled themselves like true politicians and only answered the questions they wanted to.

Dani and Petra hugged as they went their separate ways after breakfast—after Dani bussed her tray, that is. Kate made them promise to meet in her room at precisely five o'clock to get ready for the homecoming game at seven-thirty. She reminded them that the game was going to be on ESPN2, and they needed to look like superfans.

Once back in the room, Meredith pulled Dani into a healing hug. "You okay?"

"It went well," Dani said. "She was very forgiving and seemed to mean everything she said on that video."

"Is she going to have it taken down?"

"The video?"

Meredith nodded.

"No, she said even though the guy that posted it did so without her permission, she wants to leave it up there as a kind of advertisement for my campaign."

"You have a campaign? For the Student Association election?"

"I guess I do now." Dani shrugged. "And Petra volunteered to be my campaign manager."

"Wow. That's amazing."

"It's her call, but I guess she and I are friends again."

They settled down at their respective desks, determined to get their Women's Studies reading done, but Dani couldn't sit still. "Baby, I'm too antsy. Would it be okay if I texted Amanda or some of my former Indigo teammates to practice lacrosse stuff?"

"You don't have to ask my permission," Meredith said with a chuckle. "I can tell you have a lot of nervous energy. Go play. I have a ton of Spanish homework to do, anyway. These darn accents are killing me. I may ask Petra for help."

"Good idea."

Dani pulled out her phone and texted Amanda.

DANI: I can't sit still. Are you up for some LAX drills?

Amanda didn't respond right away, but Dani threw on sweats and a T-shirt anyway. She could work on feints and dodges and changing the level of her stick all by herself. She would look weird, but who cared? Her phone dinged an incoming text.

AMANDA: Perfect. Meet you at the field in fifteen. Is it okay if Suzanne comes, too?

DANI: The more, the merrier. I want to work on that reverse fake move you've perfected.

AMANDA: Glad to show you. BTW, you didn't deserve that Team Magenta move.

DANI: I don't know why I got moved. Maybe I suck.

AMANDA: No, you don't suck. I'll see you on the field in a few.

Dani put on her new Syracuse sweatshirt that her parents bought her the day she moved into the dorm and then snuck a peek at Meredith over her shoulder. Meredith often wore contact lenses, but that morning, she was wearing her black-rimmed glasses. Her hair was scattered perfectly all over the place. She was reading a workbook while chewing on the end of her felt-tip pen. She loved felt-tip pens and had them in every color imaginable. The one currently in her teeth was purple. Meredith loved purple.

"What?" Meredith said without looking. "I can feel you staring at me."

Dani shuffled over to her girlfriend and got down on her knees. She lay her head in Meredith's lap and sighed. A caressing hand reached out and stroked Dani's cheek and forehead. A finger ran the curves along Dani's ear. "You okay?" Meredith asked softly.

Dani simply nodded. She had been through so many different emotions over the past day and a half that it was nice to have a serene moment like this.

Dani sat back on her heels, looked up at her girlfriend, and said, "I love you, Merry."

Meredith smiled, nestled Dani's chin in the top of her fist, and said, "I love you, too, Dani."

"I just wanted to make sure you knew," Dani said as she stood up.

"I know," Meredith said. She swiveled in her seat as Dani made her way to the door. "Have fun, my love."

"I will." Dani raced back for one last kiss before leaving for the field.

"Mmm," Meredith said. "Don't distract me. Necesito aprender cosas nuevas."

"Ooh, that sounded good," Dani said, understanding none of it. Maybe she needed to take Spanish, too. That might help her political career at some point. "Have fun, baby."

"You, too," Meredith said and turned back to her Spanish workbook.

Dani let herself out and closed the door softly. She shrugged her lacrosse backpack on and held her stick in her hand. She flew down the four flights of stairs and then ran all the way to the field. She was out of breath when she got there, but she didn't care. She needed to get serious about her lacrosse game if she was ever going to prove to someone, anyone, that she was good enough to play on the varsity team.

"But what if no one sees me the way I see myself?" she muttered. "What if

206

I really am no good at this game?"

Chapter 22

Outliers

There was a chill in the air on Monday morning as Dani walked Meredith to her Spanish class, but Dani barely noticed because she and Meredith were holding hands the entire way. They got a few double-takes from some of the other students and even got a wolf whistle from some guy, but no one bothered them otherwise.

Dani let Meredith lead when it came time to say goodbye and was pleasantly surprised when Meredith threw her arms around Dani's neck, said she was going to miss her all day, and gave her a chaste peck on the lips. And that was fine. No, it was more than fine. For them to be able to show their affection for each other was life-alteringly amazing.

Dani, feeling good, practically skipped to the fitness center for a quick workout before hitting up the Department of Building and Property Use office at precisely nine o'clock a.m. She got in a good workout, and later, as she sat in the waiting room in the Admin Building, she smiled at the memory of Joiee commenting how much better Dani seemed that morning. Dani gave Joiee a brief summary of her weekend with Meredith, which made Joiee smile and say that she 'loved love' and that it seemed like Meredith was the perfect partner for Dani.

"She is," Dani said out loud in the waiting room.

"Who is?" a woman asked, a grin spreading on her face.

"What?" Dani realized where she was and that she'd just said the words out loud. "Oh, nothing. I'm here to see someone about reserving an indoor gym somewhere on campus."

"C'mon in," the woman said. "I believe I spoke with you last time you were here reserving the lacrosse field for your clinics or something."

"Yes, yes," Dani said. "I'm sorry, I've forgotten your name. I'm Danielle Lassiter." She stuck out her hand like a true politician and almost laughed at herself.

"Ellen Martin," the woman said and shook Dani's hand.

Once seated at Ellen's desk, Dani started at the beginning and explained how the lacrosse clinics had gotten started, but now that the cold weather was coming in, she wanted an indoor place where the kids could go and run around after school.

"Listen," Ellen said, sitting back in her swivel chair. "I appreciate your intentions."

When Ellen paused, Dani said, "I feel a 'but' coming on."

Ellen laughed. "Exactly. There is way too much liability to simply open up a gymnasium to non-university civilians. It can be done, but there's a lot of paperwork and liability on all sides."

Dani blew out a sigh, her cheeks inflating dramatically as she did so.

"I have an idea, though," Ellen said. "If you're amenable." She leaned forward and started typing something on her keyboard. "Here it is." She turned the screen to show Dani the after-school programs in the county. "It seems like the elementary school your neighborhood kids go to only has an after-hours pickup program. The kids basically sit in a classroom and do homework until their parents pick them up after work."

Dani grimaced. "Sounds like an after-school study hall. That's not fun."

"Exactly," Ellen said with a chuckle. She clicked her mouse a few times, typed something in, and turned the screen back toward Dani. "Many schools have afterschool program partners. See here?" She pointed to a list. "Griffin Elementary partners up with the YMCA. Your school, Tungsten, is close enough to a YMCA that they could partner up." She made a few more clicks, and a map popped up on the screen.

"See here? It's less than five miles from Tungsten Elementary to the YMCA on Westcott." She clicked the YMCA link and rooted around until she found what she was looking for. "Here it is. The YMCA provides transportation from the school to its center. Looks like it costs, wow, only $50

209

per semester per student."

"What if the kids can't afford the fee?"

"There may be scholarships or reduced rates or something." Ellen pulled out one of her business cards and wrote a name and number on the back of it. "Call Marguerite Reynolds at this number. Tell her Ellen Martin from SU referred you. She's a former 'close friend,' if you know what I mean, but we're still on speaking terms." She sat back and laughed. "Ahh, life."

Dani couldn't help smiling with her. "Yep, I know the feeling."

Ellen grinned at Dani, it was a knowing grin, and then she said, "You and your friends could volunteer at the Y or something. It sounds like you want to help these kids, and I'm all for that."

"We do, but I'll have to do some more research on all of this," Dani said. "This might be a good solution, though."

"You have to get the cooperation of the school, of course, but Marguerite will probably be able to help you with that or, in the least, direct you to someone who can help."

"This has been great," Dani said as she stood up. "Thank you so much for your help."

"Hey, we sapphic sisters have to help each other, right?" Ellen chuckled and shook Dani's hand.

Dani tried not to choke on Ellen's words. The woman had basically outed herself to Dani and, at the same time, seemed to know that Dani was a 'sapphic sister,' too. Wow. Maybe there was this whole network of queer people who helped each other. That was also something to look into. She said her goodbyes again and headed out the door. She wanted to run to Meredith's next class in the art building and tell her what happened, but that was silly. She would wait until this afternoon's Women's Studies class to tell her. In the meantime, she had a little reading to do for her ASL class at noon. She found a bench, pulled the hood up on her sweatshirt, and sat down. Just as she was about to take out her laptop, her phone rang.

Meredith? No, it was a number she didn't recognize, but it was an Albany area code. She usually let calls like that go to voice mail, but for some reason, she answered it.

"Hello?"

"Is this Danielle Lassiter?" It was a youngish male voice.

"Yes," she answered tentatively.

"This is Bennie Rabinowitz from Senator Winthrop's office. How are you today?"

Dani almost choked. She had almost forgotten about meeting the Senator over the weekend.

"I'm doing well, thank you. Busy, but well." She hoped that was an acceptable answer, which made her sound grown up and responsible because she wasn't sure if this Bennie person was actually interviewing her at the moment.

"Good busy, I hope," Bennie said.

"College busy," Dani said with a smile, hoping he'd hear the friendliness in her voice.

"I remember those days," he said with a teasing lilt to his voice. "Well, let me get right to it then. Senator Winthrop and his wife were quite taken with you at their alumni weekend at 'cuse, and he wanted me to reach out and walk you through the application process. If you give me your email, I'll send you the link to apply. Obviously, there are never any guarantees that he'll select you to intern for him, but he wanted me to make sure your application gets on the top of the stack. How does that sound?"

Dani chuckled. "A bit overwhelming, actually. But I am interested, and I live in the Albany area."

"Oh, that's even better. We won't have to find housing for you then."

"What exactly does an intern do?"

"All kinds of things," Bennie said. "Every day will probably be different, depending on what the needs are. You might answer phones, run errands, or do research for the senator. All in all, this opportunity might be better than any college course you could take because you'll be learning the ins and outs of the legislative process firsthand in real time."

"Sign me up," Dani said. It sounded exactly like the experience she needed. She gave him her Syracuse email address and thanked him for his time.

"I'll send that app link to you imminently," Bennie said. "If you don't get it, then call me back on this number."

Dani thanked him again, and after they said their goodbyes, she hustled to save his number in her contacts.

As she sat in the sunshine, her entire body buzzed. "Wow," she said out loud, looking but not seeing the grass in the quad. "Just. Wow."

She desperately wanted to go bug Meredith now and tell her all about her phone call, but she didn't want to seem too needy. And, besides, Meredith was in class. Dani shivered. She hadn't known early October could be so cold in Syracuse, and it wasn't even close to winter yet. She tightened the drawstring on her hoodie and got up to find a warm place to study. She had a couple of hours before her ASL class but wanted to brush up on her signs. After the break, the midterm would consist of an actual conversation in ASL with one of the TAs. The other was a written part covering the history, culture, and heritage of deaf people. Dani never knew that there were expected cultural behaviors in deaf communities, like waving, tapping someone's arm or shoulder, stamping a foot, or banging on furniture to get someone's attention. Deaf people, she learned, seemed to touch a lot during conversations and use exaggerated facial expressions.

She was heading for the building where her ASL class was held when a familiar face came into view. She stopped and waited until their paths connected.

"Hey, Kate," Dani said. "Going to class?"

"Yep," Kate said and linked arms with Dani. "Come with."

Dani looked at her like she had two heads. "Go to class with you?"

"Yep. You don't have class for a couple of hours, and I think this particular lecture will be right up your alley."

"What is—"

"It kind of fits right in with your burning desire."

Dani's eyebrows shot to the sky.

Kate burst out laughing. "Your desire to create a safe place for those neighborhood kids."

Dani groaned. "Oh, my God, Kate. You scared me."

"I know." Kate turned Dani around, and they headed back the way Dani had just come. For some reason, Dani went with her.

"Do you always drag strange people to class with you?"

Kate laughed and said, "You're not that strange." She laughed again and broke out into a semi-run, semi-walk dragging Dani behind her. "Last one in the door, busses the dinner trays." She let go of Dani's arm and sprinted ahead.

"Cheater," Dani said, hustling after Kate but letting her cheating friend win.

They found seats on one side of the lecture hall, and Dani couldn't help but feel that people were looking at her. Maybe the news that she and Meredith were a couple had begun to spread. Hopefully, Meredith wasn't feeling like a zoo animal like Dani was right now.

Kate stomped her foot, leaned over Dani, and said to a couple of her classmates in their row, "Yes, this is her."

Before she had a chance to ask Kate what she was talking about, one of the two said, "You are our hero."

Dani looked behind her.

"They're talking to you, cheeseball," Kate said with a laugh.

"Why?" Dani said directly to the one who had spoken.

"One of my floormates is in the PissyLA club and positively hates all that hate talk." She turned to her friend sitting next to her, "Right?"

"Pfft," the friend spat. "Yeah."

The first one said, "You have my vote for that student group, whatever it is."

"Thanks," Dani said, stunned.

The other said to her friend, "It's cool to see a living, breathing example of someone with integrity." She leaned over her friend and said to Dani, "We're going to tell all our friends to vote for Danielle."

"That's cool, you guys," Kate interceded. "She's one of the best candidates, if not *the* best."

Dani leaned close and whispered, "You don't know who the other candidates are."

"Hush, you," Kate said. "Petra deputized me as an assistant campaign manager." She pointed toward the front. The professor had entered the lecture hall and was getting ready to start the class.

"What class is this?" Dani whispered.

"Intro to Social Work," Kate said. She put her finger over her lips as the lights dimmed and a PowerPoint presentation shone on the big screen in the front of the hall.

"Good morning," the professor greeted the students cheerfully. "Social work, as you've been learning, is a many-faceted endeavor. Last week, we discussed Gerontology and the various programs and opportunities for working with older adults. We want to make sure they are not only taken care of but thrive. Hey, working in Gerontology is kind of a win-win because, at some point, we're all going to be part of that group."

There was a polite group chuckle, Dani included.

The professor gestured toward her PowerPoint. The title was "Child Welfare and Public Policy."

"Today is about the kids. When people hear that someone wants to be a social worker, they question why anyone would want to do it. Perhaps some of you have already gotten a raised eyebrow or two when you said you wanted to study social work."

There were many head nods in the lecture hall, Kate's included.

"And the reason people get these ideas is most likely from the movies. They always depict overworked and overtired social workers with way too many cases that can't possibly be handled properly or well, and the kids in these movies never thrive unless a superhero steps in." She took an exaggerated breath after her over-long sentence.

Once the polite chuckles died out again, she said, "Now, please let me be clear. There is a national shortage of qualified social workers. Children and families do fall through the cracks. But honestly, I'm encouraged that so many of you sitting in this lecture hall want to help. So, bravo to you." She raised her arms and clapped her hands while she took in every section of the hall. The students followed her example and clapped along with her.

"Aww, shucks," Kate said and brushed imaginary dust off her shoulder.

When the self-congratulatory applause died down, the professor said, "It's also true that there is a shortage of relevant and cost-effective programs. Funding is always a struggle. So, before we go into some case studies of various child and family well-being programs, I want to lift the curtain a bit and help you understand how these services are rendered."

She nodded at her TA who changed the slide. "You have an idea. A program to help the kids in your area or in your charge, but you need funding. Funding gets you venues, people, programs, and whatever it is you need for your great idea. What kind of program is it? Preventative, enrichment, safety, substance abuse, domestic violence? An after-school program, perhaps?"

At the mention of after-school programs, Dani went to smack Kate just as Kate went to smack Dani, and their hands cracked into each other. Dani swallowed her groan and grimaced at Kate, who seemed to be the same.

"Your state, county, city, or town may have money for you. But there's always an application and hoops to jump through, right?"

Heads nodded.

"This is a case study of a county in Florida." The professor pointed to the picture of a group of students building small robotic crawlers. "A group of college students wanted funding to host an after-school robotics club at a local high school. This particular high school had a high dropout rate, and the college students were hoping to find a way to capture the kids' interest and keep them in school.

"Apparently, the group submitted a proposal but weren't deemed funding-eligible because their program didn't satisfy the terms of the grant. The fund-granting division of that county didn't feel it had a wide enough reach that it wouldn't service enough students to be worth the amount they were asking for. So even though it fits into the category of 'Innovation Program for Youth,' they didn't get their project approved."

Dani frowned. She'd been so gung-ho about a possible YMCA after-school program for Natalie and the other kids that she hadn't realized the process would be a complicated one. The professor gave another example as the next slide popped up, showing a beautifully typed proposal.

"This proposal was for a program for at-risk youth that was beautifully

215

written, but since they'd submitted it a day after the deadline, it was rejected. One day late."

Dani groaned along with the rest of the students.

"Do you see now why due dates are so important?" She made an amused face, and the students laughed with her.

The professor's final example was of a proposal that actually managed to get funding in an Ohio county near Cincinnati. It was a program designed to give some kind of cash assistance to single mothers with children. The single mother and the children had to meet certain criteria, but the main idea was to keep families together.

"An ounce of prevention," the professor said but didn't finish her thought. "Government officials create public policies and laws that, in theory, work for the betterment of the public. What programs or situations get funding depends on these public policies. Government officials must understand what the public needs. Social work and government go hand in hand. Social workers are on the front lines. They know what the community needs. Social workers are the main group that must remind and inform our elected officials about the needs of their constituents."

"Exactly," one of the students shouted.

The professor nodded at him and then said, "Sometimes, these officials need to be educated. Many have never lived in poverty or with domestic violence or substance abuse. Many turn a blind eye to the needs of others as their aspirations for political gain take them over. They are not the enemy, though. They are the ones who hold the strings and keep our work going." She let the students absorb that information and repeated, "Government is not the enemy; government is the source. Social workers are the stewards of that source, looking after the needs of the people."

Dani wondered if there was any kind of lobby group for social workers. If the Rifle Association could have a lobby, couldn't social workers? As if reading her mind, the professor said, "The National Association of Social Workers has a great resource." She pointed to the slide that had just come up on the screen. "It's their PDF file called 'NASW Lobby Day Tool Kit' and is, of course, on your reading list. You'll use this document as a guide for a proposed meeting with a fictitious government official.

"After midterms," the professor continued, "we start field trips. This semester, we'll visit four venues. An assisted living facility, a drug treatment program, a mental health facility, and an after-school program. After the trips, you'll come up with something to lobby an elected official about.

"Obviously, we'll talk more about that part later," the professor said and looked down at her notes. "But for now, let's go back to services provided for children."

Dani listened to the lecture going on around her, but her brain was also busy trying to make sense of it all.

When the class was over, Kate wrapped her arm in Dani's again as they headed out. "What did you think?"

"This is what I want to do," Dani said as the puzzle pieces were coming together in her head.

"Be a social worker?"

"No. I mean yes, but no. Okay, kind of."

"Huh?" Kate's comically confused expression made Dani laugh. Yeah, she wasn't making any sense.

"I don't necessarily want to be the boots on the ground like you and your classmates, but I want the role of helping you all. Finding the funding. Legislating the funding. Making the laws. You know, like, I want to be part of the legislation that helps programs get implemented. I want to be the one the NASW lobbyists approach to share their thoughts and concerns. I want..." Dani hesitated because she wasn't exactly sure what she wanted. "Working at Senator Winthrop's office this summer will help me figure out if that's what I really want."

"Whoa, you're working for a senator?"

"No, not yet," Dani stammered. "I'm getting my cart before my horse." She relayed her chance meeting with the senator and his wife during the alumni weekend and added. "I mean, I haven't even filled out the application yet."

"Yeah," Kate said with a laugh. "Cart. Horse. Wrong order."

They laughed, and then Kate excused herself to run to her next class.

Energized, Dani headed to Schine for a quick bite to eat and a study period before her ASL class. Her soul was bursting. Had she found her calling? It felt like it. She resisted the burning urge to call Meredith and tell her about everything that had happened so far. Who said Mondays were the worst day of the week?

Dani tossed her lunch remnants and headed toward her noon ASL class. She jumped when her phone rang and was disappointed to see that it wasn't Meredith. Normally, she let unknown calls go directly to voice mail because, as Millie had advised her, they'll leave a message if it's important. But this wasn't a normal day.

"Hello," Dani asked cautiously, ready to hang up in an instant.

"Oh, hey," the youngish female voice said. "Joiee gave me your number. I hope that was okay. My name is Mo, and Joiee said you're looking to set up a self-defense class for your dorm floor."

"Yes, yes, yes," Dani said. "Can you help with that?"

"Absolutely," Mo said. "Joiee gave me the deets, but I wanted to go over them with you just to make sure."

They spent a few minutes talking about the basic skills Mo and her crew would go over and that a smaller group was definitely the way to go.

"I'll give your RA a call," Mo said, "and together, she and I can coordinate some dates to work with. How does that sound?"

"Like a dream," Dani said, which made Mo laugh.

"Joiee speaks quite highly of you, Dani," Mo said. "She told me not to recruit you for the Rugby club."

It was Dani's turn to laugh, and then she said, "Strictly lacrosse here."

"Ahh," Mo said. "Maybe we can change your mind sometime. At the very least, you and your friends should come down to a game after break. Joiee's the trainer for us sometimes."

"That would be cool," Dani said, and meant it. "Hey, what's this whole club thing all about, anyway? You guys play other schools and travel, right?"

Mo answered affirmative to Dani's questions and then told her that, although they weren't a varsity team, there was enough interest not only at Syracuse but all over the country for them to have competitive games.

Dani had a million more questions but couldn't ask them. "Hey, listen, Mo. I'm sorry, but I have to cut this short. I have a class to get to."

They said their goodbyes, with Mo promising to try and recruit Dani again, making Dani burst out laughing. After ending the call, Dani headed to class, floored that a Monday was turning into the complete opposite of Friday.

She got to her ASL class right on time and muttered a quote from her statistics professor, "'Outliers are anything but average.'"

Chapter 23

Be Yourself

Dani's Monday afternoon ASL class went well, and she found that communicating with sign language was becoming much more natural. She finally got to see Meredith that afternoon in the Women's Studies course they took together, but there wasn't any time before the class to tell her everything that had happened that day.

After the class, they strolled toward the dorm hand in hand. "I love this," Meredith said, squeezing Dani's hand.

Dani squeezed back. "Me, too." She was desperate to spill her news but didn't want to hog the conversation. "Tell me about your day."

They headed up the covered walkway toward their dorm, and before Meredith could say anything, Dani said, "Wait. Something's weird here."

"Whoa! They cut down the overgrown stuff," Meredith said excitedly. "Look how clearly you can see Flanagan gym."

"This is great," Dani gushed.

"Somebody in that Student Association heard you."

"Do you really think so?"

"You have a way of making people see the obvious."

Dani narrowed her eyes at Meredith as they walked up the steps. "What do you mean?"

"For instance, I didn't see my attraction to you for months," Meredith said. "Months," she repeated. "But you were calmly persistent, calmly present until I finally saw that I was in love with you."

Dani squeezed Meredith's hand again. "Well, I'm glad you finally saw it." She laughed and added, "It only took you forever."

Meredith pulled her hand from Dani's, smacked her in the chest with it, and then reached down to hold Dani's hand again.

"Ow," Dani said pitifully as she rubbed her chest with her free hand.

"Stop yer bellyaching," Meredith said, imitating Millie. She cleared her throat, leaned in, and whispered, "I'll rub that out for you when we get home."

Dani almost choked on Meredith's words. She couldn't think of an adequate reply and instead increased her speed up the steps, pulling Meredith along behind her. "Hurry," she said, making Meredith laugh.

Once inside their room, Dani kissed Meredith silly and then demanded to hear about her day.

"After the break," Meredith said without hesitating, "my art class is going to an assisted living facility for seniors, and we're going to do art therapy with the residents there. In small groups, of course. I'll have five or six people. I have to find a project that they can do. I have to submit my proposal when we get back from break."

"That's so cool. Where is the—" Dani didn't get a chance to finish.

"Did you know that within the College of Visual and Performing Arts, there's a department called Creative Arts Therapy?"

"Cool," Dani said. She had *not* known. "What does it—"

"You can get a master's degree in art therapy. A Master of Science degree." Meredith looked Dani in the eye. "This might be what I want to do, Dani."

"I can tell. I've never seen you this passionate."

Meredith scowled, and Dani quickly amended, "Passionate about school. School and careers. That's what I meant."

"Better," Meredith said, pulling Dani into a hug. She kissed Dani on the lips, released her, and said, "Tell me about your day."

"This is going to take a while," Dani said.

"Are we playing with the kids today?" Meredith interrupted.

"No, but there's a game this afternoon. Cyan versus my former Indigo."

"Let's go watch."

"O-kay," Dani said tentatively, wondering if Meredith was up to something. "Why?"

"I want to hold your hand. I want a certain someone to see us."

Dani smirked. "You have a devious mind, Ms. Bedford."

"Thank you. Now chop, chop. Time to get ready. And on the way, I want to hear all about your day."

Walking hand in hand toward the lacrosse field, Dani told Meredith about the possible YMCA after-school program, the call with the Senator's assistant, getting dragged to Kate's social work class, and finally about the call from Mo, who was going to set up the self-defense sessions for their dorm.

When Dani finally stopped to take a breath, Meredith said, "Honey, all of that is amazing. *And* you found time to work out this morning. You're superhuman."

Dani burst out laughing and said, "Like you, I may have found what I want to do with my Poly Sci degree." She relayed her epiphany about helping important programs get funding and how she would like to ensure they did by making and interpreting laws.

"That's incredible," Meredith said and added a squeeze of the hand. "I hope you get that internship with the senator. That'll open your eyes for sure."

"Right?"

They reached the fence leading into the field area, and Dani opened the gate for Meredith to pass through first.

"Always a gentlewoman," Meredith quipped.

The two teams were doing their pregame warmups on opposite ends of the field as Dani and Meredith walked toward the bleachers. Dani felt weird not being dressed and ready to play. Shoot, she hadn't thought about what her former teammates would say to her. She stiffened her spine as they walked.

"Miss Dani, Miss Dani," someone yelled.

Dani turned to find Natalie running toward them.

"Hey, kid," Dani said. "What's up?" She was super conscious of still holding Meredith's hand, but it didn't seem to faze Natalie one bit.

"I thought you said you had a game tonight." Natalie put her hands on her hips and scowled.

"I got moved down a level."

"No way," Natalie said. "Your league is stupid. How are you supposed to, like, bond with your teammates or whatever if they keep moving you around?"

"That is a really good question." Dani shrugged and said, "That's how they do it. But no worries because we have kids' day with Marti on Wednesday and another on Friday. I'll be playing on Friday with a new team, Team Magenta."

"The pink team," Natalie said glumly. "Are you going to watch this game?"

"Yep," Meredith said. "For a little while, anyway."

Dani smirked at her girlfriend. They'd stay long enough for Laura to see them holding hands or whatever else Meredith had in mind.

"C'mon," Dani said. "Let's head up the middle bleacher since we're not really rooting for any one team tonight, right?"

"Right," Natalie said as they started walking toward the stands.

"Natalie Puttman, you come here right now," a voice yelled from somewhere off to their right.

"Oh, no," Natalie said. "It's my mom."

"You have to go?" Dani asked.

"Yeah, she's home early." Natalie hung her head, took one step toward the hole in the fence, and then turned around. "What to meet my mom?"

Dani wasn't sure she wanted to, especially because Natalie's mother sounded so angry. But Natalie seemed to want her to, so she said, "Okay, lead the way."

Meredith went with them but let go of Dani's hand before reaching the hole in the fence. They didn't reach for each other's hands as they approached the car.

Natalie opened the passenger door and said, "Mom, this is Miss Dani and Miss Meredith."

"Well, it's nice to finally put faces to names," Natalie's mother said. She looked to be in her mid to late thirties and was dressed professionally. She had obviously just come from work. "All she's been talking about is lacrosse and Miss Dani this and Miss Meredith that. These lacrosse sessions you have with the kids are very generous. Thank you." Natalie's mother's smile included both Dani and Meredith.

"We're having a lot of fun, too," Dani said. She was about to tell Natalie's mother that it was nice to meet her and that she had to get back to the game, but something bubbled up inside, and she blurted out the plan about Natalie's school possibly partnering with the YMCA for after-school programs.

"They have all kinds of sports and art sessions," Dani continued. She looked at Meredith, who was smiling at the mention of art. "And transportation would be included. Of course, we haven't even gotten the ball rolling yet, but I hate to see the kids with nothing to do once our league is over."

"That is very thoughtful, Dani," Natalie's mother said. "And you had no way of knowing, but I'm a new member of her school's PTA, so I am going to chat up that group. Maybe put some pressure on the school's administration."

"That would be fantastic," Dani gushed. She wasn't sure what to add but didn't need to because apparently young Miss Natalie had a dentist appointment to go to.

"Sorry, kid," Dani said as she backed away from the car.

Natalie muttered something that Dani didn't quite catch and then said, "See you Wednesday."

"Bye, Natalie," Dani and Meredith said at the same time. They waved as the car drove away and then headed for the bleachers, holding hands.

They didn't get far. Laura stopped in front of them and said, "Can I talk to you?" This was obviously said to Dani.

"Sure," Dani said, wondering if Laura wanted to gloat or rub it in or whatever. She turned to Meredith, whose hand she was still holding, and said, "I'll be right up." She leaned in and got what she sought. A kiss. She grinned at Meredith and bopped her in the nose as if to say, "There you go. A certain someone now knows we're an item."

Laura stood with her hands on her hips and waited until Meredith walked away. "It wasn't my call. I told her not to move you, but dammit, I knew she was going to. It was personal for her."

"Stephanie?" Dani asked, utterly confused.

"Yes."

"What did I ever do to her?"

"She thought I was seeing you behind her back."

It took a moment for Laura's words to form meaning. "You're dating Stephanie?" Before Laura could answer, Dani blurted, "Behind Joiee's back." It was a statement, not a question. Dani pointedly turned her head toward Joiee.

"Yeah, I messed that one up, didn't I?"

"It's not up to me to decide," Dani said succinctly.

"I did," Laura admitted and hung her head. "Joiee's one of the good ones. I didn't want to lose her, so that's why I asked her to move in with me sophomore year." She looked up and then lickety-split changed the subject. "Two things, Dani. One, Sara from Team Magenta was as shocked as I was that you got moved to her team, so next week, she's taking my recommendation and moving you all the way up to Team Cyan."

Dani had no words. What kind of games were these people playing?

"We're not doing it out of pity or anything. You've been steadily improving, and I was going to recommend that you move up next week anyway."

"Thank you for that," Dani said, still not sure what to think. "What's the second thing?"

"I was going to ask you out for a drink, but I guess I lost my chance." She glanced up toward Meredith in the bleachers. "Is this new?"

"Me and Meredith? Not really. We've been together since May."

"Ahh," Laura said. "So, I guess my apology is overdue. I'm sorry I pulled my dumb ass Don Juan moves on you in the locker room that night. That completely wasn't fair to you."

"Thank you for the apology," Dani said, but she wasn't going to let Laura off the hook just yet. "You know Joiee told me you have a good heart."

"She said that?"

Dani nodded. "She also said you were lousy at relationships."

Laura burst out laughing. "Yeah. I have to work on that."

The teams on the field were wrapping up their pregame warmup, but an idea struck Dani right between the eyes. "Why isn't there a club lacrosse team? You know, like the club rugby team?"

"There's no varsity rugby," Laura said. "So the club is as high as they can go."

"That's what I thought, too. But softball has both a varsity team and a club team. They play different schools. They're obviously in different leagues, but everyone still gets to wear an SU jersey of one sort or another."

"Hmm," Laura said, getting a faraway look in her eye. "We should talk more about this. Have lunch. Or that drink."

Dani grinned. "No to both lunch and drinks, but yes, we should talk at some point."

Laura's expression changed, and not for the better.

"Just talk," Dani reiterated.

"Fine, fine," Laura said. "I gotta go." And without further ado, she spun around and ran back to her team.

On Wednesday afternoon, Dani headed down to the lacrosse session with the neighborhood kids by herself while Meredith went back up to the dorm to do their laundry so they could pack for their trip home Saturday morning. Seriously, fall break could not come soon enough. Dani wanted to pack dirty clothes and have her mom do them at home, but Meredith just blinked at her and said, "It puts the dirties in the basket." Dani had to give in, but obviously, this would mean that Dani owed Meredith one laundry day after break. And that was okay. She would do anything for Meredith.

Wednesday with the kids felt really good. Her old Indigo teammate Amanda came by, and together, they showed off some of the new moves they'd both been learning, like the hitch dodge, which still fooled Amanda and allowed Dani to score every time. Natalie, in particular, cheered Dani on every time. Dani hadn't quite mastered the rocker dodge, though. She kept losing her focus on the goal when she changed direction. She'd get it, though. She could feel it.

Thursday's classes went well, and then Friday came. It had been a long week, and she was kind of tired. Probably because it had been one whole week since she'd emotionally fled the PSLA meeting. When she walked in with Petra that morning, though, no one seemed to pay them any attention. It was as if the life-altering debate had never happened. Petra must have been feeling the same way because as they took their usual seats, she shrugged at Dani. Dani shrugged back as if to say she was also clueless.

Dani was about to say to Petra that this might be her last PSLA meeting, but Mae, the president of the Student Association, cleared her throat and asked for quiet. So even though Dani didn't voice her thoughts verbally, she was sure Petra heard them anyway. As a bonus, she'd get an hour back every Friday morning.

"Elections will be next week," Mae said. "A link to vote will go out electronically to all registered first-year students. If you've decided *not* to run for a position and your name is on our list, then you'll need to inform us before you leave here today. Otherwise, you'll still be on the ballot and taking votes away from other candidates."

Dani sighed. She should take her name off that list. She didn't think she had the strength to deal with those Student Association members every Monday evening. Their values and hers didn't quite match up.

"After the elections," Mae continued. "This first-year PSLA group will no longer exist, and you all will join the bigger group, which meets right after this time slot, right here in this very room. And now, let me remind you that PSLA stands for Political Science Leadership Association, and our focus will shift to guest speakers who will drop by our meetings to tell us what leadership means to them."

Mae gestured to Wayne to take over. Wayne told them that the mayor of a small upstate town was going to talk to them next Friday about her role as overseer of her town. She would take questions at the end, so please be prepared to voice intelligent questions.

Dani was having second thoughts about dropping out of the PSLA group now. She would love to hear what the mayor of a small town did. Yes, that sounded really interesting, and Dani found herself leaning toward staying. She'd talk to Petra afterward and ask what she thought.

After the PSLA meeting, Dani and Petra agreed to stay in the PSLA now that the classmate bashing was hopefully over. They met Meredith and Kate for lunch, and Dani was so relieved that their happy little friends' group was okay. After lunch, Dani's heart fluttered when Meredith walked her to her ASL class and then kissed her on the lips in front of other students. One guy catcalled at them in a good-natured way. That embarrassed Dani a little. Public displays of affection were still kind of new to her.

After her ASL class, Dani changed in the restroom and then hustled over to the field to work with Marti and the neighborhood kids. Meredith said she was finishing up an art project and would be there for the actual game later.

To Dani's surprise, Amanda showed up for the kids' practice.

"I didn't know you were coming today," Dani said as she stretched in a circle with the kids.

"This is so much fun, so I thought I'd come help again." Amanda wore practice gear and was ready to play. "I thought maybe you could practice some of your feint moves before you play for Team Magenta this afternoon."

Dani was floored. Why was Amanda doing this? With Dani out of the way, Amanda could shine and get moved up to Cyan instantly. But Dani understood that she had been misjudging a lot of people lately. So, the only thing she said was, "Thank you."

"Just remember to do a few face dodges before going for the hitch dodge. That way, they think you only have that one move."

"Yep, yep," Dani said, feeling the amazing stretch of her hamstring muscles.

"But then later," Amanda gushed, her excitement palpable, "plant your foot like you're going to bring the stick across your face for the dodge, but then don't. Burst up field and score."

Dani grinned at Amanda's enthusiasm. "And the hitch..." She raised her eyebrows, clearly waiting for Dani to finish the sentence like they were in class or something.

"The hitch freezes the defense, and then—"

"Score," they burst together.

Once they stopped laughing, Amanda got serious. "Dani, I don't know what's going on, but you so don't belong on Team Magenta." She whispered the last two words. "Something fishy. That's for sure. You and I should be heading for Team Cyan any day now."

Dani wished she could confide in Amanda but didn't want to stir that pot. She simply shrugged and went back to stretching. The thing that had happened between her and Laura was private. There was no real sense in bringing it up or the fact that Stephanie was being vindictive.

Amanda smiled at her sympathetically and then went over to help a young boy use better form stretching so he wouldn't hurt himself.

Dani's phone rang in her pocket. She instinctively pulled it out in case Meredith needed her. She didn't recognize the number, but it was a 315 Syracuse area code, so she answered it.

"Hello?" Dani said and walked away from the group. She put one finger up toward Natalie, who wanted to have a catch with her.

"Danielle Lassiter?" the middle-aged female voice asked.

"Yes?"

"This is Marguerite Reynolds from YMCA outreach programs."

"Oh, hi," Dani said, surprised.

"Ellen Martin called me and told me about the after-school program you want to investigate."

"Yes," Dani said and explained how they'd accidentally started the lacrosse clinics for the neighborhood kids and that she was hoping to facilitate not only something more stable and organized for the kids but something meaningful they could do after school in the winter months.

"Winter," Marguerite chuckled. "You mean from August to June?"

Dani laughed. "I'm from downstate and haven't experienced a Syracuse winter yet."

"You're in for a treat," Marquerite chided. "And you're saying it wrong, by the way. It's pronounced Siber-a-cuse."

Dani burst out laughing. Wait 'til she told Meredith that one.

"Let me get down to brass tacks here. We here at the YMCA on Westcott have the facilities and the staff for an after-school program. We already have one going for another elementary school on the other side of us. And although we appreciate your desire for the kids to have somewhere to go, we'll need to officially work with the school itself."

"I don't work for the school," Dani said, "but I think I might be able to get that ball rolling. I have a contact in the PTA, and she is enthusiastic about a program like this for her fifth-grade daughter."

There was surprise in Marguerite's voice when she said, "Get me that contact ASAP. Let's make this happen. If your contact doesn't want to give me their number, please give them mine, and let's make this thing happen."

"Fantastic," Dani said. "I'll see if I can reach her this evening."

They spoke about a few details Dani would need to convey to Natalie's mom, and then they ended the call. Shoot, she'd taken up more time than she'd intended. She looked up to find Natalie and was relieved to see her having a catch with Amanda. Good.

Since it was getting close to game time with her new team, Dani made sure that she and Amanda showed the kids the feint dodges that they'd been working on. Marti and her crew nodded and told Dani they'd work on that today, along with throwing and catching.

"Perfect," Dani said. "I have to get going now."

Out of the blue, Natalie raced for her and hugged her. "Have a good game."

Dani patted the top of Natalie's head. "Thanks, kid. I hope I don't move down again next week."

"Pfft," Natalie spat. "Not a chance. Just be yourself."

"Hey, that's what I always tell you guys."

"Take your own advice, Miss Dani." Natalie sounded so grown up that Dani simply grinned, grabbed her gear, and headed toward her new coach.

After Dani's tenth goal, her new coach, Sara, pulled her out.

"It's 10-0, Dani," Sara said. Her dark hair was pulled back under a bandana, giving her a flower-child vibe. "I have to let Team Teal save a little face."

"I feel good today," Dani said, wishing she could stay in the game. She'd taken Amanda's advice and used her old moves a few times before breaking out the newly minted rocker and hitch dodges. The defense had been completely clueless.

"That backhanded scoop on your fifth goal?" Sara's expression was one of complete disbelief. "Total poetry. It's my call, and I'm moving you all the way to Team Cyan next week. Laura's on board." She grinned at Dani. "That okay with you?"

"More than okay," Dani said. "More than okay."

"Good," Sara said. "Now, stay warm. You never know if the tide will turn, and I need you to score another ten."

Dani scoffed and headed for her water bottle. She looked into the stands and was surprised to see Meredith sitting with Natalie and Natalie's mom. It looked like the three of them were having an animated conversation about something.

As it turned out, Team Teal did manage to score a few goals, but Team Magenta ended up winning the game by a score of 12-3. Dani thanked Sara and her teammates and headed toward Meredith.

"Great game, Miss Dani," Natalie said.

"Thanks, kid," Dani said.

"See? I told you you shouldn't have been moved down."

Dani chuckled. "It felt good."

"Quite impressive, young lady," Natalie's mother said to Dani. "Meredith here has been filling us in on your quest to make the varsity team."

"She has, has she?" Dani raised a playful eyebrow at her girlfriend.

"I hope that was okay," Meredith said, panic in her voice.

"I'm teasing," Dani said quickly. "It's fine." She turned to Natalie's mother and said, "Thanks for staying to watch the game."

Natalie's mother nodded and said, "I needed to see who my daughter is hanging around with after school when she's supposed to be in the locked house doing her homework."

Natalie looked down at the ground, clearly admitting her disobedience.

"It's not safe for kids to be unsupervised," Dani said, sounding like an old grandma or something. "That's why I want to find some kind of after-school program for them." She then relayed the phone call she'd had with the YMCA liaison and gave Natalie's mother the phone number.

"I will call this evening and leave a message," Natalie's mother said. "I've spoken informally with some of the other parents, and there is enthusiasm for the program. I'll get it on the agenda for the next PTA meeting. Of course, I have to get the details from this Marguerite Reynolds first."

"Of course," Dani said with a nod. "Tell her Danielle Lassiter gave you her phone number. That way, she knows who you are."

"Sounds good." Natalie's mother looked down at her daughter. "Time to head home. Dinner, shower, then homework."

Natalie made a show of smelling under her armpits. "Maybe the shower should come first."

Dani, Meredith, and Natalie's mother burst out laughing, and then they parted ways.

Dani reached for Meredith's hand as they headed toward the gate leading to their dorm.

"Hey, Dani," an out-of-breath voice called. It was Laura.

Dani stopped and turned around. She didn't let go of Meredith's hand, though. Whatever Laura had to say could and would be said in front of Meredith.

"Hey," Laura said to Meredith, but before Meredith could get out a return greeting, Laura asked Dani, "Did Sara tell you you'd be moving up to Cyan next week?"

"She did," Dani said.

"That's great, honey," Meredith said and rubbed Dani's arm.

Dani tried not to grin. She knew Meredith was miffed about being dismissed by Laura, so she was asserting herself in the conversation. Good for her. The old Meredith never would have done that.

"I checked into that club thing," Laura said. "And it seems that you actually can have a club and varsity teams in the same sport. Who knew?"

"We do now," Dani said. "What do we have to do?"

"There's an online application due next week."

"Hey, at least we didn't miss it, right?"

"I'll send you the link to the app. We should fill it out together." Laura turned toward Meredith and said, "If it's okay with you."

"I'm Meredith, by the way," Meredith said, sticking out her hand.

Laura shook Meredith's hand. "Laura."

"I know."

Dani's stomach tightened as she squelched a laugh. Who was this woman at her side? The high school Meredith she'd fallen in love with was coming out of her shell for sure.

Laura nodded, and then the awkward silence Dani figured would happen…happened.

"So, can I text her?" Laura said to Meredith. "No meetings alone with her. Promise." She put up a hand as if taking an oath.

"You may," Meredith said.

Dani pressed her lips together. This was too rich.

"Cool." Laura seemed to take Meredith's responses in stride. "Dani, the intramural games kept you active in lacrosse, but I'm hoping a club team will give you the experience the varsity coaches said you lack. Hopefully, this will get you some real competition. You deserve a shot at that varsity team."

"Thanks, Laura," Dani said, and it was funny. Dani believed she was sincere. Maybe Laura did have a good heart after all.

Meredith squeezed Dani's hand, and Dani took that as the cue to head back to the dorm.

"We have to head back," Dani said.

Laura nodded. "I'll text you that link."

Dani simply nodded and she and Meredith headed toward the path leading to the dorm. Once they were out of earshot, Dani said, "You know…Petra, Kate, and a lot of people are already gone for break, and the dorm will be pretty quiet."

"It's quiet already," Meredith said. "I stopped there before coming to your game." She looked at Dani in a way that said she wanted Dani to continue with this line of thinking.

"So," Dani said slowly, "maybe we could, uh…" She felt her face flush. She felt too shy to suggest it.

"We could what?" Meredith asked in a sultry tone that sent shivers through Dani's core.

"Um, well," Dani stammered. She leaned closer but didn't dare look at Meredith. "There won't be anybody around, and we could, um…"

"You're killing me here," Meredith said with a chuckle.

"I mean, I have to shower, anyway, and we could, you know, save water by, uh…"

"By doing what?"

Oh, now Meredith was just enjoying Dani's discomfort. She knew perfectly well what Dani was suggesting.

Dani leaned closer and whispered, "We could shower togeth—"

"Yes," Meredith burst and doubled her speed. She practically pulled Dani up the hill.

Dani matched her speed but protested, "Baby, I need to eat before the dining hall closes."

Meredith chuckled. "I'm kind of hungry, too, I guess. And, sure, we need to fuel up because tomorrow we go home and spend three nights apart from each other."

"I'm not going to survive that," Dani said. "But we have tonight to make up for it."

Meredith increased her speed, and Dani obliged.

Chapter 24

Circuit Breaker

Dani pulled her dad's pickup truck into one of the visitor spots at the apartment complex on Grove Street. She'd driven past this complex many times growing up in Whickett but never knew it was a complex for senior citizens. The sun was low in the sky, but made the cream-colored bricks shine bright orange.

"Beautiful golden twilight right now," Meredith said from the passenger seat. Her artist's soul loved natural light like this. "The lovers' light."

"Mmm. It's nice." Dani undid her seatbelt, looked over at Meredith, and said, "Ready?"

"Not yet."

Meredith took off her own seatbelt and leaned closer. Dani took the hint by kissing her on the lips and then wrapping her in a soothing hug. Meredith sat back with a sigh. "I missed you last night."

"We've only spent one night apart so far," Dani said with a chuckle.

"I know, but that bus ride home was way too long. It made so many stops. And then coming out to my parents last night. Oh, my God, I feel like a million years have passed since we left campus."

"I know. I felt weird picking you up just now. Like I couldn't tell if your parents hate me now."

"No," Meredith said. "They don't hate you. My mom came up to my room at bedtime and said she wanted me to make sure this is what I really wanted. She said it might not be an easy road for us. She included you in that statement."

"Really."

"Mm hmm. Dad seemed kind of okay about it, though."

"He did?"

"Yeah," Meredith said with a laugh. "I think he kind of wants someone to pal around with. Talk sports and all that. You know?"

Dani laughed. "Well, sure, I'm good for that. But I hope they understand that I love you and I'm taking care of you."

Meredith's face scrunched up with emotion. "And I'm taking care of you, too, baby."

"You absolutely do."

"You said coming out to your parents went okay?" This, Meredith asked softly.

"Yeah," Dani said. "My mom said she already had an inkling. They both seemed to take it in stride. I mean, they weren't jumping for joy at the news, but at least I wasn't packing my bags."

"I know what you mean," Meredith said. "My folks love me. I know that. But you hear so many horror stories about kids getting thrown out of their homes over stuff like this."

"We got lucky, I guess." Dani smiled to try to reassure Meredith that all was well with her family. "My parents made Laney and me rake leaves together this morning."

"That seems kind of random."

"Actually," Dani said, "I'm pretty sure it was planned. I think my mom wanted Laney and me to bond or talk or whatever. And, bonus, the backyard gets raked."

"And did you?"

"What? Bond?"

Meredith nodded.

"Yes, we did. Laney wanted advice about running for office. I told her to be herself, speak her truths, and not compromise by saying things she thinks her classmates, or the administration want to hear."

"Wise advice there, big sis," Meredith said.

Dani chuckled. "She told me that she knew I liked girls. She said when I was a junior, she overheard me on the phone talking to my first girlfriend."

"Whose name was not Meredith," Meredith said and crossed her arms in mock hurt.

"Nope," Dani said. "But you are my second."

"And your last," Meredith scolded.

"And my last," Dani repeated and then chuckled. "Laney thoroughly approves of you, by the way."

"Really?"

"Mm hmm," Dani said. "She thinks you're 'cool' and really 'pretty.' And so do I."

Meredith blushed. "Tell Laney I think she's cool, too. I'm looking forward to getting to know her better."

"Laney said she knew something was going on between you and me last summer."

"How did she know? We were so careful."

Dani chuckled. "Armor All. She said that every time I went over to your house, I would Armor All the interior of Dad's truck before I went. I usually washed it, too. Dad certainly wasn't complaining."

"I never said anything to you, but I noticed the fresh, clean smell every time I got in the truck." Meredith smiled, but then her smile faded. She sighed and said, "I had the weirdest feeling this morning. I was helping mom make breakfast. Mikey was babbling about karate—"

"Tae kwon do," Dani corrected.

"I don't know why I can't remember that," Meredith said with a tiny self-deprecating scoff. "But, anyway, Dad was at the table talking about his wage increase, which is awesome, but I couldn't help thinking that I should be so happy that I was home. I mean, I am. I miss my parents and Mikey. I was happy, but I wasn't. I was missing you. We've spent every night together since late August, and now it's October."

"It's only for a few nights, sweetie," Dani said gently. "Maybe you're just overtired."

"Maybe, but I was wondering if this is ever going to truly be my home again. I know I'll always be welcomed here, and I should help out with Mikey, but—" She sighed and didn't finish her thought.

237

"You called our dorm room *home* the other day."

"I did?"

Dani nodded. "Monday afternoon. We were walking back to the dorm after our Women's Studies class. You smacked me in the chest, and when I protested, you said you would rub it for me 'when we get back *home.*'"

"I don't remember saying that, but I do remember the rubbing later." Meredith laughed devilishly.

"Me, too," Dani said and waggled her eyebrows. She checked her watch. "We should get in there, but before we do, just know that wherever you are feels like home to me."

"Aww," Meredith said and splayed a hand over her chest. "You say the sweetest things."

"C'mon, let's see if we can help with dinner."

They didn't hold hands on their way to Esther and Millie's door because they didn't want to cause trouble for their older friends.

Dani barely got one knock on the door when Esther flung it open.

"Girls," Esther gushed. "Come in. Come in." She hugged them both at the same time. "We've missed you so much." She turned toward Millie, who was slowly getting up from the couch. "Haven't we, dearest?"

"We sure have," Millie said. Her short silver hair looked like it needed cutting, but maybe because she'd been so sick, she hadn't felt up to it. She was a bit hunched over as she made her way to the door, but she had much better color in her face than the last time they had video-chatted together.

"We've missed you both, too," Meredith said.

"Can I take your jackets?" Esther asked. Her smile and the twinkle in her eye made Dani feel cozy inside. Esther's snow-white hair had been artfully pulled up into a manageable bun on top of her head. It was cute.

"I'm good," Dani said. "It's a little chilly out there, and I still need to warm up."

"Me, too," Meredith said.

The truth was Esther and Millie's apartment was cold. Was their furnace working properly? Were they trying to save money, and had it turned low? Dani wasn't sure how to ask, so she decided it wasn't any of her business. She and Meredith called them their honorary grandmothers, but Dani didn't want to overstep.

When offered drinks, Meredith said, "Agua, por favor," and then had to explain that she was practicing her Spanish because midterms were next week.

"Never went to college," Millie said and resumed her spot on the couch. On the side table next to her was an open crossword puzzle book and several well-worn pencils. There was a prescription bottle of some kind and a tablet, which was probably the tablet they used for video chats.

Esther excused herself to check on the meatloaf, and Meredith followed her into the small kitchen to help.

Dani sat where Millie pointed. "I'd give you a tour," Millie said with a grin, "but this is about it. One bedroom down the hall past the one bathroom. Kitchen that way."

"Bigger than our dorm room," Dani quipped. When Millie asked her how school was going, Dani gave her the highlight reel of college life, including her courses, lacrosse, Meredith's art exhibit, football games, and the new friends they were making.

"Sounds like you two are settling in just fine," Esther said from the open doorway to the kitchen. "Come fill your plates in the kitchen, and then we'll sit at the table there."

It was a bit difficult to maneuver in their small apartment because there were piles of boxes and bags everywhere. Dani supposed that with Esther's recent hip fracture and Millie's even more recent stomach issues, they hadn't had the time or the energy to unpack.

"Smells so good," Dani said as she picked up a paper plate from the countertop. "Meatloaf and macaroni and cheese."

"The mac n cheese is Millie's specialty," Meredith informed Dani. She must have just learned that bit of information.

"Oh, yeah? You'll have to give Meredith the recipe so she can make it for me," Dani quipped, earning her a smack from her girlfriend.

"Why am I always the one cooking dinner for you?" Meredith bugged out her eyes playfully, making both Esther and Millie laugh.

"I don't know how to cook," Dani protested weekly.

"Sounds like you better learn how, youngin," Millie said and patted Dani on the back.

"Ya think?" It was Dani's turn to bug out her eyes.

"You girls are so much fun," Esther said. "Come, sit."

The food Esther and Millie made for them was truly good old home cooking. The food in the dining hall was fine, but this had clearly been made with love. While they ate, Esther and Millie reassured them that Millie was on the mend and that the infection seemed to be cleared up. A controlled diet and exercise were clearly the keys to good health, and they had been taking daily walks around the apartment complex.

"How are you going to get your walks in during the winter?" Meredith asked.

Esther and Millie exchanged a glance, and an eerie feeling crept up Dani's spine.

"What?" Dani asked, sitting back in the kitchen chair.

"I'm sure you've noticed the boxes by now," Millie said.

"Yeah, I was wondering about that," Dani said.

"We're moving to Florida," Esther blurted out, completely cutting off anything Millie was about to say.

"Way to break it to them gently, Esther," Millie scolded, but it was a gentle scolding.

"We're so excited," Esther said. "These New York winters are for the birds." She rolled her eyes and added to Millie, "We did think about being snowbirds, you know. Half the time in Florida and half the time here."

"But maintaining two homes just didn't make sense," Millie said.

"She'd be worrying about the water heater or whatever up here while we were down there and vice versa," Esther clarified.

"And financially, it makes more sense to have one residence," Millie said with a practical tone.

"We'll miss you," Meredith said softly. It almost broke Dani's heart to hear the disappointment in her girlfriend's voice.

"We will," Dani said.

"Bah," Millie said and looked away, but not fast enough. Dani saw the tears in her eyes.

"We know, girls," Esther said. "You two are probably the only people we're going to miss if we're being honest."

"What she means," Millie said, "is that all our friends have moved away, and we lost our sense of community. And now that the old painted lady is being taken care of and thriving again, we have nothing to hold us back."

"Except you two," Esther said. "Of course, we wanted to see you when you came home for your holiday from school, but we also wanted to make sure we said goodbye to you face to face."

Meredith wiped away some tears, and Esther handed her a box of tissues.

Dani frantically searched for something to say. "We're very happy for you both, but where in Florida are you going?"

"Show them, dearest," Esther said and stood up. "Go get your tablet with the video while I clear the dishes. I'll put some water on for tea."

Millie pushed her chair back, but Dani stopped her.

"I'll get it." She leaped to her feet, fetched the tablet from the side table, and handed it to Millie. "Here you go."

"Thank you," Millie said. She fumbled with the casing and then raised her head as if remembering something. "Esther, don't forget the apple pie."

"Of course not," Esther called from the kitchen. "Sweets with this one. What am I going to do with her?"

"Keep her," Meredith said as she carried a stack of dirty dishes toward the kitchen. The kitchen was too small for Dani to go in as well, so she gathered up the drinking glasses and handed them to Meredith at the doorway.

Once the tea was made, the pie sliced, and the ice cream scooped, they sat back down at the now clean table and watched a real estate agent take them on a live virtual tour of a retirement village south of Tampa. The realtor in the video was speaking directly to Esther and Millie, obviously addressing some of their concerns.

"Those tiny houses are so cute," Meredith said. "Look at the palm trees, Dani."

"The landscaping looks well taken care of," Dani added.

"There are more videos from Susie," Millie said, "but we won't bore you with them."

"We're flying down next weekend," Esther said. "Susie will take us on a tour and hopefully, we'll find a unit we both like. She thinks we will. Hopefully, we can make an offer on one while we're there."

"Sounds like a lovely trip," Meredith said. "I only wish we were here to drive you to the airport."

"No worries," Millie said. "I know an Uber driver."

"She's up on that modern stuff," Esther said with a laugh.

Dani took a bite of the warmed pie and moaned. "This is so good."

"Esther's specialty," Millie said. "She's been spoiling me with that pie for forty years."

Esther and Millie smiled at each other, still so obviously in love all that time. Dani shot Meredith a look. She tried to convey that she wanted the same with Meredith. Meredith smiled back, probably thinking the same thing.

"We haven't told you the best thing, though," Millie said.

Esther took up the telling. "It's a women's community. Mostly lesbian or bi or trans or all the alphabets, but we hope to find a real community of people where we can finally be out and be our natural selves."

"It's not a cult or anything, is it?" Dani asked half-seriously. "Like some kind of work commune?"

Esther and Millie burst out laughing. Meredith smacked Dani on the thigh.

"No, dear," Esther said. "You can look them up on the internet. 'Google it.' as Millie says."

Millie swiped at her tablet and then turned it around to show them some pictures. "This is the clubhouse and the recreation hall."

"They're huge," Meredith said.

"They have concerts there and comedians and shows," Esther said.

"My goal," Millie said, "is to be sitting in that recreation hall surrounded by women sharing Thanksgiving dinner and then watching football on that big screen TV while in a food coma."

"Gotta have goals," Dani said with a laugh.

"But more seriously," Esther said, "this seems like a place where the residents look out for each other. We miss being part of a community. They have a walking club and pool aerobics and even arts and crafts." Esther looked at Meredith when she said the last part.

"It sounds so great," Meredith said. "Like a resort. Dani and I are so happy for you. I only wish we could help you pack and move and then unpack you."

"We've got it covered," Millie said. "We've hired a company to move all the boxes once we've purchased our home there and have a date set. The community has Uber drivers in residence, too, so we'll be able to have an Uber scheduled to pick us up from the airport and bring us right there."

"Sounds like you've got it all figured out," Dani said. Her heart was breaking a little bit, but she was happy for her honorary grandmothers.

"We want you to visit us," Esther said. "They have these furnished park models, that's what they call them, that can be rented out. So, you girls could come and stay in your own little house and check up on us."

"I would love that," Meredith said. "You'll keep us posted as to your moving dates and all of that, right?"

"Of course," Esther said and stood up to clear the dessert dishes. Once again, Meredith helped out, and the two of them went off into the kitchen.

"Come," Millie said leading the way back to the living room seating. "It sounds like you have an awful lot on your plate, kid."

"I do," Dani said. "We both do, but we have each other to lean on, vent to, and cry with."

"I'm glad."

Dani was about to say something, but they were plunged into darkness.

"Dammit," Esther cursed from the kitchen.

"I'll get it," Millie said, fumbling around near her chair. "Dang it. Where's my flashlight?"

"Here." Dani tapped on her phone's flashlight feature.

"To the circuit breaker box in the hallway," Millie said, leading the way. "You can't overload the system. Esther forgets and runs too many appliances at the same time. That's another reason we're ready to move. I used to be the one fixing everything, but now that we live in an apartment, I can't fuss with stuff. We're on the list for a service call, but who knows?" She shrugged and opened the door to the breaker panel.

"Look at all these breakers," Millie said, pointing to the entire panel. "None of them seem tripped. They all seem fine, right?"

"Right," Dani said, shining her flashlight on the panel.

"But one of them is tripped. One of them needs our help." Millie reached to the right side of the panel and said, "See it now? That one is slightly off its mark."

Dani did see it. "I hadn't noticed that."

Millie flipped the breaker all the way off and then flipped it back on. The lights came back on in the small apartment, accompanied by cheers from the two women in the kitchen.

"So, you need to notice," Millie said, her tone very serious. "You need to notice when your girl is off kilter or when you yourself are not right. It could be a small thing or something big. You need to make sure you're paying attention."

"I will," Dani said, feeling like she was receiving wisdom from a wise sage.

"Make sure you two learn how to communicate with each other. Learn how to argue but with respect. Learn to read her signs. Hopefully, she'll learn to read yours, too."

Dani nodded as they stood there in front of the now-fixed breaker box.

"And the reason this breaker tripped," Millie continued, "is because it was overloaded. Someone thought it could handle all the loads put on it. But it can't. Promise me that you will not be an overloaded circuit. Become your own breaker with help from your girl, of course. Promise me you'll pay attention to all the stuff that gets put on you. Promise me you'll know your limits and not be like this guy here." She pointed to the breaker and then closed the panel door.

"I promise," Dani said with a grin. "That is a great analogy."

"Don't trip your circuit breaker," Millie said with a laugh.

When they all gathered in the living room for more conversation, Dani said, "Wait a minute. I just thought of something. You said you were flying down. How are you going to get your car down there?"

"We're not," Esther said. She exchanged another glance with Millie and nodded to her.

Millie reached into the pocket of her flannel shirt and tossed Dani a set of keys. Dani was confused. Did they expect her to drive the car down for them? She wouldn't have time for that. She had classes and then there was the full time job of training for the lacrosse team.

"Millie," Esther scolded, "she looks frightened. Tell her."

"It's all set up and done," Millie said, not clearing up anything. "That car out front? The Ford Taurus? It's yours."

"What?" Dani was still very confused.

Esther spoke first. "We contacted your parents about our plans, Dani. Yours, too, Meredith. We wanted to let them know that we were moving." Esther turned her attention back to Dani. "Your parents made an offer on the car."

"It's in your father's name right now," Millie added, "but he says he and your mom were buying it for you. And I think they understood that Meredith means a lot to you because your mom said it would be so much easier for the 'kids' to come home from college if 'they' had a car of their own."

"She meant me?" Meredith asked, eyebrows raised.

"She did," Esther said. "There was no mistaking her meaning."

"Hmm," Dani said, exchanging a glance with Meredith and then said to Meredith, "I think you were right when you said our parents already knew we were together."

Meredith nodded. "They were waiting for us to tell them, I guess."

Dani turned back to the older women. "I don't know what to say, you guys. This is so generous of you. I…" She really didn't know what to say.

"We're going to miss you so much," Meredith burst out, fresh tears streaming down her face.

Meredith's emotions got to Dani that time, and she teared up as well. Soon, all four of them were laughing, crying, and passing around the box of tissues.

"We'll still do our video chats," Dani said. "If you want to."

"Absolutely," Millie said. "I was going to ask if that would still be okay."

"More than okay."

Meredith couldn't help herself and leaped up to hug Esther and Millie. Dani did the same, and when they sat back down, they chatted about less emotional things like Meredith's art show and Dani's ASL course. She had to demonstrate a few sentences to them, of course, but she didn't mind at all. The conversation eventually turned back to Esther and Millie's new beginning at the women's community in Florida and Dani felt her heart get warm for them. They were truly hopeful for a new start in a new place.

Funny how she and Meredith had the exact same goals at Syracuse.

Chapter 25

Red Flags, Red Shirts

Although first-year students weren't supposed to have cars, Dani and Meredith drove back to Syracuse in Dani's new-to-her Ford Taurus. They arranged to park it at Joiee's apartment complex until Dani could get approval to have a car as a freshman and keep it in her dorm parking lot. On the two-and-a-half-hour trip back from Albany, they decided that even if Natalie's elementary school didn't partner up with the YMCA, Dani and Meredith would volunteer there anyway—starting after midterm exams, of course. Dani planned to put volunteering down as one of her main reasons for needing a car on campus.

Once they got back to campus, it seemed like they hit the ground running. Dani did indeed get moved up to Team Cyan and was stoked to find that Amanda had also been moved up. Neither of them had any idea if anyone had been moved down, but they didn't want to ask, so they didn't. In that first game with Team Cyan, neither of them started, but when they finally got in the game, Dani scored a respectable three goals, and Amanda scored one. Laura, their new team captain, gave them both high fives when the game was over and told them that Team Cyan's practices were on Tuesdays and Thursdays. Apparently, they were the only intramural team that actually practiced during the season.

Dani had no idea how she was going to work in an entire day's worth of classes *and* lacrosse. But, she reasoned, that would be her life on the varsity team if she made it next year, so maybe it would be best to get used to it now. Meredith would be affected, too, so this was a good dress rehearsal for her, too.

Midterm week was incredibly harrowing, with everyone, Dani and Meredith included, losing their minds. When the first day of exams was complete, Dani decided she couldn't continue at that high stress level. Meredith laughed when Dani told her about overloading your circuits in Millie's circuit breaker analogy. Meredith confided that Esther had also taken her aside and advised her to always be present for her partner and to look for changes in mood. "You can't ignore the little things," Esther had told Meredith, "because little things tend to grow bigger."

Dani was touched that their two older friends made sure to give them advice. It was nice to have caring people like that in your life. And in terms of not overloading the circuits, Dani reasoned that over their four years of college, there would only be eight midterm periods, so there was no sense in losing your mind every time. She convinced a few people to relax more and take in the experience because it was inevitable. Kate was one of those losing her mind, but between Dani, Meredith, and Petra, Kate managed to take a breath on occasion.

Because it was midterm week, there was only one lacrosse game, but Dani felt the most amazing satisfaction when Laura not only started her against Dani's old Team Indigo, but she scored five goals on top of that. She and Amanda made it a regular thing to teach each other and practice any moves or strategies each one had learned. It became a challenge to find and bring a new skill to Amanda, but Dani was up for it. Meredith laughed at Dani sitting at her desk watching lacrosse videos instead of doing school work. She said it looked like Dani was taking another course, this one in advanced lacrosse. Dani agreed. There was a lot to take in.

Meredith was also super busy after their return from fall break. One Saturday morning, she went with her art class to an assisted living facility, where they conducted art classes for a group of senior citizens. She said it was an incredible experience and definitely something she wanted to do again, but she also wanted to see what working with younger kids would be like, too. On her own, Meredith called the YMCA and spoke with someone about volunteer opportunities. Apparently, there was an online application that needed to be filled out. When midterm exams were finally over, they spent an entire evening filling out and submitting the applications.

The rest of October was a bit of a blur, but Dani and Meredith managed to find time to go for walks and check out the fall foliage. The park with the rose garden became a favorite destination. Meredith, of course, took a bunch of pictures of the colorful leaves for one art project or another. Dani enjoyed Meredith's enthusiasm. But October had come and gone, and the early days of November were upon them. Thank goodness her load was about to lighten up because her very last intramural lacrosse game was that afternoon. The games started at 4:00 now because the sun just refused to stay out much longer after that.

"You go on," Meredith said out of breath. "Don't be late."

"You sure?" Dani asked. "Are you okay?"

"I'm fine. Just out of shape." Meredith waved her on. "Go, go."

Dani blew her a kiss and jogged the rest of the way to the field. Today was the final championship game of the fall, and as expected, Team Cyan was taking on Team Indigo for the trophy. And there were real trophies, too. How about that?

Dani wasn't exactly late, but most of her teammates were already there warming up. She threw herself on the ground and whipped on her cleats. Before pulling out her goggles and mouthguard case, she glanced around, taking in the sounds of the players warming up, the blue but chilly sky overhead, and the fading green grass. This was her sanctuary, her first love after Meredith, of course.

Dani shoved her sneakers in the bag and zipped it closed.

"Right on time," Laura said as she walked over. "Where's the wife?"

Dani pointed toward the path. Meredith was just now strolling toward the field.

"Cool," Laura said. "Important game tonight. This one's for all the chips."

"Yeah," Dani said. She liked winning, but honestly, it was an intramural game, and she just wanted to play well.

"Just do what you do," Laura said. "No heroics. You've made amazing strides, and these guys accept you as one of their own now." She gestured to their teammates warming up on the field.

"Okay," Dani said, not knowing what to add. Laura was giving her some kind of weird pep talk. "Thanks," she finally added, but when an awkward silence fell between them, Dani said, "I'm going to warm up."

"Good idea," Laura said with a nod.

Yeah. Weird.

Dani stretched for a minute and went for a quick run up the sideline. She passed Joiee and made faces at her as she went by. The sound of Joiee's laughter followed her.

"You're weird, Dani," Joiee called after her.

Dani threw one thumb up overhead but didn't turn back. She sprinted to the end line, turned around, did side hops for a bit, and then turned and sprinted toward Joiee again. She raised her hand just like she'd done every game since joining Team Cyan and slapped Joiee's hand as she went by.

The pregame warmup felt good. She was with a group of players who played the game well and knew how to win. Dani loved the vibe. Laura called the team together for one last pep talk, and then they took the field. Dani waved to Meredith, Kate, Petra, Natalie, and the rest of the neighborhood kids in the stands and found her favorite spot on the field for the opening draw. Her heart practically melted when they all waved the 'I love you' sign back at her. She returned it quickly and refocused on the game ahead.

And with the official's whistle, the championship game was on. She, Amanda, and one of the original Team Cyan attackers were unstoppable. Dani didn't hear the crowd, although afterward, Meredith said she had a sore throat from all the yelling and cheering.

"You're on fire," Dani yelled in Amanda's ear after Amanda scored another goal.

"Caught it from you," Amanda said. She retrieved her stick after the stick check, a requirement after each goal, and called to Dani, "Your turn."

And Dani did take her turn again and again and again. She easily summed up Team Indigo's weaknesses, something she'd never really been able to do in the past, but now she did fairly easily. Laura's practices on Tuesdays and Thursdays, especially the one yesterday, often focused on the mental aspects of the game. Laura was a really good coach, and Dani was glad she had finally been able to get past that initial locker room harassment.

The game hardly seemed like a fair fight with Team Cyan whooping Team Indigo by a score of 21 – 5.

"Victory," Laura shouted when the game ended. "Trophy time."

A woman who looked official but who Dani had never seen before stood behind the trophy table that had been moved out to the center line. She had short, wavy brown hair and an athlete's gait. She stood tall and held a cordless microphone. "That was inspiring lacrosse, ladies." Cheers went up on the field from both teams and the crowd.

Dani snuck a peek at the stands and made a small wave at Meredith and her friends. They all cheered and waved back, calling Dani's name.

"Second place trophy goes to a hardworking team who never gave up," the official-looking woman said. "Sometimes, when faced with overwhelming odds, you have to create different goals. You did that and slowed down this team trying to steamroll you, but then you actually came out with five goals of your own because of it." She picked up the trophy and said, "In second place, Team Indigo."

The players and fans cheered and clapped as Stephanie stepped up to shake Laura's hand first and then the official-looking woman's hand. She took the trophy and held it high over her head. Her teammates surrounded her and cheered.

"And in first place," the woman continued, "a team that has had a lot of growth all season. I've seen players on this team go from mediocre to outstanding. I've seen defensive players read their opponents' offense and make changes. The same goes for the offense. They found weaknesses and exploited them again and again and again. Twenty-one goals in a championship game is quite impressive."

She picked up the first-place trophy and said, "In first place, the defending league champions, Team Cyan!" She shook hands with Laura and then handed her the trophy.

Laura thrust the trophy high overhead and was instantly swallowed up by her teammates, Dani included. Dani wished Laura had gone over to shake

Stephanie's hand, though. Apparently, Laura had broken things off with Stephanie after Stephanie moved Dani down to Team Magenta. "Not a cool move," Laura had said to Dani when they were working on the club lacrosse application. "I can't be with someone who would be that vindictive."

Dani hoped Laura would turn that lens inward and understand how much she had hurt Joiee. Dani wasn't going to get involved, though. That was Laura's life, not hers.

"Great game, you guys," Laura said. "Look for that club lacrosse announcement. Fingers crossed that we get approved."

Dani's teammates chattered excitedly about the possibility of the club team. Dani was excited, too. She and Laura had worked together to complete the application as thoroughly as they could. Laura suggested that Dani be the one to submit it because it had been Dani's idea to begin with. That had been incredibly cool of her to do.

Working with Laura on the application and having her as a coach made Dani understand what Joiee meant when she said Laura had a good heart. She did. Even Meredith came to see Laura as a nice person, flawed like all humans, but nice. Dani and Meredith both agreed that they weren't ready to call Laura a friend just yet and were still keeping her several arms' length away. Friendship was going to take some time, given Dani's history with Laura and given what Laura had done to Joiee.

Dani blew out a sigh. She plopped down on the ground and took off her cleats. Ugh. The ground was cold and wet from the evening dew. She pulled her sneakers out of her bag, but before she had a chance to put them on, Laura and the official-looking woman were heading right for her. Dani stood up.

"Dani, this is Coach Manzetti. She's one of the assistant varsity coaches."

"Nice to meet you, Dani," Coach Manzetti said and stuck out her hand.

Dani shook it and awkwardly remembered to speak. "Nice to meet you, too."

"I'll let you two talk," Laura said and excused herself.

"You had a good game, Dani. Given the competition, that is."

"Thanks. I love this game." Dani tried not to grimace at her cheesy response.

"Laura put you on my radar early on," Coach Manzetti said. "I watched a couple of the first few games you played with Team Indigo, and it was obvious how green you were, but Laura begged me to come back. She said you'd been putting in the time to improve your skills and develop new ones. And it shows. I went back to find your student athlete information sheet, and I see why we stopped recruiting you."

Dani tried not to look down ashamed. She held the coach's gaze with what she hoped was a neutral expression even though she'd just been told she hadn't measured up. The cold, damp grass seeped up Dani's socks as she stood there in front of the coach. That was fine. It fit the mood she now found herself in.

The coach continued, "There were some red flags which made us pause. You haven't been on any travel teams or been to any camps that we could find. But then again, watching these last few games you've played in, you do seem to be a leader and not a showboat. That's good. Your skills have definitely improved, and you seem to be a game player, meaning you turn it on when it's game time. That is a good thing.

"So, I won't take up much more of your time," the coach continued, "but I wanted to let you know that I'm putting you on my recruiting list for next year's team. Not this season, mind you. We're too far along already, and all the slots and then some have been filled."

"Thank you," Dani said. "I appreciate the opportunity," she added, knowing she sounded like a dork.

"And I heard through the grapevine that there is a very good chance that a women's club lacrosse team will be approved for the spring."

"Really? Are you sure?"

"It's not a done deal, but I have a friend who...you know. Anyway, she said it just had to get the final stamp of approval from the committee."

"That would be so awesome," Dani said as much to the coach as to herself.

"I'll need you to play there, and we'll keep looking at you, but I need to lay all the cards on the table. It's quite possible the head coach may ask you to redshirt next season."

"What does that mean, exactly?" Dani tried to remember what Laura had told her about her own redshirt season but couldn't recall a dang thing. Her racing pulse was causing memory loss or something.

"It means that you would practice and scrimmage with the team but not play in games so that we can extend your period of playing eligibility. You'd be developing your skills and getting stronger in the meantime."

"Oh," Dani said, trying not to sound disappointed. Redshirting was not what she wanted to do, but if that's what was offered, then there it was.

"Since you'd most likely be redshirting in your sophomore year, that means you'd still have four more years of eligibility after that," the coach said with a happy lilt to her voice.

Dani wasn't sure how that kind of math worked but then remembered Laura telling her that people sometimes took five or six years to finish their bachelor's degrees. A hollow feeling hit her stomach. *Six years?*

"Find a camp, Dani. Play on a summer traveling team. Try out for a U20 league. You probably won't make the team, but it will be a learning experience for you. Live, breathe, eat lacrosse."

The pit in Dani's stomach refused to be ignored. "What does that look like? Living, breathing, eating lacrosse?" She didn't mean to sound flippant or snarky, but she wasn't quite sure what the coach meant.

"Well, if you do join us next year in whatever capacity, you'll take a reduced course load. You'll be provided with tutors. You'll have a limited social life. Laura already told you that relationships suffer. She knows firsthand. Vacations belong to the team. Lacrosse is first. School is second. Everything else is a distant, a far distant third. You have to want this, Dani. You have to want it with everything you have. I can't impress that upon you enough."

Dani decided to find the positives. "I appreciate your candor, coach. Thank you for taking my cause seriously."

"Your 'cause,'" the coach repeated. "I love that." She tapped Dani's shoulder and said, "I have to get going."

"Thanks," Dani said.

The coach turned away, and Dani closed her eyes and sighed. That was a lot of information.

"You okay?" Meredith asked, sidling up to Dani's side. "That looked serious."

"She was one of the varsity coaches," Dani said. "She gave me a lot of information and a lot to think about." She looked into Meredith's face and found what she hoped to find there. Sympathy and support with a dash of curiosity. "Can we—I have to—" Dani sighed forcefully. Her brain was overloading. "I'm hungry."

Meredith burst out laughing. "Yeah, c'mon, the gang's starving, too. They were too scared to come up to you after your talk with the varsity coach."

"*Assistant* coach," Dani clarified, wondering why she felt the need to make that distinction. Was she trying to diminish the coach's stature because she said Dani's skills were lacking?

"Stop," Meredith said.

"Huh?"

"You're going down some rabbit hole or another," Meredith said.

"You're right." Dani plopped her wet butt down on the equally wet grass and put her wet socks into her soon-to-be wet sneakers. She leaped to her feet and said quick goodbyes to a few people, including Joiee, who made her promise to text later and tell her how the meeting with the coach went. She made a point of thanking Natalie and the other kids for coming out to the game, and she hoped to see them at the YMCA if the program got approved. Natalie looked emotional, and Dani realized that this might be the last time they saw each other. Then, it was Dani's turn to be emotional.

"Hey, we'll be back on this field sometime in March," Dani said to Natalie and pointed to the field. "One way or another, we'll be back."

"Promise?" Natalie asked, her lower lip sticking out.

"Yes," Dani said.

"Yes," Meredith echoed. "I'll make sure she doesn't get lost on her way to see you."

Natalie grinned, gave each of them another hug, and turned to run home through the hole in the fence,

Kate and Petra patted her on the back and told her she had a great game.

"Thanks, you guys," Dani said. "Now that it's over, I'm not going to know what to do with myself in the afternoons now."

"Oh," Kate said comically, "I think you two will find something to do."

Meredith screeched in laughter, which started a mega amount of teasing from Kate all the way back to the dining hall.

Chapter 26

The Luckiest Person

Dani plopped down on the floor of their dorm room and sighed. "One more day of classes, and we have a week off."

"With two weekends on either side," Meredith added. "Personally, I'm a bit scared about our families having Thanksgiving dinner together." This Meredith said as she continued to pack her suitcase for Thanksgiving break. Dani had yet to pull her own suitcase out from under her bed. Maybe she wouldn't bring anything home.

She groaned.

"What, baby?" Meredith asked but didn't stop folding her shirt.

"I don't know what to do."

"It's only been two weeks since you talked with Coach Manzetti. You don't have to decide today."

"I know. But…"

Meredith placed her neatly folded shirt in her suitcase and sat in Dani's desk chair. "Tell me."

Dani looked up from her prone position on the floor and decided to unleash. "We got approved to volunteer at the YMCA."

"Yes, we did, which helped get your parking pass approved. Yay," Meredith said, clapping those cute little angel claps she always did. It was one of the adorable things Dani loved about her girlfriend.

"Club Lacrosse is set to have tryouts in January," Dani said. "The first game is February 25th against Ithaca, and it's a home game."

"Amanda got the club lacrosse Instagram page up already."

Dani bolted upright. "She did? Did she get the announcement out for spring tryouts? Let me see." She reached for her phone in her pocket but then thought better of it. "No, no. That can wait. We're frying other fish right now."

"Yes, we are, baby," Meredith said in an even keel. "Let me recap your commitments. One—YMCA volunteering three times a week, possibly for Natalie's after-school program if the school gets off their butt and decides. Two—Club Lacrosse from January to mid-April with eight regular season games, two of which are away games at Albany State and Rochester Tech."

"I can't believe I'm going to be able to play in a Syracuse jersey back home in Albany," Dani said wistfully. "I wish Esther and Millie were still going to be around to come to the game."

"I know. Apparently, all their stuff is on a moving truck heading to Florida without them at this very moment."

"When do they fly down?"

"Saturday sometime, I think," Meredith said.

Dani raised an eyebrow. "Are you thinking what I'm thinking?"

"Yes, yes, yes," Meredith said. "We get home tomorrow night. We can drive them to the airport on Saturday and call dibs on last hugs."

"Aww, yeah," Dani said. "I'll text Millie about it later." Dani leaned back against the leg of her bed.

"Back to the list," Meredith said. "One—YMCA. Two—club lacrosse. Three—newly elected freshmen representative in the Student Association with meetings every Monday evening. Four—increased course load because someone decided to minor in Social Work."

"Just like someone else decided to minor in Art Therapy." Dani sat up on her knees and knee-walked over to her girlfriend. She lay her head in Meredith's lap and got her head petted softly as expected.

"Five—," Meredith continued, "interning for incumbent state senator Winthrop next summer and possibly over spring break. Six—A semester abroad in England during junior year. Seven—making certain, absolutely certain, your girlfriend is happy."

"Wait," Dani said, picking her head up. "No way are you seventh on my list. Redo it. One— Meredith. Two—" She stopped talking when Meredith put a hand over her mouth.

"I appreciate the gesture, but we have to meet the gang for dinner in a few minutes."

"Fine," Dani mumbled under the hand. When the hand released her lips, she said. "Now for the other list. If I somehow make the varsity team, there will be no time for the YMCA. No club lacrosse because it will be varsity lacrosse. I'd have to resign as a Student Association rep, reduce my courseload because of the lacrosse commitment, and take five or six years to complete my bachelor's degree." Dani groaned at the next one. "And I'd have to give up my internship for Senator Winthrop."

"That one hurts, doesn't it," Meredith asked, twirling Dani's short hair around one finger.

"They all hurt."

"And don't forget having to give up a semester in London."

"Yeah." Dani sat back and looked Meredith right in the eye. "But I think the worst one is that Meredith would be way down on the list."

For the life of her, Dani could not read Meredith's expression.

After a few more beats, Meredith said, "You don't have to decide today, baby."

Dani groaned and fell back flat on the floor again. "I know, but I have to decide sometime soon for my own sanity. I have to know where to put my energy. My brain can't take much more of this back and forth."

"I know. You just want it settled." Meredith helped her off the floor, and they headed to the dining hall to meet their friends. They scanned their cards and walked in to see Kate, Petra, and that bearded guy Edward sitting at their table. Dani waved and then motioned they would be right over after filling their trays.

Once at the shared table, Kate said, "Last night before Thanksgiving break."

"I think I'm going to sleep the entire time," Petra said with a laugh.

"Me, too," Meredith said in commiseration.

Edward cleared his throat, and all gazes went toward him. Edward was truly a nice guy, Dani had come to realize, and she was glad that he and

Meredith had been able to reconnect after so many years. "I'm not going home until Monday," Edward announced.

"Because?" Meredith asked.

Edward looked like the cat that had caught the canary. "Derek invited me to stay over." He squealed like a little girl.

He ate up the congratulations and best wishes from the four young women at the table, and then Meredith said to him, "Safety first."

Edward, always the dramatist, inhaled sharply and splayed a hand over his chest. "Of course, mademoiselle. What do you take me for? Easy?"

"Yes," came four loud voices in agreement.

He looked offended and said, "I resemble that remark."

After the laughter died down, Dani blurted, "You guys, what do I do?" She put her hands on top of her head dramatically. It was partly for Edward's benefit. He did like camp, that was for sure.

"Dani," Kate said, "you don't have to decide now."

"No, I get it," Petra said. "She wants her future to be clear. She wants to make that decision and be done with it once and for all."

"Ahh," Kate said. "To play or not to play."

"That is the question," Petra said. "But either way, she'll play whether it's on varsity or the new club team. She'll still have lacrosse in one form or another." It was kind of funny how they were talking about her as if she wasn't sitting right there.

"True, true," Kate said.

"Hey, why aren't you eating?" Dani asked Kate. She'd just noticed that everyone had a tray in front of them except Kate, who held onto a small glass of water. And Kate was dressed up and wore makeup and everything.

"I have a date," Kate said and sat up taller.

"With who?" Dani asked. "Or is it 'whom'?"

"I think it's 'whom,'" Meredith said. "Because then she can answer, 'with him.' Get it? Whom and him? Both end with the letter m?"

"Oh, that makes sense." Dani turned back to Kate. "With *whom*?"

Kate didn't answer. She just looked up and pointed.

Dani heard the strangled sound that came out of her throat as she saw the person walking toward them.

"What's up, ladies and gentle-man?" Joiee asked, adjusting the collar on her dress shirt. Dani had never seen her friend look so spiffy.

"It took her forever to ask me out," Kate said behind her hand, even though Joiee clearly heard it.

"What can I say?" Joiee said and sat at the table next to Kate. "Pretty women are intimidating."

"Yes, they are," Dani said and gave Meredith a loving expression.

"Aww, so cute," Edward said, and the others echoed his sentiment.

Dani didn't have time to process the fact that her friend, who she thought was straight and who'd had a boyfriend in high school, was dating a woman. And not just any woman. Her two friends were dating each other.

"You look like a deer in the headlights, Dani," Joiee said. Her cologne wafted over. It was nice. Joiee must really be interested in Kate.

"What are your intentions with my honorary sister?" Dani asked half-seriously.

Joiee burst out laughing. She turned to Kate, "You were right. She *is* protective." She turned back to face Dani. "We're going for dinner at Enzo's on the Lake and then maybe a strip joint after that."

Dani's eyes widened beyond measure, making everyone laugh.

"Dani, relax," Kate said. "We're going to the Coffee Ring after dinner to hang out."

"They have retro pinball machines," Joiee said, her eyes lighting up.

"Carry on," Dani said. "Just be safe. Both of you."

"Yes, Mom," Kate said with a chuckle.

"So, I interrupted a conversation," Joiee said. "Carry on," she mimicked Dani.

"She doesn't know what to do," Meredith said.

"You don't have to decide now," Joiee said, obviously knowing what Dani's dilemma was.

The entire table, including Dani, groaned in frustration. Dani pushed her tray out of the way and clunked her forehead on the table. "Carry on without me," she said meekly.

"So, Edward," Meredith said, clearly changing the subject, "call me when you get home. Maybe you can drive up for a visit. I'm sure my parents would love to see you again. And it's been years since you've seen Mikey."

"Who's Mikey again?" Kate asked.

The conversation turned into a discussion of siblings and families and went on without Dani's participation. As confused as ever, Dani sighed. A hand came to rest on her back. Meredith. She was letting Dani know she saw the struggle and was there for support.

Comforted, Dani let her brain circle back to the many arguments and counterarguments she'd gotten lost in over the past two weeks since talking to Coach Manzetti. If she gave up all the things she'd worked toward at Syracuse, she might be giving them up for nothing because she might not even make the varsity team, or possibly worse. She might have to redshirt. And even that wasn't guaranteed because she might not be good enough to redshirt. Although her high school coach had made lacrosse challenging and fun, she hadn't been knowledgeable about guiding her players to the next level. Her former coach never suggested summer camps or traveling teams, so Dani never knew she should seek those out. Her skills had clearly suffered because of it. Dani had spent several days being angry about that, but Meredith helped her accept that it was what it was, and she couldn't change it now. There was no point in wallowing over it. She also pointed out that Dani had been doing just fine growing and improving on her own.

Dani felt an epiphany blossoming as her friends' conversation continued in the background. If she played on the varsity team, she might have to wait until her junior year to see any playing time. A junior! She'd be twenty years old at that point.

She heard Kate laugh at something Meredith said, which made Dani also realize that she would be so committed to a Division 1 sport that she wouldn't be part of her friends' lives anymore. Not every day like this, anyway. She'd have to give up so many things she'd fostered in the short time she'd been at Syracuse. She was about to revisit everything she'd have to give up but told herself, *No, I won't go over all of it again.*

She lifted her head off the table and sat up. A hush fell over her friends as if they expected her to speak. All gazes were on her. Oh, they did expect that.

"I've dreamed of playing varsity women's lacrosse at Syracuse University ever since I was a little girl," Dani began. The hand resting on her back stroked her a few times. "Practically from the time I picked up my first lacrosse stick way back in the day."

Her head hurt from all of her thinking, but she glanced over at Meredith. Dang, she wore another one of those nondescript expressions. She had no idea what Meredith was thinking.

"But I think I have to amend that dream," Dani said slowly as if testing out the words.

"Dreams change if you let them, Dani," Petra said softly.

"New goals emerge the more information you get," Joiee added.

Dani nodded to both of them. She then took in Kate's sympathetic expression and Edward's neutral but quiet respect. Lastly, she looked back at Meredith, hoping to get validation for her decision. Nope. For the life of her, Dani couldn't read what Meredith was thinking. Meredith was going to make her do this on her own, wasn't she?

Dani took a deep breath, let it out quickly, and blurted, "I'm *not* going to try out for the varsity team." There. She said it. She slapped the table with the palm of her hand as if officially stamping her final decision.

Joiee reached across the table and patted her hand. "Tough decision, Dani. We all support you."

"She could always change her mind lat—" Edward howled in pain and didn't finish his sentence.

Dani whipped her head around. He was clutching his shin and mouthing to Meredith, "That hurt."

Dani glanced surreptitiously at Meredith and saw her glaring at Edward wide-eyed. *OMG*, Dani thought. She kicked him to get him to shut up about Dani possibly changing her mind later. Finally, with amazing relief, Dani knew how Meredith felt about the decision. Dani's heart swelled because she now understood that Meredith had allowed Dani space to make her own decision without biased influence.

"Thank you," Dani said to Meredith.

"For what?"

"Supporting me in my wishy-washiness."

"Always and forever," Meredith said.

"Isn't that a song?" Edward asked, making everyone laugh, which happily broke the tension.

"Are you sure, Dani?" Kate asked.

"No, but I think I'm seriously leaning in that direction. I mean, I would have to give up too much. I'd never see you guys, and…" She had to stop talking because a giant lump had developed in her throat.

"Aww," Kate said and leaped from her seat. "We love you, too." She wrapped her arms around Dani from behind. Petra, Edward, and Joiee joined in the hug while Meredith held both of Dani's hands.

"You are very loved," Meredith said. "By all of us."

When the hug ended, Joiee said, "I hate to break up this love fest, but I have a date." She turned to Kate and said, "Your arm looks so heavy. Here, let me hold it up for you."

Kate slid her arm through Joiee's and then turned around with an expression that said, "Isn't she romantic?"

"Be safe, you two," Dani said. She knew she sounded like an infinite loop but couldn't help it.

"We will," Kate said. "Someone at this table made us take self-defense classes in the dorm, and now I'm a ninja warrior in a dress."

Everyone laughed, and then the two women turned to head toward the exit.

Dani called after them, "Bring her home by midnight." Joiee and Kate laughed. Joiee didn't turn around but simply raised one hand and waved.

Kate turned her head and said, "Don't wait up, Petra."

A chorus of teasing catcalls followed them out the door.

After bussing their trays and wishing Edward a good break, Dani, Meredith, and Petra headed back to their dorm.

"Did you know about this date?" Dani asked Petra.

"I knew she was going on a date, but she was tight-lipped about who she was going out with."

"What about her boyfriend, Stevie, back home?" Meredith asked as they got into the elevator.

"Apparently, they broke up at the end of the summer," Petra said. "Kate told me that he wanted the space and freedom to explore other relationships in college. But she always thought he'd change his mind and come back to her."

"Aww," Meredith said. "I'm guessing that didn't happen."

Petra shook her head. "She admitted to me that she hadn't really loved him. She was just miffed that he had the audacity not to love her."

Dani bit back a laugh. "That sounds like our Kate, doesn't it?"

Petra chuckled. "It does."

They reached their floor, and Petra said, "Have a good break, you guys."

"You, too," Dani and Meredith said simultaneously and then laughed.

"We have our group chat," Dani said to Petra. "You know, if you need support."

"Thanks," Petra said. "I might. Mom will be cooking all my favorite foods." She rolled her eyes. "But I have appointments set up with my old therapist if I need her."

"You're strong," Meredith said. "But, yes, use our chat if you need help. Or call. We're here for you."

Tears welled up in Petra's eyes, and Dani didn't hesitate to pull her into a hug. Meredith lay a calming hand on Petra's back.

"You're okay," Meredith said softly.

"I know," Petra said, pulling out of the hug. She wiped her eyes. "I'm just grateful I found such amazing friends."

"We are, too," Meredith said. Dani nodded her agreement.

"I'm okay," Petra said.

"You know, we have to have a group chat, anyway," Dani said emphatically. "We have to find out how Kate's big date went, right?"

Petra laughed, and it was reassuring that she truly looked like she would be okay. They hugged again and wished each other a good break, although Dani would see Petra in their Poly Sci Discussion group first thing in the morning and then at the PSLA meeting after that.

Once back in their room, Meredith stood tall with her arms folded across her chest. Uh, oh. Dani knew that look. Dani had messed up somewhere somehow.

Meredith simply pointed to Dani's suitcase underneath her bed.

"Packing will commence in three, two, one," Dani said, pulling out the dusty suitcase. "How does dust get all the way under there?"

"One of life's big mysteries, I suppose," Meredith said, turning to finish packing her own suitcase. Meredith pulled her hair up and out of her face and fastened it down with a giant plastic clip that you could probably use to keep a potato chip bag closed. Meredith had called it a tortoiseshell clip or something.

As Dani started packing, she grinned because she loved having a femme partner. Not that she was into gender roles or anything like that, but she loved that Meredith liked to dress up, fuss with her hair, and wear makeup. She loved holding hands with her and loved when Meredith snaked her hand under Dani's arm and held on as they walked. It was a declaration that they needed each other, and this was their way of showing affection. She loved showing the world this affection, too.

"You know," Meredith said, "I think it's all about balance."

Dani took three T-shirts out of her suitcase. She was only going away for nine days and had clothes at home. What the heck? Her brain wasn't thinking properly. "What's about balance, baby?"

"You're not a one-trick pony, Dani," Meredith said without answering Dani's question. "I wasn't sure which way you were leaning."

Oh, this was about the lacrosse decision. Of course, it was.

Meredith continued, "You thrive when you talk politics. You beam when you work with the kids. You support me like crazy, and I think you would be miserable if you didn't have those other outlets besides lacrosse."

"I think you're—"

"I think college is about finding those things that fulfill us, you know?"

"I think you're—"

Meredith interrupted again. "Like the way I wasn't sure what my art could contribute to the world, but then I found the art-as-therapy program, and my heart and soul just sang." She stopped folding a sweatshirt and turned to face Dani. "Baby, your heart sings when you do all those other things. It also sings when you play lacrosse. You're starting a legacy with this new lacrosse club. You're a founding member, which is incredible. I'm so amazed by the things you do."

Dani didn't say a thing. She couldn't. That stupid lump was back in her throat. People spent lifetimes trying to find what she'd found with Meredith, and she was proud to show the entire world.

Dani stopped all movement and turned to look at her girlfriend.

"What?" Meredith said, a grin growing on her face.

Dani's smile also grew. "I can't wait to spend the rest of my life with you." She abandoned all pretense of packing and pulled Meredith into her arms. "I can't wait to see where life takes us."

"Wherever it is," Meredith murmured into Dani's neck, "I want you with me."

"Yep," Dani said to the universe. "I am the luckiest person in the whole wide world."

"And don't you forget it," Meredith said.

Dani pulled her into a kiss, and soon, the suitcases, lacrosse decisions, and the rest of the world were long forgotten.

~~~ The End ~~~

Newsletter Signup

Sign up for Barbara L. Clanton's newsletter to keep up with new (and revised) releases. She also likes to provide writing tips for writers and recommend books to read (other than her own, of course).

Sign Up on the official website: www.BLClanton.com

Resources

lgbt national help center
https://lgbthotline.org/

From the lgbt national help center website:

"All of our support volunteers identify as part of the LGBTQIA+ family, and are here to serve the entire community, by providing free & confidential peer-support, information, and local resources through national hotlines and online programs."

LGBT National Hotline: 888-843-4564
LGBT National Coming Out Support Hotline: 888-688-5428
LGBT National Youth Talkline: 800-246-7743
LGBT National Senior Hotline: 888-234-7243

Volunteering Opportunities with the YMCA
https://www.ymca.org/get-involved/volunteer/opportunities

From the YMCA.org website:

"The YMCA welcomes volunteers of all ages and backgrounds to share their time and talent. Our volunteers are critical to strengthening communities, improving lives and helping people reach their potential. Learn more about how you can get involved at the Y and help create a connected community where everyone can thrive."

About the Author

Barbara L. Clanton

Barbara L. Clanton is a native New Yorker who left those "New York minutes" for a slower-paced life in central Florida. While in middle and high schools, she played any sport she could find—softball, volleyball, basketball, and field hockey. During high school, she could even be found in the upstairs gym
playing handball with her friends. She played softball at Princeton University and was the team captain during her Ivy-league champion senior year.

She has spent her career teaching computer science and mathematics at college preparatory schools in New York and Florida. She also coached softball and basketball in both states as well. As an amateur softball player, she was inducted into the ASANA's (Amateur Sports Alliance of North America) Hall of Fame.

Somewhere in adulthood, she picked up a new hobby. "Dr. Barb" plays the bass guitar and has been in several pop-rock bands, playing in notable events such as Gay Days Orlando.

When asked why she started writing, she said she was writing the books she wished she had in high school to help her make sense of her "differentness." Although the world is evolving, it's still not easy to come out to yourself or the world. She hopes her books will help.

Barbara L. Clanton's Website:
http://www.blclanton.com

Barbara L. Clanton's Instagram:
https://www.instagram.com/barbara.clanton14

Barbara L. Clanton's Facebook:
https://www.facebook.com/BassGuitarGirl

Barbara L. Clanton's Goodreads Page:
https://www.goodreads.com/author/show/3072442.Barbara_L_Clanton

Barbara L. Clanton's Author Page on Amazon:
https://www.amazon.com/Barbara-L-Clanton

Books by Barbara L. Clanton

THE WHICKETT SERIES (Young Adult & New Adult)

The Whickett Series follows two young women who discover a close friendship. For Meredith, their friendship has always been about friendship and nothing more. For Danielle, it has always been about more, but she respects the friendship and resigns herself to remaining friend-zoned because it's a way to keep Meredith in her life. This series starts following the two young women in their second semester of senior year in high school. Book one is the young adult novel: "Art for Art's Sake: Meredith's Story." The series continues into their first semester of college in the new adult novel: "More Than Roommates: Dani's Story." Somewhere along the way, their definition of friendship changes.

Art for Art's Sake: Meredith's Story
(Book One in the Whickett Series)

A young adult lesbian romance.

High school senior Meredith Bedford is a social outcast. Her family recently moved from the Catskill Mountains to the sprawling suburbs of Albany, the capital of New York State. Shy and self-conscious about her acne scars, she stays to herself and tries to remain invisible. Her twelve-year-old brother, Mikey, has Down Syndrome, and she tries hard not to blame her troubles on him. Despite verbal and sometimes physical harassment, she survives because she has her art. She was selected to be part of the elite Advanced Placement art class and is quite good at capturing the emotions of her subjects in her portraits. Besides her family, art is the one thing that helps her cope with her outcast status.

One day, at a senior class meeting, she sees Dani Lassiter, president of the senior class and captain of the lacrosse team, and knows that she must paint this enigmatic young woman. One class period later, Dani manipulates things to have Meredith as her partner for a history project. Meredith is suspicious of Dani's motives but takes a chance. And it pays off. Meredith slowly sheds her invisibility cloak and allows Dani in - a little at a time. They explore an old Victorian house for their history project and become close with Esther and Millie, the two older women who own the house and who've lived together for about forty years. But, when Dani reveals to Meredith that she is gay, Meredith simply can't deal with the news. How had she not known? What is it that won't allow her to come to terms with this unexpected news? Will Meredith control her own homophobia, or will she reject the one person who had taken a chance on her and made her feel human?

ISBN: 978-1-953734-34-1 (eBook)
ISBN: 978-1-953734-35-8 (Paperback)

More Than Roommates: Dani's Story
(Book Two in the Whickett Series)

A new adult lesbian romance.

This new adult lesbian romance is the story of Danielle (Dani) Lassiter as she heads off to Syracuse University for her freshman year of college. And as far as any of their new college friends know, she and her girlfriend Meredith are just roommates and nothing more. And for a little while, they are able to keep it their private secret.

Dani has goals for her college career. She wants to get involved in campus politics and get elected as one of the freshmen representatives of the Student Association. She's also set her sights on improving her lacrosse skills so she can be good enough to make the varsity women's lacrosse team.

Reality hits hard and fast, though, when she discovers that things aren't coming as easily to her in college as they did in high school. An older female student assaults her. A lacrosse coach tells her she isn't good enough. And, the worst thing, her relationship with her not-just-a-roommate Meredith lands on shaky ground from both sides.

Dani accidentally starts an informal after-school program teaching young neighborhood children lacrosse. At one point, she advises them to just "be themselves." She tells them that good things will happen if they do that. It is only when ten-year-old Natalie reminds her to do that for herself that she becomes unsure of what it means to "be herself." Who is Danielle Lassiter, really? Unsteady and unsure, Dani has difficult decisions to make. And one of those decisions includes whether or not she should stay at Syracuse University. Running away to Albany State might be easier on everyone, including herself.

ISBN: 978-1-953734-36-5 (eBook)
ISBN: 978-1-953734-37-2 (Paperback)

THE CLARKSONVILLE SERIES (Young Adult)

The Clarksonville Series follows four high school girls in upstate New York as they maneuver the difficult process of coming out to themselves, each other, and their families. And it doesn't always go well. The four friends have a mutual love of softball, which helps them bond and find love. Each book is from a different character's point of view, but all four main characters are present in each book. There are currently eight books in the series.

Out of Left Field: Marlee's Story
(Book One in the Clarksonville Series)

A young adult lesbian romance.

High school junior Marlee McAllister lives and breathes softball. She's the pitcher for the Clarksonville Cougars in the North Country of upstate New York. With the season opener approaching, Marlee and her best friend, Jeri D'Amico, go to scout their rivals, the East Valley Panthers. The Panthers' star pitcher, Christy Loveland, took the All-county pitching title the preceding year. It is a title Marlee covets. Marlee and Jeri settle in for the game, but as the Panthers take the field, Marlee finds herself staring at Susie Torres, the Panther left fielder.

For reasons Marlee doesn't understand, she's drawn to Susie. Over the next few weeks, Marlee and Susie will slowly act on their mutual attraction. But suddenly, Susie pulls away without explanation, and Marlee realizes it has to do with Christy. Susie won't explain the bond she and Christy share, but whatever it is, it threatens Marlee's burgeoning relationship with Susie.

Struggling to maintain her grades, dealing with the ever-increasing estrangement from her best friend Jeri, and handling the pressures of the All-county pitching competition, Marlee also has to confront the bittersweet realities of what it might mean to be gay.

ISBN: 978-1-953734-04-4 (eBook)
ISBN: 978-1-953734-16-7 (Paperback)

Tools of Ignorance: Lisa's Story
(Book Two in the Clarksonville Series)

A young adult lesbian romance.

Lisa Brown is the starting catcher for the Clarksonville Cougars High School softball team, and she has a major crush on her pitcher, Marlee. Lisa continues to carry her torch for Marlee, even when Sam, a rival softball player, flirts sweetly. However, Lisa becomes more confused than ever when Tara, the first girl she ever kissed and the first girl who ever broke her heart, resurfaces. Since Marlee doesn't know Lisa's alive, should Lisa give up on her once and for all?

Sam seems to have secrets of her own, but Lisa wonders if she should overlook them and allow her fledging attraction to grow for the pretty blonde, or should she fan the tiny flame still burning in her heart for Tara? Lisa faces these problems and deals with society's tools of ignorance in her quest for love and acceptance.

ISBN: 978-1-953734-06-8 (eBook)
ISBN: 978-1-953734-17-4 (Paperback)

Going, Going, Gone: Susie's Story
(Book Three in the Clarksonville Series)

A young adult lesbian romance.

Susie Torres planned to spend most of the summer before her senior year of high school with her girlfriend, Marlee McAllister, but that's proving to be quite challenging. Marlee works at D'Amico's restaurant, and Susie babysits for Mrs. Johnson, her mother's boss. Susie hates the job because she not only works like a slave but almost gets paid like one. Susie is desperate to take her physical relationship with Marlee further, but she knows she has to go at Marlee's slower pace. Complicating things is the attention that a pretty blonde softball player from another team shows Marlee, and Susie falls into a funk when Marlee seems to enjoy it.

On top of that, nothing she does seems to be good enough for her summer softball coach. Frustrated with life, Susie accidentally, on purpose, comes out to her mother. It would be an understatement to say that her mother didn't take it well. Can Susie deal with a girlfriend whose head has possibly been turned by another, an employer who treats her like dirt, a coach who doesn't respect her, and a mother who tells her she is unnatural? Can she get her life back on track before senior year starts?

ISBN: 978-1-953734-05-1 (eBook)
ISBN: 978-1-953734-18-1 (Paperback)

Stealing Second: Sam's Story
(Book Four in the Clarksonville Series)

A young adult lesbian romance

Samantha Rose Payton likes girls, but her parents don't know that. And Sam would like to keep it that way because her parents are ultra-conservative Republicans. They live in a mansion and have servants and chauffeurs. However, instead of playing the dutiful debutante who plays the violin and still has a nanny at age seventeen, Sam would rather watch ice hockey on TV and play second base on her summer softball team. Having to hide her relationship with her girlfriend, Lisa, from her parents is becoming an agonizing struggle. Not only are her friends pressuring her to come out to her parents, but they are also trying to convince her to attend a very public gay pride festival at the local college.

At least she has her nanny Helene to confide in, but for how much longer? Sam is acutely aware that the time for Helene to move on may be fast approaching. And if that isn't enough, Sam's summer softball coach gives her no end of grief after an error-filled game and isn't afraid of making an example out of her. Will Sam remain the perfect princess her parents expect? Will her beloved nanny leave her forever? Will her girlfriend get fed up about being kept hidden? Will her friends continue to pressure her about coming out? Will Coach Greer make her life miserable? All of these questions are answered in Stealing Second: Sam's Story.

ISBN: 978-1-953734-07-5 (eBook)
ISBN: 978-1-953734-19-8 (Paperback)

Out at Home

(Book Five in the Clarksonville Series)

A young adult lesbian romance

Marlee McAllister just wants to fit in. She didn't know she didn't fit in until Kate and Rita – the prettiest girls in the senior class - pointed it out. Even Marlee's grandmother declared that Marlee was too old for "this tomboy nonsense." All the other girls at school have long hair except Marlee. All the other girls wear something other than jeans, a T-shirt, and sneakers to school every day. Except for Marlee. All the other girls fit in except Marlee.

Marlee decides to grow out her short hair, buy femmy girly clothes, and pretend she has a boyfriend named Ronnie. Really, though? She has the most amazing girlfriend in Susie Torres. Susie is everything Marlee hoped for - sweet, sexy, kind, athletic, pretty. And best of all? She loves Marlee as much as Marlee loves her. Although their parents know about their relationship, not many other people do.

Marlee is out at home but not to anyone else. And if anyone else finds out she's into girls, Kate and Rita especially, the entire school and her grandparents will know within a day. Life as she knows it will be over.

Out at Home is the story of Marlee McAllister's life-altering struggle to fit in.

ISBN: 978-1-953734-20-4 (eBook)
ISBN: 978-1-953734-24-2 (Paperback)

Tools of the Devil
(Book Six in the Clarksonville Series)

A young adult lesbian romance

Seventeen-year-old Lisa Brown loved going to church. Oh sure, sometimes she'd rather sleep in, but she liked the calming and empowering strength of her faith. Sundays revitalized her spirit when she thanked God for the wonderful things in her life, like her loving family and amazing girlfriend, Samantha Rose. One day, she hoped to marry Sam, have a house and yard, and have babies together. One day.

But then it happened. That fateful Sunday, the guest preacher stepped behind the pulpit and spoke four words that would change Lisa's world forever. "Homosexuality is a sin," he said. Had she heard him right? She knew she had when her mother put a hand on her forearm. Every muscle in her body tensed, and she forgot to breathe. What was happening?

The church she'd been baptized in, grown up in, and wanted to get married in had, in one instant, turned against her. Still not quite believing what she'd heard, she mumbled, "Ignorance is a sin, Reverend." Never one to back down from a challenge, she scanned the congregation but didn't find a single soul who looked upset by his statement. On the contrary, many nodded in agreement. Under her breath, she muttered, "Game on, people. Game on."

ISBN: 978-1-953734-21-1 (eBook)
ISBN: 978-1-953734-25-9 (Paperback)

Going Under
(Book Seven in the Clarksonville Series)

A young adult lesbian romance

Susie Torres is a second-semester senior with devoted friends and an amazing girlfriend in Marlee McAllister. Susie's father has a job that takes him away from home on frequent business trips, but lately, his trips seem to be longer and more frequent. Tensions rise at home when Susie's mother challenges him about that. At first, Susie and her younger brother Miguel hide in her room when their parents' frequent squabbles elevate to out-and-out yelling matches. But as her parents' war escalates further, Susie finds other ways to escape the tension.

A fake ID becomes a clear and easy way to anesthetize herself with alcohol. Her crumbling home life becomes momentarily forgotten whenever she swims in a sea of peaceful drunken bliss. Unfortunately, Susie doesn't realize she is alienating everyone around her with her attempts to cope with her parents' possible divorce, including Marlee. Her best friend Sam tries to warn her that her excessive drinking is driving away all of her friends, but Sam's well-meaning advice isn't heard. Will Susie finally realize that it is her own actions that are making her life fall apart around her? That her new love of drinking is getting in the way of everything good in her life? That her amazingly patient girlfriend isn't going to put up with much more?

ISBN: 978-1-953734-22-8 (eBook)
ISBN: 978-1-953734-26-6 (Paperback)

Stealing Hope
(Book Eight in the Clarksonville Series)

A young adult lesbian romance

Sam Payton is a high school senior with a bit of an identity crisis. Raised in a well-to-do family, she dutifully plays the role of Samantha Rose Payton, the wealthy debutante. Now, almost one full year into her life-changing relationship with Lisa Brown, Sam is hit with many life-challenging events. Her best friend, Susie Torres, struggles with alcohol addiction and a wrecked home life as her parents go through a bitter divorce, and Sam tries to help her friend keep her head above water. In another struggle, two friends cross the line between friendship and intimacy—a line that should not have been approached. Sam finds herself trying to make them see how incredibly egregious the transgressions are for all involved. And to top it all off, Sam's mother is diagnosed with a serious illness.

Through the love of her parents and her girlfriend, Sam navigates these challenges the best way she can, all while trying to fulfill everyone's varying expectations of her. Sam struggles to break free of the preconceived roles she seems bound by to figure out who she really is. It ultimately comes down to whether Sam can make everyone see that she is both a softball-playing, ice-hockey-loving lesbian named Sam as well as a classically-music-trained debutante named Samantha Rose.

ISBN: 978-1-953734-23-5 (eBook)
ISBN: 978-1-953734-27-3 (Paperback)

THE GRASSE RIVER SERIES (Young Adult)

Quite an Undertaking: Devon's Story
(Book One in the Grasse River Series)

A young adult interracial lesbian romance

Devon Raines, a sixteen-year-old journalism nerd, was happily minding her own business when, wham, her life was turned upside down. She struggled with grief when her grandmother died from a sudden heart attack. But it was at her grandmother's wake that she locked eyes with the most beautiful black girl she'd ever seen. No, Rebecca Washington was the most beautiful *girl* she'd ever seen, period. Would this beautiful dancer freak out if she knew Devon was gay and attracted?

Enter Jessie Crowler, Rebecca's basketball-playing best friend. Or were they only friends? Devon tried to hide her attraction for the ebony dancer, but would fate allow Rebecca to look her way? Would Jessie get in the way? Would the difference in skin color keep them apart? All this adds up to quite an undertaking in Devon's formerly quiet existence.

Rebecca's Story
(Book Two in the Grasse River Series)

< Coming Soon >

THE GIRLS' SPORTS SERIES (Children's Books Ages 9-12)

Bases Loaded

Sixth-grader Mackenzie Kelly's first love was soccer until her best friend talked her into playing summer softball. Now Mack is eager to be on her school's softball team and dreams of playing in the Olympics with her idol, Cat Osterman. But first, she needs to bring up her failing English grade to stay on the team. When she learns softball has been cut from the Olympics, she's determined somehow to get it back into the Olympic Games so she can fulfill her dream.

> *"I just wanted to let you know I received the book and*
> *I think it is FANTASTIC!"*
> – Jessica Mendoza, *US Olympic Softball Team*

ASIN: B00094IT3RK (eBook)
ISBN 978-1-934452-79-0 (Paperback)

Side Out

Seventh-grader Dina Jacobs feels like she's landed on another planet when her family moves from Long Island, New York to Indiana. She tries out for the seventh-grade volleyball team, and her new friend, Christine, introduces her to Olympic volleyball. Now Dina dreams of playing in the Olympics like her newfound idol, Logan Tom. Indiana doesn't seem so bad until Dina's Jewish faith crashes against her coach's win-at-all-costs attitude. Miserable, Dina is torn between staying true to her religious customs or putting them aside to play the game she loves.

ASIN: B005HM9CUU (eBook)
ISBN 978-1-934452-65-3 (Paperback)

Live, Love, Lacrosse

Addie Coleburn, fresh out of the sixth grade, is spending the summer at her grandmother's house in Syracuse with her mother and brother. Kimi Takahashi, a girl who lives up the street, invites Addie to go to the park and play lacrosse. Addie hasn't the first clue what lacrosse is and would rather sit on Grandma's front porch eating potato chips, drinking sodas, and reading books. But then again, spending the summer dealing with her younger brother isn't appealing, either, so she goes to the park with Kimi. Within a week, she's hooked on lacrosse. She's overweight and can't keep up with the faster, stronger girls. She has to find a way to lose her excess weight quickly or risk getting cut from the team.

ASIN: B09GPYMHDK (eBook)
ISBN 978-1-943837-50-2 (Paperback)

www.ingramcontent.com/pod-product-compliance
Lightning Source LLC
Chambersburg PA
CBHW061543170626
46811CB00001B/70